The Unclassed

George Gissing

Contents

THE UNCLASSED

BY

George Gissing

The Unclassed by George Gissing

CHAPTER I
SCHOOL

There was strange disorder in Miss Rutherford's schoolroom, wont to be the abode of decorum. True, it was the gathering-time after the dinner-hour, and Miss Rutherford herself was as yet out of sight; but things seemed to be going forward of a somewhat more serious kind than a game of romps among the children. There were screams and sobbings, hysterical cries for help; some of the little girls were crowding round an object in one corner of the room, others appeared to be getting as far away from it as possible, hiding their pale faces in their hands, or looking at one another with terrified eyes. At length one more thoughtful than the rest sped away out of the room, and stood at the bottom of the stairs, calling out her teacher's name as loud as she could. A moment, and Miss Rutherford came hastening down, with alarmed aspect, begging to be told what was the matter. But the summoner had turned and fled at the first sight of the lady's garments. Miss Rutherford darted into the schoolroom, and at once there was quietness, save for half-choked sobs here and there, and a more ominous kind of moaning from the crowded corner.

"Gracious goodness, children, what is it? Who's that lying on the floor? Harriet Smales! What *ever* has happened?"

The cluster of children had fallen aside, exposing a strange picture. On the ground lay a girl of twelve, her face deadly pale, save in the places where it was dabbled with fresh blood, which still streamed from a gash on the right side of her forehead. Her eyes were half opened; she was just recovering consciousness; a moan came from her at intervals. She had for support the lap and arms of a little girl, perhaps two years younger than herself. Heedless of the flowing blood, this child was pressing her pale cheek against that of the wounded one, whose name she kept murmuring in pitiful accents, mixed with endearing epithets. So unconscious was she of all around, that the falling back of the other children did not cause her to raise her eyes; neither was she aware of Miss Rutherford's first exclamations, nor yet of the question which was next addressed to her by the horrified schoolmistress.

"How did it happen? Some of you run at once for a doctor--Dr. Williams in Grove Road--Oh, quick!--Ida Starr, how *did* it happen?"

Ida did not move, but seemed to tighten her embrace. The other pupils all looked fearfully hither and thither, but none ventured to speak.

"Ida!" repeated Miss Rutherford, dropping on her knees by the two, and beginning to wipe away some of the blood with her handkerchief. "Speak, child! Has some one gone for the doctor? How was it done?"

The face at length turned upon the questioner was almost as ghastly and red-stained as that it had been pressed against. But it had become self-controlled; the dark eyes looked straight forward with an expression marvellously full of meaning in one so young; the lips did not tremble as they spoke.

"I did it, Miss Rutherford. I have killed Harriet. I, and nobody else."

"You? How, child?"

"I killed her with the slate, Miss Rutherford; this slate, look."

She pointed to a slate without a frame which lay on the floor. There were sums worked on the uppermost side, and the pencil-marks were half obliterated. For a moment the schoolmistress's amazement held her motionless, but fresh and louder moans recalled her to the immediate necessities of the case. She pushed Ida Starr aside, and, with the help of a servant-girl who had by this time appeared in the room, raised the sufferer into a chair, and began to apply what remedies suggested themselves. The surgeon, whom several of the children had hastened to seek, only lived a few yards away, and his assistant was speedily present. Harriet Smales had quite recovered consciousness, and was very soon able to give her own account of the incident. After listening to her, Miss Rutherford turned to the schoolchildren, who were now seated in the usual order on benches, and spoke to them with some degree of calm.

"I am going to take Harriet home. Lucy Wood, you will please to see that order is preserved in my absence; I shall only be away twenty minutes, at the most. Ida Starr, you will go up into my sitting-room, and remain there till I come to you. All take out your copy-books; I shall examine the lines written whilst I am away."

The servant, who had been despatched for a cab, appeared at the door. Harriet Smales was led out. Before leaving the house, Miss Rutherford whispered to the servant an order to occupy herself in the sitting-room, so as to keep Ida Starr in sight.

Miss Rutherford, strict disciplinarian when her nerves were not unstrung, was as good as her promise with regard to the copy-books. She had returned within the twenty minutes, and the first thing she did was to walk along all the benches, making a comment here, a correction there, in another place giving a word of praise. Then she took her place at the raised desk whence she was wont to survey the little room.

There were present thirteen pupils, the oldest of them turned fifteen, the youngest scarcely six. They appeared to be the daughters of respectable people, probably of tradesmen in the neighbourhood. This school was in Lisson Grove, in the northwest of London; a spot not to be pictured from its name by those ignorant of the locality; in point of fact a dingy street, with a mixture of shops and private houses. On the front door was a plate displaying Miss Rutherford's name,--nothing more. That lady herself was middle-aged, grave at all times, kindly, and, be it added, fairly competent as things go in the world of school. The room was rather bare, but the good fire necessitated by the winter season was not wanting, and the plain boarding of the floor showed itself no stranger to scrubbings. A clock hanging on the wall ticked very loudly in the perfect stillness as the schoolmistress took her seat.

She appeared to examine a book for a few moments, then raised her head, looked at the faces before her with a troubled expression, and began to speak.

"I wish to know who can give me any account of the way in which Harriet Smales received her hurt. Stop! Hands only, please. And only those raise their hands who actually saw the blow struck, and overheard **all** that led to it. You understand, now? One, two, three--seven altogether, that is quite enough. Those seven will wait in the room at four o'clock till the others have all gone. Now I will give the first class their sums."

The afternoon passed Very slowly to teacher and pupils alike. When the clock struck four, work was put away with more than the usual noise and hurry. Miss

Rutherford seemed for a time to be on the point of making some new address to the school before the children departed, but eventually she decided to keep silence, and the dismissal was got over as quickly as possible. The seven witnesses remained, solemnly seated at their desks, all anxious-looking.

"Lucy Wood," Miss Rutherford began, when the door was closed and quiet, "you are the eldest. Please tell me all you can of this sad affair."

There was one of the seven faces far more discomposed than the rest, a sweet and spiritual little countenance; it was tear-stained, red-eyed; the eager look, the trembling lips spoke some intimate cause of sympathy. Before the girl addressed had time to begin her answer, this other, one would have said in spite of herself, intervened with an almost agonised question.

"Oh, Miss Rutherford, is Harriet really dead?"

"Hush, hush!" said the lady, with a shocked look. "No, my dear, she is only badly hurt."

"And she really won't die?" pleaded the child, with an instant brightening of look.

"Certainly not, certainly not. Now be quiet, Maud, and let Lucy begin."

Lucy, a sensible and matter-of-fact girl, made a straightforward narration, the facts of which were concurred in by her companions. Harriet Smales, it seemed, had been exercising upon Ida for some days her utmost powers of irritation, teasing her, as Lucy put it, "beyond all bearing." The cause of this was not unknown in the school, and Miss Rutherford remembered the incident from which the malice dated. Harriet had copied a sum in class from Ida's slate--she was always copying from somebody--and the teacher, who had somehow detected her, asked Ida plainly whether such was not the case. Ida made no reply, would not speak, which of course was taken as confirmatory evidence, and the culprit had accordingly received an imposition. Her spleen, thus aroused, Harriet vented upon the other girl, who, she maintained, ought to have stoutly denied the possibility of the alleged deceit, and so have saved her. She gave poor Ida no rest, and her persecution had culminated this afternoon; she began to "call Ida's mother names," the result of which was that the assailed one suddenly snatched up her slate, and, in an uncontrollable fit of passion, struck her tormentor a blow with it upon the forehead.

"What did she call Ida's mother?" inquired Miss Rutherford, all at once changing her look curiously.

"She called her a bad woman."

"Was that all?"

"No, please, Miss Rutherford," put in Maud eagerly. "She said she got her living in the streets. And it isn't true. Ida's mother's a lady, and doesn't sell things in the streets!"

The teacher looked down and was silent.

"I don't think I need ask any more questions," she said presently. "Run away home all of you. What is it, my dear?"

Maud, she was about eleven, and small for her age, had remained behind, and was looking anxiously up into Miss Rutherford's face.

"May I wait for Ida, please," she asked, "and--and walk home with her? We go the same way."

"Not to-night, dear; no, not to-night. Ida Starr is in disgrace. She will not go home just yet. Run away, now, there's a good girl."

Sadly, sadly was the command obeyed, and very slowly did Maud Enderby walk along the streets homeward, ever turning back to see whether perchance Ida might not be behind her.

Miss Rutherford ascended to her sitting-room. The culprit was standing in a corner with her face to the wall.

"Why do you stand so?" asked the teacher gravely, but not very severely.

"I thought you'd want me to, Miss Rutherford."

"Come here to me, child."

Ida had clearly been crying for a long time, and there was still blood on her face. She seemed to have made up her mind that the punishment awaiting her must be dreadful, and she resolved to bear it humbly. She came up, still holding her hands behind her, and stood with downcast eyes. The hair which hung down over her shoulders was dark brown, her eye-brows strongly marked, the eyes themselves rather deep-set. She wore a pretty plum-coloured dress, with a dainty little apron in front; her whole appearance bespeaking a certain taste and love of elegance in the person who had the care of her.

"You will be glad to hear," said Miss Rutherford, "that Harriet's hurt is not as serious as we feared at first. But she will have to stay at home for some days."

There was no motion, or reply.

"Do you know that I am quite afraid of you, Ida? I had no idea that you were so passionate. Had you no thought what harm you might do when you struck that terrible blow?"

But Ida could not converse; no word was to be got from her.

"You must go home now," went on the schoolmistress after a pause, "and not come back till I send for you. Tell your mother just what you have done, and say that I will write to her about you. You understand what I say, my child?"

The punishment had come upon her. Nothing worse than this had Ida imagined; nay, nothing so bad. She drew in her breath, her fingers wreathed themselves violently together behind her back. She half raised her face, but could not resolve to meet her teacher's eyes. On the permission to go being repeated, she left the room in silence, descended the stairs with the slow steps of an old person, dressed herself mechanically, and went out into the street. Miss Rutherford stood for some time in profound and troubled thought, then sighed as she returned to her usual engagements.

The following day was Saturday, and therefore a half-holiday. After dinner, Miss Rutherford prepared herself for walking, and left home. A quarter of an hour brought her to a little out-of-the-way thoroughfare called Boston Street, close to the west side of Regent's Park, and here she entered a chemist's shop, over which stood the name Smales. A middle-aged man of very haggard and feeble appearance stood behind the counter, and his manner to the lady as she addressed him was painfully subservient. He spoke very little above a whisper, and as though suffering from a severe sore throat, but it was his natural voice.

"She's better, I thank you, madam; much better, I hope and believe; yes, much better."

He repeated his words nervously, rubbing his hands together feverishly the while, and making his eye-brows go up and down in a curious way.

"Might I see her for a few moments?"

"She would be happy, madam, very happy: oh yes, I am sure, very happy If--if you would have the kindness to come round, yes, round here, madam, and--and to excuse our poor sitting-room. Thank you, thank you. Harriet, my dear, Miss Rutherford has had the great, the very great, goodness to visit you--to visit you personally--yes. I will leave you, if--if you please--h'm, yes."

He shuffled away in the same distressingly nervous manner, and closed the door behind him. The schoolmistress found herself in a dark little parlour, which smelt even more of drugs than the shop itself. The window looked out into a dirty back-yard, and was almost concealed with heavy red curtains. As the eyes got accustomed to the dimness, one observed that the floor was covered with very old oil-cloth, and that the articles of furniture were few, only the most indispensable, and all very shabby. Everything seemed to be dusty and musty. The only approach to an ornament was a framed diploma hanging over the mantelpiece, certifying that John Alfred Smales was a duly qualified pharmaceutical chemist. A low fire burned in the grate, and before it, in a chair which would probably have claimed the title of easy, sat the girl Harriet Smales, her head in bandages.

She received Miss Rutherford rather sulkily, and as she moved, groaned in a way which did not seem the genuine utterance of pain. After a few sympathetic remarks, the teacher began to touch upon the real object of her visit.

"I have no intention of blaming you, Harriet; I should not speak of this at all, if it were not necessary. But I must ask you plainly what reason you had for speaking of Ida Starr's mother as they say you did. Why did you say she was a bad woman?"

"It's only what she is," returned Harriet sullenly, and with much inward venom.

"What do you mean by that? Who has told you anything about her?"

Only after some little questioning the fact was elicited that Harriet owed her ideas on the subject to a servant girl in the house, whose name was Sarah.

"What does Sarah say, then?" asked Miss Rutherford.

"She says she isn't respectable, and that she goes about with men, and she's only a common street-woman," answered the girl, speaking evidently with a very clear understanding of what these accusations meant. The schoolmistress looked away with a rather shocked expression, and thought a little before speaking again.

"Well, that's all I wanted to ask you, Harriet," she said. "I won't blame you, but I trust you will do as I wish, and never say such things about any one again, whoever may tell you. It is our duty never to speak ill of others, you know; least of all when we know that to do so will be the cause of much pain and trouble. I hope you will very soon be able to come back again to us. And now I will say good-bye."

In the shop Miss Rutherford renewed to the chemist her sincere regret for what had taken place.

"Of course I cannot risk the recurrence of such a thing," she said. "The child who did it will not return to me, Mr. Smales."

Mr. Smales uttered incoherent excuses, apologies, and thanks, and shufflingly escorted the lady to his shop-door.

Miss Rutherford went home in trouble. She did not doubt the truth of what Harriet Smales had told her, for she herself had already entertained uneasy suspicions, dating indeed from the one interview she had had with Mrs. Starr, when Ida was first brought to the school, and deriving confirmation from a chance meeting in the street only a few days ago. It was only too plain what she must do, and the necessity grieved her. Ida had not shown any especial brilliancy at her books, but the child's character was a remarkable one, and displayed a strength which might eventually operate either for good or for evil. With careful training, it seemed at present very probable that the good would predominate. But the task was not such as the schoolmistress felt able to undertake, bearing in mind the necessity of an irreproachable character for her school if it were to be kept together at all. The disagreeable secret had begun to spread; all the children would relate the events of yesterday in their own homes; to pass the thing over was impossible. She sincerely regretted the step she must take, and to which she would not have felt herself driven by any ill-placed prudery of her own. On Monday morning it must be stated to the girls that Ida Starr had left.

In the meantime, it only remained to write to Mrs. Starr, and make known this determination. Miss Rutherford thought for a little while of going to see Ida's mother, but felt that this would be both painful and useless. It was difficult even to write, desirous as she was of somehow mitigating the harshness of this sentence of expulsion. After half-an-hour spent in efforts to pen a suitable note, she gave up the attempt to write as she would have wished, and announced the necessity she was under in the fewest possible words.

CHAPTER II
MOTHER AND CHILD

Ida Starr, dismissed by the schoolmistress, ran quickly homewards. She was unusually late, and her mother would be anxious. Still, when she came within sight of the door, she stopped and stood panting. How should she tell of her disgrace? It was not fear that made her shrink from repeating Miss Rutherford's message; nor yet shame, though she would gladly have hidden herself away somewhere in the dark from every eye; her overwhelming concern was for the pain she knew she was going to cause one who had always cherished her with faultless tenderness,--tenderness which it had become her nature to repay with a child's unreflecting devotion.

Her home was in Milton Street. On the front-door was a brass-plate which bore the inscription: "Mrs. Ledward, Dressmaker;" in the window of the ground-floor was a large card announcing that "Apartments" were vacant. The only light was one which appeared in the top storey, and there Ida knew that her mother was waiting for her, with tea ready on the table as usual. Mrs. Starr was seldom at home during the child's dinner-hour, and Ida had not seen her at all to-day. For it was only occasionally that she shared her mother's bedroom; it was the rule for her to sleep with Mrs. Ledward, the landlady, who was a widow and without children. The arrangement had held ever since Ida could remember; when she had become old enough to ask for an explanation of this, among other singularities in their mode of life, she was told that her mother slept badly, and must have the bed to herself.

But the night had come on, and every moment of delay doubtless increased the anxiety she was causing. Ida went up to the door, stood on tiptoe to reach the knocker, and gave her usual two distinct raps. Mrs. Ledward opened the door to her in person; a large woman, with pressed lips and eyes that squinted very badly; attired, however, neatly, and looking as good-natured as a woman who was at once landlady and dressmaker could be expected to look.

"How 's 't you're so late?" she asked, without looking at the child; her eyes, as far as one could guess, fixed upon the houses opposite, her hands in the little pocket on each side of her apron. "Your mother's poorly."

"Oh, then I shall sleep with her to-night?" exclaimed Ida, forgetting her trouble for the moment in this happy foresight.

"Dessay," returned Mrs. Ledward laconically.

Ida left her still standing in the doorway, and ran stairs. The chamber she went into--after knocking and receiving permission to enter, according to the rule which had been impressed upon her--was a tolerably-furnished bedroom, which, with its bright fire, tasteful little lamp, white coverlets and general air of fresh orderliness, made a comfortable appearance. The air was scented, too, with some pleasant odour of a not too pungent kind. But the table lacked one customary feature; no tea was laid as it was wont to be at this hour. The child gazed round in surprise. Her mother was in bed, lying back on raised pillows, and with a restless, half-pettish look on her face.

"Where have you been?" she asked querulously, her voice husky and feeble, as if from a severe cold. "Why are you so late?"

Ida did not answer at once, but went straight to the bed and offered the accustomed kiss. Her mother waved her off.

"No, no; don't kiss me. Can't you see what a sore throat I've got? You might catch it. And I haven't got you any tea," she went on, her face growing to a calmer expression as she gazed at the child "Ain't I a naughty mother? But it serves you half right for being late. Come and kiss me; I don't think it's catching. No, perhaps you'd better not."

But Ida started forward at the granted leave, and kissed her warmly.

"There now," went on the hoarse voice complainingly, "I shouldn't wonder if you catch it, and we shall both be laid up at once. Oh, Ida, I do feel that poorly, I do! It's the draught under the door; what else can it be? I do, I do feel that poorly!"

She began to cry miserably. Ida forgot all about the tale she had to tell; her own eyes overflowed in sympathy. She put her arm under her mother's neck, and pressed cheek to cheek tenderly.

"Oh, how hot you are, mother! Shall I get you a cup of tea, dear? Wouldn't it make your throat better?"

"Perhaps it would; I don't know. Don't go away, not just yet. You'll have to be a mother to me to-night, Ida. I almost feel I could go to sleep, if you held me like that."

She closed her eyes, but only for a moment, then started up anxiously.

"What am I thinking about! Of course you want your tea."

"No, no; indeed I don't, mother."

"Nonsense; of course you do. See, the kettle is on the bob, and I think it's full. Go away; you make me hotter. Let me see you get your tea, and then perhaps it'll make me feel I could drink a cup. There, you've put your hair all out of order; let me smooth it. Don't trouble to lay the cloth; just use the tray; it's in the cupboard."

Ida obeyed, and set about the preparations. Compare her face with that which rested sideways upon the pillows, and the resemblance was as strong as could exist between two people of such different ages: the same rich-brown hair, the same strongly-pencilled eye-brows; the deep-set and very dark eyes, the fine lips, the somewhat prominent jaw-bones, alike in both. The mother was twenty-eight, the daughter ten, yet the face on the pillow was the more childish at present. In the mother's eyes was a helpless look, a gaze of unintelligent misery, such as one could not conceive on Ida's countenance; her lips, too, were weakly parted, and seemed trembling to a sob, whilst sorrow only made the child close hers the firmer. In the one case a pallor not merely of present illness, but that wasting whiteness which is only seen on faces accustomed to borrow artificial hues; in the other, a healthy pearl-tint, the gleamings and gradations of a perfect complexion. The one a child long lost on weary, woful ways, knowing, yet untaught by, the misery of desolation; the other a child still standing upon the misty threshold of unknown lands, looking around for guidance, yet already half feeling that the sole guide and comforter was within.

It was strange that talk which followed between mother and daughter. Lotty Starr (that was the name of the elder child, and it became her much better than any more matronly appellation), would not remain silent, in spite of the efforts it cost her to speak, and her conversation ran on the most trivial topics. Except at occasional moments, she spoke to Ida as to one of her own age, with curious neglect of the relationship between them; at times she gave herself up to the luxury of feeling like an infant dependent on another's care; and cried just for the pleasure of being petted and consoled. Ida had made up her mind to leave her disclosure till the next morning; impossible to grieve her mother with such shocking news when she was so poorly. Yet the little girl with difficulty kept a cheerful countenance; as often as a moment's silence left her to her own reflections she was reminded of the heaviness of heart which made speaking an effort. To bear up under the secret thought of her crime and its consequences required in Ida Starr a courage different alike in quality and degree from that of which children are ordinarily capable. One compensation alone helped her; it was still early in the evening, and she knew there were before her long hours to be spent by her mother's side.

"Do you like me to be with you, mother?" she asked, when a timid question had at length elicited assurance of this joy. "Does it make you feel better?"

"Yes, yes. But it's my throat, and you can't make that better; I only wish you could. But you are a comfort to me, for all that; I don't know what I should do without you. Oh, I sha'n't be able to speak a word soon, I sha'n't!"

"Don't, don't talk, dear. I'll talk instead, and you listen. Don't you think, mother dear, I could--could always sleep with you? I wouldn't disturb you; indeed, indeed I wouldn't! You don't know how quiet I lie. If I'm wakeful ever I seem to have such a lot to think about, and I lie so still and quiet, you can't think. I never wake Mrs. Led ward, indeed. Do let me, mother; just try me!"

Lotty broke out into passionate weeping, wrung her hands, and hid her face in the pillow. Ida was terrified, and exerted every effort to console this strange grief. The outburst only endured a minute or two, however; then a mood of vexed impatience grew out of the anguish and despair, and Lotty pushed away the child fretfully.

"I've often told you, you can't, you mustn't bother me. There, there; you don't mean any harm, but you put me out, bothering me, Ida. Tell me, what do you think about when you lay awake? Don't you think you'd give anything to get off to sleep again? I know I do; I can't bear to think; it makes my head ache so."

"Oh, I like it. Sometimes I think over what I've been reading, in the animal book, and the geography-book; and--and then I begin my wishing-thoughts. And oh, I've such lots of wishing-thoughts, you couldn't believe!"

"And what are the wishing-thoughts about?" inquired the mother, in a matter-of-fact way.

"I often wish I was grown up. I feel tired of being a child; I want to be a woman. Then I should know so much more, and I should be able to understand all the things you tell me I can't now. I don't care for playing at games and going to school."

"You'll be a woman soon enough, Ida," said Lotty, with a quiet sadness unusual in her. "But go on; what else?"

"And then I often wish I was a boy. It must be so much nicer to be a boy. They're stronger than girls, and they know more. Don't you wish I was a boy, mother?"

"Yes, I do, I often do!" exclaimed Lotty. "Boys aren't such a trouble, and they can go out and shift for themselves."

"Oh, but I won't be a trouble to you," exclaimed Ida. "When I'm old enough to leave school--"

She interrupted herself, for the moment she had actually forgotten the misfortune which had come upon her. But her mother did not observe the falling of her countenance, nor yet the incomplete sentence.

"Ida, have I been a bad mother to you?" Lotty sobbed out presently. "If I was to die, would you be sorry?"

"Mother!"

"I've done my best, indeed I've done my best for yon! How many mothers like me would have brought you up as I've done? How many, I'd like to know? And some day you'll hate me; oh yes, you will! Some day you'll wish to forget all about me, and you'll never come to see where I'm buried, and you'll get rid of everything that could remind you of me. How I wish I'd never been born!"

Ida had often to comfort her mother in the latter's fits of low spirits, but had never heard such sad words as these before. The poor child could say nothing in reply; the terrible thought that she herself was bringing new woes to be endured almost broke her heart She clung about her mother's neck and wept passionately.

Lotty shortly after took a draught from a bottle which the child reached out of a drawer for her, and lay pretty still till drowsiness came on. Ida undressed and crept to her side. They had a troubled night, and, when the daylight came again, Lotty was no better. Ida rose in anguish of spirit, torturing herself to find a way of telling what must be told. Yet she had another respite; her mother said that, as it was Saturday, she might as well stay away from school and be a little nurse. And the dull day wore through; the confession being still postponed.

But by the last post at night came Miss Rutherford's letter. Ida was still sitting up, and Lotty had fallen into a doze, when the landlady brought the letter upstairs.

The child took it in, answered an inquiry about her mother in a whisper, and returned to the bedside. She knew the handwriting on the envelope. The dreaded moment had come.

She must have stood more than a quarter of an hour, motionless, gazing on her mother's face, conscious of nothing but an agonised expectation of seeing the sleeper's eyes open. They did open at length, and quickly saw the letter.

"It's from Miss Rutherford, mother," said Ida, her own voice sounding very strange to herself.

"Oh, is it?" said Lotty, in the hoarse whisper which was all she could command "I suppose she wants to know why you didn't go. Read it to me."

Ida read, and, in reading, suffered as she never did again throughout her life.

"DEAR MRS. STARR,--I am very sorry to have to say that Ida must not return to school. I had better leave the explanation to herself; she is truthful, and will tell you what has compelled me to take this step. I grieve to lose her, but have really no choice.--I am, yours truly,

H. RUTHERFORD."

No tears rose; her voice was as firm as though she had been reading in class; but she was pale and cold as death.

Lotty rose in bed and stared wildly.

"What have you done, child?--what ever have you done? Is--is it anything--about *me*."

"I hit Harriet Smales with a slate, and covered her all over with blood, and I thought I'd killed her."

She could not meet her mother's eyes; stood with head hung down, and her hands clasped behind her.

"What made you do it?" asked Lotty in amazement.

"I couldn't help it, mother; she--she said you were a bad woman."

Ida had raised her eyes with a look of love and proud confidence. Lotty shrank before her, clutched convulsively at the bed-clothes, then half raised herself and dashed her head with fearful violence against the wall by which the bed stood. She fell back, half stunned, and lay on the pillows, whilst the child, with outstretched hands, gazed horror-struck. But in a moment Ida had her arms around the distraught woman, pressing the dazed head against her breast. Lotty began to utter incoherent self-reproaches, unintelligible to her little comforter; her voice had become the merest whisper; she seemed to have quite exhausted herself. Just now there came a knock at the door, and Ida was relieved to see Mrs. Ledward, whose help she begged. In a few minutes Lotty had come to herself again, and whispered that she wished to speak to the landlady alone. The latter persuaded Ida to go downstairs for a while, and the child, whose tears had begun to flow, left the room, sobbing in anguish.

"Ain't you better then?" asked the woman, with an apparent effort to speak in a sympathetic tone which did not come easily to her.

"I'm very bad," whispered the other, drawing her breath as if in pain.

"Ay, you've got a bad cold, that's what it is. I'll make you some gruel presently, and put some rum in it. You don't take care of yourself: I told you how it 'ud be when you came in with those wringin' things on, on Thursday night."

"They've found out about me at the school," gasped Lotty, with a despairing look, "and Ida's got sent away."

"She has? Well, never mind, you can find another, I suppose. I can't see myself what she wants with so much schoolin', but I suppose you know best about your own affairs."

"Oh, I feel that bad! If I get over this, I'll give it up--God help me, I will! I'll get my living honest, if there's any way. I never felt so bad as I do now."

"Pooh!" exclaimed the woman. "Wait a bit till you get rid of your sore throat, and you'll think different. Poorly people gets all sorts o' fancies. Keep a bit quiet now, and don't put yourself out so."

"What are we to do? I've only got a few shillings--"

"Well, you'll have money again some time, I suppose. You don't suppose I'll turn you out in the streets? Write to Fred on Monday, and he'll send you something."

They talked till Lotty exhausted herself again, then Ida was allowed to re-enter the room. Mrs. Ledward kept coming and going till her own bed-time, giving what help and comfort she could in her hard, half-indifferent way. Another night passed, and in the morning Lotty seemed a little better. Her throat was not so painful, but she breathed with difficulty, and had a cough. Ida sat holding her mother's hand. It was a sunny morning, and the bells of neighbouring churches began to ring out clearly on the frosty air.

"Ida," said the sick woman, raising herself suddenly, "get me some note-paper and an envelope out of the box; and go and borrow pen and ink, there's a good child."

The materials were procured, and, with a great effort, Lotty managed to arrange herself so as to be able to write. She covered four pages with a sad scrawl, closed the envelope, and was about to direct it, but paused.

"The bells have stopped," she said, listening. "It's half-past eleven. Put on your things, Ida."

The child obeyed, wondering.

"Give me my purse out of the drawer. See, there's a shilling. Now, say this after me: Mr. Abra'm Woodstock, Number--, St. John Street Road."

Ida repeated the address.

"Now, listen, Ida. You put this letter in your pocket; you go down into the Mary'bone road; you ask for a 'bus to the Angel. When you get to the Angel, you ask your way to Number--, St. John Street Road; it isn't far off. Knock at the door, and ask if Mr. Abra'm Woodstock is in. If he is, say you want to see him, and then give him this letter,--into his own hands, and nobody else's. If he isn't in, ask when he will be, and, if it won't be long, wait."

Ida promised, and then, after a long gaze, her mother dropped back again on the pillow, and turned her face away. A cough shook her for a few moments. Ida waited.

"Well, ain't you gone?" asked Lotty faintly.

"Kiss me, mother."

They held each other in a passionate embrace, and then the child went away.

She reached Islington without difficulty, and among the bustling and loitering crowd which obstructs the corner at the Angel, found some one to direct her to the street she sought. She had to walk some distance down St. John Street Road, in the direction of the City, before discovering the house she desired to find. When she reached it, it proved to be a very dingy tenement, the ground-floor apparently used as offices; a much-worn plate on the door exhibited the name of the gentleman to whom her visit was, with his professional description added. Mr. Woodstock was an accountant.

She rang the bell, and a girl appeared. Yes, Mr. Woodstock was at home. Ida was told to enter the passage, and wait.

A door at her right hand as she entered was slightly ajar, and voices could be heard from the other side of it. One of these voices very shortly raised itself in a harsh and angry tone, and Ida could catch what was said.

"Well, Mr. What's-your-name, I suppose I know my own business rather better than you can teach me. It's pretty clear you've been doing your best for some time to set the people against me, and I'm damned if I'll have it! You go to the place on religious pretences, and what your real object may be I don't know; but I do know one thing, and that is, I won't have you hanging about any longer. I'll meet you there myself, and if it's a third-floor window you get pitched out of, well, it won't be my fault. Now I don't want any more talk with you. This is most folks' praying-time; I wonder you're not at it. It's *my* time for writing letters, and I'd rather have your room than your company. I'm a plain-spoken man, you see, a man of business, and I don't mince matters. To come and dictate to me about the state of my houses and of my tenants ain't a business-like proceeding, and you'll excuse me if I don't take it kindly. There's the door, and good morning to you!"

The door opened, and a young man, looking pale and dismayed, came out quickly, and at once left the house. Behind him came the last speaker. At the sight of the waiting child he stood still, and the expression of his face changed from sour annoyance to annoyed surprise.

"Eh? Well?" he exclaimed, looking closely at Ida, his eye-brows contracting.

"I have a letter for Mr. Abra'm Woodstock, sir."

"Well, give it here. Who's it from?"

"Mrs. Starr, sir."

"Who's Mrs. Starr? Come in here, will you?"

His short and somewhat angry tone was evidently in some degree the result of the interview that had just closed, but also pretty clearly an indication of his general manner to strangers. He let the child pass him, and followed her into the room with the letter in his hand. He did not seem able to remove his eyes from her face. Ida, on her side, did not dare to look up at him. He was a massively built, grey-headed man of something more than sixty. Everything about him expressed strength and determination, power alike of body and mind. His features were large and heavy, but the forehead would have become a man of strong intellect; the eyes were full of astonishing vital force, and the chin was a physiognomical study, so strikingly did its moulding express energy of character. He was clean-shaven, and scarcely a seam or wrinkle anywhere broke the hard, smooth surface of his visage, its complexion clear and rosy as that of a child.

Still regarding Ida, he tore open the envelope. At the sight of the writing he, not exactly started, but moved his head rather suddenly, and again turned his eyes upon the messenger.

"Sit down," he said, pointing to a chair. The room was an uncomfortable office, with no fire. He himself took a seat deliberately at a desk, whence he could watch Ida, and began to read. As he did so, his face remained unmoved, but he looked away occasionally, as if to reflect.

"What's your name?" he asked, when he had finished, beginning, at the same time, to tear the letter into very small pieces, which he threw into a waste-paper basket.

"Ida, sir,--Ida Starr."

"Starr, eh?" He looked at her very keenly, and, still looking, and still tearing up the letter, went on in a hard, unmodulated voice. "Well, Ida Starr, it seems your mother wants to put you in the way of earning your living." The child looked up in fear and astonishment. "You can carry a message? You'll say to your mother that I'll undertake to do what I can for you, on one condition, and that is that she puts you in my hands and never sees you again."

"Oh, I can't leave mother!" burst from the child's lips involuntarily, her horror overcoming her fear of the speaker.

"I didn't ask you if you could," remarked Mr. Woodstock, with something like a sneer, tapping the desk with the fingers of his right hand. "I asked whether you could carry a message. Can you, or not?"

"Yes, I can," stammered Ida.

"Then take *that* message, and tell your mother it's all I've got to say. Run away."

He rose and stood with his hands behind him, watching her. Ida made what haste she could to the door, and sped out into the street.

CHAPTER III
ANTECEDENTS

It would not have been easy to find another instance of a union of keen intellect and cold heart so singular as that displayed in the character of Abraham Woodstock. The man s life had been strongly consistent from the beginning; from boyhood a powerful will had borne him triumphantly over every difficulty, and in each decisive instance his will had been directed by a shrewd intelligence which knew at once the strength of its own resources and the multiplied weaknesses of the vast majority of men. In the pursuit of his ends he would tolerate no obstacle which his strength would suffice to remove. In boyhood and early manhood the exuberance of his physical power was wont to manifest itself in brutal self-assertion. At school he was the worst kind of bully, his ferociousness tempered by no cowardice. Later on, he learned that a too demonstrative bearing would on many occasions interfere with his success in life; he toned down his love of muscular victory, and only allowed himself an outbreak every now and then, when he felt he could afford the indulgence. Put early into an accountant's office, and losing his father about the same time (the parent, who had a diseased heart, was killed by an outburst of fury to which Abraham gave way on some trivial occasion), he had henceforth to fight his own battle, and showed himself very capable of winning it. In many strange ways he accumulated a little capital, and the development of commercial genius put him at a comparatively early age on the road to fortune. He kept to the business of an accountant, and by degrees added several other distinct callings. He became a lender of money in several shapes, keeping both a loan-office and a pawnbroker's shop. In middle age he frequented the race-course, but, for sufficient reasons, dropped that pursuit entirely before he had turned his fiftieth year. As a youth he had made a good thing of games of skill, but did not pursue them as a means of profit when he no longer needed the resource.

He married at the age of thirty. This, like every other step he took, was well planned; his wife brought him several thousand pounds, being the daughter of a retired publican with whom Woodstock had had business relations.

Two years after his marriage was born his first and only child, a girl whom they called Lotty. Lotty, as she grew up, gradually developed an unfortunate combination of her parents' qualities; she had her mother's weakness of mind, without her mother's moral sense, and from her father she derived an ingrained stubbornness, which had nothing in common with strength of character. Doubly unhappy was it that she lost her mother so early; the loss deprived her of gentle guidance during her youth, and left her without resource against her father's coldness or harshness. The result was that the softer elements of her character unavoidably degenerated and found expression in qualities not at all admirable, whilst her obstinacy grew the ally of the weakness from which she had most to fear.

Lotty was sent to a day-school till the age of thirteen, then had to become her father's housekeeper. Her friends were very few, none of them likely to be of use to her. Left very much to her own control, she made an acquaintance which led to secret intimacy and open disaster. Rather than face her father with such a disclosure, she left home, and threw herself upon the mercy of the man who had assisted her to go astray. He was generous enough to support her for about a year, during which time her child was born. Then his help ceased.

The familiar choice lay before her--home again, the streets, or starvation. Hardship she could not bear; the second alternative she shrank from on account of her child; she determined to face her father. For him she had no affection, and knew that he did not love her; only desperation could drive her back. She came one Sunday evening, found Mr. Woodstock at home, and, without letting the servant say who was come, went up and entered his presence, the child in her arms. Abraham rose and looked at her calmly. Her disappearance had not troubled him, though he had exerted himself to discover why and whither she was gone, and her return did not visibly affect him. She was a rebel against his authority--so he viewed the matter--and consequently quite beyond the range of his sympathies. He listened to all she had to say, beheld unmoved her miserable tears, and, when she became silent, coolly delivered his ultimatum. For her he would procure a situation, whereby she could earn her living, and therewith his relations to her would end; the child he would put into other hands and have it cared for, but Lotty would lose sight of it for ever. The girl hesitated, but the maternal instinct was very strong in her; the little one began to cry, as if fearing separation from its mother; she decided to refuse.

"Then I shall go on the streets!" she exclaimed passionately. "There's nothing else left for me."

"You can go where you please," returned Abraham.

She tried to obtain work, of course fruitlessly. She got into debt with her land-lady, and only took the fatal step when at length absolutely turned adrift.

That was not quite ten years gone by; she was then but eighteen. Let her have lost her child, and she would speedily have fallen into the last stages of degradation. But the little one lived. She had called it Ida, a name chosen from some tale in the penny weeklies, which were the solace of her misery. She herself took the name of Starr, also from a page of fiction.

Balancing the good and evil of this life in her dark little mind, Lotty determined that one thing there was for which it was worth while to make sacrifices, one end which she felt strong enough to keep persistently in view. Ida should be brought up "respectably"--it was her own word; she should be kept absolutely free from the contamination of her mother's way of living; nay, should, when the time came, go to school, and have good chances. And at the end of all this was a far-off hope, a dim vision of possibilities, a vague trust that her daughter might perchance prove for her a means of returning to that world of "respectability" from which she was at present so hopelessly shut out. She would keep making efforts to get into an honest livelihood as often as an occasion presented itself; and Ida should always live with "respectable" people, cost what it might.

The last resolution was only adhered to for a few months. Lotty could not do without her little one, and eventually brought it back to her own home. It is not an infrequent thing to find little children living in disorderly houses. In the profession Lotty had chosen there are, as in all professions, grades and differences. She was by no means a vicious girl, she had no love of riot for its own sake; she would greatly have preferred a decent mode of life, had it seemed practicable. Hence she did not associate herself with the rank and file of abandoned women; her resorts were not the crowded centres; her abode was not in the quarters consecrated to her business. In all parts of London there are quiet by-streets of houses given up to lodging-letting, wherein are to be found many landladies, who, good easy souls, trouble little about the private morals of their lodgers, so long as no positive disorder comes about and no public scandal is occasioned. A girl who says that she is occupied in a workroom is never presumed to be able to afford the luxury of strict virtue, and if such a one, on taking a room, says that "she supposes she may have friends come to see her?" the landlady will understand quite well what is meant, and will either accept or refuse her for a lodger as she sees good. To such houses as these Lotty confined herself. After some three or four years of various experiences, she hit upon the abode in Milton Street, and there had dwelt ever since. She got on well with Mrs. Ledward, and had been able to make comfortable arrangements for Ida. The other lodgers in the house were generally very quiet and orderly people, and she herself was quite successful in arranging her affairs so as to create no disturbance. She had her regular *clientele*; she frequented the roads about Regent's Park and Primrose Hill; and she supported herself and her child.

Ida Starr's bringing up was in no respect inferior to that she would have received in the home of the average London artisan or small tradesman. At five years old she had begun to go to school; Mrs. Ledward's daughter, a girl of seventeen, took her backwards and forwards every day. At this school she remained three years and a half; then her mother took her away, and put her under the care of Miss Rutherford, a better teacher. When at home, she either amused herself in Lotty's room, or, when that was engaged, made herself comfortable with Mrs. Ledward's family, with one or other of whom she generally passed the night. She heard no bad language, saw nothing improper, listened to no worse conversation than any of the other children at Miss Rutherford's. Even at her present age of ten it never occurred to her to inquire how her mother supported herself. The charges brought by Harriet Smales conveyed to her mind no conception of their true meaning; they were to her mere general calumnies of vague application. Her mother "bad," indeed! If so, then what was the meaning of goodness? For poor Lotty's devotion to the child had received its due reward herein, that she was loved as purely and intensely as any most virtuous parent could hope to be; so little regard has nature for social codes, so utterly is she often opposed to all the precepts of respectability. This phrase of Harriet's was the very first breathing against her mother's character that Ida had ever heard. Lotty had invented fables, for the child's amusement, about her own earlier days. The legend was, that her husband had died about a year after marriage. Of course Ida implicitly believed all this. Her mind contained pictures of a beautiful little house just outside London in which her mother had once lived, and her imagination busied itself with the time when they would both live in just that same way. She was going to be a teacher, so it had been decided in confidential chats, and would one day have a school of her own. In such a future Lotty herself really believed. The child seemed to her extraordinarily clover, and in four more years she would be as old as a girl who had assisted with the little ones in the first school she went to. Lotty was ambitious. Offers of Mrs. Ledward to teach Ida dressmaking, she had put aside; it was not good enough.

Yet Ida was not in reality remarkable either for industry or quickness in learning. At both schools she had frequently to be dealt with somewhat severely. Ability she showed from time to time, but in application she was sadly lacking. Books were distasteful to her, more even than to most children; she learned sometimes by listening to the teacher, but seldom the lessons given her to prepare. At home there were no books to tempt her to read for herself; her mother never read, and would not have known how to set about giving her child a love for such occupation, even had she deemed it needful. And yet Ida always seemed to have abundance to think about; she would sit by herself for hours, without any childlike employment, and still not seem weary. When asked what her thoughts ran upon, she could not give very satisfactory answers; she was always rather slow in expressing herself, and never chattered, even to her mother. One queer and most unchildlike habit she had, which, as if thinking it wrong, she only indulged when quite alone; she loved to sit before a looking-glass and gaze into her own face. At such times her little countenance became very sad without any understood reason.

The past summer had been to her a time of happiness, for there had come comparatively little bad weather, and sunshine was like wine to Ida. The proximity of the park was a great advantage. During the weeks of summer holiday, she spent whole days wandering about the large, grassy tracts by herself, rejoicing in the sensation of freedom from task-work. If she were especially in luck, a dog would come and play about her, deserting for a minute its lawful master or mistress, and the child would roll upon the grass in delighted sport. Or she would find out a warm, shady nook quite near to the borders of the Zoological Gardens, and would lie there with ear eager to catch the occasional sounds from the animals within. The roar of the lion thrilled her with an exquisite trembling; the calls of the birds made her laugh with joy. Once, three years ago, her mother had taken her to Hastings for a week, and when she now caught the cry of the captive sea-gulls, it brought back marvellous memories of the ocean flashing in the sun, of the music of breakers, of the fresh smell of the brine.

Now there had come upon her the first great grief. She had caused her mother bitter suffering, and her own heart was filled with a commensurate pain. Had she been a little older she would already have been troubled by another anxiety; for the last two years her mother's health had been falling away; every now and then had come a fit of illness, and at other times Lotty suffered from a depression of spirits which left her no energy to move about. Ida knew that her mother was often un-happy, but naturally could not dwell long on this as soon as each successive occa-sion had passed away. Indeed, in her heart, she almost welcomed such times, since she was then allowed to sleep upstairs, one of her greatest joys. Lotty was only too well aware of the physical weakness which was gaining upon her. She was mentally troubled, moreover. Ida was growing up; there would come a time, and that very shortly, when it would be necessary either for them to part, or else for herself to change her mode of life. Indeed, she had never from the first quite lost sight of her intention to seek for an honest means of support; and of late years the conscious-ness of her hopeless position had grown to an ever-recurring trouble. She knew the proposed step was in reality impossible to her, yet she persistently thought and talked of it. To Mrs. Ledward she confided at least once a week, generally when she paid her rent, her settled intention to go and find work of some kind in the course of the next two or three days; till at length this had become a standing joke with the landlady, who laughed merrily as often as the subject was mentioned. Lotty had of late let her thoughts turn to her father, whom she had never seen since their part-ing. Not with any affection did she think of him, but, in her despairing moments, it seemed to her impossible that he should still refuse aid if she appealed to him for it. Several times of late she had been on the point of putting her conviction to the test. She had passed his house from time to time, and knew that he still lived there. Perhaps the real reason of her hesitation was, not fear of him, but a dread, which she would not confess to herself, lest he should indeed prove obdurate, and so put an end to her last hope. For what would become of her and of Ida if her health absolutely failed? The poor creature shrank from the thought in horror. The hope connected with her father grew more and more strong. But it needed some very decided crisis to bring her to the point of overcoming all the apprehensions which lay in the way of an appeal to the stern old man This crisis had arrived. The illness which was now upon her she felt to be more serious than any she had yet suffered. Suppose she were to die, and Ida to be left alone in the world Even before she heard of the child's dismissal from school she had all but made up her mind to write to her father, and the shock of that event gave her the last impulse. She wrote a letter of pitiful entreaty. Would he help her to some means of earning a living for herself and her child? She could not part from Ida. Perhaps she had not long to live, and to ask her to give up her child would be too cruel. She would do anything, would go into service, perform the hardest and coarsest toil. She told him how Ida had been brought up, and implored his pity for the child, who at all events was innocent.

When Ida reached home from her visit to the City, she saw her mother risen and sitting by the fire. Lotty had found the suspense insupportable as she lay still, and, though the pains in her chest grew worse and the feeling of lassitude was gaining upon her, she had half-dressed, and even tried to move about. Just before the child's appearance, she seemed to have sunk into something of a doze on her chair, for, as the door opened, she started and looked about her in doubt.

"Where have you been so long?" she asked impatiently.

"I got back as quickly as I could, mother," said Ida, in some surprise.

"Got back? Is school over?"

"From the--the place you sent me to, mother."

"What am I thinking of!" exclaimed Lotty, starting to consciousness. "Come here, and tell me. Did you see--see him, Ida? Mr. Woodstock, you know."

"Yes, mother," began the child, with pale face, "and he--he said I was to tell you--"

She burst into tears, and flew to her mother's neck.

"Oh, you won't send me away from you, mother dear? I can't go away from you!"

Lotty felt she knew what this meant. Fear and trouble wrought with her physical weakness to drive her almost distracted. She sprang up, caught the child by the shoulders, and shook her as if in anger.

"Tell me, can't you?" she cried, straining her weak voice. "What did he say? Don't be a little fool! Can't the child speak?"

She fell back again, seized with a cough which choked her. Ida stayed her sobbing, and looked on in terror. Her mother motioned constantly to her to proceed.

"The gentleman said," Ida continued, with calm which was the result of extreme self-control, "that he would take me; but that you were never to see me again."

"Did he say anything else about me?" whispered Lotty.

"No, nothing else."

"Go--go and tell him you'll come,--you'll leave me."

Ida stood in anguish, speechless and motionless. All at once her mother seemed to forget what she was saying, and sat still, staring into the fire. Several times she shivered. Her hands lay listlessly on her lap; she breathed with difficulty.

Shortly afterwards, the landlady came into the room. She was alarmed at Lotty's condition. Her attempts to arouse the sick woman to consciousness were only partly successful. She went downstairs again, and returned with another woman, a lodger in the house. These two talked together in low tones. The result of their colloquy was that Mrs. Ledward dressed Lotty as well as she could, whilst the other left the house and returned with a cab.

"We're going to take your mother to the hospital," said Mrs. Ledward to the child. "You wait here till we come back, there's a good girl. Now, hold up a bit, Lotty; try and walk downstairs. That's better, my girl."

Ida was left alone.

CHAPTER IV
CHRISTMAS IN TWO HOMES

When Ida Starr was dismissed from school it wanted but a few days to the vacations. The day which followed her mother's removal to the hospital was Christmas Eve. For two hours on the afternoon of Christmas Day, Ida sat in silence by the bedside in the ward, holding her mother's hand. The patient was not allowed to speak, seemed indeed unable to do so. The child might not even kiss her. The Sister and the nurse looked pityingly at Ida when they passed by, and, when the visitors' time was at an end, and she had to rise and go, the Sister put an orange into her hand,

and spoke a few hopeful words.

Night was setting in as she walked homewards; it was cold, and the sky threatened snow. She had only gone a few yards, when there came by a little girl of her own age, walking with some one who looked like a nurse-maid. They were passing; but all at once the child sprang to Ida's side with a cry of recognition. It was little Maud Enderby.

"Where have you been, Ida? Where are you going? Oh, I'm so glad; I wanted so to see you. Miss Rutherford told us you'd left school, and you weren't coming back again. Aren't you really? And sha'n't I see you?"

"I don't know, I think not," said Ida. In her premature trouble she seemed so much older than her friend.

"I told Miss Rutherford you weren't to blame," went on Maud eagerly. "I told her it was Harriet's own fault, and how shockingly she'd behaved to you. I expect you'll come back again after the holidays, don't you?"

Ida shook her head, and said nothing.

"But I shall see you again?" pleaded the little maid. "You know we're always going to be friends, aren't we? Who shall I tell all my dreams to, if I lose you?"

Dreams, in the literal sense of the word. Seldom a week went by, but Maud had some weird vision of the night to recount to her friend, the meaning of which they would together try to puzzle out; for it was an article of faith with both that there were meanings to be discovered, and deep ones.

Ida promised that she would not allow herself to be lost to her friend, and they kissed, and went their several ways.

Throughout the day the door of Mr. Smales's shop had been open, though the shutters were up. But at nightfall it was closed, and the family drew around the tea-table in the parlour which smelt so of drugs. It was their only sitting-room, for as much of the house as could be was let to another family. Besides Mr. Smales and his daughter Harriet, there sat at the table a lad of about thirteen, with a dark, handsome face, which had something of a foreign cast His eyes gleamed at all times with the light of a frank joyousness; he laughed with the unrestraint of a perfectly happy nature. His countenance was capable, too, of a thoughtfulness beyond his years, a gravity which seemed to come of high thoughts or rich imagination. He bore no trace of resemblance to either the chemist or his daughter, yet was their relative.

Mr. Smales had had a sister, who at an early age became a public singer, and so far prospered as to gain some little distinction in two or three opera seasons. Whilst thus engaged, she made the acquaintance of an Italian, Casti by name, fell in love with him, and subsequently followed him to Italy. Her courage was rewarded, for there she became the singer's wife. They travelled for two years, during which time a son was born to them. The mother's health failed; she was unable henceforth to travel with her husband, and, after living in Rome for nearly four years, she died there. The boy was shortly brought back to England by his father, and placed in the care of Mr. Smales, on the understanding that a sum of money should be paid yearly for his support and education. From that day to the present nothing more had been heard of Signor Casti, and all the care of his sister's child had fallen upon poor Smales, who was not too well provided with means to support his own small household. However, he had not failed in the duty, and Julian (his name had been Englished) was still going to school at his uncle's expense. It was by this time understood that, on leaving school, he should come into the shop, and there qualify himself for the business of a chemist.

Had it not been for Julian, the back parlour would have seen but little cheerfulness to-night. Mr. Smales himself was always depressed in mind and ailing in body. Life had proved too much for him; the burden of the recurring daylight was beyond his strength. There was plainly no lack of kindliness in his disposition, and this never failed to come strongly into his countenance as often as he looked at Harriet. She was his only child. Her mother had died of consumption early in their married life, and it was his perpetual dread lest he should discover in Harriet a disposition to the same malady.

His fears had but too much stimulus to keep them alive. Harriet had passed through a sickly childhood, and was growing up with a feeble constitution. Body and mind were alike unhealthy. Of all the people who came in contact with her, her father alone was blind to her distorted sense of right, her baseless resentments, her malicious pleasures, her depraved intellect. His affection she repaid with indifference. At present, the only person she appeared to really like was the servant Sarah, a girl of vicious character.

Harriet had suffered more from Ida's blow than had at first appeared likely. The wound would not heal well, and she had had several feverish nights. For her convenience, the couch had been drawn up between the fire and the table; and, reclining here, she every now and then threw out a petulant word in reply to her father's or Julian's well-meant cheerfulness. But for the boy, the gloomy silence would seldom have been broken. He, however, was full to-night of a favourite subject, and kept up a steady flow of bright narrative. At school he was much engaged just now with the history of Rome, and it was his greatest delight to tell the listeners at home the glorious stories which were his latest acquisitions. All to-day he had been reading Plutarch. The enthusiasm with which he spoke of these old heroes and their deeds went beyond mere boyish admiration of valour and delight in bloodshed; he seemed to be strongly sensible of the real features of greatness in these men's lives, and invested his stories with a glow of poetical colour which found little appreciation in either of his hearers.

"And I was born in Rome, wasn't I, uncle?" he exclaimed at last. "*I* am a Roman; **Romanus sum**!"

Then he laughed with his wonted bright gleefulness. It was half in jest, but for all that there was a genuine warmth on his cheek, and lustre in his fine eyes.

"Some day I will go to Rome again," he said, "and both of you shall go with me. We shall see the Forum and the Capitol! Sha'n't you shout when you see the Capitol, uncle?"

Poor Smales only smiled sadly and shook his head. It was a long way from Marylebone to Rome; greater still the distance between the boy's mind and that of his uncle.

Sarah took Harriet to bed early. Julian had got hold of his Plutarch again, and read snatches of it aloud every now and then. His uncle paid no heed, was sunk in dull reverie. When they had sat thus for more than an hour, Mr. Smales began to exhibit a wish to talk.

"Put the book away, and draw up to the fire, my boy," he said, with as near an approach to heartiness as he was capable of. "It's Christmas time, and Christmas only comes once a year."

He rubbed his palms together, then began to twist the corners of his handkerchief.

"Well, Julian," he went on, leaning feebly forward to the fire, "a year more school, I suppose, and then--business; what?"

"Yes, uncle."

The boy spoke cheerfully, but yet not in the same natural way as before.

"I wish I could afford to make you something better, my lad; you ought to be something better by rights. And I don't well know what you'll find to do in this little shop. The business might be better; yes, might be better. You won't have much practice in dispensing, I'm afraid, unless things improve. It is mostly hair-oil,--and the patent medicines. It's a poor look-out for you, Julian."

There was a silence.

"Harriet isn't quite well yet, is she?" Smales went on, half to himself.

"No, she looked poorly to-night."

"Julian," began the other, but paused, rubbing his hands more nervously than ever.

"Yes, uncle?"

"I wonder what 'ud become of her if I--if I died now? You're growing up, and you're a clever lad; you'll soon be able to shift for yourself. But what'll Harriet do? If only she had her health. And I shall have nothing to leave either her or you, Julian,--nothing,--nothing! She'll have to get her living somehow. I must think of some easy business for her, I must. She might be a teacher, but her head isn't strong enough, I fear. Julian--"

"Yes, uncle?"

"You--you are old enough to understand things, my boy," went on his uncle, with quavering voice. "Suppose, after I'm dead and gone, Harriet should want help. She won't make many friends, I fear, and she'll have bad health. Suppose she was in want of any kind,--you'd stand by her, Julian, wouldn't you? You'd be a friend to her,--always?"

"Indeed I would, uncle!" exclaimed the boy stoutly.

"You promise me that, Julian, this Christmas night?--you promise it?"

"Yes, I promise, uncle. You've always been kind and good to me, and see if I'm not the same to Harriet."

His voice trembled with generous emotion.

"No, I sha'n't see it, my boy," said Smales, shaking his head drearily; "but the promise will be a comfort to me at the end, a comfort to me. You're a good lad, Julian!"

Silence came upon them again.

In the same district, in one of a row of semi-detached houses standing in gardens, lived Ida's little friend, Maud Enderby, with her aunt, Miss Bygrave, a lady of forty-two or forty-three. The rooms were small and dark; the furniture sparse, old-fashioned, and much worn; there were no ornaments in any of the rooms, with the exception of a few pictures representing the saddest incidents in the life of Christ. On entering the front door you were oppressed by the chill, damp atmosphere, and by a certain unnatural stillness. The stairs were not carpeted, but stained a dark colour; a footfall upon them, however light, echoed strangely as if from empty chambers above. There was no sign of lack of repair; perfect order and cleanliness wherever the eye penetrated; yet the general effect was an unspeakable desolation.

Maud Enderby, on reaching home after her meeting with Ida, entered the front parlour, and sat down in silence near the window, where faint daylight yet glimmered. The room was without fire. Over the mantelpiece hung an engraving of the Crucifixion; on the opposite wall were the Agony in the Garden, and an Entombment; all after old masters. The centre table, a few chairs, and a small sideboard were the sole articles of furniture. The table was spread with a white cloth; upon it were a loaf of bread, a pitcher containing milk, two plates, and two glasses.

Maud sat in the cold room for a quarter of an hour; it became quite dark. Then was heard a soft footstep descending the stairs; the door opened, and a lady came in, bearing a lighted lamp, which she stood upon the table. She was tall, very slender, and with a face which a painter might have used to personify the spiritual life. Its outlines were of severe perfection; its expression a confirmed grief, subdued by, and made subordinate to, the consciousness of an inward strength which could convert suffering into triumph. Her garment was black, of the simplest possible design. In looking at Maud, as the child rose from the chair, it was scarcely affection that her eyes expressed, rather a grave compassion. Maud took a seat at the table without speaking; her aunt sat down over against her. In perfect silence they partook of the milk and the bread. Miss Bygrave then cleared the table with her own hands, and took the things out of the room. Maud still kept her place. The child's manner was not at all constrained; she was evidently behaving in her wonted way. Her eyes wandered about the room with rather a dreamy gaze, and, as often as they fell upon her aunt's face, became very serious, though in no degree expressive of fear or even awe.

Miss Bygrave returned, and seated herself near the little girl; then remained thoughtful for some minutes. The breath from their lips was plainly visible on the air. Maud almost shivered now and then, but forced herself to suppress the impulse. Her aunt presently broke the silence, speaking in a low voice, which had nothing of tenderness, but was most impressive in its earnest calm.

"I wish to speak to you before you go upstairs, Maud; to speak of things which you cannot understand fully as yet, but which you are old enough to begin to think about."

Maud was surprised. It was the first time that her aunt had ever addressed her in this serious way. She was used to being all but ignored, though never in a manner which made her feel that she was treated unkindly. There was nothing like confidence between them; only in care for her bodily wants did Miss Bygrave fill the place of the mother whose affection the child had never known. Maud crossed her hands on her lap, and looked up with respectful attention upon her pale sweet little face.

"Do you wonder at all," Miss Bygrave went on, "why we never spend Christmas like your friends do in their homes, with eating and drinking and all sorts of merriment?"

"Yes, aunt, I do."

It was evidently the truth, and given with the simple directness which characterised the child.

"You know what Christmas Day means, Maud?"

"It is the day on which Christ was born."

"And for what purpose did Christ come as a child on earth?"

Maud thought for a moment. She had never had any direct religious teaching; all she knew of these matters was gathered from her regular attendance at church. She replied in a phrase which had rested in her mind, though probably conveying little if any meaning to her.

"He came to make us free from sin."

"And so we should rejoice at His coming. But would it please Him, do you think, to see us showing our joy by indulging in those very sins from which He came to free us?"

Maud looked with puzzled countenance.

"Is it a sin to like cake and sweet things, aunt?"

The gravity of the question brought a smile to Miss Bygrave's close, strong lips.

"Listen, Maud," she said, "and I will tell you what I mean. For you to like such things is no sin, as long as you are still too young to have it explained to you why you should overcome that liking. As I said, you are now old enough to begin to think of more than a child's foolishness, to ask yourself what is the meaning of the life which has been given you, what duties you must set before yourself as you grow up to be a woman. When once these duties have become clear to you, when you understand what the end of life is, and how you should seek to gain it, then many things become sinful which were not so before, and many duties must be performed which previously you were not ready for."

Miss Bygrave spoke with effort, as if she found it difficult to express herself in sufficiently simple phraseology. Speaking, she did not look at the child; and, when the pause came, her eyes were still fixed absently on the picture above the mantel-piece.

"Keep in mind what I shall tell you," she proceeded with growing solemnity, "and some day you will better understand its meaning than you can now. The sin which Christ came to free us from was--fondness for the world, enjoyment of what we call pleasure, desire for happiness on earth. He Himself came to set us the example of one to whom the world was nothing, who could put aside every joy, and make His life a life of sorrows. Even that was not enough. When the time had come, and He had finished His teaching of the disciples whom He chose, He willingly underwent the most cruel of all deaths, to prove that His teaching had been the truth, and to show us that we must face any most dreadful suffering rather than desert what we believe to be right."

She pointed to the crucified figure, and Maud followed the direction of her hand with awed gaze.

"And this," said Miss Bygrave, "is why I think it wrong to make Christmas a time of merriment. In the true Christian, every enjoyment which comes from the body is a sin. If you feel you *like* this or that, it is a sign that you must renounce it, give it up. If you feel fond of life, you must force yourself to hate it; for life is sin. Life is given to us that we may conquer ourselves. We are placed in the midst of sin that we may struggle against its temptations. There is temptation in the very breath you draw, since you feel a dread if it is checked. You must live so as to be ready at any moment to give up your life with gladness, as a burden which it has been appointed you to bear for a time. There is temptation in the love you feel for those around you; it makes you cling to life; you are tempted to grieve if you lose them, whereas death is the greatest blessing in the gift of God. And just because it is so, we must not snatch at it before our time; it would be a sin to kill ourselves, since that would be to escape from the tasks set us. Many pleasures would seem to be innocent, but even these it is better to renounce, since for that purpose does every pleasure exist. I speak of the pleasures of the world. One joy there is which we may and must pursue, the joy of sacrifice. The more the body suffers, the greater should be the delight of the soul; and the only moment of perfect happiness should be that when the world grows dark around us, and we feel the hand of death upon our hearts."

She was silent, and both sat in the cold room without word or motion.

CHAPTER V
POSSIBILITIES

Christmas passed, and the beginning of the New Year drew nigh. And, one morning, as Mr. Woodstock was glancing up and down the pages of a ledger, a telegram was delivered to him. It was from a hospital in the north-west of London. "Your daughter is dying, and wishes to see you. Please come at once."

Lotty's ailment had declared itself as pneumonia. She was frequently delirious, and the substance of her talk at such times led the attendant Sister to ask her, when reason returned, whether she did not wish any relative to be sent for. Lotty was frightened, but, as long as she was told that there was still hope of recovery, declined to mention any name. The stubborn independence which had supported her through these long years asserted itself again, as a reaction after her fruitless appeal; at moments she felt that she could die with her lips closed, and let what might happen to her child. But when she at length read upon the faces of those about her that her fate hung in the balance, and when she saw the face of little Ida, come there she knew not how, looking upon her from the bedside, then her purpose yielded, and in a whisper she told her father's address, and begged that he might be apprised of her state.

Abraham Woodstock arrived at the hospital, but to no purpose. Lotty had lost her consciousness. He waited for some hours; there was no return of sensibility. When it had been long dark, and he had withdrawn from the ward for a little, he was all at once hastily summoned back. He stood by the bedside, his hands behind his back, his face set in a hard gaze upon the pale features on the pillow. Opposite to him stood the medical man, and a screen placed around the bed shut them off from the rest of the ward. All at once Lotty's eyes opened. It seemed as though she recognised her father, for a look of surprise came to her countenance. Then there was a gasping for breath, a struggle, and the eyes saw no more, for all their staring.

Mr. Woodstock left the hospital. At the first public-house he reached he entered and drank a glass of whisky. The barman had forgotten the piece of lemon, and was rewarded with an oath considerably stronger than the occasion seemed to warrant. Arrived at certain cross-ways, Mr. Woodstock paused. His eyes were turned downwards; he did not seem dubious of his way, so much as in hesitation as to a choice of directions. He took a few steps hither, then back; began to wend thither, and again turned. When he at length decided, his road brought him to Milton Street, and up to the door on which stood the name of Mrs. Ledward.

He knocked loudly, and the landlady herself opened.

"A Mrs. Starr lived here, I believe?" he asked.

"She does live here, sir, but she's in the orspital at present, I'm sorry to say."

"Is her child at home?"

"She is, sir."

"Let me see her, will you? In some room, if you please."

Mrs. Ledward's squinting eyes took shrewd stock of this gentleman, and, with much politeness, she showed him into her own parlour. Then she summoned Ida from upstairs, and, the door being closed upon the two, she held her ear as closely as possible to the keyhole.

Ida recognised her visitor with a start, and drew back a little. There were both fear and dislike in her face, fear perhaps predominating.

"You remember coming to see me," said Mr. Woodstock, looking down upon the child, and a trifle askance.

"Yes, sir," was Ida's reply.

"I have just been at the hospital. Your mother is dead."

His voice gave way a little between the first and the last letter of the last word. Perhaps the sound was more to his ear than the thought had been to his mind. Perhaps, also, he felt when it was too late that he ought to have made this announcement with something more of preparation. Ida's eyes were fixed upon his face, and seemed expanding as they gazed; her lips had parted; she was the image of sudden dread. He tried to look away from her, but somehow could not. Then two great tears dropped upon her cheeks, and her mouth began to quiver. She put her hands up to her face, and sobbed as a grown woman might have done.

Mr. Woodstock turned away for a minute, and fingered a china ornament on the mantelpiece. He heard the sobs forcibly checked, and, when there was silence, again faced his grandchild.

"You'll be left all alone now, you see," he said, his voice less hard. "I was a friend of your mother's, and I'll do what I can for you. You'd better come with me to my house."

Ida looked at him in surprise, tempered with indignation.

"If you were a friend of mother's," she said, "why did you want to take me away from her and never let her see me again?"

"Well, you've nothing to do with that," said Abraham roughly. "Go and put your things on, and come with me."

"No," replied Ida firmly. "I don't want to go with you."

"What you want has nothing to do with it. You will do as I tell you."

Abraham felt strangely in this interview. It was as though time were repeating itself, and he was once more at issue with his daughter's childish wilfulness.

Ida did not move.

"Why won't you come?" asked Mr. Woodstock sharply.

"I don't want to," was Ida's answer.

"Look here, then," said the other, after a brief consideration. "You have the choice, and you're old enough to see what it means. You can either come with me and be well cared for, or stay here and shift as best you can; now, be sharp and make up your mind."

"I don't wish to go with you, I'll stay here and do my best."

"Very well."

Mr. Woodstock whistled a bar of an air, stepped from the room, and thence out into the streets.

It was not his intention really to go at once. Irritation had made it impossible for him to speak longer with the child; he would walk the length of the street and return to give her one more chance. Distracted in purpose as he had never been in his life before, he reached Marylebone Road; rain was just beginning to fall, and he had no umbrella with him. He stood and looked back. Ida once out of his sight, that impatient tenderness which her face inspired failed before the recollection of her stubbornness. She had matched her will with his, as bad an omen as well could be. What was the child to him, or he to her? He did not feel capable of trying to make her like him; what good in renewing the old conflicts and upsetting the position of freedom he had attained? Doubtless she inherited a fatal disposition. In his mind lurked the foreknowledge that he might come to be fond of this little outcast, but Woodstock was incapable as yet of understanding that love must and will be its own reward. The rain fell heavier, and at this moment an omnibus came up. He hailed it, saying to himself that he would think the matter over and come back on the morrow. The first part of his purpose he fulfilled; but to Milton Street he never returned.

As soon as he had left the house, Mrs. Ledward bounced into the room where Ida stood.

"You little idjot!" she exclaimed. "What do you mean by refusing a offer like that!--Why, the gentleman's your own father."

"My father!" repeated Ida, in scornful astonishment. "My father died when I was a baby. Mother's told me so often."

"If you believe all your mother told you,--Well, well, you have been a little wooden-head. What made you behave like that to him?--Where does he live, eh?"

"I don't know."

"You do know. Why, I heard him say you'd been to see him. And what are you going to do, I'd like to know? You don't expect me to keep you, I s'pose. Tell me at once where the gentleman lives, and let me take you there. The idea of your turning against your own father!"

"He's **not** my father!" cried Ida passionately. "My father is dead; and now mother's dead, and I'm alone." She turned and went from the room, weeping bitterly.

CHAPTER VI
AN ADVERTISEMENT

In a morning newspaper of March 187--, that is to chapter, appeared a singular advertisement.

"WANTED, human companionship. A young man of four-and-twenty wishes to find a congenial associate of about his own age. He is a student of ancient and modern literatures, a free-thinker in religion, a lover of art in all its forms, a hater of conventionalism. Would like to correspond in the first instance. Address O. W., City News Rooms, W.C."

An advertisement which, naturally, might mean much or little, might be the outcome of an idle whim, or the despairing cry of a hungry heart. It could not be expected to elicit many replies; and brought indeed but one.

Behind the counter of a chemist's shop in Oxford Street there served, day after day, a young assistant much observed of female customers. The young man was handsome, and not with that vulgar handsomeness which is fairly common among the better kind of shop-walkers and counter-keepers. He had rather long black hair, which arranged itself in silky ripples about a face of perfectly clear, though rather dark, complexion. When he smiled, as he frequently did, the effect was very pleasant. He spoke, too, with that musical intonation which is always more or less suggestive of musical thought. He did not seem by any means ideally adapted to the place he occupied here, yet filled it without suspicion of constraint or uneasiness: there was nothing in him to make one suppose that he had ever been accustomed to a better sphere of life.

He lived in the house above the shop, and had done so for about two years; previously he had held a like position in a more modest establishment. His bed-room, which had to serve him as sitting-room also during his free hours, gave indications of a taste not ordinarily found in chemists' assistants. On the walls were several engravings of views in Rome, ancient and modern; and there were two bookcases filled with literature which had evidently known the second-hand stall,--most of the Latin poets, a few Italian books, and some English classics. Not a trace anywhere of the habits and predilections not unfairly associated with the youth of the shop, not even a pipe or a cigar-holder. It was while sitting alone here one evening, half musing, half engaged in glancing over the advertisements in a paper two days old, that the assistant had been attracted by the insertion just quoted. He read and re-read it, became more thoughtful, sighed slightly. Then he moved to the table and took some note-paper out of a writing-case. Still he seemed to be in doubt, hesitated in pressing a pen against his thumb-nail, was on the point of putting the note-paper away again. Ultimately, however, he sat down to write. He covered four pages with a letter, which he then proceeded deliberately to correct and alter, till he had cut it down by about half. Then came another period of doubt before he decided to make a fair copy. But it was finally made, and the signature at the foot was: Julian Casti.

He went out at once to the post.

Two days later he received a reply, somewhat longer than his own epistle. The writer was clearly keeping himself in a tentative attitude. Still, he wrote something about his own position and his needs. He was a teacher in a school in South London, living in lodgings, with his evenings mostly unoccupied. His habits, he declared, were Bohemian. Suppose, by way of testing each other's dispositions, they were to interchange views on some book with which both were likely to be acquainted: say, Keats's poems? In conclusion, the "O. W." of the advertisement signed himself Osmond Waymark.

The result was that, a week after, Casti received an invitation to call on Way-mark, at the latter's lodgings in Walcot Square, Kennington. He arrived on a Saturday evening, just after eight o'clock. The house he sought proved to be one of very modest appearance; small, apparently not too clean, generally uninviting. But a decent-looking woman opened the door, and said that Mr. Waymark would be found in response to a knock at the first-floor front. The visitor made his way up the dark, narrow stair-case, and knocked as bidden. A firm voice summoned him to enter.

From a seat by a table which was placed as near as possible to a very large fire rose a young man whose age might have been either twenty-three or twenty-six. Most people would have inclined to give him the latter figure. He was rather above the average stature, and showed well-hung limbs, with a habit of holding himself which suggested considerable toughness of sinews; he moved gracefully, and with head well held up. His attire spoke sedentary habits; would have been decidedly shabby, but for its evident adaptation to easy-chair and fireside. The pure linen and general tone of cleanliness were reassuring; the hand, too, which he extended, was soft, delicate, and finely formed. The head was striking, strongly individual, set solidly on a rather long and shapely neck; a fine forehead, irregular nose, rather prominent jaw-bones, lips just a little sensual, but speaking good-humour and intellectual character. A heavy moustache; no beard. Eyes dark, keen, very capable of tenderness, but perhaps more often shrewdly discerning or cynically speculative. One felt that the present expression of genial friendliness was unfamiliar to the face, though it by no means failed in pleasantness. The lips had the look of being frequently gnawed in intense thought or strong feeling. In the cheeks no healthy colour, but an extreme sallowness on all the features. Smiling, he showed imperfect teeth. Altogether, a young man upon whom one felt it difficult to pronounce in the earlier stages of acquaintance; whose intimacy but few men would exert themselves to seek; who in all likelihood was chary of exhibiting his true self save when secure of being understood.

Julian Casti was timid with strangers; his eyes fell before the other's look, and he shook hands without speaking. The contrast in mere appearance between the two was very pronounced; both seemed in some degree to be aware of it. Waymark seemed more rugged than in ordinary companionship; the slightly effeminate beauty of Casti, and his diffident, shyly graceful manners, were more noticeable than usual. Waymark inspected his visitor closely and directly; the latter only ventured upon one or two quick side glances. Yet the results were, on the whole, mutually satisfactory.

Julian's eyes glistened at the sight of two goodly bookcases, reaching from floor to ceiling. There were, too, pictures of other than the lodging-house type; engraved heads of the great in art and science, and a few reproductions in pencil or chalk of known subjects, perchance their possessor's own work. On the table lay traces of literary occupation, sheets of manuscript, open books, and the like. On another table stood a tray, with cups and saucers. A kettle was boiling on the fire.

Waymark helped the conversation by offering a cup of coffee, which he himself made.

"You smoke, I hope?" he asked, reaching some cigars from the mantelpiece.

Julian shook his head, with a smile.

"No? How on earth do you support existence?--At all events, you don't, as the railway-carriage phrase has it, object to smoking?"

"Not at all. I like the scent, but was never tempted to go further."

Waymark filled his pipe, and made himself conformable in a low cane-bottom chair, which had stood folded-up against the wall. Talk began to range over very various topics, Waymark leading the way, his visitor only gradually venturing to take the initiative. Theatres were mentioned, but Julian knew little of them; recent books, but with these he had small acquaintance; politics, but in these he had clearly no interest.

"That's a point of contact, at all events," exclaimed Waymark. "I detest the very name of Parliament, and could as soon read Todhunter on Conic Sections as the reports of a debate. Perhaps you're a mathematician?" This with a smile.

"By no means," was the reply. "In fact," Casti went on, "I'm afraid you begin to think my interests are very narrow indeed. My opportunities have been small. I left a very ordinary school at fourteen, and what knowledge I have since got has come from my own efforts. I am sure the profit from our intercourse would be entirely on my side. I have the wish to go in for many things, however,--"

"Oh," broke in the other, "don't suppose that I am a scholar in any sense of the word, or a man of more than average culture. My own regular education came to an end pretty much at the same age, and only a certain stubbornness has forced me into an intellectual life, if you can call it so. Not much intellect required in my every-day business, at all events. The school in which I teach is a fair type of the middle-class commercial 'academy;' the headmaster a nincompoop and charlatan, my fellow-assistants poor creatures, who must live, I suppose,--though one doesn't well understand why. I had always a liking for Greek and Latin and can make shift to read both in a way satisfactory to myself, though I dare say it wouldn't go for much with college examiners. Then, as for my scribbling, well, it has scarcely yet passed the amateur stage. It will some day; simply because I've made up my mind that it shall; but as yet I haven't got beyond a couple of weak articles in weak maga-zines, and I don't exactly feel sure of my way. I rather think we shall approach most nearly in our taste for poetry. I liked much what you had to say about Keats. It de-cided me that we ought to go on."

Julian looked up with a bright smile.

"What did you think at first of my advertisement, eh?" cried Waymark, with a sudden burst of loud laughter. "Queer idea, wasn't it?"

"It came upon me curiously. It was so like a frequent thought of my own actu-ally carried out."

"It was? You have felt that same desperate need of congenial society?"

"I have felt it very strongly indeed. I live so very much alone, and have always done so. Fortunately I am of a very cheerful disposition, or I might have suffered much. The young fellows I see every day haven't much intellect, it must be con-fessed. I used to try to get them under the influence of my own enthusiasms, but they didn't seem to understand me. They care only for things which either repel me, or are utterly without interest."

"Ha! you understand what that means!" Waymark had risen from his low chair, and stood with his back to the fire. His eyes had a new life, and he spoke in a strong, emphatic way which suited well with his countenance. "You know what it is to have to do exclusively with fools and brutes, to rave under the vile restraints of Philistine surroundings? Then you can form some notion of the state I was in when I took the step of writing that advertisement; I was, I firmly believe, on the verge of lunacy! For two or three days I had come back home from the school only to pace up and down the room in an indescribable condition. I get often like that, but this time things seemed reaching a head. Why, I positively cried with misery, absurd as it may sound. My blood seemed too hot, seemed to be swelling out the veins beyond endurance. As a rule I get over these moods by furious walking about the streets half through the night, but I couldn't even do that. I had no money to go in for dissipation: that often helps me. Every book was loathsome to me. My landlady must have overheard something, for she came in and began a conversation about God knows what; I fear I mortally offended her; I could have pitched the poor old woman out of the window! Heavens, how did I get through those nights?"

"And the fit has passed?" inquired Julian when the other ceased.

"The Lord be praised; yes!" Waymark laughed half-scornfully. "There came an editor's note, accepting a thing that had been going from magazine to magazine for three months. This snatched me up into furious spirits. I rushed out to a theatre, drank more than was good for me, made a fool of myself in general,--and then received your letter. Good luck never comes singly."

Julian had watched the strange workings of Waymark's face with close interest. When the latter suddenly turned his eyes, as if to see the effect of all his frankness, Casti coloured slightly and looked away, but with a look of friendly sympathy.

"Do I shock you?" asked the other. "Do you think me rather too much of an animal, for all my spiritual longings?"

"Certainly not, I can well understand you, I believe."

The conversation passed to quieter things. Julian seemed afraid of saying too much about his own experiences, but found opportunities of showing his acquaintance with English poetry, which was quite as extensive as that of his new friend, excepting in the case of a few writers of the day, whom he had not been able to procure. He had taught himself Italian, too, and had read considerably in that language. He explained that his father was an Italian, but had died when he himself was still an infant.

"You have been in Italy?" asked Waymark, with interest.

A strange look came over Julian's features, a look at once bright and melancholy; his fine eyes gleamed as was their wont eight years ago, in the back-parlour in Boston Street, when he was telling tales from Plutarch.

"Not," he said, in a low voice charged with feeling, "since I was three years old.--You will think it strange, but I don't so much long for the modern Italy, for the beautiful scenery and climate, not even for the Italy of Raphael, or of Dante. I think most of classical Italy. I am no scholar, but I love the Latin writers, and can forget myself for hours, working through Livy or Tacitus. I want to see the ruins of Rome; I want to see the Tiber, the Clitumnus, the Aufidus, the Alban Hills, Lake Trasimenus,--a thousand places! It is strange how those old times have taken hold upon me. The mere names in Roman history make my blood warm.--And there is so little chance that I shall ever be able to go there; so little chance."

Waymark had watched the glowing face with some surprise.

"Why, this is famous!" he exclaimed. "We shall suit each other splendidly.

Who knows? We may see Italy together, and look back upon these times of miserable struggle. By the by, have you ever written verses?"

Julian reddened, like a girl.

"I have tried to," he said.

"And do still?"

"Sometimes."

"I thought as much. Some day you shall let me hear them; won't you? And I will read you some of my own. But mine are in the savage vein, a mere railing against the universe, altogether too furious to be anything like poetry; I know that well enough. I have long since made up my mind to stick to prose; it is the true medium for a polemical egotist. I want to find some new form of satire; I feel capabilities that way which shall by no means rust unused. It has pleased Heaven to give me a splenetic disposition, and some day or other I shall find the tongue."

It was midnight before Julian rose to leave, and he was surprised when he discovered how time had flown. Waymark insisted on his guest's having some supper before setting out on his walk home; he brought out of a cupboard a tin of Australian mutton, which, with bread and pickles, afforded a very tolerable meal after four hours' talk. They then left the house together, and Waymark accompanied his friend as far as Westminster Bridge.

"It's too bad to have brought you so far at this hour," said Julian, as they parted.

"Oh, it is my hour for walking," was the reply. "London streets at night are my element. Depend upon it, Rome was poor in comparison!"

He went off laughing and waving his hand.

CHAPTER VII
BETWEEN OLD AND NEW

Julian Casti's uncle had been three years dead. It was well for him that he lived no longer; his business had continued to dwindle, and the last months of the poor man's life were embittered by the prospect of inevitable bankruptcy. He died of an overdose of some opiate, which the anguish of sleeplessness brought him into the habit of taking. Suicide it might have been, yet that was scarcely probable; he was too anxious on his daughter's account to abandon her in this way, for certainly his death could be nothing to her profit. Julian was then already eighteen, and quickly succeeded in getting a situation. Harriet Smales left London, and went to live with her sole relative, except Julian, an aunt who kept a stationer's shop in Colchester. She was taught the business, and assisted her aunt for more than two years, when, growing tired of the life of a country town, she returned to London, and succeeded in getting a place at a stationer's in Gray's Inn Road. This was six months ago. Having thus established herself, she wrote to Julian, and told him where she was.

Julian never forgot the promise he had made to his uncle that Christmas night, eight years ago, when he was a lad of thirteen. Harriet he had always regarded as his sister, and never yet had he failed in brotherly duty to her. When the girl left Colchester, she was on rather bad terms with her aunt, and the latter wrote to Julian, saying that she knew nothing of Harriet's object in going to London, but that it was certainly advisable that some friend should be at hand, if possible, to give her advice; though advice (she went on to say) was seldom acceptable to Harriet. This letter alarmed Julian, as it was the first he had heard of his cousin's new step; the letter from herself at the end of a week's time greatly relieved him, and he went off as soon as possible to see her. He found her living in the house where she was engaged, apparently with decent people, and moderately contented; more than this could never be said of the girl. Since then, he had seen her at least once every week. Sometimes he visited her at the shop; when the weather was fine, they spent the Sunday afternoon in walking together. Harriet's health seemed to have improved since her return to town. Previously, as in her childhood, she had always been more or less ailing. From both father and mother she had inherited an unhealthy body; there was a scrofulous tendency in her constitution, and the slightest casual ill-health, a cold or any trifling accident, always threatened her with serious results. She was of mind corresponding to her body; restless, self-willed, discontented, sour-tempered, querulous. She certainly used no special pains to hide these faults from Julian, perhaps was not herself sufficiently conscious of them, but the young man did not seem to be repelled by her imperfections; he invariably treated her with gentle forbearance, pitied her sufferings, did many a graceful little kindness in hope of pleasing her.

The first interview between Julian and Waymark was followed by a second a few days after, when it was agreed that they should spend each Sunday evening together in Kennington; Julian had no room in which he could well receive visitors. The next Sunday proved fine; Julian planned to take Harriet for a walk in the afternoon, then, after accompanying her home, to proceed to Walcot Square. As was usual on these occasions, he was to meet his cousin at the Holborn end of Gray's Inn Road, and, as also was the rule, Harriet came some twenty minutes late. Julian was scrupulously punctual, and waiting irritated him not a little, but he never allowed himself to show his annoyance. There was always the same kind smile on his handsome face, and the pressure of his hand was warm.

Harriet Smales was about a year younger than her cousin. Her dress showed moderately good taste, with the usual fault of a desire to imitate an elegance which she could not in reality afford. She wore a black jacket, fur-trimmed, over a light grey dress; her black straw hat had a few flowers in front. Her figure was good and her movements graceful; she was nearly as tall as Julian. Her face, however, could not be called attractive; it was hollow and of a sickly hue, even the lips scarcely red. Grey eyes, beneath which were dark circles, looked about with a quick, suspicious glance; the eye-brows made almost a straight line. The nose was of a coarse type, the lips heavy and indicative of ill-temper. The disagreeable effect of these lineaments was heightened by a long scar over her right temple; she evidently did her best to conceal it by letting her hair come forward very much on each side, an arrangement in itself unsuited to her countenance.

"I think I'm going to leave my place," was her first remark to-day, as they turned to walk westward. She spoke in a dogged way with which Julian was familiar enough, holding her eyes down, and, as she walked, swinging her arms impatiently.

"I hope not," said her cousin, looking at her anxiously. "What has happened?"

"Oh, I don't know; it's always the same; people treat you as if you was so much dirt. I haven't been accustomed to it, and I don't see why I should begin now. I can soon enough get a new shop."

"Has Mrs. Ogle been unkind to you?"

"Oh, I don't know, and I don't much care. You're expected to slave just the same, day after day, whether you're feeling well or not."

This indirect and querulous mode of making known her grievances was characteristic of the girl. Julian bore with it very patiently.

"Haven't you been feeling well?" he asked, with the same kindness.

"Well, no, I haven't. My head fairly splits now, and this sun isn't likely to make it any better."

"Let us cross to the shady side."

"'Twon't make any difference; I can't run to get out of the way of horses."

Julian was silent for a little.

"Why didn't you write to me in the week?" she asked presently. "I'm sure it would be a relief to hear from somebody sometimes. It's like a year from one Sunday to another."

"Did I promise to write? I really didn't remember having done so; I'm very sorry. I might have told you about a new friend I've got."

Harriet looked sharply into his face. Julian had made no mention of Waymark on the preceding Sunday; it had been a rainy day, and they had only spent a few minutes together in the parlour which Mrs. Ogle, the keeper of the shop, allowed them to use on these occasions.

"What sort of a friend?" the girl inquired rather sourly.

"A very pleasant fellow, rather older than myself; I made his acquaintance by chance."

Julian avoided reference to the real circumstances. He knew well the difficulty of making Harriet understand them.

"We are going to see each other every Sunday," he went on.

"Then I suppose you'll give up coming for me?"

"Oh no, not at all. I shall see him at night always, after I have left you."

"Where does he live?"

"Rather far off; in Kennington."

"What is he?"

"A teacher in a school. I hope to get good from being with him; we're going to read together, and so on. I wish you could find some pleasant companion of the same kind, Harriet; you wouldn't feel so lonely."

"I dare say I'm better off without anybody. I shouldn't suit them. It's very few people I do suit, or else people don't suit me, one or the other. What's his name, your new friend's?"

"Waymark."

"And he lives in Kennington? Whereabouts?"

"In Walcot Square. I don't think you know that part, do you?"

"What number?"

Julian looked at her with some surprise. He found her eyes fixed with penetrating observation upon his face. He mentioned the number, and she evidently made a mental note of it. She was silent for some minutes.

"I suppose you'll go out at nights with him?" was her next remark.

"It is scarcely likely. Where should we go to?"

"Oh, I don't know, and I don't suppose it matters much, to me."

"You seem vexed at this, Harriet. I'm very sorry. Really, it's the first friend I've ever had. I've often felt the need of some such companionship."

"I'm nobody?" she said, with a laugh, the first today.

Julian's face registered very perfectly the many subtle phases of thought and emotion which succeeded each other in his mind. This last remark distressed him for a moment; he could not bear to hurt another's feelings.

"Of course I meant male friend," he said quickly. "You are my sister."

"No, I'm not," was the reply; and, as she spoke, Harriet glanced sideways at him in a particularly unpleasant manner. She herself meant it to be pleasant.

"Oh yes, you are, Harriet," he insisted good-humouredly. "We've been brother and sister ever since we can remember, haven't we?"

"But we aren't really, for all that," said the girl, looking away. "Well, now you've got somebody else to take you up, I know very well I shall see less of you. You'll be making excuses to get out of the rides when the summer comes again."

"Pray don't say or think anything of the kind, Harriet," urged Julian with feeling. "I should not think of letting anything put a stop to our picnics. It will soon be getting warm enough to think of the river, won't it? And then, if you would like it, there is no reason why my friend shouldn't come with us, sometimes."

"Oh, nonsense! Why, you'd be ashamed to let him know me."

"Ashamed! How can you possibly think so? But you don't mean it; you are joking."

"I'm sure I'm not. I should make mistakes in talking, and all sorts of things. You don't think much of me, as it is, and that would make you like me worse still."

She tossed her head nervously, and swung her arms with the awkward restlessness which always denoted some strong feeling in her.

"Come, Harriet, this is too bad," Julian exclaimed, smiling. "Why, I shall have to quarrel with you, to prove that we're good friends."

"I wish you *would* quarrel with me sometimes," said the girl, laughing in a forced way. "You take all my bad-temper always just in the same quiet way. I'd far rather you fell out with me. It's treating me too like a child, as if it didn't matter how I went on, and I wasn't anything to you."

Of late, Harriet had been getting much into the habit of this ambiguous kind of remark when in her cousin's company. Julian noticed it, and it made him a trifle uneasy. He attributed it, however, to the girl's strangely irritable disposition, and never failed to meet such outbreaks with increased warmth and kindness of tone. To-day, Harriet's vagaries seemed to affect him somewhat unusually. He became silent at times, and then tried to laugh away the unpleasantness, but the laughter was not exactly spontaneous. At length he brought back the conversation to the point from which it had started, and asked if she had any serious intention of leaving Mrs. Ogle.

"I'm tired of being ordered about by people!" Harriet exclaimed. "I know I sha'n't put up with it much longer. I only wish I'd a few pounds to start a shop for myself."

"I heartily wish I had the money to give you," was Julian's reply.

"Don't you save anything at all?" asked his cousin, with affected indifference.

"A little; very little. At all events, I think we shall be able to have our week at the seaside when the time comes. Have you thought where you'd like to go to?"

"No; I haven't thought anything about it. What time shall you get back home to-night?"

"Rather late, I dare say. We sit talking and forget the time. It may be after twelve o'clock."

Harriet became silent again. They reached Hyde Park, and joined the crowds of people going in all directions about the walks. Harriet had always a number of ill-natured comments to make on the dress and general appearance of people they passed. Julian smiled, but with no genuine pleasure. As always, he did his best to lead the girl's thoughts away from their incessant object, hers, elf.

They were back again at the end of Gray's Inn Road by half-past four.

"Well, I won't keep you," said Harriet, with the sour smile. "I know you're in a hurry to be off. Are you going to walk?"

"Yes; I can do it in about an hour."

The girl turned away without further leave-taking, and Julian walked south-wards with a troubled face.

Waymark expected him to tea. At this, their third meeting, the two were al-ready on very easy terms. Waymark did the greater share of the talking, for Julian was naturally of fewer words; from the beginning it was clear that the elder of the friends would have the initiative in most things. Waymark unconsciously displayed something of that egoism which is inseparable from force of character, and to the other this was far from disagreeable; Julian liked the novel sensation of having a strong nature to rely upon. Already he was being led by his natural tendency to hero-worship into a fervid admiration for his friend.

"What have you' been doing with yourself this fine day?" Waymark asked, as they sat down to table.

"I always spend Sunday afternoon with a cousin of mine," replied Julian, with the unhesitating frankness which was natural to him.

"Male or female?"

"Female." There was a touch of colour on his face as he met the other's eye, and he continued rather quickly. "We lived together always as children, and were only separated at my uncle's death, three years ago. She is engaged at a stationer's shop."

"What is a fellow to do to get money?" Waymark exclaimed, when his pipe was well alight. "I'm growing sick of this hand-to-mouth existence. Now if one had a bare competency, what glorious possibilities would open out. The vulgar saying has it that 'time is money;' like most vulgar sayings putting the thing just the wrong way about. 'Money is time,' I prefer to say; it means leisure, and all that follows. Why don't you write a poem on Money, Casti? I almost feel capable of it myself. What can claim precedence, in all this world, over hard cash? It is the fruitful soil wherein is nourished the root of the tree of life; it is the vivifying principle of hu-man activity. Upon it luxuriate art, letters, science; rob them of its sustenance, and they droop like withering leaves. Money means virtue; the lack of it is vice. The devil loves no lurking-place like an empty purse. Give me a thousand pounds to-morrow, and I become the most virtuous man in England. I satisfy all my instincts freely, openly, with no petty makeshifts and vile hypocrisies. To scorn and revile wealth is the mere resource of splenetic poverty. What cannot be purchased with coin of the realm? First and foremost, freedom. The moneyed man is the sole king; the herds of the penniless are but as slaves before his footstool. He breathes with a sense of proprietorship in the whole globe-enveloping atmosphere; for is it not in his power to inhale it wheresoever he pleases? He puts his hand in his pocket, and bids with security for every joy of body and mind; even death he faces with the comforting consciousness that his defeat will only coincide with that of human science. He buys culture, he buys peace of mind, he buys love.--You think not! I don't use the word cynically, but in very virtuous earnest. Make me a millionaire, and I will purchase the passionate devotion of any free-hearted woman the world contains!"

Waymark's pipe had gone out; he re-lit it, with the half-mocking smile which always followed upon any more vehement utterance.

"That I am poor," he went on presently, "is the result of my own pigheaded-ness. My father was a stock-broker, in anything but flourishing circumstances. He went in for some cursed foreign loan or other,--I know nothing of such things,-- and ruined himself completely. He had to take a subordinate position, and died in it. I was about seventeen then, and found myself alone in the world. A friend of my father's, also a city man, Woodstock by name, was left my guardian. He wanted me to begin a business career, and, like a fool, I wouldn't hear of it. Mr. Woodstock and I quarrelled; he showed himself worthy of his name, and told me plainly that, if I didn't choose to take his advice, I must shift for myself. That I professed myself perfectly ready to do; I was bent on an intellectual life, forsooth; couldn't see that the natural order of things was to make money first and be intellectual afterwards. So, lad as I was, I got a place as a teacher, and that's been my business ever since."

Waymark threw himself back and laughed carelessly. He strummed a little with his fingers on the arm of the chair, and resumed:

"I interested myself in religion and philosophy; I became an aggressive disciple of free-thought, as it is called. Radicalism of every kind broke out in me, like an ailment. I bought cheap free-thought literature; to one or two papers of the kind I even contributed. I keep these effusions carefully locked up, for salutary self-humiliation at some future day, when I shall have grown conceited. Nay, I went further. I delivered lectures at working-men's clubs, lectures with violent titles. One, I remember, was called 'The Gospel of Rationalism.' And I was enthusiastic in the cause, with an enthusiasm such as I shall never experience again. Can I imagine myself writing and speaking such things now-a-days? Scarcely: yet the spirit remains, it is only the manifestations which have changed. I am by nature combative; I feel the need of attacking the cherished prejudices of society; I have a joy in outraging what are called the proprieties. And I wait for my opportunity, which has yet to come."

"How commonplace my life has been, in comparison," said Julian, after an interval of thoughtfulness.

"Your nature, I believe, is very pure, and therefore very happy. *I* am what Browning somewhere calls a 'beast with a speckled hide,' and happiness, I take it, I shall never know."

Julian could begin to see that his friend took something of a pleasure in showing and dwelling upon the worst side of his own character.

"You will be happy," he said, "when you once find your true work, and feel that you are doing it well."

"But the motives, the motives!--Never mind, I've talked enough of myself for one sitting. Don't think I've told you everything. Plenty more confessions to come, when time and place shall serve. Little by little you will get to know me, and by then will most likely have had enough of me."

"That is not at all likely; rather the opposite."

When they left the house together, shortly after eleven, Julian's eye fell upon the dark figure of a girl, standing by a gas-lamp on the opposite side of the way. The figure held his gaze. Waymark moved on, and he had to follow, but still looked back. The girl had a veil half down upon her face; she was gazing after the two. She moved, and the resemblance to Harriet was so striking that Julian again stopped. As he did so, the figure turned away, and walked in the opposite direction, till it was lost in the darkness.

Julian went on, and for a time was very silent.

CHAPTER VIII
ACADEMICAL

The school in which Osmond Waymark taught was situated in "a pleasant suburb of southern London" (Brixton, to wit); had its "spacious playground and gymnasium" (the former a tolerable back-yard, the latter a disused coach-house); and, as to educational features, offered, at the choice of parents and guardians, either the solid foundation desirable for those youths predestined to a commercial career, or the more liberal training adapted to minds of a professional bias. Anything further in the way of information was to be obtained by applying to the headmaster, Dr. Tootle.

At present the number of resident pupils was something under forty. The marvel was how so many could be accommodated in so small a house. Two fair-sized bedrooms, and a garret in which the servants could not be persuaded to sleep, served as dormitories for the whole school; the younger children sleeping two together.

Waymark did not reside on the premises. For a stipulated sum of thirteen pounds per quarter he taught daily from nine till five, with an interval of an hour and a half at dinner-time, when he walked home to Walcot Square for such meal as the state of his exchequer would allow. Waymark occupied a prominent place in Dr. Tootle's prospectus. As Osmond Waymark, B.A.,--the degree was a ***bona fide*** one, of London University,--he filled the position of Senior Classical Master; anonymously he figured as a teacher of drawing and lecturer on experimental chemistry. The other two masters, resident, were Mr. O'Gree and Herr Egger; the former, teacher of mathematics, assistant classical master, and professor of gymnastics; the latter, teacher of foreign languages, of music, and of dancing. Dr. Tootle took upon himself the English branches, and, of course, the arduous duty of general superintendence. He was a very tall, thin, cadaverous, bald-headed man. Somehow or other he had the reputation of having, at an earlier stage in his career, grievously over-exerted his brain in literary labour; parents were found, on the whole, ready to accept this fact as an incontestable proof of the doctor's fitness to fill his present office, though it resulted in entire weeks of retreat from the school-room under the excuse of fearful headaches. The only known product of the literary toil which had had such sad results was a very small English Grammar, of course used in the school, and always referred to by the doctor as "my little compendium."

Now and then, Waymark sought refuge from the loneliness of his room in a visit to his colleagues at the Academy. The masters' sitting-room was not remarkable for cosiness, even when a fire burnt in the grate and the world of school was for the time shut out. The floor was uncarpeted, the walls illustrated only with a few maps and diagrams. There was a piano, whereon Herr Egger gave his music lessons. Few rooms in existence could have excelled this for draughts; at all times there came beneath the door a current of wind which pierced the legs like a knife; impossible to leave loose papers anywhere with a chance of finding them in the same place two minutes after.

When Waymark entered this evening, he found his colleagues seated together in silence. Mr. Philip O'Gree--"fill-up" was his own pronunciation of the name--would have been worse than insignificant in appearance, but for the expression of good-humour and geniality which possessed his irregular features. He was red-headed, and had large red whiskers.

Herr Egger was a gentleman of very different exterior. Tall, thick, ungainly, with a very heavy, stupid face, coarse hands, outrageous lower extremities. A mass of coal-black hair seemed to weigh down his head. His attire was un-English, and, one might suspect, had been manufactured in some lonely cottage away in the remote Swiss valley which had till lately been the poor fellow's home. Dr. Tootle never kept his foreign masters long. His plan was to get hold of some foreigner without means, and ignorant of English, who would come and teach French or German in return for mere board and lodging; when the man had learnt a little English, and was in a position to demand a salary, he was dismissed, and a new professor obtained. Egger had lately, under the influence of some desperate delusion, come to our hospitable clime in search of his fortune. Of languages he could not be said to know any; his French and his German were of barbarisms all compact; English as yet he could use only in a most primitive manner. He must have been the most unhappy man in all London. Finding himself face to face with large classes of youngsters accustomed to no kind of discipline, in whom every word he uttered merely excited outrageous mirth, he was hourly brought to the very verge of despair. Constitutionally he was lachrymose; tears came from him freely when distress had reached a climax, and the contrast between his unwieldy form and this weakness of demeanour supplied inexhaustible occasion for mirth throughout the school. His hours of freedom were spent in abysmal brooding.

Waymark entered in good spirits. At the sight of him, Mr. O'Gree started from the fireside, snatched up the poker, brandished it wildly about his head, and burst into vehement exclamations.

"Ha! ha! you've come in time, sir; you've come in time to hear my resolution. I can't stand ut any longer; I won't stand ut a day longer! Mr. Waymark, you're a witness of the outrageous way in which I'm treated in this academy--the way in which I'm treated both by Dr. Tootle and by Mrs. Tootle. You were witness of his insulting behaviour this very afternoon. He openly takes the side of the boys against me; he ridicules my accent; he treats me as no gentleman can treat another, unless one of them's no gentleman at all! And, Mr. Waymark, I won't stand ut!"

Mr. O'Gree's accent was very strong indeed, especially in his present mood. Waymark listened with what gravity he could command.

"You're quite right," he said in reply. "Tootle's behaviour was especially scandalous to-day. I should certainly take some kind of notice of it."

"Notuss, sir, notuss! I'll take that amount of notuss of it that all the metropoluss shall hear of my wrongs. I'll assault 'um, sir; I'll assault 'um in the face of the school,--the very next time he dares to provoke me! I'll rise in my might, and smite his bald crown with his own ruler! I'm not a tall man, Mr. Waymark, but I can reach his crown, and that he shall be aware of before he knows ut. He sets me at naught in my own class, sir; he pooh-poohs my mathematical demonstrations, sir; he encourages my pupils in insubordination! And Mrs. Tootle! Bedad, if I don't invent some device for revenging myself on that supercilious woman. The very next time she presumes to address me disrespectfully at the dinner-table, sir, I'll rise in my might, sir,--see if I don't!--and I'll say to her, 'Mrs. Tootle, ma'am, you seem to forget that I'm a gentleman, and have a gentleman's susceptibilities. When I treat *you* with disrespect, ma'am, pray tell me of ut, and I'll inform you you speak an untruth!'"

Waymark smiled, with the result that the expression of furious wrath immediately passed from his colleague's countenance, giving place to a broad grin.

"Waymark, look here!" exclaimed the Irishman, snatching up a piece of chalk, and proceeding to draw certain outlines upon a black-board. "Here's Tootle, a veritable Goliath;--here's me, as it were David. Observe; Tootle holds in his hand his 'little compendium,' raised in haughty superciliousness. Observe me with the ruler!--I am on tiptoe; I am taking aim; there is wrath in every sinew of my arrum! My arrum descends on the very centre of Tootle's bald pate--"

"Mr. O'Gree!"

The tableau was most effective. Unnoticed by either the Irishman or Way-mark, the door had opened behind them, and there had appeared a little red-faced woman, in slatternly dress. It was Mrs. Tootle. She had overheard almost the whole of O'Gree's vivid comment upon his graphic illustration, in silence, until at length she could hold her peace no longer, and gave utterance to the teacher's name in a voice which trembled with rage and mortification.

"Mr. O'Gree! Are you aware of my presence, sir?"

The chalk dropped from O'Gree's fingers, but otherwise his attitude remained unaltered; struck motionless with horror, he stood pointing to the drawing on the board, his face pale, his eyes fascinated by those of Mrs. Tootle. The latter went on in a high note.

"Well, sir, as soon as you have had enough of your insulting buffoonery, per-haps you will have the goodness to attend to me, and to your duty! What do you mean by allowing the dormitories to get into this state of uproar? There's been a pillow-fight going on for the last half-hour, and you pay no sort of attention; the very house is shaking?"

"I protest I had not heard a sound, ma'am, or I should have--"

"Perhaps you hear nothing now, sir,--and the doctor suffering from one of his very worst headaches, utterly unable to rest even if the house were perfectly quiet!"

O'Gree darted to the door, past Mrs. Tootle, and was lost to sight. There was indeed a desperate uproar in the higher regions of the house. In a moment the noise increased considerably. O'Gree had rushed up without a light, and was battling desperately in the darkness with a score of pillow-fighters, roaring out threats the while at the top of his voice. Mrs. Tootle retired from the masters' room with much affectation of dignity, leaving the door open behind her.

Waymark slammed it to, and turned with a laugh to the poor Swiss.

"In low spirits to-night, I'm afraid, Mr. Egger?"

Egger let his chair tilt forward, rose slowly, drew a yellow handkerchief from his mouth and wiped his eyes with it, then exclaimed, in the most pitiful voice--

"Mr. Waymark, I have made my possible!--I can no more!"

It was his regular phrase on these occasions; Waymark had always much ado to refrain from laughter when he heard it repeated, but he did his best to be seriously sympathetic, and to attempt consolation in such German as was at his command. Egger's despondency only increased, and he wept afresh to hear accents which were intelligible to him. Mr. O'Gree re-entered the room, and the Swiss retired to his comer.

Philip was hot with excitement and bodily exertion; he came in mopping his forehead, and, without turning to Waymark, stood with eyes fixed on the chalk caricatures. Very gradually he turned round. Waymark was watching him, on his face an expression of subdued mirth. Their looks met, and both exploded in laughter.

"Bedad, my boy," exclaimed O'Gree, "I'm devilish sorry! I wouldn't have had it happen for a quarter's salary,--though I sadly need a new pair of breeches. She's a supercilious cat-o-mountain, and she loses no opportunity of insulting me, but after all she's a woman."

"By-the-by, Waymark," he added in a moment, "what a stunner the new governess is! You're a lucky dog, to sit in the same room with her. What's her name, I say?"

"Miss Enderby. You've seen her, have you?"

"I caught a glimpse of her as she came downstairs; it was quite enough; she floored me. She's never been out of my thoughts for a minute since I saw her. 'I love her, I love her, and who shall dare, to chide me for loving that teacher fair!'"

"Well, yes," said Waymark, "she has a tolerable face; seems to me a long way too good to be teaching those unlicked cubs. The dragon wasn't too civil to her, though it was the first day."

"Not civil to her? If I were present, and heard that woman breathe the slight eat incivility, I'd--"

He broke off in the midst of his vehemence with a startled look towards the door.

"Mr. Egger," he exclaimed, "a song; I beg, a song. Come, I'll lead off.

'Miss Enderby hath a beaming eye'--
Bah! I'm not in voice to-night."

Egger was persuaded to sit down to the piano. It was a mournful instrument, reduced to discordant wheeziness by five-finger exercises, but the touch of the Swiss could still evoke from it some kind of harmony. He sang a Volkslied, and in a way which showed that there was poetry in the man's nature, though his outward appearance gave so little promise of it. His voice was very fair, and well suited to express the tender pathos of these inimitable melodies. Waymark always enjoyed this singing; his eyes brightened, and a fine emotion played about his lips. And as he walked along the dark ways to his lodgings, Egger's voice was still in his ears--

"*Der Mensch wenn er fortgeht, der kommt nimmermefr*."

"Heaven be thanked, no!" the young man said to himself.

Poverty was his familiar companion, and had been so for years. His rent paid each week, there often remained a sum quite insufficient for the absolute necessities of existence; for anything more, he had to look to chance pupils in the evenings, and what little he could earn with his pen. He wrote constantly, but as yet had only succeeded in getting two articles printed. Then, it was a necessity of his existence to mix from time to time in the life of the town, and a stroll into the Strand after nightfall inevitably led to the expenditure of whatever cash his pocket contained. He was passionately found of the theatre; the lights about the open entrance drew him on irresistibly, and if, as so often, he had to choose between a meal and a seat in the gallery, the meal was sacrificed. Hunger, indeed, was his normal state; semi-starvation, alternating with surfeits of cheap and unwholesome food, brought about an unhealthy condition of body. Often he returned to Walcot Square from his day-long drudgery, and threw himself upon the bed, too exhausted to light a fire and make his tea,--for he was his own servant in all things except the weekly cleaning-out of the room. Those were dark hours, and they had to be struggled through in solitude.

Weary as he was he seldom went to bed before midnight, sometimes long after, for he clung to those few hours of freedom with something like savage obstinacy; during this small portion of each day at least, he would possess his own soul, be free to think and read. Then came the penalty of anguish unutterable when the morning had to be faced. These dark, foggy February mornings crushed him with a recurring misery which often drove him to the verge of mania. His head throbbing with the torture of insufficient sleep, he lay in dull half-conscious misery till there was no longer time to prepare breakfast, and he had to hasten off to school after a mouthful of dry bread which choked him. There had been moments when his strength failed, and he found his eyes filling with tears of wretchedness. To face the hideous drudgery of the day's teaching often cost him more than it had cost many men to face the scaffold. The hours between nine and one, the hours between half-past two and five, Waymark cursed them minute by minute, as their awful length was measured by the crawling hands of the school-clock. He tried sometimes, in mere self-defence, to force himself into an interest in his work, that the time might go the quicker; but the effort was miserably vain. His senses reeled amid the din and rattle of classes where discipline was unknown and intelligence almost indiscoverable. Not seldom his temper got the better even of sick lassitude; his face at such times paled with passion, and in ungoverned fury he raved at his tormentors. He awed them, too, but only for the moment, and the waste of misery swallowed him up once more.

Was this to be his life?--he asked himself. Would this last for ever?

For some reason, the morning after the visit to the masters' room just spoken of found him in rather better spirits than usual. Perhaps it was that he had slept fairly well; a gleam of unwonted sunshine had doubtless something to do with it. Yet there was another reason, though he would scarcely admit it to himself. It was the day on which he gave a drawing-lesson to Dr. Tootle's two eldest children. These drawing-lessons were always given in a room upstairs, which was also appropriated to the governess who came every morning to teach three other young Tootles, two girls and a boy, the latter considered not yet old enough to go into the school. On the previous day, Waymark had been engaged in the room for half an hour touching up some drawings of boys in the school, which were about to be sent home. He knew that he should find a fresh governess busy with the children, the lady hitherto employed having gone at a moment's notice after a violent quarrel with Mrs. Tootle, an incident which had happened not infrequently before. When he entered the room, he saw a young woman seated with her back to him, penning a copy, whilst the children jumped and rioted about her in their usual fashion. The late governess had been a mature person of features rather serviceable than handsome; that her successor was of a different type appeared sufficiently from the fair round head, the gracefully handed neck, the perfect shoulders, the slight, beautiful form. Waymark took his place and waited with some curiosity till she moved. When she did so, and, rising, suddenly became aware of his presence, there was a little start on both sides; Miss Enderby--so Waymark soon heard her called by the pupils--had not been aware, owing to the noise, of a stranger's entrance, and Waymark on his side was so struck with the face presented to him. He had expected, at the most, a pretty girl of the commonplace kind: he saw a countenance in which refinement was as conspicuous as beauty. She was probably not more than eighteen or nineteen. In speaking with the children she rarely if ever smiled, but exhibited a gentle forbearance which had something touching in it; it was almost as though she appealed for gentleness in return, and feared a harsh word or look.

"That's Mr. Waymark," cried out Master Percy Tootle, when his overquick eyes perceived that the two had seen each other. "He's our drawing-master. Do you like the look of him?"

Miss Enderby reddened, and laid her hand on the boy's arm, trying to direct his attention to a book. But the youngster shook off her gentle touch, and looked at his brothers and sisters with a much too knowing grin. Waymark had contented himself with a slight bow, and at once bent again over his work.

Very shortly the two eldest children, both girls, came in, and with them their mother. The latter paid no attention to Waymark, but proceeded to cross-examine the new governess as to her methods of teaching, her experience, and so on, in the coarse and loud manner which characterised Mrs. Tootle.

"You'll find my children clever," said Mrs. Tootle, "at least, that has been the opinion of all their teachers hitherto. If they don't make progress, it certainly will not be their own fault. At the same time, they are high-spirited, and require to be discreetly managed. This, as I previously informed you, must be done without the help of punishment in any shape; I disapprove of those methods altogether. Now let me hear you give them a lesson in geography."

Waymark retired at this juncture; he felt that it would be nothing less than cruelty to remain. The episode, however, had lightened his day with an interest of a very unusual kind. And so it was that, on the following morning, not only the gleam of watery sunshine, but also the thought of an hour to be spent in the presence of that timid face, brought him on his way to the school with an unwonted resignation. Unfortunately his drawing lessons were only given on two mornings in the week. Still, there would be something in future to look forward to, a novel sensation at The Academy.

CHAPTER IX
THE COUSINS

Harriet Smales had left home in a bad temper that Sunday afternoon, and when she came back to tea, after her walk with Julian, her state of mind did not appear to have undergone any improvement. She took her place at the tea-table in silence. She and Mrs. Ogle were alone this evening; the latter's husband--he was a journeyman printer, and left entirely in his wife's hands the management of the shop in Gray's Inn Road--happened to be away. Mrs. Ogle was a decent, cheerful woman, of motherly appearance. She made one or two attempts to engage Harriet in conversation, but, failing, subsided into silence, only looking askance at the girl from time to time. When she had finished her tea and bread-and-butter, Harriet coughed, and, without facing her companion, spoke in rather a cold way.

"I may be late back to-night, Mrs. Ogle. You won't lock the door?"

"I sha'n't go to bed till eleven myself," was the reply.

"But it may be after twelve when I get back."

"Where are you going to, Harriet?"

"If you must know always, Mrs. Ogle, I'm going to see my friend in Westminster."

"Well, it ain't no business of mine, my girl," returned the woman, not unkindly, "but I think it's only right I should have some idea where you spend your nights. As long as you live in my house, I'm responsible for you, in a way."

"I don't want any one to be responsible for me, Mrs. Ogle."

"Maybe not, my girl. But young people ain't always the best judges of what's good for them, and what isn't. I don't think your cousin 'ud approve of your being out so late. I shall sit up for you, and you mustn't be after twelve."

It was said very decidedly. Harriet made no reply, but speedily dressed and went out. She took an omnibus eastward, and sought a neighbourhood which most decently dressed people would have been chary of entering after nightfall, or indeed at any other time, unless compelled to do so. The girl found the object of her walk in a dirty little public-house at the corner of two foul and narrow by-ways. She entered by a private door, and passed into a parlour, which was behind the bar.

A woman was sitting in the room, beguiling her leisure with a Sunday paper. She was dressed with vulgar showiness, and made a lavish display of jewellery, more or less valuable. Eight years ago she was a servant in Mr. Smales's house, and her name was Sarah. She had married in the meanwhile, and become Mrs. Sprowl.

She welcomed her visitor with a friendly nod, but did not rise.

"I thought it likely you'd look in, as you missed larst week. How's things goin' in your part o' the world?"

"Very badly," returned Harriet, throwing off her hat and cloak, and going to warm her hands and feet at the fire. "It won't last much longer, that's the truth of it."

"Eh well, it's all in a life; we all has our little trials an' troubles, as the sayin' is."

"How's the baby?" asked Harriet looking towards a bundle of wrappers which lay on a sofa.

"I doubt it's too good for this world," returned the mother, grinning in a way which made her ugly face peculiarly revolting. "Dessay it'll join its little brother an' sister before long. Mike put it in the club yes'day."

The burial-club, Mrs. Sprowl meant, and Harriet evidently understood the allusion.

"Have you walked?" went on the woman, doubling up her paper, and then throwing it aside. "Dessay you could do with somethin' to take the cold orff yer chest.--Liz," she called out to some one behind the bar, with which the parlour communicated by an open door; "two Irish!"

The liquor was brought. Presently some one called to Mrs. Sprowl, who went out. Leaning on the counter, in one of the compartments, was something which a philanthropist might perhaps have had the courage to claim as a human being; a very tall creature, with bent shoulders, and head seeming to grow straight out of its chest; thick, grizzled hair hiding almost every vestige of feature, with the exception of one dreadful red eye, its fellow being dead and sightless. He had laid on the counter, with palms downward as if concealing something, two huge hairy paws. Mrs. Sprowl seemed familiar with the appearance of this monster; she addressed him rather bad-temperedly, but otherwise much as she would have spoken to any other customer.

"No, you don't, Slimy! No, you don't! What you have in this house you pay for in coppers, so you know. Next time I catch you tryin' to ring the changes, I'll have you run in, and then you'll get a warm bath, which you wouldn't partic'lar care for."

The creature spoke, in hoarse, jumbled words, not easy to catch unless you listened closely.

"If you've any accusion to make agin me, Mrs. Sprowl, p'r'aps you'll wait till you can prove it. I want change for arf a suvrin: ain't that straight, now?"

"Straight or not, you won't get no change over this counter, so there you've the straight tip. Now sling yer 'ook, Slimy, an' get it somewhere else."

"If you've any accusion to make--"

"Hold yer noise!--What's he ordered, Liz?"

"Pot o' old six," answered the girl.

"Got sixpence, Slimy?"

"No, I ain't, Mrs. Sprowl," muttered the creature. "I've got arf a suvrin."

"Then go an' get change for it. Now, once more, sling yer 'ook."

The man moved away, sending back a horrible glare from his one fiery eye-ball.

Mrs. Sprowl re-entered the parlour.

"I wish you'd take me on as barmaid, Sarah," Harriet said, when she had drunk her glass of spirits.

"Take you on?" exclaimed the other, with surprise. "Why, have you fallen out with your cousin? I thought you was goin' to be married soon."

"I didn't say for sure that I was; I only said I might be. Any way it won't be just yet, and I'm tired of my place in the shop."

"Don't you be a fool, Harriet," said the other, with genial frankness. "You're well enough off. You stick where you are till you get married. You wouldn't make nothin' at our business; 'tain't all sugar an' lemon, an' sittin' drinkin' twos o' whisky till further orders. You want a quiet, easy business, you do, an' you've got it. If you keep worritin' yerself this way, you won't never make old bones, an' that's the truth. You wait a bit, an' give yer cousin a chance to arst you,--if that's what you're troublin' about."

"I've given him lots o' chances," said Harriet peevishly.

"Eh well, give him lots more, an' it'll all come right. We're all born, but we're not buried.--Hev' another Irish?"

Harriet allowed herself to be persuaded to take another glass.

When the clock pointed to half-past nine, she rose and prepared to depart. She had told Mrs. Sprowl that she would take the 'bus and go straight home; but something seemed to have led her to alter her purpose, for she made her way to Westminster Bridge, and crossed the river. Then she made some inquiries of a policeman, and, in consequence, got into a Kennington omnibus. Very shortly she was set down close by Walcot Square. She walked about till, with some difficulty in the darkness, she had discovered the number at which Julian had told her his friend lived. The house found, she began to pace up and down on the opposite pavement, always keeping her eyes fixed on the same door. She was soon shivering in the cold night air, and quickened her walk. It was rather more than an hour before the door she was watching at length opened, and two friends came out together. Harriet followed them as closely as she could, until she saw that she herself was observed. Thereupon she walked away, and, by a circuit, ultimately came back into the main road, where she took a 'bus going northwards.

Harriet's cousin, when alone of an evening, sat in his bedroom, the world shut out, his thoughts in long past times, rebuilding the ruins of a fallen Empire.

When he was eighteen, the lad had the good luck to light upon a cheap copy of Gibbon in a second-hand book-shop. It was the first edition; six noble quarto volumes, clean and firm in the old bindings. Often he had turned longing eyes upon newer copies of the great book, but the price had always put them beyond his reach. That very night he solemnly laid open the first volume at the first page, propping it on a couple of meaner books, and, after glancing through the short Preface, began to read with a mind as devoutly disposed as that of any pious believer poring upon his Bible. "In the second century of the Christian AEra, the empire of Rome comprehended the fairest part of the earth, and the most civilised portion of mankind.

The frontiers of that extensive monarchy were guarded by ancient renown and disciplined valour." With what a grand epic roll, with what anticipations of solemn music, did the noble history begin! Far, far into the night Julian turned over page after page, thoughtless of sleep and the commonplace duties of the morrow.

Since then he had mastered his Gibbon, knew him from end to end, and joyed in him more than ever. Whenever he had a chance of obtaining any of the writers, ancient or modern, to whom Gibbon refers, he read them and added to his knowledge. About a year ago, he had picked up an old Claudian, and the reading of the poet had settled him to a task which he had before that doubtfully sought. He wanted to write either a poem or a drama on some subject taken from the "Decline and Fall," and now, with Claudian's help, he fixed upon Stilicho for his hero. The form, he then decided, should be dramatic. Upon "Stilicho" he had now been engaged for a year, and to-night he is writing the last words of the last scene. Shortly after twelve he has finished it, and, throwing down his pen, he paces about the room with enviable feelings.

He had not as yet mentioned to Waymark the work he was engaged upon, though he had confessed that he wrote verses at times. He wished to complete it, and then read it to his friend. It was now only the middle of the week, and though he had decided previously to wait till his visit to Walcot Square next Sunday before saying a word about "Stilicho," he could not refrain now from hastily penning a note to Waymark, and going out to post it at once.

When the day came, the weather would not allow the usual walk with Harriet, and Julian could not help feeling glad that it was so. He was too pre-occupied to talk in the usual way with the girl, and he knew how vain it would be to try and make her understand his state of mind. Still, he went to see her as usual, and sat for an hour in Mrs. Ogle's parlour. At times, throughout the week, he had thought of the curious resemblance between Harriet and the girl he had noticed on leaving Waymark's house last Sunday, and now he asked her, in a half-jesting way, whether it had really been she.

"How could it be?" said Harriet carelessly. "I can't be in two places at once."

"Did you stay at home that evening?"

"No,--not all the evening."

"What friends are they you go to, when you are out at night, Harriet?"

"Oh, some relations of the Colchester people.--I suppose you've been spending most of your time in Kennington since Sunday?"

"I haven't left home. In fact, I've been very busy. I've just finished some work that has occupied me for nearly a year."

After all, he could not refrain from speaking of it, though he had made up his mind not to do so.

"Work? What work?" asked Harriet, with the suspicious look which came into her grey eyes whenever she heard something she could not understand.

"Some writing. I've written a play."

"A play? Will it be acted?"

"Oh no, it isn't meant for acting."

"What's the good of it then?"

"It's written in verse. I shall perhaps try to get it published."

"Shall you get money for it?"

"That is scarcely likely. In all probability I shall not be able to get it printed at all."

"Then what's the good of it?" repeated Harriet, still suspicious, and a little contemptuous.

"It has given me pleasure, that's all."

Julian was glad when at length he could take his leave. Waymark received him with a pleased smile, and much questioning.

"Why did you keep it such a secret? I shall try my hand at a play some day or other, but, as you can guess, the material will scarcely be sought in Gibbon. It will be desperately modern, and possibly not altogether in accordance with the views of the Lord Chamberlain. What's the time? Four o'clock. We'll have a cup of coffee and then fall to. I'm eager to hear your 'deep-chested music,' your 'hollow oes and aes.'"

The reading took some three hours; Waymark smoked a vast number of pipes the while, and was silent till the close. Then he got up from his easy-chair, took a step forward, and held out his hand. His face shone with the frankest enthusiasm. He could not express himself with sufficient vehemence. Julian sat with the manuscript rolled up in his hands, on his face a glow of delight.

"It's very kind of you to speak in this way," he faltered at length.

"Kind! How the deuce should I speak? But come, we will have this off to a publisher's forth with. Have you any ideas for the next work?"

"Yes; but so daring that they hardly bear putting into words."

"Try the effect on me."

"I have thought," said Julian, with embarrassment, "of a long poem--an Epic. Virgil wrote of the founding of Rome; her dissolution is as grand a subject. It would mean years of preparation, and again years in the writing. The siege and capture of Rome by Alaric--what do you think?"

"A work not to be raised from the heat of youth, or the vapours of wine. But who knows?"

There was high talk in Walcot Square that evening. All unknown to its other inhabitants, the poor lodging-house was converted into a temple of the Muses, and harmonies as from Apollo's lyre throbbed in the hearts of the two friends. The future was their inexhaustible subject, the seed-plot of strange hopes and desires. They talked the night into morning, hardly daunted when perforce they remembered the day's work.

CHAPTER X
THE WAY OUT

The ruling spirit of the Academy was Mrs. Tootle. Her husband's constitutional headache, and yet more constitutional laziness, left to her almost exclusively the congenial task of guiding the household, and even of disciplining the school. In lesson-time she would even flit about the classrooms, and not scruple to administer sharp rebukes to a teacher whose pupils were disorderly, the effect of this naturally being to make confusion worse confounded. The boys of course hated her with the hatred of which schoolboys alone are capable, and many a practical joke was played at her expense, not, however, with impunity. Still more pronounced, if possible, was the animus entertained against Mrs. Tootle's offspring, and it was upon the head of Master Felix that the full energy of detestation concentrated itself. He was, in truth, as offensive a young imp as the soil of a middle-class boarding-school could well produce. If Mrs. Tootle ruled the Academy, he in turn ruled Mrs. Tootle, and on all occasions showed himself a most exemplary autocrat. His position, however, as in the case of certain other autocratic rulers, had its disadvantages; he could never venture to wander out of earshot of his father or mother, who formed his body-guard, and the utmost prudence did not suffice to protect him from an occasional punch on the head, or a nip in a tender part, meant probably as earnest of more substantial kindnesses to be conferred upon him at the very earliest opportunity.

To poor Egger fell the unpleasant duty of instructing these young Tootles in the elements of the French language. For that purpose he went up every morning to the class-room on the first floor, and for a while relieved Miss Enderby of her charge. With anguish of spirit he felt the approach of the moment which summoned him to this dread duty, for, in addition to the lively spite of Master Felix and the other children, he had to face the awful superintendence of Mrs. Tootle herself; who was invariably present at these lessons. Mrs. Tootle had somehow conceived the idea that French was a second mother-tongue to her, and her intercourse with Mr. Egger was invariably carried on in that language. Now this was a refinement of torture, seeing that it was often impossible to gather a meaning from her remarks, whilst to show any such difficulty was to incur her most furious wrath. Egger trembled when he heard the rustle of her dress outside, the perspiration stood on his forehead as he rose and bowed before her.

"Bon jour, Monsieur," she would come in exclaiming. "Quel un beau matin! Vous trouverez les jeunes dames et messieurs en bons esprits ce matin."

The spirits of Master Felix had manifested themselves already in his skilfully standing a book upright on the teacher's chair, so that when Egger subsided from his obeisance he sat down on a sharp edge and was thrown into confusion.

"Monsieur Felix," cried his mother, "que faites-vous la?--Les jeunes messieurs anglais sont plus spirituels que les jeunes messieurs suisses, n'est ce pas, Monsieur Egger?"

"En effet, madame," muttered the teacher, nervously arranging his books.

"Monsieur Egger," exclaimed Mrs. Tootle, with a burst of good humour, "est-ce vrai ce qu'on dit que les Suisses sont si excessivement sujets a etre ***chez-malades***?"

The awful moment had come. What on earth did ***chez-malades*** mean? Was he to answer yes or no? In his ignorance of her meaning, either reply might prove offensive. He reddened, fidgeted on his chair, looked about him with an anguished mute appeal for help. Mrs. Tootle repeated her question with emphasis and a change of countenance which he knew too well. The poor fellow had not the tact to appear to understand, and, as he might easily have done, mystify her by some idiomatic remark. He stammered out his apologies and excuses, with the effect of making Mrs. Tootle furious.

Then followed a terrible hour, at the end of which poor Egger rushed down to the Masters' Room, covered his head with his hands and wept, regardless of the boy strumming his exercises on the piano. Waymark shortly came in to summon him to some other class, whereupon he rose, and, with gestures of despair, groaned out--

"Let me, let me!--I have made my possible; I can no more!"

Waymark alone feared neither Mrs. Tootle nor her hopeful son, and, in turn, was held in some little awe by both of them. The lady had at first tried the effect of interfering in his classes, as she did in those of the other masters, but the result was not encouraging.

"Don't you think, Mr. Waymark," she had said one day, as she walked through the school-room and paused to listen to our friend's explanation of some rule in English grammar; "don't you think it would be better to confine yourself to the terms of the doctor's little compendium? The boys are used to it."

"In this case," replied Waymark calmly, "I think the terms of the compendium are rather too technical for the fourth class."

"Still, it is customary in this school to use the compendium, and it has never yet been found unsatisfactory. Whilst you are discoursing at such length, I observe your class gets very disorderly."

Waymark looked at her, but kept silence. Mrs. Tootle stood still.

"What are you waiting for, Mr. Waymark?" she asked sharply.

"Till your presence has ceased to distract the boys' attention, Mrs. Tootle," was the straightforward reply.

The woman was disconcerted, and, as Waymark preserved his calm silence, she had no alternative but to withdraw, after giving him a look not easily forgotten.

But there was another person whose sufferings under the tyranny of mother and children were perhaps keenest of all. Waymark had frequent opportunities of observing Miss Enderby under persecution, and learned to recognise in her the signs of acutest misery. Many times he left the room, rather than add to her pain by his presence; very often it was as much as he could do to refrain from taking her part, and defending her against Mrs. Tootle. He had never been formally introduced to Miss Enderby, and during several weeks held no kind of communication with her beyond a "good morning" when he entered the room and found her there. The first quarter of a year was drawing to a close when there occurred the first conversation between them. Waymark had been giving some of the children their drawing-lesson, whilst the governess taught the two youngest. The class-time being over, the youngsters all scampered off. For a wonder, Mrs. Tootle was not present, anti Waymark seized the opportunity to exchange a word with the young lady.

"I fear your pupils give you dreadful trouble," he said, as he stood by the window pointing a pencil.

She started at being spoken to.

"They are full of life," she replied, in the low sad voice which was natural to her.

"Which would all seem to be directed towards shortening that of others," said Waymark, with a smile.

"They are intelligent," the governess ventured to suggest, after a silence. "It would be a pleasure to teach them if they--if they were a little more orderly."

"Certainly. If their parents had only common sense--"

He stopped. A flush had risen to the girl's face, and a slight involuntary motion of her hand seemed to warn him. The reason was that Mrs. Tootle stood in the doorway, to which he had his back turned. Miss Enderby said a quick "good morning" and left him.

He was taking up some papers, preparatory to leaving the room, when he noticed that the governess had left behind her a little book in which she was accustomed to jot down lessons for the children. He took it up and examined it. On the first page was written "Maud Enderby, South Bank, Regent's Park." He repeated the name to himself several times. Then he smiled, recalling the way in which the governess had warned him that Mrs. Tootle could overhear what he said. Somehow, this slight gesture of the girl's had seemed to bring them closer to each other; there was an unpremeditated touch of intimacy in the movement, which it pleased him to think of. This was by no means the first time that he had stood with thoughts busied about her, but the brief exchange of words and what had followed gave something of a new complexion to his feelings. Previously he had been interested in her; her striking features had made him wonder what was the history which their expression concealed; but her extreme reticence and the timid coldness of her look had left his senses unmoved. Now he all at once experienced the awakening of quite a new interest; there had been something in her eyes as they met his which seemed to desire sympathy; he was struck with the possibilities of emotion in the face which this one look had revealed to him. Her situation seemed, when he thought of it, to affect him more strongly than hitherto; he felt that it would be more difficult henceforth to maintain his calmness when he saw her insulted by Mrs. Tootle or disrespectfully used by the children.

Nor did the new feelings subside as rapidly as they had arisen. At home that night he was unable to settle to his usual occupations, and, as a visit to his friends in the Masters' Room would have been equally distasteful, he rambled about the streets and so tired himself. His duties did not take him up to the children's classroom on the following morning, but he invented an excuse for going there, and felt rewarded by the very faint smile and the inclination of the head with which Miss Enderby returned his "good morning." Day after day, he schemed to obtain an opportunity of speaking with her again, and he fancied that she herself helped to remove any chances that might have occurred. Throughout his lessons, his attention remained fixed upon her; he studied her face intently, and was constantly discovering in it new meanings. When she caught his eyes thus busy with her, she evinced, for a moment, trouble and uneasiness; he felt sure that she arranged her seat so as to have her back to him more frequently than she had been accustomed to do. Her work appeared to him to be done with less self-forgetfulness than formerly; the rioting and impertinence of the children seemed to trouble her more; she bore Mrs. Tootle's interference with something like fear. Once, when Master Felix had gone beyond his wonted licence, in his mother's absence, Waymark went so far as to call him to order. As soon as he had spoken, the girl looked up at him in a startled way, and seemed silently to beg him to refrain. All this only strengthened the influence she exercised upon Waymark.

Since the climax of wretchedness which had resulted in his advertisement and the forming of Julian Casti's acquaintance, a moderate cheerfulness had possessed him. Now he once more felt the clouds sinking about him, was aware of many a threatening portent, the meaning whereof he too well understood. There had been a week or two of prevailing bad weather, a state of things which always wrought harmfully upon him; his thoughts darkened under the dark sky, and the daily downpour of rain sapped his energies. It was within a few days of Easter, but the prospect of a holiday had no effect upon him. Night after night he lay in fever and unrest. He felt as though some voice were calling upon him to undertake a vaguely hazardous enterprise which yet he knew not the nature of.

On one of these evenings, Mr. O'Gree announced to him that Miss Enderby was going to give up her position at the end of the quarter. Philip had gathered this from a conversation heard during the day between Dr. Tootle and his wife.

"The light of my life will be gone out," exclaimed O'Gree, "when I am no longer able to catch a glimpse of her as she goes past the schoolroom door. And I've never even had a chance of speaking to her. You know the tale of Raleigh and Queen Elizabeth. Suppose I were to rush out and throw my top-coat on the muddy door-step, just as she's going out; d'ye think she'd say thank you?"

"Probably," muttered Waymark, without knowing what he said. It was Mr. O'Gree's habit to affect this violent devotion to each new governess in turn, but Waymark did not seem to find the joke amusing at present.

"Bedad, I'll do it then! Or, rather, I would, if I'd two top-coats. Hang it! There's no behaving like a gentleman on twenty-five pounds a year."

Waymark walked about the streets the greater part of the night, and the next morning came to school rather late. Dr. Tootle had to consult with him about some matter as soon as he arrived.

"You seem indisposed, Mr. Waymark," the doctor remarked, when he had in vain tried to elicit intelligible replies to his questions.

"I am a little out of sorts," the other returned carelessly. "Perhaps we could talk about these things to-morrow."

"As you please," said Dr. Tootle, a little surprised at his assistant's indifference.

It was a drawing-lesson morning. As he went upstairs, his ears apprised him of the state of things he would find in Miss Enderby's room. The approach of the Easter holidays was making the youngsters even more than usually uproarious, and their insubordination had passed beyond all pretence of attending to tasks. When

Waymark entered, his first glance, as always, was towards the governess. She looked harassed and ill; was in vain endeavouring to exert some authority with her gentle voice. Her eyes showed unmistakable gratitude as the teacher appeared, for his approach meant that she would be relieved from the three elder children. Waymark called sharply to his pupils to come and take their places, but without any attention on their part. Master Felix openly urged the rest to assume a defiant attitude, and began to improvise melodies on a trumpet formed by rolling up a copy-book.

"Felix," said Miss Enderby, "give me your copy-book and go to the drawing-lesson."

The boy removed the trumpet from his mouth, and, waving it once round his head, sent it flying across the room at the speaker; it hit her on the cheek. In the same minute, Waymark had bent across his knee a large pointer which stood in a corner of the room, and had snapped it into two pieces. Holding the lighter of these in one hand, with the other hand he suddenly caught Master Felix by the coat-collar, and in a second had him out of the room and on to the landing. Then did the echoes of the Academy wake to such a bellowing as they had probably never heard before. With a grip impossible even to struggle against, Waymark held the young imp under his arm, and plied the broken pointer with great vigour; the stripes were almost as loud as the roarings. There was a rush from the rooms below in the direction of the disturbance; all the boys were in a trice leaping about delightedly on the stairs, and behind them came O'Gree, Egger, and Dr. Tootle himself. From the room above rushed out all the young Tootles, yelling for help. Last of all, from still higher regions of the house there swept down a vision of disordered female attire, dishevelled hair, and glaring eyes; it was Mrs. Tootle, disturbed at her toilet, forgetting all considerations of personal appearance at the alarming outcry. Just as she reached the spot, Waymark's arm dropped in weariness; he flung the howling young monkey into one corner, the stick into another, and deliberately pulled his coat-sleeves into position once more. He felt vastly better for the exercise, and there was even a smile on his heated face.

"You brutal ruffian!" shrieked Mrs. Tootle. "How dare you touch my child? You shall answer for this in the police court, sir."

"Waymark," cried her husband, who had struggled to the scene through the crowd of cheering boys, "what's the meaning of this? You forget yourself, sir. Who gave you authority to use corporal chastisement?"

"The boy has long deserved a good thrashing," he said, "and I'm glad I lost my temper sufficiently to give him a portion of his deserts. If you wish to know the immediate cause, it simply was that he threw a book at his governess's head and hit her."

"Mr. O'Gree," called out the doctor, "take your boys back to their duties, sir! I am quite unable to understand this disgraceful lack of discipline. Every boy who is not at his seat in one minute will have five hundred verses of the Psalms to write out!--Mr. Waymark, I shall be obliged to you if you will step into my study."

Five minutes after, Waymark was closeted with Dr. Tootle. The latter had all at once put off his appearance of indignation.

"Really," he began, "it's a great pity you let yourself be carried away like that. I think it very probable indeed that Felix deserved castigation of some kind, but you would have done much better to report him to me, you know, and let me see to it. You have put me in an awkward position. I fear you must make an apology to Mrs. Tootle, and then perhaps the matter can be allowed to blow over."

"I think not," replied Waymark, whose mind was evidently made up. There was a look of recklessness on his face which one could at any time have detected lurking beneath the hard self-control which usually marked him. "I don't feel disposed to apologise, and I am tired of my position here. I must give it up."

Dr. Tootle was annoyed. It would not be easy to get another teacher of the kind at so cheap a rate.

"Come, you don't mean this," he said. "You are out of temper for the moment. Perhaps the apology could be dispensed with; I think I may promise that it can be. The lad will be no worse for his little correction. Possibly we can come to some more satisfactory arrangements for the future--"

"No," interposed Waymark; "I have quite made up my mind. I mean to give up teaching altogether; it doesn't suit me. Of course I am willing to come as usual the next two days."

"You are aware that this notice should have been given me at the beginning of the quarter?" hinted the principal.

"Oh yes. Of course you will legally owe me nothing. I am prepared for that."

"Well, I shall have to consider it. But I still think that you--"

"As far as I am concerned, the matter is decided. I go at Easter."

"Very well. I think you are blind to your own interest, but of course you do as you please. If Mrs. Tootle should press me to take out a summons against you for assault, of course I--"

"Good morning, Dr. Tootle."

The summons was not taken out, but Waymark's resolution suffered no change. There was another interview between him and the principal, from which he issued with the sum of six pounds ten in his pocket, being half the quarter's salary. He had not applied for this, but did not refuse it when it was offered. Seeing that the total amount of cash previously in his possession was something less than five shillings, he did wisely, perhaps, to compromise with his dignity, and let Dr. Tootle come out of the situation with a certain show of generosity.

CHAPTER XI
BY THE WAYSIDE

"So there ends another chapter. How many more to the end of the story? How many more scenes till the farce is played out? There is something flattering to one's vanity in this careless playing with fate; it is edifying, moreover, to sot circumstances at defiance in this way, now and then, to assert one's freedom. Freedom! What a joke the word must be to whoever is pulling the wires and making us poor puppets dance at his pleasure. Pity that we have to pay the piper so heavily for our involuntary jigging!"

A passage from the letter Waymark wrote to his friend Casti, on the evening when his school-work came to an end. That night he sought rest early, and slept well. The sensations with which he woke next morning were such as he had not experienced for a long time. He was at liberty,--with six pounds ten in his pocket. He could do what he liked and go whither he liked,--till lack of a dinner should remind him that a man's hardest master is his own body. He dressed leisurely, and, having dressed, treated himself to an egg for breakfast. Absolutely no need for hurry; the thought of school-hours dismissed for ever; a horizon quite free from the vision of hateful toil; in the real sky overhead a gleam of real sunshine, as if to make credible this sudden change. His mood was still complete recklessness, a revolt against the idea of responsibility, indifference to all beyond the moment.

It was Thursday; the morrow would be Good Friday; after that the intervention of two clear days before the commencement of a new week In the meantime the sun was really shining, and the fresh spring air invited to the open ways. Waymark closed the door of his room behind him, and went downstairs, whistling to himself. But, before reaching the bottom, he turned and went back again. It seemed warm enough to sit in one of the parks and read. He laid his hand on a book, almost at haphazard, to put in his pocket. Then he walked very leisurely along Kennington Road, and on, and on, till he had crossed the river.

Wondering in which direction he should next turn, he suddenly found himself repeating, with unaccountable transition of thought, the words "South Bank, Regent's Park." In all likelihood, he said to himself presently, they were suggested by some inscription on a passing omnibus, noted unconsciously. The address was that he had read in Miss Enderby's note-book. Why not ramble in that direction as well as another, and amuse himself by guessing which house it was that the governess lived in? He had not seen her since the uproar which had terminated his connection with the young Tootles. Was it true that she had then already decided to give up her position? If not, his outbreak of temper had doubtless resulted unpleasantly for her, seeing that Mrs. Tootle would almost certainly dismiss her out of mere spite. Several times during the last two days he had thought of conveying to her a note by some means, to express in some way or other this fear, and the regret it caused him; the real motive, he knew well enough, would be a hope of receiving a reply from her. But now she had perhaps left the school, and he did not know her exact address. He made his way across the Park in the direction of St. John's Wood, and had soon reached South Bank.

He had walked once the length of the road, and was looking at the nearest houses before he turned, when a lady came round the corner and paused to avoid him, as he stood in the middle of the pavement. It was Miss Enderby herself. Her embarrassment was apparently not as great as his own. She smiled with friendliness; seemed indeed in a happier frame of mind than any in which Waymark had as yet seen her. But she did not offer her hand, and the other, having raised his hat, was almost on the point of passing on, when he overcame his diffidence and spoke.

"I came here to try and discover where you lived, Miss Enderby."

There was something grotesque in this abruptness; his tone only saved it from impertinence. The girl looked at him with frank surprise.

"Pray don't misunderstand me," he went on hurriedly. "I wished, if possible, to--well, to tell you that I feared I acted thoughtlessly the other day; without regard, I mean, to any consequences it might have for yourself."

"Rather I ought to thank you for defending me. It made no difference in the way you mean. It had already been decided that I should leave. I did not suit Mrs. Tootle."

It was very pleasant to look down into her earnest face, and watch it as she spoke in this unrestrained way. She seemed so slight and frail, evidently thought so depreciatingly of herself, looked as though her life had in it so little joy, that Waymark had speedily assumed a confident attitude, and gazed at her as a man does at one whom he would gladly guard and cherish.

"You were certainly unsuited for the work, in every way," he said, with a smile. "Your efforts were quite wasted there. Still, I am sorry you have left."

"I am going into a family," were her next words, spoken almost cheerfully. "It is in the country, in Essex. There are only two children, quite young. I think I shall succeed better with them; I hope so."

"Then I suppose," Waymark said, moving a little and keeping his eyes fixed on her with an uneasy look, "I shall--I must say good-bye to you, for the last time?"

A scarcely heard "yes" fell from her lips. Her eyes were cast down.

"I am going to make a bold request," Waymark exclaimed, with a sort of recklessness, though his voice expressed no less respect than hitherto. "Will you tell me where you are going to?"

She told him, without looking up, and with a recurrence to the timid manner which had marked her in the schoolroom. This gave Waymark encouragement; his confidence grew as hers diminished.

"Will you let me write to you--occasionally? Would you let me keep up our acquaintance in this way,--so that, if you return to London, I might look forward to meeting you again some time?"

The girl answered timidly--

"I shall be glad to keep up our acquaintance. I shall be glad to hear from you."

Then, at once feeling that she had gone too far, her confusion made her pale. Waymark held out his hand, as if to take leave.

"Thank you very much," he said warmly. "I am very grateful."

She gave him a quick "good-bye," and then passed on. Waymark moved at once in the opposite direction, turning the corner. Then he wished to go back and notice which house she entered, but would not do so lest she should observe him. He walked straight forwards.

How the aspect of the world had changed for him in these few minutes; what an incredible revolution had come to pass in his own desires and purposes t The intellectual atmosphere he breathed was of his own creation; the society of cultured people he had never had an opportunity of enjoying. A refined and virtuous woman had hitherto existed for him merely in the sanctuary of his imagination; he had known not one such. If he passed one in the street, the effect of the momentary proximity was only to embitter his thoughts, by reminding him of the hopeless gulf fixed between his world and that in which such creatures had their being. In revenge, he tried to soil the purity of his ideals; would have persuaded himself that the difference between the two spheres was merely in externals, that he was imposed upon by wealth, education, and superficial refinement of manners. Happily he had never really succeeded in thus deceiving himself, and the effort had only served to aggravate his miseries. The habit of mind, however, had shown itself in the earlier stages of his acquaintance with Miss Enderby. The first sight of her had moved him somewhat, but scarcely with any foreshadowing of serious emotion. He felt that she was different from any woman with whom he had ever stood on an equal footing; but, at the same time, the very possibility of establishing more or less intimate relations with her made him distrustful of his judgment. In spite of himself, he tried to disparage her qualities. She was pretty, he admitted, but then of such a feeble, characterless type; doubtless her understanding corresponded with the weakness of her outward appearance. None the less, he had continued to observe her keenly, and had noted with pleasure every circumstance which contradicted his wilful depreciation of her. His state of mind after the thrashing he gave to young Tootle had been characteristic. What had been the cause of his violence? Certainly not uncontrollable anger, for he had in reality been perfectly cool throughout the affair; simply, then, the pleasure of avenging Miss Enderby. And for this he had sacrificed his place, and left himself without resources. He had acted absurdly; certainly would not have repeated the absurdity had the scene been to act over again. This was not the attitude of one in love, and he knew it. Moreover, though he had thought of writing to her, it would in reality have cost him nothing if she had forthwith passed out of his sight and knowledge. Now how all this had been altered, by a mere chance meeting. The doubts had left him; she was indeed the being from a higher world that he would have liked to believe her from the first; the mysterious note of true sympathy had been struck in that short exchange of words and looks, and, though they had taken leave of each other for who could say how long, mutual knowledge was just beginning, real intercourse about to be established between them. He might write to her, and of course she would reply.

He walked without much perception of time or distance, and found himself at home just before nightfall. He felt disposed for a quiet evening, to be spent in the companionship of his thoughts. But when he had made his coffee and eaten with appetite after the day's rambling, restlessness again possessed him. After all, it was not retirement that he needed; these strange new Imaginings would consort best with motion and the liveliness of the streets. So he put out his lamp, and once more set forth. The night air freshened his spirits; he sang to himself as he went along. It was long since he had been to a theatre, and just now he 'vas so hopelessly poor that he could really afford a little extravagance. So he was soon sitting before the well-known drop of a favourite play-house, as full of light-hearted expectancy as a boy who is enjoying a holiday. The evening was delightful, and passed all too quickly.

The play over, he was in no mood to go straight home. He lit a cigar and drifted with the current westward, out of the Strand and into Pall Mall. A dispute between a cabdriver and his fare induced him to pause for a moment under the colonnade, and, when the little cluster of people had moved on, he still stood leaning against one of the pillars, enjoying the mild air and the scent of his cigar. He felt his elbow touched, and, looking round with indifference, met the kind of greeting for which he was prepared. He shook his head and did not reply; then the sham gaiety of the voice all at once turned to a very real misery, and the girl began to beg instead of trying to entice him in the ordinary way. He looked at her again, and was shocked at the ghastly wretchedness of her daubed face. She was ill, she said, and could scarcely walk about, but must get money somehow; if she didn't, her landlady wouldn't let her sleep in the house again, and she had nowhere else to go to. There could be no mistake about the genuineness of her story, at all events as far as bodily suffering went. Waymark contrasted her state with his own, and took out what money he had in his pocket; it was the change out of a sovereign which he had received at the theatre, and he gave her it all. She stared, and did not understand.

"Are you coming with me?" she asked, feeling obliged to make a hideous attempt at professional coaxing in return for such generosity.

"Good God, no!" Waymark exclaimed. "Go home and take care of yourself."

She thanked him warmly, and turned away at once. As his eye followed her, he was aware that somebody else had drawn near to him from behind. This also was a girl, but of a different kind. She was well dressed, and of graceful, rounded form; a veil almost hid her face, but enough could be seen to prove that she had good looks.

"That a friend of yours?" she asked abruptly, and her voice was remarkably full, clear, and sweet.

Waymark answered with a negative, looking closely at her.

"Then why did you give her all that money?"

"How do you know what I gave her?"

"I was standing just behind here, and could see."

"Well?"

"Nothing; only I should think you are one out of a thousand. You saved me a sovereign, too; I've watched her begging of nearly a dozen people, and I couldn't have stood it much longer."

"You would have given her a sovereign?"

"I meant to, if she'd failed with you."

"Is she a friend of yours?"

"Never saw her before to-night."

"Then you must be one out of a thousand."

The girl laughed merrily.

"In that case," she said, "we ought to know each other, shouldn't we?"

"If we began by thinking so well of each other," returned Waymark, smiling, "we should not improbably suffer a grievous disappointment before long."

"Well, *you* might. You have to take my generosity on trust, but I have proof of yours."

"You're an original sort of girl," said Waymark, throwing away the end of his cigar. "Do you talk to everybody in this way?"

"Pooh, of course not. I shouldn't be worth much if I couldn't suit my conversation to the man I want to make a fool of. Would you rather have me talk in the usual way? Shall I say--"

"I had rather not."

"Well, I knew that."

"And how?"

"Well, *you* don't wear a veil, if I do."

"You can read faces?"

"A little, I flatter myself. Can you?"

"Give me a chance of trying."

She raised her veil, and he inspected her for some moments, then looked away.

"Excellently well, if God did all," he observed, with a smile.

"That's out of a play," she replied quickly. "I heard it a little time ago, but I forget the answer. I'd have given anything to be able to cap you! Then you'd have put me down for a clever woman, and I should have lived on the reputation henceforth and for ever. But it's all my own, indeed; I'm not afraid of crying."

"*Do* you ever cry? I can't easily imagine it."

"Oh yes, sometimes," she answered, sighing, and at the same time lowering her veil again. "But you haven't read my face for me."

"It's a face I'm sorry to have seen."

"Why?" she asked, holding her hands clasped before her, the palms turned outwards.

"I shall think of it often after tonight, and imagine it with all its freshness gone, and marks of suffering and degradation upon it."

"Suffering, perhaps; degradation, no. Why should I be degraded?"

"You can't help yourself. The life you have chosen brings its inevitable consequences."

"Chosen!" she repeated, with an indignant face. "How do you know I had any choice in the matter? You have no right to speak contemptuously, like that."

"Perhaps not. Certainly not. I should have said--the life you are evidently leading."

"Well, I don't know that it makes so much difference. I suppose everybody has a choice at all events between life and death, and you mean that I ought to have killed myself rather than come to this. That's my own business, however, and--"

A man had just passed behind them, and, catching the sound of the girl's voice, had turned suddenly to look at her. She, at the same moment, looked towards him, and stopped all at once in her speech.

"Are you walking up Regent Street?" she asked Waymark, in quite a different voice. "Give me your arm, will you?"

Waymark complied, and they walked together in the direction she suggested.

"What is the matter with you?" he asked. "Why are you trembling?"

"Don't look round. It's that fellow behind us; I know he is following."

"Somebody you know?"

"Yes, and hate. Worse than that, I'm afraid of him. Will you keep with me till he's gone?"

"Of course I will. What harm can he do you though?"

"None that I know of. It's a strange stupid feeling I have. I can't bear the sight of him. Don't look round!"

"Has he been a--a friend of yours?"

"No, no; not in that way. But he follows me about. He'll drive me out of London, I know."

They had reached Piccadilly Circus.

"Look back now," she said, "and see if he's following still."

Waymark turned his head; the man was at a little distance behind. He stopped when he saw himself observed, and stood on the edge of the pavement, tapping his boot with his cane. He was a tall and rather burly fellow, well dressed, with a clean-shaven face.

"Let's make haste round the corner," the girl said, "and get into the restaurant. You must have some supper with me."

"I should be very happy, had I a penny in my pocket."

"See how easily good deeds are forgotten," returned the other, laughing in the old way. "Now comes my turn to give proof of generosity. Come and have some supper all the same."

"No; that's out of the question."

"Fiddlestick Surely you won't desert me when I ask your protection? Come along, and pay me back another time, if you like."

They walked round the corner, then the girl started and ran at her full speed. Waymark followed in the same way, somewhat oppressed by a sense of ridiculousness. They reached the shelter of the restaurant, and the girl led the way upstairs, laughing immoderately.

Supper was served to them, and honoured with due attention by both. Waymark had leisure to observe his companion's face in clearer light. It was beautiful, and, better still, full of character.

He presently bent forward to her, and spoke in a low voice.

"Isn't this the man who followed us just coming in now? Look, he has gone to the table on the right."

She looked round hastily, and shuddered, for she had met the man's eyes.

"Why did you tell me?" she exclaimed impatiently. "Now I can't finish my supper. Wait till he has given his order, and then we will go."

Waymark examined this mysterious persecutor. In truth, the countenance was no good one, and a woman might well dislike to have such eyes turned upon her. It was a strong face; coarse originally, and, in addition to the faults of nature, it now bore the plainest traces of hard living. As soon as he perceived Waymark and his companion, he fixed them with his eyes, and scarcely looked away as long as they remained in the room. The girl seemed shrinking under this gaze, though she sat almost with her back to him. She ceased talking, and, as soon as she saw that Waymark had finished, made a sign to him to pay quickly (with a sovereign she pushed across the table) and let them be gone. They rose, accordingly, and left. The man watched them, but remained seated.

"Are you in a hurry to get home?" the girl asked, when they were in the street again.

"No; time is of no consequence to me."

"Do you live far off?"

"In Kennington. And you?"

"If you like, I'll show you. Let us walk quickly. I feel rather cold."

She led the way into the Strand. At no great distance from Temple Bar she turned off into a small court.

"This is a queer place to live in," observed Waymark, as he looked up at the dark houses.

"Don't be afraid," was the good-humoured reply, as she opened the door with a latch-key. They went up two flights of stairs, then entered a room where a bright fire was burning. Waymark's conductor held a piece of paper to the flame, and lit a lamp. It was a small, pleasantly furnished sitting-room.

"Do you play?" Waymark asked, seeing an open piano, with music upon it.

"I only wish I could. My landlady's daughter is giving me lessons. But I think I'm getting on. Listen to me do this exercise."

She sat down, and, with much conscientious effort, went over some simple bars. Then she looked up at her companion and caught him smiling.

"Well," she exclaimed, in a pet, "you must begin at the beginning in everything, mustn't you? Come and let me hear what you can do."

"Not even so much."

"Then don't laugh at a poor girl doing her best. You have such a queer smile too; it seems both ill-natured and good-natured at the same time. Now wait a minute till I come back."

She went into an inner room, and closed the door behind her. In five minutes it opened again. She appeared in a dressing gown and with her feet in slippers. Her fine hair fell heavily about her shoulders; in her arms she held a beautiful black cat, with white throat and paws.

"This is my child. Don't you admire him? Shake hands, Grim."

"Why Grim?"

"It's short for Grimalkin. The name of a cat in a hook of fairy tales I used to be fond of reading. Don't you think he's got a beautiful face, and a good deal more intelligent than some people we could mention? I picked him up on our door-step, two months ago. Oh, you never saw such a wretched little object, dripping with rain, and with such a poor starved little face, and bones almost coming through the skin. He looked up at me, and begged me as plain as plain could be to have pity on him and help him; didn't you, Grimmy? And so I brought him upstairs, and made him comfortable, and now we shall never part.--Do you like animals?"

"Yes."

The door of the room suddenly opened, and there sprang in a fresh-coloured young girl in hat and jacket, short, plump, pretty, and looking about seventeen. She started back on seeing that the room was occupied.

"What is it, Sally?" asked Grim's mistress, with a good-natured laugh.

"Why, Mrs. Walter told me you wasn't in yet; I'm awful sorry, I beg your pardon."

She spoke with a strong south-west-country accent.

"Do you want me?"

"It's only for Grim," returned Sally, showing something which she held wrapped up in paper. "I'd brought un home a bit o' fish, a nice bit without bone; it'll just suit he."

"Then come and give it he," said the other, with a merry glance at Waymark. "But he mustn't make a mess on the hearthrug."

"Oh, trust un for that," cried Sally. "He won't pull it off the paper."

Grim was accordingly provided with his supper, and Sally ran away with a "good-night."

"Who's that?" Waymark asked. "Where on earth does she come from?"

"She's from Weymouth. They talk queerly there, don't they? She lives in the house, and goes to business. Sally and I are great friends."

"Do you come from the country?" Waymark inquired, as she sat down in an easy-chair and watched the cat eating.

"No, I'm a London girl. I've never been out of the town since I was a little child."

"And how old are you now?"

"Guess."

"Not twenty."

"Eighteen a month ago. All my life before me, isn't it?"

Waymark kept silence for a moment.

"How do you like my room?" she asked suddenly, looking round.

"It's very comfortable. I always thought there were nothing but business places all about here. I should rather like to live in the very middle of the town, like this."

"Should you? That's just what I like. Oh, how I enjoy the noise and the crowds! I should be ill if I had to live in one of those long, dismal streets, where the houses are all the same shape, and costermongers go bawling about all day long. I suppose you live in a place like that?"

"Very much the same."

In taking his handkerchief out, Waymark just happened to feel a book in his overcoat-pocket. He drew it forth to see what it was, having forgotten entirely that he had been carrying the volume about with him since morning.

"What's that?" asked the girl. "Will you let me look? Is it a tale? Lend it me; will you?"

"Do you read books?"

"Oh yes; why not? Let me keep this till you come again. Is this your name written here--Osmond Waymark?"

"Yes. And what is your name?"

"Ida Starr."

"Ida? That's a beautiful name. I was almost afraid to ask you, for fear it should be something common."

"And why shouldn't I have a common name?"

"Because you are by no means a common girl."

"You think not? Well, perhaps you are right. But may I keep the book till I see you again?"

"I had better give it you, for it isn't very likely you will see me again."

"Why not?"

"My acquaintance would be anything but profitable to you. I often haven't enough money to live on, and--"

Ida stooped down and played for a few moments with Grim, who turned over lazily on to his back, and stroked his mistress's hands delicately with his soft white paws.

"But you are a gentleman," she said, rising again, and rustling over the pages of the book she still held. "Are you in the city?"

"The Lord deliver me!"

"What then?"

"I am nothing."

"Then you must be rich."

"It by no means follows. Yesterday I was a teacher in a school. To-day I am what is called out of work."

"A teacher. But I suppose you'll get another place."

"No. I've given it up because I couldn't endure it any longer."

"And how are you going to live?"

"I have no idea."

"Then you must have been very foolish to give away your money like that to-night."

"I don't pretend to much wisdom. If I had had another sovereign in my pocket, no doubt I should have given it you before this, and you wouldn't have refused it."

"How do you know?" she asked sharply. "Why should you think me selfish?"

"Certainly I have no reason to. And by the by, I already owe you money for the supper. I will send it you to-morrow."

"Why not bring it?"

"Better not. I have a good deal of an unpleasant quality which people call pride, and I don't care to make myself uncomfortable unnecessarily."

"You can't have more pride than I have. Look." She held out her hands. "Will you be my friend, really my friend? You understand me?"

"I think I understand, but I doubt whether it is possible."

"Everything is possible. Will you shake hands with me, and, when you come to see me again, let us meet as if I were a modest girl, and you had got to know me in a respectable house, and not in the street at midnight?"

"You really wish it? You are not joking?"

"I am in sober earnest, and I wish it. You won't refuse?"

"If I did I should refuse a great happiness."

He took her hand and again released it.

"And now look at the time," said she, pointing to a clock on the mantelpiece. "Half-past one. How will you get home?"

"Walk. It won't take me more than an hour. May I light my pipe before I start?"

"Of course you may. When shall I see you again?"

"Shall we say this night next week?"

"Very well. Come here any time you like in the evening. I will be at home after six. And then I can give you your book back."

Waymark lit his pipe, stooped to give Grim a stroke, and buttoned up his coat. Ida led the way downstairs. They shook hands again, and parted.

CHAPTER XII
RENT DAY

It was much after his usual hour when Waymark awoke on Good Friday morning. He had been troubled throughout the night with a strangely vivid dream, which seemed to have repeated itself several times; when he at length started into consciousness the anguish of the vision was still upon him.

He rose at once, and dressed quickly, doing his best to shake off the clinging misery of sleep. In a little while it had passed, and he tried to go over in his mind the events of the preceding day. Were they, too, only fragments of a long dream? Surely so many and strange events could not have crowded themselves into one period of twelve hours; and for him, whose days passed with such dreary monotony. The interview with Maud Enderby seemed so unnaturally long ago; that with Ida Starr, so impossibly fresh and recent. Yet both had undoubtedly taken place. He, who but yesterday morning had felt so bitterly his loneliness in the world, and, above all, the impossibility of what he most longed for--woman's companionship--found himself all at once on terms of at least friendly intimacy with two women, both young, both beautiful, yet so wholly different. Each answered to an ideal which he cherished, and the two ideals were so diverse, so mutually exclusive. The experience had left him in a curious frame of mind. For the present, he felt cool, almost indifferent, to both his new acquaintances. He had asked and obtained leave to write to Maud Enderby; what on earth could he write about? How could he address her? He had promised to go and see Ida Starr, on a most impracticable footing. Was it not almost certain that, before the day came round, her caprice would have vanished, and his reception would prove anything but a flattering one? The feelings which both girls had at the time excited in him seemed artificial; in his present mood he in vain tried to resuscitate his interest either in the one or the other. It was as though he had over-exerted his emotional powers, and they lay exhausted. Weariness was the only reality of which he was conscious. He must turn his mind to other things. Having breakfasted, he remembered what day it was, and presently took down a volume of his Goethe, opening at the Easter morning scene in Faust, favourite reading with him. This inspired him with a desire to go into the open air; it was a bright day, and there would be life in the streets. Just as he began to prepare himself for walking, there came a knock at his door, and Julian Casti entered.

"Halloa!" Waymark cried. "I thought you told me you were engaged with your cousin to-day."

"I was, but I sent her a note yesterday to say I was unable to meet her."

"Then why didn't you write at the same time and tell me you were coming? I might have gone out for the day."

"I had no intention of coming then."

"What's the matter? You look out of sorts."

"I don't feel in very good spirits. By the by, I heard from the publishers yesterday. Here's the note."

It simply stated that Messrs. So-and-so had given their best attention to the play of "Stilicho," which Mr. Casti had been so good as to submit to them, and regretted their inability to make any proposal for its publication, seeing that its subject was hardly likely to excite popular interest. They thanked the author for offering it to them, and begged to return the MS.

"Well, it's a disappointment," said Waymark, "but we must try again. I myself am so hardened to this kind of thing that I fear you will think me unsympathetic. It's like having a tooth out. You never quite get used to it, but you learn after two or three experiments to gauge the moment's torture at its true value. Re-direct your parcel, and fresh hope beats out the old discouragement."

"It wasn't altogether that which was making me feel restless and depressed," Casti said, when they had left the house and were walking along. "I suppose I'm not quite right in health just at present. I seem to have lost my natural good spirits of late; the worst of it is, I can't settle to my day's work as I used to. In fact, I have just been applying for a new place, that of dispenser at the All Saints' Hospital. If I get it, it would make my life a good deal more independent. I should live in lodgings of my own, and have much more time to myself."

Waymark encouraged the idea strongly. But his companion could not be roused to the wonted cheerfulness. After a long silence, he all at once put a strange question, and in an abashed way.

"Waymark, have you ever been in love?"

Osmond laughed, and looked at his friend curiously.

"Many thousand times," was his reply.

"No, but seriously," urged Julian.

"With desperate seriousness for two or three days at a time. Never longer."

"Well now, answer me in all earnestness. Do you believe it possible to love a woman whom in almost every respect you regard as your inferior, who you know can't understand your thoughts and aspirations, who has no interest in anything above daily needs?"

"Impossible to say. Is she good-looking?"

"Suppose she is not; yet not altogether plain."

"Then does she love you?"

Julian reddened at the direct application.

"Suppose she seems to."

"Seems to, eh?--On the whole, I should say that I couldn't declare it possible or the contrary till I had seen the girl. I myself should be very capable of falling desperately in love with a girl who hadn't an idea in her head, and didn't know her letters. All I should ask would be passion in return, and--well, yes, a pliant and docile character."

"You are right; the character would go for much. Never mind, we won't speak any more of the subject. It was an absurd question to ask you."

"Nevertheless, you have made me very curious."

"I will tell you more some other time; not now. Tell me about your own plans. What decision have you come to?"

Waymark professed to have formed no plan whatever. This was not strictly true. For some months now, ever and again, as often indeed as he had felt the burden of his schoolwork more than usually intolerable, his thoughts had turned to the one person who could be of any assistance to him, and upon whom he had any kind of claim; that was Abraham Woodstock, his father's old friend. He had held no communication with Mr. Woodstock for four years; did not even know whether he was living. But of him he still thought, now that absolute need was close at hand, and, as soon as Julian Casti had left him to-day, he examined a directory to ascertain whether the accountant still occupied the house in St. John Street Road. Apparently he did. And the same evening Waymark made up his mind to visit Mr. Woodstock on the following day.

The old gentleman was sitting alone when the servant announced a visitor. In personal appearance he was scarcely changed since the visit of his little grand-daughter. Perhaps the eye was not quite so vivid, the skin on forehead and cheeks a trifle less smooth, but his face had the same healthy colour; there was the same repose of force in the huge limbs, and his voice had lost nothing of its resonant firmness.

"Ah!" he exclaimed, as Waymark entered. "You! I've been wondering where you were to be found."

The visitor held out his hand, and Abraham, though he did not rise, smiled not unpleasantly as he gave his own.

"You wanted to see me?" Waymark asked.

"Well, yes. I suppose you've come about the mines."

"Mines? What mines?"

"Oh, then you haven't come about them. You didn't know the Llwg Valley people have begun to pay a dividend?"

Waymark remembered that one of his father's unfortunate speculations had been the purchase of certain shares in some Welsh mines. The money thus invested had remained, for the last nine years, wholly unproductive. Mr. Woodstock explained that things were looking up with the company in question, who had just declared a dividend of 4 per cent. on all their paid-up shares.

"In other words," exclaimed Waymark eagerly, "they owe me some money?"

"Which you can do with, eh?" said Abraham, with a twinkle of good-humoured commiseration in his eye.

"Perfectly. What are the details?"

"There are fifty ten-pound shares. Dividend accordingly twenty pounds."

"By Jingo! How is it to be got at?"

"Do you feel disposed to sell the shares?" asked the old man, looking up side-ways, and still smiling.

"No; on the whole I think not."

"Ho, ho, Osmond, where have you learnt prudence, eh?--Why don't you sit down?--If you didn't come about the mines, why did you come, eh?"

"Not to mince matters," said Waymark, taking a chair, and speaking in an off-hand way which cost him much effort, "I came to ask you to help me to some way of getting a living."

"Hollo!" exclaimed the old man, chuckling. "Why, I should have thought you'd made your fortune by this time. Poetry doesn't pay, it seems?"

"It doesn't. One has to buy experience. It's no good saying that I ought to have been guided by you five years ago. Of course I wish I had been, but it wasn't possible. The question is, do you care to help me now?"

"What's your idea?" asked Abraham, playing with his watch-guard, a smile as of inward triumph flitting about his lips.

"I have none. I only know that I've been half-starved for years in the cursed business of teaching, and that I can't stand it any longer. I want some kind of occupation that will allow me to have three good meals every day, and leave me my evenings free. That isn't asking much, I imagine; most men manage to find it. I don't care what the work is, not a bit. If it's of a kind which gives a prospect of getting on, all the better; if that's out of the question, well, three good meals and a roof shall suffice."

"You're turning out a devilish sensible lad, Osmond," said Mr. Woodstock, still smiling. "Better late than never, as they say. But I don't see what you can do. You literary chaps get into the way of thinking that any fool can make a man of business, and that it's only a matter of condescending to turn your hands to desk work and the ways clear before you. It's a mistake, and you're not the first that'll find it out."

"This much I know," replied Waymark, with decision. "Set me to anything that can be learnt, and I'll be perfect in it in a quarter the time it would take the average man."

"You want your evenings free?" asked the other, after a short reflection. "What will you do with them?"

"I shall give them to literary work."

"I thought as much. And you think you can be a man of business and a poet at the same time? No go, my boy. If you take up business, you drop poetising. Those two horses never yet pulled at the same shaft, and never will."

Mr. Woodstock pondered for a few moments. He thrust out his great legs with feet crossed on the fender, and with his hands jingled coin in his trouser-pockets.

"I tell you what," he suddenly began. "There's only one thing I know of at present that you're likely to be able to do. Suppose I gave you the job of collecting my rents down east."

"Weekly rents?"

"Weekly. It's a rough quarter, and they're a shady lot of customers. You wouldn't find the job over-pleasant, but you might try, eh?"

"What would it bring me in,--to go at once to the point?"

"The rents average twenty-five pounds. Your commission would be seven per cent. You might reckon, I dare say, on five-and-thirty shillings a week."

"What is the day for collecting?"

"Mondays; but there's lots of 'em you'd have to look up several times in a week. If you like I'll go round myself on Tuesday--Easter Monday's no good--and you can come with me."

"I will go, by all means," exclaimed Waymark

Talk continued for some half-hour. When Waymark rose at length, he expressed his gratitude for the assistance promised.

"Well, well," said the other, "wait till we see how things work. I shouldn't wonder if you throw it up after a week or two. However, be here on Tuesday at ten. And prompt, mind: I don't wait for any man."

Waymark was punctual enough on the following Tuesday, and the two drove in a hansom eastward. It was rather a foggy morning, and things looked their worst. After alighting they had a short walk. Mr. Woodstock stopped at the end of an alley.

"You see," he said, "that's Litany Lane. There are sixteen houses in it, and they're all mine. Half way down, on the left, runs off Elm Court, where there are fourteen houses, and those are all mine, too."

Waymark looked. Litany Lane was a narrow passage, with houses only on one side; opposite to them ran a long high wall, apparently the limit of some manufactory. Two posts set up at the entrance to the Lane showed that it was no thoroughfare for vehicles. The houses were of three storeys. There were two or three dirty little shops, but the rest were ordinary lodging-houses, the front-doors standing wide open as a matter of course, exhibiting a dusky passage, filthy stairs, with generally a glimpse right through into the yard in the rear. In Elm Court the houses were smaller, and had their fronts whitewashed. Under the archway which led into the Court were fastened up several written notices of rooms to be let at this or that number. The paving was in evil repair, forming here and there considerable pools of water, the stench and the colour whereof led to the supposition that the inhabitants facilitated domestic operations by emptying casual vessels out of the windows. The dirty little casements on the ground floor exhibited without exception a rag of red or white curtain on the one side, prevailing fashion evidently requiring no corresponding drapery on the other. The Court was a *cul de sac*, and at the far end stood a receptacle for ashes, the odour from which was intolerable. Strangely enough, almost all the window-sills displayed flower-pots, and, despite the wretched weather, several little bird-cages hung out from the upper storeys. In one of them a lark was singing briskly.

They began their progress through the tenements, commencing at the top of Litany Lane. Many of the rooms were locked, the occupiers being away at their work, but in such case the rent had generally been left with some other person in the house, and was forthcoming. But now and then neither rent nor tenant was to be got at, and dire were the threats which Abraham bade the neighbours convey to the defaulters on their return. His way with one and all was curt and vigorous; to Waymark it seemed needlessly brutal. A woman pleading inability to make up her total sum would be cut short with a thunderous oath, and the assurance that, if she did not pay up in a day or two, every stick would be carried off. Pitiful pleading for time had absolutely no effect upon Abraham. Here and there e tenant would complain of high rent, and point out a cracked ceiling, a rotten piece of stairs, or something else imperatively calling for renovation. "If you don't like the room, clear out," was the landlord's sole reply to all such speeches.

In one place they came across an old Irish woman engaged in washing. The room was hung with reeking clothes from wall to wall. For a time it was difficult to distinguish objects through the steam, and Waymark, making his way in, stumbled and almost fell over an open box. From the box at once proceeded a miserable little wail, broken by as terrible a cough as a child could be afflicted with; and Waymark then perceived that the box was being used as a cradle, in which lay a baby gasping in the agonies of some throat disease, whilst drops from the wet clothing trickled on to its face.

On leaving this house, they entered Elm Court. Here, sitting on the doorstep of the first house, was a child of apparently nine or ten, and seemingly a girl, though the nondescript attire might have concealed either sex, and the face was absolutely sexless in its savagery. Her hair was cut short, and round her neck was a bit of steel chain, fastened with string. On seeing the two approach, she sprang up, and disappeared with a bound into the house.

"That's the most infernal little devil in all London, I do believe," said Mr. Woodstock, as they began to ascend the stairs. "Her mother owes two weeks, and if she don't pay something to-day, I'll have her out. She'll be shamming illness, you'll see. The child ran up to prepare her."

The room in question was at the top of the house. It proved to be quite bare of furniture. On a bundle of straw in one corner was lying a woman, to all appearances *in extremis*. She lay looking up to the ceiling, her face distorted into the most ghastly anguish, her lips foaming; her whole frame shivered incessantly.

"Ha, I thought so," exclaimed Abraham as he entered. "Are you going to pay anything this week?"

The woman seemed to be unconscious.

"Have you got the rent?" asked Mr. Woodstock, turning to the child, who had crouched down in another corner.

"No, we ain't," was the reply, with a terribly fierce glare from eyes which rather seemed to have looked on ninety years than nine.

"Then out you go! Come, you, get up now; d' you hear? Very well; come along, Waymark; you take hold of that foot, and I'll take this. Now, drag her out on to the landing."

They dragged her about half-way to the door, when suddenly Waymark felt the foot he had hold of withdrawn from his grasp, and at once the woman sprang upright. Then she fell on him, tooth and nail, screaming like some evil beast. Had not Abraham forthwith come to the rescue, he would have been seriously torn about the face, but just in time the woman's arms were seized in a giant grip, and she was flung bodily out of the room, falling with a crash upon the landing. Then from her and the child arose a most terrific uproar of commination; both together yelled such foulness and blasphemy as can only be conceived by those who have made a special study of this vocabulary, and the vituperation of the child was, if anything, richer in quality than the mother's. The former, moreover, did not confine herself to words, but all at once sent her clenched fist through every pain of glass in the window, heedless of the fearful cuts she inflicted upon herself, and uttering a wild yell of triumph at each fracture. Mr. Woodstock was too late to save his property, but he caught up the creature like a doll, and flung her out also on to the landing, then coolly locked the door behind him, put the key in his pocket, and, letting Waymark pass on first, descended the stairs. The yelling and screeching behind them continued as long as they were in the Court, but it drew no attention from the neighbours, who were far too accustomed to this kind of thing to heed it.

In the last house they had to enter they came upon a man asleep on a bare bedstead. It was difficult to wake him. When at length he was aroused, he glared at them for a moment with one blood-shot eye (the other was sightless), looking much like a wild beast which doubts whether to spring or to shrink back.

"Rent, Slimy," said Mr. Woodstock with more of good humour than usual.

The man pointed to the mantelpiece, where the pieces of money were found to be lying. Waymark looked round the room. Besides the bedstead, a table was the only article of furniture, and on it stood a dirty jug and a glass. Lying about was a strange collection of miscellaneous articles, heaps of rags and dirty paper, bottles, boots, bones. There were one or two chairs in process of being new-caned; there was a wooden frame for holding glass, such as is carried about by itinerant glaziers, and, finally, there was a knife-grinding instrument, adapted for wheeling about the streets. The walls were all scribbled over with obscene words and drawings. On the inside of the door had been fitted two enormous bolts, one above and one below.

"How's trade, Slimy?" inquired Mr. Woodstock.

"Which trade, Mr. Woodstock?" asked the man in return, in a very husky voice.

"Oh, trade in general."

"There never was sich times since old Scratch died," replied Slimy, shaking his head. "No chance for a honest man."

"Then you're in luck. This is the new collector, d'you see."

"I've been a-looking at him," said Slimy, whose one eye, for all that, had seemed busy all the time in quite a different direction. "I seen him somewheres, but I can't just make out where."

"Not many people you haven't seen, I think," said Abraham, nodding, as he went out of the room. Waymark followed, and was glad to get into the open streets again.

CHAPTER XIII
A MAN-TRAP

Julian Casti was successful in his application for the post of dispenser at the All Saints' Hospital, and shortly after Easter he left the shop in Oxford Street, taking lodgings in Beaufort Street, Chelsea. His first evening there was spent in Waymark's company, and there was much talk of the progress his writing would make, now that his hours of liberty were so considerably extended. For the first time in his life he was enjoying the sense of independence. Waymark talked of moving from Walcot Square, in order to be nearer to his friend. He, too, was possessed of more freedom than had been the case for a long time, and his head was full of various fancies. They would encourage each other in their work, afford by mutual appreciation that stimulus which is so essential to the young artist.

But in this world, though man may propose, it is woman who disposes. And at this moment, Julian's future was being disposed of in a manner he could not well have foreseen.

Harriet Smales had heard with unconcealed pleasure of his leaving the shop and taking lodgings of his own. She had been anxious to come and see the rooms, and, though the following Sunday was appointed for her visit, she could not wait so long, but, to her cousin's surprise, presented herself at the house one evening, and was announced by the landlady, who looked suspicious. Julian, with some nervousness, hastened to explain that the visitor was a relative, which did not in the least alter his landlady's preconceived ideas. Harriet sat down and looked about her with a sigh of satisfaction. If she could but have such a home! Girls had no chance of getting on as men did. If only her father could have lived, things would have been different. Now she was thrown on the world, and had to depend upon her own hard work. Then she gave way to an hysterical sob, and Julian--who felt sure that the landlady was listening at the door--could only beg her nervously not to be so down-hearted.

"Whatever success I have," he said to her, "you will share it."

"If I thought so!" she sighed, looking down at the floor, and moving the point of her umbrella up and down. Harriet had saturated her mind with the fiction of penny weeklies, and owed to this training all manner of awkward affectations which she took to be the most becoming manifestations of a susceptible heart. At times she would express herself in phrases of the most absurdly high-flown kind, and lately she had got into the habit of heaving profound sighs between her sentences. Julian was not blind to the meaning of all this. His active employments during the past week had kept his thoughts from brooding on the matter, and he had all but dismissed the trouble it had given him. But this visit, and Harriet's demeanour throughout it, revived all his anxieties. He came back from accompanying his cousin part of her way home in a very uneasy frame of mind. What could he do to disabuse the poor girl of the unhappy hopes she entertained? The thought of giving pain to any most humble creature was itself a pain unendurable to Julian. His was one of those natures to which self-sacrifice is infinitely easier than the idea of sacrificing another to his own desires or even necessities, a vice of weakness often more deeply and widely destructive than the vices of strength.

The visit having been paid, it was arranged that on the following Sunday Julian should meet his cousin at the end of Gray's Inn Road as usual. On that day the weather was fine, but Harriet came out in no mood for a walk. She had been ailing for a day or two, she said, and felt incapable of exertion; Mrs. Ogle was away from home for the day, too, and it would be better they should spend the afternoon together in the house. Julian of course assented, as always, and they established themselves in the parlour behind the shop. In the course of talk, the girl made mention of an engraving Julian had given her a week or two before, and said that she had had it framed and hung it in her bed-room.

"Do come up and look at it," she exclaimed; "there's no one in the house. I want to ask you if you can find a better place for it. It doesn't show so well where it is."

Julian hesitated for a moment, but she was already leading the way, and he could not refuse to follow. They went up to the top of the house, and entered a little chamber which might have been more tidy, but was decently furnished. The bed was made in a slovenly way, the mantelpiece was dusty, and the pictures on the walls hung askew. Harriet closed the door behind them, and proceeded to point out the new picture, and discuss the various positions which had occurred to her. Julian would have decided the question as speedily as possible, and once or twice moved to return downstairs, but each time the girl found something new to detain him. Opening a drawer, she took out several paltry little ornaments, which she wished him to admire, and, in showing them, stood very close by his side. All at once the door of the room was pushed open, and a woman ran in. On seeing the stranger present, she darted back with an exclamation of surprise.

"Oh, Miss Smales, I didn't know as you wasn't alone! I heard you moving about, and come just to arst you to lend me--but never mind, I'm so sorry; why didn't you lock the door?"

And she bustled out again, apparently in much confusion.

Harriet had dropped the thing she held in her hand, and stood looking at her cousin as if dismayed.

"I never thought any one was in," she said nervously. "It's Miss Mould, the lodger. She went out before I did, and I never heard her come back. Whatever will she think!"

"But of course," he stammered, "you will explain everything to her. She knows who I am, doesn't she?"

"I don't think so, and, even if she did--"

She stopped, and stood with eyes on the ground, doing her best to display maiden confusion. Then she began to cry.

"But surely, surely there is no need to trouble yourself," exclaimed Julian, almost distracted, beginning to be dimly conscious of all manner of threatening possibilities. "I will speak to the woman myself, and clear you of every--. Oh, but this is all nonsense. Let us go down at once, Harriet. What a pity you asked me to come up here!"

It was the nearest to a reproach that he had ever yet addressed to her. His face showed clearly how distressed he was, and that on his own account more than hers, for he could not conceive any blame save on himself for being so regardless of appearances.

"Go as quietly as ever you can," Harriet whispered. "The stairs creak so. Step very softly."

This was terrible to the poor fellow. To steal down in this guilty way was as bad as a confession of evil intentions, and he so entirely innocent of a shadow of evil even in his thought. Yet he could not but do as she bade him. Even on the stairs she urged him in a very loud whisper to be yet more cautious. He was out of himself with mortification; and felt angry with her for bringing him into such ignominy. In the back parlour once more, he took up his hat at once.

"You mustn't go yet," whispered Harriet. "I'm sure that woman's listening on the stairs. You must talk a little. Let's talk so she can hear us. Suppose she should tell Mrs. Ogle."

"I can't see that it matters," said Julian, with annoyance. "I will myself see Mrs. Ogle."

"No, no! The idea! I should have to leave at once. Whatever shall I do if she turns me away, and won't give me a reference or anything!"

Even in a calmer mood, Julian's excessive delicacy would have presented an affair of this kind in a grave light to him; at present he was wholly incapable of distinguishing between true and false, or of gauging these fears at their true value. The mere fact of the girl making so great a matter out of what should have been so easy to explain and have done with, caused an exaggeration of the difficulty in his own mind. He felt that he ought of course to justify himself before Mrs. Ogle, and would have been capable of doing so had only Harriet taken the same sensible view; but her apparent distress seemed--even to him--so much more like conscious guilt than troubled innocence, that such a task would cost him the acutest suffering. For nearly an hour he argued with her, trying to convince her how impossible it was that the woman who had surprised them should harbour any injurious suspicions.

"But she knows--" began Harriet, and then stopped, her eyes falling.

"What does she know?" demanded her cousin in surprise; but could get no reply to his question. However, his arguments seemed at length to have a calming effect, and, as he took leave, he even affected to laugh at the whole affair. For all that, he had never suffered such mental trouble in his life as during this visit and throughout the evening which followed. The mere thought of having been obliged to discuss such things with his cousin filled him with inexpressible shame and misery. Waymark came to spend the evening with him, but found poor entertainment. Several times Julian was on the point of relating what had happened, and asking for advice, but he found it impossible to broach the subject. There was an ever-recurring anger against Harriet in his mind, too, for which at the same time he reproached himself. He dreaded the next meeting between them.

Harriet, though herself quite innocent of fine feeling and nice complexities of conscience, was well aware of the existence of such properties in her cousin. She neither admired nor despised him for possessing them; they were of unknown value, indifferent to her, indeed, until she became aware of the practical use that might be made of them. Like most narrow-minded girls, she became a shrewd reader of character, when her affections and interests were concerned, and could calculate Julian's motives, and the course wherein they would lead him, with much precision. She knew too well that he did not care for her in the way she desired, but at the same time she knew that he was capable of making almost any sacrifice to spare her humiliation and trouble, especially if he felt that her unhappiness was in any way caused by himself.

Thus it came about that, on the Tuesday evening of the ensuing week, Julian was startled by his landlady's announcing another visit from Miss Smales. Harriet came into the room with a veil over her face, and sank on a chair, sobbing. What she had feared had come to pass. The lodger had told Mrs. Ogle of what had taken place in her absence on the Sunday afternoon, and Harriet had received notice that she must find another place at once. Mrs. Ogle was a woman of severe virtue, and would not endure the suspicion of wrong-doing under her roof. To whom could she come for advice and help, but to Julian?

Julian was overwhelmed. His perfectly sincere nature was incapable of suspecting a far more palpable fraud. He started up with the intention of going forthwith to Gray's Inn Road, but Harriet clung to him and held him back. The idea was vain. The lodger, Miss Mould, had long entertained a spite against her, Harriet said, and had so exaggerated this story in relating it to Mrs. Ogle, that the latter, and her husband, had declared that Casti should not as much as put foot in their shop again.

"If you only knew what they've been told!" sobbed the girl, still clinging to Julian. "They wouldn't listen to a word you said. As if I could have thought of such a thing happening, and that woman to say all the bad things of us she can turn her tongue to! I sha'n't never get another place; I'm thrown out on the wide world!"

It was a phrase she had got out of her penny fiction; and very remarkable indeed was the mixture of acting and real sentiment which marked her utterances throughout.

Julian's shame and anger began to turn to compassion. A woman in tears was a sight which always caused him the keenest distress.

"But," he cried, with tears in his own eyes, "it is impossible that you should suffer all this through me, and I not even make an attempt to clear you of such vile charges!"

"It was my own fault. I was thoughtless. I ought to have known that people's always ready to think harm. But I think of nothing when I'm with you, Julian!"

He had disengaged himself from her hands, and was holding one of them in his own. But, as she made this last confession, she threw her arms about his neck and drooped her head against his bosom.

"Oh, if you only felt to me like I do to you!" she sobbed.

No man can hear without some return of emotion a confession from a woman's lips that she loves him. Harriet was the only girl whom Julian had ever approached in familiar intercourse; she had no rival to fear amongst living women; the one rival to be dreaded was altogether out of the sphere of her conceptions,--the ideal love of a poet's heart and brain. But the ideal is often least present to us when most needed. Here was love; offer but love to a poet, and does he pause to gauge its quality? The sudden whirl of conflicting emotions left Julian at the mercy of the instant's impulse. She was weak; she was suffering through him; she loved him.

"Be my wife, then," he whispered, returning her embrace, "and let me guard you from all who would do you harm."

She uttered a cry of delight, and the cry was a true one.

CHAPTER XIV
NEAR AND FAR

Osmond Waymark was light-hearted; and with him such a state meant something not at all to be understood by those with whom lightness of heart is a chronic affection. The man who dwells for long periods face to face with the bitter truths of life learns so to distrust a fleeting moment of joy, gives habitually so cold a reception to the tardy messenger of delight, that, when the bright guest outdares his churlishness and perforce tarries with him, there ensues a passionate revulsion unknown to hearts which open readily to every fluttering illusive bliss. Illusion it of course remains; is ever recognised as that; but illusion so sweet and powerful that he thanks the god that blinds him, and counts off with sighs of joy the hours thus brightly winged.

He awaited with extreme impatience the evening on which he would again see Ida. Distrustful always, he could not entirely dismiss the fear that his first impressions might prove mistaken in the second interview; yet he tried his best to do so, and amused himself with imagining for Ida a romantic past, for her and himself together a yet more romantic future. In spite of the strange nature of their relations, he did not delude himself with the notion that the girl had fallen in love with him at first sight, and that she stood before him to take or reject as he chose. He had a certain awe of her. He divined in her a strength of character which made her his equal; it might well be, his superior. Take, for instance, the question of the life she was at present leading. In the case of an ordinary pretty and good-natured girl falling in his way as Ida Starr had done, he would have exerted whatever influence he might acquire over her to persuade her into better paths. Any such direct guidance was, he felt, out of the question here. The girl had independence of judgment; she would resent anything said by him on the assumption of her moral inferiority, and, for aught he knew, with justice. The chances were at least as great that he might prove unworthy of her, as that she should prove unworthy of him.

When he presented himself at the house in the little court by Temple Bar, it was the girl Sally who opened the door to him. She beckoned him to follow, and ran before him upstairs. The sitting-room presented the same comfortable appearance, and Grim, rising lazily from the hearthrug, came forward purring a welcome, but Ida was not there.

"She was obliged to go out," said Sally, in answer to his look of inquiry. "She won't be long, and she said you was to make yourself comfortable till she came back."

On a little side-table stood cups and saucers, and a box of cigars. The latter Sally brought forward.

"I was to ask you to smoke, and whether you'd like a cup of coffee with it?" she asked, with the curious *naivete* which marked her mode of speech.

"The kettle's boiling on the side," she added, seeing that Waymark hesitated. "I can make it in a minute."

"In that case, I will."

"You don't mind me having one as well?"

"Of course not."

"Shall I talk, or shall I keep quiet? I'm not a servant here, you know," she added, with an amusing desire to make her position clear. "Ida and me's friends, and she'd do just as much for I."

"Talk by all means," said Waymark, smiling, as he lit his cigar. The result was that, in a quarter of an hour Sally had related her whole history. As Ida had said, she came from Weymouth, where her father was a fisherman, and owner of bumboats. Her mother kept a laundry, and the family had all lived together in easy circumstances. She herself had come to London--well, just for a change. And what was she doing? Oh, getting her living as best she could. In the day-time she worked in a city workroom.

"And how much do you think I earn a week?" she asked.

"Fifteen shillings or so, I suppose?"

"Ah, that's all you know about it! Now, last week was the best I've had yet, and I made seven shillings."

"What do you do?"

"Machine work; makin' ulsters. How much do you think we get, now, for makin' a ulster--one like this?" pointing to one which hung behind the door.

"Have no idea."

"Well,--*fourpence*: there now!"

"And how many can you make in a day?"

"I can't make no more than two. Some make three, but it's blessed hard work. But I get a little job now and then to do at home."

"But you can't live on seven shillings a week?"

"I sh'd think not, indeed. We have to make up the rest as best we can, s'nough."

"But your employers must know that?"

"In course. What's the odds? All us girls are the same; we have to keep on the two jobs at the same time. But I'll give up the day-work before long, s'nough. I come home at night that tired out I ain't fit for nothing. I feel all eyes, as the sayin' is. And it's hard to have to go out into the Strand, when you're like that."

"But do they know about all this at home?"

"No fear! If our father knew, he'd be down here precious soon, and the house wouldn't hold him. But I shall go back some day, when I've got a good fit-out."

The door opened quietly, and Ida came in.

"Well, young people, so you are making yourselves at home."

The sweet face, the eyes and lips with their contained mirth, the light, perfect form, the graceful carriage,--Waymark felt his pulses throb at the sound of her voice and the touch of her hand.

"You didn't mind waiting a little for me? I really couldn't help it. And then, after all, I thought you mightn't come."

"But I promised to."

"Promises, promises, oh dear!" laughed Ida. "Sally, here's an orange for you."

"You *are* a duck!" was the girl's reply, as she caught it, and, with a nod to Waymark, left the room.

"And so you've really come," Ida went on, sitting down and beginning to draw off her gloves.

"You find it surprising? To begin with, I have come to pay my debts."

"Is there another cup of coffee?" she asked, seeming not to have heard. "I'm too tired to get up and see."

Waymark felt a keen delight in waiting upon her, in judging to a nicety the true amount of sugar and cream, in drawing the little table just within her reach.

"Mr. Waymark," she exclaimed, all at once, "if you had had supper with a friend, and your friend had paid the bill, should you take out your purse and pay him back at your next meeting?"

"It would depend entirely on circumstances."

"Just so. Then the present circumstances don't permit anything of the kind, and there's an end of *that* matter. Light another cigar, will you?"

"You don't dislike the smoke?"

"If I did, I should say so."

Having removed her outer garments one by one, she rose and took them into the inner room. On reappearing, she went to the sitting-room door and turned the key in the lock.

"Could you let me have some more books to read?" she asked.

"I have brought one, thinking you might be ready for it."

It was "Jane Eyre." She glanced over the pages eagerly.

"I don't know how it is," she said, "I have grown so hungry for reading of late. Till just now I never cared for it. When I was a child and went to school, I didn't like my lessons. Still I learned a good deal, for a little girl, and it has stayed by me. And oh, it seems so long ago! Never mind, perhaps I will tell you all about that some day."

They were together for an hour or so. Waymark, uneasily watching his companion's every movement, rose as soon as she gave sign of weariness, and Ida did not seek to detain him.

"I shall think much of you," he said.

"The less the better," was Ida's reply.

For his comfort, yes,--Waymark thought, as he walked homewards. Ida had already a dangerous hold upon him; she possessed his senses, and set him on fire with passionate imaginings. Here, as on every hand, his cursed poverty closed against him the possibilities of happiness. That she should ever come to love him, seemed very unlikely; the alliance between them could only be a mere caprice on her part, such as girls of her kind are very subject to; he might perhaps fill up her intervals of tedium, but would have no share in her real life. And the thought of that life fevered him with jealousy. She might say what she liked about never having known love, but it was of course impossible that she should not have a preference among her lovers. And to think of the chances before such a girl, so blessed with rare beauty and endless charms. In the natural order of events she would become the mistress of some rich man; might even, as at times happens, be rescued by marriage; in either case, their acquaintance must cease. And, indeed, what right had he to endeavour to gain her love having nothing but mere beggarly devotion to offer her in return? He had not even the excuse of one who could offer her married life in easy circumstances,--supposing that to be an improvement on her present position. Would it not be better at once to break off these impossible relations? How often he had promised himself, in moments of clear thought, never again to enter on a course which would obviously involve him in futile suffering. Why had he not now the strength to obey his reason, and continue to possess his soul in the calm of which he had enjoyed a brief taste?

The novel circumstances of the past week had almost driven from his mind all thought of Maud Enderby. He regretted having asked and obtained permission to write to her. She seemed so remote from him, their meeting so long past. What could there be in common between himself and that dim, quiet little girl, who had excited his sympathy merely because her pretty face was made sad by the same torments which had afflicted him? He needed some strong, vehement, original nature, such as Ida Starr's; how would Maud's timid conventionality--doubtless she was absolutely conventional--suit with the heresies of which he was all compact? Still, he could not well ignore what had taken place between them, and, after all, there would be a certain pleasant curiosity in awaiting her reply. In any case, he would write just such a letter as came naturally from him. If she were horrified, well, there was an end of the matter.

Accordingly, he sat down on the morning after his visit to Ida, and, after a little difficulty in beginning, wrote a long letter. It was mainly occupied with a description of his experiences in Litany Lane and Elm Court. He made no apology for detailing such unpleasant matters, and explained that he would henceforth be kept in pretty close connection with this unknown world. Even this, he asserted, was preferable to the world of Dr. Tootle's Academy. Then he dwelt a little on the contrast between this life of his and that which Maud was doubtless leading in her home on the Essex coast; and finally he hoped she would write to him when she found leisure, and be able to let him know that she was no longer so unhappy as formerly.

This he posted on Friday. On the following Monday morning, the post brought two letters for him, both addressed in female hand, one bearing a city, the other a country, post-mark. Waymark smiled as he compared the two envelopes, on one of which his name stood in firm, upright characters, on the other in slender, sloping, delicate writing. The former he pressed to his lips, then tore open eagerly; it was the promised intimation that Ida would be at home after eight o'clock on Wednesday and Friday evenings, nothing more. The second letter he allowed to lie by till he had breakfasted. He could see that it contained more than one sheet. When at length he opened it, he read this:--

"DEAR MR. WAYMARK,--I have an hour of freedom this Sunday afternoon, and I will spend it in replying as well as I can to your very interesting letter. My life is, as you say, very quiet and commonplace compared with that you find yourself suddenly entering upon. I have no such strange and moving things to write about, but I will tell you in the first place how I live and what I do, then put down some of the thoughts your letter has excited in me.

"The family I am with consists of very worthy but commonplace people. They treat me with more consideration than I imagine governesses usually get, and I am grateful to them for this, but their conversation, especially that of Mrs. Epping, I find rather wearisome. It deals with very trivial concerns of everyday life, in which I vainly endeavour to interest myself.

"Then there is the religious formalism of the Eppings and their friends. They are High Church. They discuss with astonishing vigour and at dreadful length what seems to me the most immaterial points in the Church service, and just at present an impulse is given to their zeal by the fact of their favourite clergyman being threatened with a prosecution for ritualistic practices. Of course I have to feign a becoming interest in all this, and to take part in all their religious forms and ceremonies. And indeed it is all so new to me that I have scarcely yet got over the first feelings of wonder and curiosity.

"Have I not, then, you will ask, the courage of my opinions? But indeed my religious opinions are so strangely different from those which prevail here, that I fear it would be impossible to make my thoughts clear to these good people. They would scarcely esteem me a Christian; and yet I cannot but think that it is they who are widely astray from Christian belief and practice. The other evening the clergyman dined with us, and throughout the meal discussions of the rubric alternated with talk about delicacies of the table! That the rubric should be so interesting amazes me, but that an earnest Christian should think it compatible with his religion to show the slightest concern in what he shall eat or drink is unspeakably strange to me. Surely, if Christianity means anything it means asceticism. My experience of the world is so slight. I believe this is the first clergyman I ever met in private life. Surely they cannot all be thus?

"I knew well how far the world at large had passed from true Christianity; that has been impressed upon me from my childhood. But how strange it seems to me to hear proposed as a remedy the formalism to which my friends here pin their faith! How often have I burned to speak up among them, and ask--'What think ye, then, of Christ? Is He, or is He not, our exemplar? Was not His life meant to exhibit to us the ideal of the completest severance from the world which is consistent with human existence? To follow Him, should we not, at least in the spirit, cast off everything which may tempt us to consider life, as life, precious?' We cannot worship both God and the world, and yet nowadays Christians seem to make a merit of doing so. When I conceive a religious revival, my thought does not in the least concern itself with forms and ceremonies. I imagine another John the Baptist inciting the people, with irresistible fervour, to turn from their sins--that is, from the world and all its concerns--and to purify themselves by Renunciation. What they call 'Progress,' I take to be the veritable Kingdom of Antichrist. The world is evil, life is evil; only by renunciation of the very desire for life can we fulfil the Christian idea. What then of the civilisation which endeavours to make the world more and more pleasant as a dwelling-place, life more and more desirable for its own sake?

"And so I come to the contents of your own letter. You say you marvel that these wretched people you visited do not, in a wild burst of insurrection, overthrow all social order, and seize for themselves a fair share of the world's goods. I marvel also;--all the more that their very teachers in religion seem to lay such stress on the joys of life. And yet what profit would a real Christian preacher draw for them from this very misery of their existence! He would teach them that herein lay their supreme blessing, not their curse; that in their poverty and nakedness lay means of grace and salvation such as the rich can scarcely by any means attain to; that they should proudly, devoutly, accept their heritage of woe, and daily thank God for depriving them of all that can make life dear. Only awaken the spirit in these poor creatures, and how near might they be to the true Kingdom of Heaven! And surely such a preacher will yet arise, and there will be a Reformation very different from the movement we now call by that name. But I weary you, perhaps. It may be you have no interest in all this. Yet I think you would wish me to write from what I am.

"It would interest me to hear your further experiences in the new work. Believe me to be your sincere friend,

"MAUD ENDERBY."

Waymark read, and thought, and wondered.

Then it was time to go and collect his rents.

CHAPTER XV
UP THE RIVER

Here is an extract from a letter written by Julian Casti to Waymark in the month of May. By this time they were living near to each other, but something was about to happen which Julian preferred to communicate in writing.

"This will be the beginning of a new life for me. Already I have felt a growth in my power of poetical production. Verse runs together in my thoughts without effort; I feel ready for some really great attempt. Have you not noticed something of this in me these last few days? Come and see me to-night, if you can, and rejoice with me."

This meant that Julian was about to be married. Honeymoon journey was out of the question for him. He and his wife established themselves in the lodgings which he was already occupying. And the new life began.

Waymark had made Harriet's acquaintance a couple of weeks before; Julian had brought her with him one Sunday to his friend's room. She was then living alone, having quitted Mrs. Ogle the day after that decisive call upon Julian. There was really no need for her to have done so, Mrs. Ogle's part in the comedy being an imaginary one of Harriet's devising. But Julian was led entirely by his cousin, and, as she knew quite well, there was not the least danger of his going on his own account to the shop in Gray's Inn Road; he dreaded the thought of such an interview.

Waymark was not charmed with Miss Smales; the more he thought of this marriage, the more it amazed him; for, of course, he deemed it wholly of his friend's bringing about.

The marriage affected their intercourse. Harriet did not like to be left alone in the evening, so Julian could not go to Waymark's, as he had been accustomed to, and conversation in Mrs. Casti's presence was, of course, under restraint. Waymark bore this with impatience, and even did his best to alter it. One Sunday afternoon, about three weeks after the marriage, he called and carried Julian off to his room across the street. Harriet's face sufficiently indicated her opinion of this proceeding, and Julian had difficulty in appearing at his case. Waymark understood what was going on, and tried to discuss the matter freely, but the other shrank from it.

"I am grievously impatient of domestic arrangements," Waymark said. "I fancy it would never do for me to marry, unless I had limitless cash, and my wife were as great a Bohemian as myself. By the by, I have another letter from Maud. Her pessimism is magnificent. This intense religiousness is no doubt a mere phase; it will pass, of course; I wonder how things would arrange themselves if she came back to London. Why shouldn't she come here to sit and chat, like you do?"

"That would naturally lead to something definite," said Casti, smiling.

"Oh, I don't know. Why should it? I'm a believer in friendship between men and women. Of course there is in it the spice of the difference of sex, and why not accept that as a pleasant thing? How much better if, when we met a woman we liked, we could say frankly, 'Now let us amuse each other without any *arriere pensee*. If I married you to-day, even though I feel quite ready to, I should ten to one see some one next week who would make me regret having bound myself. So would you, my dear. Very well, let us tantalise each other agreeably, and be at ease in the sense that we are on the right side of the illusion.' You laugh at the idea?"

Julian laughed, but not heartily. They passed to other things.

"I'm making an article out of Elm Court," said Waymark. "Semi-descriptive, semi-reflective, wholly cynical Maybe it will pay for my summer holiday. And, apropos of the same subject, I've got great ideas. This introduction to such phases of life will prove endlessly advantageous to me, artistically speaking. Let me get a little more experience, and I will write a novel such as no one has yet ventured to write, at all events in England. I begin to see my way to magnificent effects; ye gods, such light and shade! The fact is, the novel of every-day life is getting worn out. We must dig deeper, get to untouched social strata. Dickens felt this, but he had not the courage to face his subjects; his monthly numbers had to lie on the family tea-table. Not *virginibus puerisque* will be my book, I assure you, but for men and women who like to look beneath the surface, and who understand that only as artistic material has human life any significance. Yes, that is the conclusion I am working round to. The artist is the only sane man. Life for its own sake?--no; I would drink a pint of laudanum to-night. But life as the source of splendid pictures, inexhaustible material for effects--*that* can reconcile me to existence, and that only. It is a delight followed by no bitter after-taste, and the only such delight I know."

Harriet was very quiet when Julian returned. She went about getting the tea with a sort of indifference; she let a cup fall and break, but made no remark, and left her husband to pick up the pieces.

"Waymark thinks I'm neglecting him," said Julian, with a laugh, as they sat down together.

"It's better to neglect him than to neglect me, I should think," was Harriet's reply, in a quiet ill-natured tone which she was mistress of.

"But couldn't we find out some way of doing neither, dear?" went on Julian, playing with his spoon. "Now suppose I give him a couple of hours one evening every week? You could spare that, couldn't you? Say, from eight to ten on Wednesdays?"

"I suppose you'll go if you want to." said Harriet, rising from the tea-table, and taking a seat sulkily by the window.

"Come, come, we won't say any more about it, if it's so disagreeable to you," said Julian, going up to her, and coaxing her back to her place. "You don't feel well to-day, do you? I oughtn't to have left you this afternoon, but it was difficult to refuse, wasn't it?"

"He had no business to ask you to go. He could see I didn't like it."

Waymark grew so accustomed to receiving Ida's note each Monday morning, that when for the first time it failed to conic he was troubled seriously. It happened, too, that he was able to attach a particular significance to the omission. When they had last parted, instead of just pressing her hand as usual, he had raised it to his lips. She frowned and turned quickly away, saying no word. He had offended her by this infringement of the conditions of their friendship; for once before, when he had uttered a word which implied more than she was willing to allow, Ida had engaged him in the distinct agreement that he should never do or say anything that approached love-making. As, moreover, it was distinctly understood that he should never visit her save at times previously appointed, he could not see her till she chose to write. After waiting in the vain expectation of some later post bringing news, he himself wrote, simply asking the cause of her silence. The reply came speedily.

"I have no spare time in the week. I thought you would understand this.

I. S."

It was her custom to write without any formal beginning or ending; yet Waymark felt that this note was briefer than it would have been, had all been as usual between them. The jealousy which now often tortured him awoke with intolerable vehemence. He spent a week of misery.

But late on Saturday evening came a letter addressed in the well-known hand. It said--

"Sally and I are going up the river to-morrow, if it is fine. Do you care to meet us on the boat which reaches Chelsea Pier at 10.30?

I. S."

It seemed he did care; at all events he was half an hour too soon at the pier. As the boat approached his eye soon singled out two very quietly-dressed girls, who sat with their backs to him, and neither turned nor made any sign of expecting any addition to their party. With like undemonstrativeness he took a seat at Ida's side, and returned Sally's nod and smile. Ida merely said "Good morning;" there was nothing of displeasure on her face, however, and when he began to speak of indifferent things she replied with the usual easy friendliness.

It was the first time he had seen her by daylight. He had been uncertain whether she used any artificial colour on her cheeks; seemingly she did, for now she looked much paler than usual. But the perfect clearness of her complexion, the lustre of her eyes, appeared to indicate complete health. She breathed the fresh sun-lit air with frank enjoyment, and smiled to herself at objects on either side of the river.

"By the by," Waymark said, when no words had been exchanged for some minutes, "you didn't tell me where you were going; so I took no ticket, and left matters to fate."

"Are you a good walker?" Ida asked.

"Fairly good, I flatter myself."

"Then this is what I propose. It's a plan I carried out two or three times by myself last summer, and enjoyed. We get off at Putney, walk through Roehampton, then over the park into Richmond. By that time we shall be ready for dinner, and I know a place where we can have it in comfort."

There was little thought of weariness throughout the delightful walk. All three gave themselves up for the time to simple enjoyment; their intercourse became that of children; the troubles of passion, the miseries of self-consciousness, the strain of mutual observation fell from them as the city dropped behind; they were once more creatures for whom the external world alone had reality. There was a glorious June sky; there were country roads scented with flower and tree; the wide-gleaming common with its furze and bramble; then the great park, with felled trunks to rest upon, and prospects of endlessly-varied green to soothe the eye. The girls exhibited their pleasure each in her own way. Sally threw off restraint, and sprang about in free happiness, like one of the young roes, the sight of which made her utter cries like a delighted child. She remembered scenes of home, and chattered in her dialect of people and places strange enough to both her companions. She was in constant expectation of catching a glimpse of the sea; in spite of all warnings it was a great surprise and disappointment to her that Richmond Hill did not end in cliffs and breakers. Ida talked less, but every now and then laughed in her deep enjoyment. She had no reminiscence of country life it was enough that all about her was new and fresh and pure; nothing to remind her of Regent Street and the Strand. Waymark talked of he knew not what, cheerful things that came by chance to his tongue, trifling stories, descriptions of places, ideal plans for spending of ideal holidays; but nothing of London, nothing of what at other times his thoughts most ran upon. He came back to himself now and then, and smiled as he looked at the girls, but this happened seldom.

The appetites of all three were beyond denying when they had passed the "Star and Garter" and began to walk down into the town. Waymark wondered whither their guide would lead them, but asked no questions. To his surprise, Ida stopped at a small inn half way down the hill.

"You are to go straight in," she said, with a smile, to Waymark, "and are to tell the first person you meet that three people want dinner. There's no choice--roast beef and vegetables, and some pudding or other afterwards. Then you are to walk straight upstairs, as if you knew your way, and we will follow."

These directions were obeyed, with the result that all reached an upper chamber, wherein a table was cleanly and comfortably laid, as if expecting them. French windows led out on to a quaint little verandah at the back of the house, and the view thence was perfect. The river below, winding between wooded banks, and everywhere the same splendour of varied green which had delighted their eyes all the morning. Just below the verandah was the tiled roof of an outhouse, whereon lay a fine black and white cat, basking in the hot sun. Ida clapped her hands.

"He's like poor old Grim," she cried. Then, turning to Waymark: "If you are good, you may bring out a chair and smoke a cigar here after dinner."

They had just began to eat, when footsteps were heard coining up the stairs.

"Oh bother!" exclaimed Sally. "There's some one else a-comin', s'nough."

There was. The door opened, and two gentlemen walked in. Waymark looked up, and to his astonishment recognised his old friends O'Gree and Egger. Mr. O'Gree was mopping his face with a handkerchief, and looked red and hungry; Mr. Egger was resplendent in a very broad-brimmed straw hat, the glistening newness of which contrasted with the rest of his attire, which had known no variation since his first arrival at Dr. Tootle's. He, too, was perspiring profusely, and, as he entered, was just in the act of taking out the great yellow handkerchief which Waymark had seen him chewing so often in the bitterness of his spirit.

"Hollo, Waymark, is it you?" cried Mr. O'Gree, forgetting the presence of the strangers in his astonishment. "Sure, and they told us we'd find a *gentleman* here."

"And I was the last person you would have thought of as answering that description?"

"Well, no, I didn't mean that. I meant there was no mention of the ladies."

Waymark flashed a question at Ida with his eyes, and understood her assent in the smile and slight motion of the head.

"Then let me introduce you to the ladies."

The new-comers accordingly made the acquaintance of Miss Starr and Miss Fisher (that was Sally's name), and took seats at the table, to await the arrival of their dinners. Both were on their good behaviour. Mr. O'Gree managed to place himself at Sally's left hand, and led the conversation with the natural ease of an Irishman, especially delighted if Sally herself seemed to appreciate his efforts to be entertaining.

"Now, who'd have thought of the like of this." he exclaimed. "And we came in here by the merest chance; sure, there's a fatality in these things. We've walked all the way from Hammersmith."

"And we from Putney," said Waymark.

"You don't mean it? It's been a warm undertaking."

"How did you find the walk, Mr. Egger?"

"Bedad," replied that gentleman, who had got hold of his friend's exclamation, and used it with killing effect; "I made my possible, but, bedad, I could not much more."

"You both look warm," Waymark observed, smiling. "I fear you hurried. You should have been leisurely, as we were."

"Now that's cruel, Waymark. You needn't have reflected upon our solitariness. If we'd been blessed with society such as you had, we'd have come slow enough. As it was, we thought a good deal of our dinners."

No fresh guests appeared to disturb the party. When all had appeased their hunger, Waymark took a chair out on to the verandah for Ida. He was spared the trouble of providing in the same way for Sally by Mr. O'Gree's ready offices. Poor Egger, finding himself deserted, opened a piano there was in the room, and began to run his finger over the keys.

"Let us have one of your German songs, my boy," cried O'Gree.

"But it is the Sunday, and we arc still in England," said the Swiss, hesitating.

"Pooh, never mind," said Waymark. "We'll shut the door. Sing my favourite, Mr. Egger,--' ***Wenn's Mailufterl***.'"

When they left the inn, Waymark walked first with Ida, and Mr. O'Gree followed with Sally. Egger brought up the rear; he had relapsed into a dreamy mood, and his mind seemed occupied with unearthly things.

With no little amusement Waymark had noted Sally's demeanour under Mr. O'Gree's attentions. The girl had evidently made up her mind to be absolutely proper. The Irishman's respectful delicacy was something so new to her and so pleasant, and the question with her was how she could sufficiently show her appreciation without at the same time forfeiting his good opinion for becoming modesty. All so new to her, accustomed to make an art of forwardness, and to school herself in the endurance of brutality. She was constantly blushing in the most unfeigned way at his neatly-turned little compliments, and, when she spoke, did so with a pretty air of self-distrust which sat quite charmingly on her. Fain, fain would O'Gree have proposed to journey back to London by the same train, but good taste and good sense prevailed with him. At the ticket-barrier there was a parting.

"How delightful it would be, Miss Fisher," said Mr. O'Gree, in something like a whisper, "if this lucky chance happened again. If I only knew when you were coming again, there's no telling but it might."

Sally gave her hand, smiled, evidently wished to say something, but ended by turning away and running after her companions.

CHAPTER XVI
EXAMPLE WITHOUT PRECEPT

Waymark was grateful for the help Mr. Woodstock had given him. Indeed, the two soon began to get on very well together. In a great measure, of course, this was due to the change in Waymark's philosophy; whereas his early idealism had been revolted by what he then deemed Mr. Woodstock's crass materialism and vulgarity, the tolerance which had come with widened experience now made him regard these characteristics with far less certainty of condemnation. He was often merely amused at what had formerly enraged and disgusted him. At the same time, there were changes in Abraham himself, no doubt--at all events in his manner to the young man. He, on his side, was also far more tolerant than in the days when he had growled at Osmond for a conceited young puppy.

One Sunday morning in early July, Waymark was sitting alone in his room, when he noticed that a cab stopped before the house. A minute after, there was a knock at his door, and, to his great surprise, Mr. Woodstock entered, bearing a huge volume in his arms. Abraham deposited it on a chair, wiped his forehead, and looked round the room.

"You smoke poor tobacco," was his first remark, as he sniffed the air.

"Good tobacco happens to be expensive," was the reply. "Will you sit down?"

"Yes, I will." The chair creaked under him. "And so here you hang out, eh? Only one room?"

"As you see."

"Devilish unhealthy, I should think."

"But economical."

"Ugh!"

The grunt meant nothing in particular. Waymark was eyeing the mighty volume on the chair, and had recognised it Some fortnight previously, he had come upon Abraham, in the latter's study, turning over a collection of Hogarth's plates, and greatly amusing himself with the realism which so distinctly appealed to his taste in art. The book had been pledged in the shop, and by lapse of time was become Abraham's property. It was the first time that Waymark had had an opportunity of examining Hogarth; the pictures harmonised with his mood; they gave him a fresh impulse in the direction his literary projects were taking. He spent a couple of hours in turning the leaves, and Mr. Woodstock had observed his enjoyment. What meant the arrival of the volume here in Beaufort Street?

Abraham lit a cigar, still looking about the room.

"You live alone?" he asked, in a matter-of-fact way.

"At present."

"Ha! Didn't know but you might have found it lonely; I used to, at your age."

Then, after a short silence--

"By-the-by, it's your birthday."

"How do you know?"

"Well, I shouldn't have done, but for an old letter I turned up by chance the other day. How old are you?"

"Five-and-twenty."

"H'm. I am sixty-nine. You'll be a wiser man when you get to my age.--Well, if you can find room anywhere for that book there, perhaps you'd like to keep it!"

Waymark looked up in astonishment.

"A birthday present!" he exclaimed. "It's ten years since I had one. Upon my word, I don't well know how to thank you!"

"Do you know what the thing was published at?" asked Abraham in an off-hand way.

"No."

"Fifty pounds."

"I don't care about the value. It's the kindness. You couldn't have given me anything, either, that would have delighted me so much."

"All right; keep it, and there's an end of the matter. And what do you do with yourself all day, eh? I didn't think it very likely I should find you in."

"I'm writing a novel."

"H'm. Shall you get anything for it?"

"Can't say. I hope so."

"Look here. Why don't you go in for politics?"

"Neither know nor care anything about them."

"Would you like to go into Parliament?"

"Wouldn't go if every borough in England called upon me to-morrow?"

"Why not?"

"Plainly, I think myself too good for such occupation. If you once succeed in getting *outside* the world, you have little desire to go back and join in its most foolish pranks."

"That's all damned nonsense! How can any one be too good to be in Parliament? The better men you have there, the better the country will be governed, won't it?"

"Certainly. But the best man, in this case, is the man who sees the shortest distance before his nose. If you think the world worth all the trouble it takes to govern it, go in for politics neck and crop, by all means, and the world will no doubt thank you in its own way."

Abraham looked puzzled, and half disposed to be angry.

"Then you think novel-writing better than governing the country?" he asked.

"On its own merits, vastly so."

"And suppose there was no government What about your novels then?"

"I'd make a magnificent one out of the spectacle of chaos."

"But you know very well you're talking bosh," exclaimed Abraham, somewhat discomfited. "There must be government, and there must be order, say what you like. Its nature that the strong should rule over the weak, and show them what's for their own good. What else are we here for? if you're going to be a parson, well and good; then cry down the world as much as you please, and think only about heaven and hell. But as far as I can make out, there's government there too. The devil rebelled and was kicked out. Serve him right If he wasn't strong enough to hold his own, he'd ought to have kept quiet."

"You're a Conservative, of course," said Waymark, smiling. "You believe only in keeping the balance. You don't are about reform."

"Don't be so sure of that Let me have the chance and he power, and I'd reform hard enough, many a thing."

"Well, one might begin on a small scale. Suppose one took in hand Litany Lane and Elm Court? Suppose we exert our right as the stronger, and, to begin with, do a little whitewashing? Then sundry stairs and ceilings might be looked to. No doubt there'd be resistance, but on the whole it would be for the people's own good. A little fresh draining mightn't be amiss, or--"

"What the devil's all this to do with politics?" cried Abraham, whose face had grown dark.

"I should imagine, a good deal," returned Waymark, knocking out his pipe. "If you're for government, yen mustn't be above considering details."

"And so you think you have a hit at me, eh? Nothing of the kind. These are affairs of private contract, and no concern of government at all. In private contract a man has only a right to what he's strong enough to exact If a tenant tells me my houses ain't fit to live in, I tell him to go where he'll be better off' and I don't hinder him; I know well enough in a day or two there'll come somebody else. Ten to one he can't go, and he don't. Then why should I be at unnecessary expense in making the places better? As Boon as I can get no tenants I'll do so; not till then."

"You don't believe in works of mere humanity?"

"What the devil's humanity got to do with business?" cried Abraham.

"True," was Waymark's rejoinder.

"See, we won't talk of these kind of things," said Mr. Woodstock. "That's just what we always used to quarrel about, and I'm getting too old for quarrelling. Got any engagement this afternoon?"

"I thought of looking in to see a friend here in the street"

"Male or female?"

"Both; man and wife."

"Oh, then you have got some friends? So had I when I was your age. They go somehow when you get old. Your father was the last of them, I think. But you're not much like him, except a little in face. True, he was a Radical, but you,--well, I don't know what you are. If you'd been a son of mine, I'd have had you ill Parliament by now, somehow or other."

"I think you never had a son?" said Way mark, observing the note of melancholy which every now and then came up in the old man's talk.

"No."

"But you had some children, I think?"

"Yes, yes,--they're dead."

He had walked to the window, and suddenly turned round with a kind of impatience.

"Never mind the friend to-day; come and have some dinner with me. I seem to want a bit of company."

This was the first invitation of the kind Waymark had received. He accepted it, and they went out together.

"It's a pleasant part this," Mr. Woodstock said, as they walked by the river. "One might build himself a decent house somewhere about here, eh?"

"Do you think of doing so?"

"I think of doing so! What's the good of a house, and nobody to live in it?"

Waymark studied these various traits of the old man's humour, and constantly felt more of kindness towards him.

On the following day, just as he had collected his rents, and was on his way out of Litany Lane, Waymark was surprised at coming face to face with Mrs. Casti; yet more surprised when he perceived that she had come out from a public-house. She looked embarrassed, and for a moment seemed about to pass without recognising him; but he had raised his hat, and she could not but move her head in reply. She so obviously wished to avoid speaking, that he walked quickly on in another direction. He wondered what he could be doing in such a place as this. It could hardly be that she had acquaintances or connections here. Julian had not given him any particulars of Harriet's former life, and his friend's marriage was still a great puzzle to him. He knew well that the girl had no liking for himself; it was not improbable that this casual meeting would make their intercourse yet more strained. He thought for a moment of questioning Julian, but decided that the matter was no business of his.

It was so rare for him to meet an acquaintance in the streets, that a second chance of the same kind, only a few minutes later, surprised him greatly. This time the meeting as a pleasant one; somebody ran across to him from over the way, and he saw that it was Sally Fisher. She looked pleased. The girl had preserved a good deal of her sea-side complexion through the year and a half of town life, and, when happy, glowed all over her cheeks with the healthiest hue. She held out her hand in the usual frank, impulsive way.

"Oh, I thought it was you! You won't see I no more at the old place."

"No? How's that?"

"I'm leavin' un to-morrow. I've got a place in a shop, just by here,--a chandler's shop, and I'm going to live in."

"Indeed? Well, I'm glad to hear it. I dare say you'll be better off."

"Oh, I say,--you know your friend?"

"The Irishman?"

"Yes."

"What about him?" asked the other, smiling as he looked into the girl's pretty face.

"Well," said Sally, "I don't mind you telling un where I live now,--if you like.--Look, there's the address on that paper; you can take it."

"Oh, I see. In point of fact, you *wish* me to tell him?"

"Oh, I don't care. I dessay he don't want to know anything about I. But you can if you like."

"I will be sure to, and no doubt he will be delighted. He's been growing thin since I told him you declined to renew his acquaintance."

"Oh, don't talk! And now I must be off. Good-bye. I dessay I shall see you sometimes?"

"Without doubt. We'll have another Sunday at Richmond soon. Good-bye."

It was about four in the afternoon when Sally reached home, and she ran up at once to Ida's room, and burst in, crying out, "I've got it! I've got it!" with much dancing about and joyous singing. Ida rose with a faint smile of welcome. She had been sitting at the window, reading a book lent her by Waymark.

"They said they liked my appearance," Sally went on, "and 'ud give me a try. I go in to-morrow. It won't be a over easy place, neither. I've to do all the cleaning in the house, and there's a baby to look after when I'm not in the shop."

"And what will they give you?"

"Ten shillings a month for the first half-year; then a rise."

"And you're satisfied?"

"Oh, it'll do till something better turns up. Oh, I say, I met your friend just after I'd come away."

"Did you?" said Ida quietly.

"Yes; and I told him he could tell his friend where I was, if he liked."

"His friend?"

"The Irishman, you know," explained Sally, moving about the room. "I told you he'd been asking after me."

Ida seemed all at once to awake from a dream. She uttered a long "Ah!" under her breath, and for a moment looked at the girl like one who is struck with an unexpected explanation. Then she turned away to the window, and again gazed up at the blue sky, standing so for nearly a minute.

"Are you engaged to-night?" Sally asked presently.

"No; will you sit with me?"

"You're not feeling very well to-day, are you?"

"I think not," replied Ida, passing her hand over her forehead. "I've been thinking of going out of London for a few days, perhaps to the seaside."

"Go to Weymouth!" cried Sally, delighted at the thought. "Go and see my people, and tell un how I'm getting on. They'll make you hide with un all the time you're there, s'nough. It isn't a big house, but it's comfortable, and see if our mother wouldn't look after you! It's three weeks since I wrote; if I don't mind there'll be our father up here looking after I. Now, do go!"

"No, it's too far. Besides, if I go, I shall want to be quite alone."

On the following evening Waymark was expected. At his last visit he had noticed that Ida was not in her usual spirits. To-night he saw that something was clearly wrong, and when Ida spoke of going to the seaside, he strongly urged her to do so.

"Where should you go to?" he asked.

"I think to Hastings. I went there once, when I was a child, with my mother--I believe I told you. I had rather go there than anywhere else."

"I feel the need of a change myself," he said, a moment after, and without looking at her. "Suppose I were to go to Hastings, too--at the same time that you're there--would you dislike it?"

She merely shook her head, almost indifferently. She did not care to talk much to-night, and frequently nodded instead of replying with words.

"But--you would rather I didn't?" he urged.

"No, indeed," still in the same indifferent way. "I should have company, if I found it dull."

"Then let us go down by the same train--will you, Ida?"

As far as she remembered, it was the first time that he had ever addressed her thus by her name. She looked up and smiled slightly.

"If you like," was her answer.

CHAPTER XVII
THE MISSING YEARS

"Why shouldn't life be always like this?" said Waymark, lying on the upper beach and throwing pebbles into the breakers, which each moment drew a little further hack and needed a little extra exertion of the arm to reach them. There was small disturbance by people passing, here some two miles up the shore east-ward from Hastings. A large shawl spread between two walking-sticks stuck up-right gave, at this afternoon hour, all the shade needful for two persons lying side by side, and, even in the blaze of unclouded summer, there were pleasant airs flit-ting about the edge of the laughing sea. "Why shouldn't life be always like this? It might be--sunshine or fireside--if men were wise. Leisure is the one thing that all desire, but they strive for it so blindly that they frustrate one another's hope. And so at length they have come to lose the end in the means; are mad enough to set the means before them as in itself an end."

"We must work to forget our troubles," said his companion simply.

"Why, yes, and those very troubles are the fit reward of our folly. We have not been content to live in the simple happiness of our senses. We must be learned and wise, forsooth. We were not content to enjoy the beauty of the greater and the lesser light. We must understand whence they come and whither they go--after that, what they are made of and how much they weigh. We thought for such a long time that our toil would end in something; that we might become as gods, knowing good and evil. Now we are at the end of our tether, we see clearly enough that it has all been worse than vain; how good if we could unlearn it all, scatter the building of phantasmal knowledge in which we dwell so uncomfortably! It is too late. The gods never take back their gifts; we wearied them with our prayers into granting us this one, and now they sit in the clouds and mock us."

Ida looked, and kept silent; perhaps scarcely understood.

"People kill themselves in despair," Waymark went on, "that is, when they have drunk to the very dregs the cup of life's bitterness. If they were wise, they would die at that moment--if it ever comes--when joy seems supreme and stable. Life can give nothing further, and it has no more hellish misery than disillusion following upon delight."

"Did you ever seriously think of killing yourself?" Ida asked, gazing at him closely.

"Yes. I have reached at times the point when I would not have moved a muscle to escape death, and from that it is not far to suicide. But my joy had never come, and it is hard to go away without that one draught.--And you!"

"I went so far once as to buy poison. But neither had I tasted any happiness, and I could not help hoping."

"And you still wait--still hope?"

Ida made no direct answer. She gazed far off at the indistinguishable borderland of sea and sky, and when she spoke it was in a softened tone.

"When I was here last, I was seven years old. Now I am not quite nineteen. How long I have lived since then--how long! Yet my life did not really begin till I was about eleven. Till then I was a happy child, understanding nothing. Between then and now, if I have discovered little good either in myself or in others, I have learned by heart everything that is bad in the world. Nothing in meanness or vileness or wretchedness is a secret to me. Compare me with other girls of nineteen--perhaps still at school. What sort of a companion should I be for one of those, I wonder! What strange thoughts I should have, if ever I talked with such a girl; how old I should feel myself beside her!"

"Your knowledge is better in my eyes than their ignorance. My ideal woman is the one who, knowing every darkest secret of life, keeps yet a pure mind--as you do, Ida."

She was silent so long that Waymark spoke again.

"Your mother died when you were eleven!"

"Yes, and that was when my life began. My mother was very poor, but she managed to send me to a pretty good school. But for that, my life would have been very different; I should not have understood myself as well as I always have done. Poor mother,--good, good mother! Oh, if I could but have her now, and thank her for all her love, and give her but one year of quiet happiness. To think that I can see her as if she were standing before me, and yet that she is gone, is nowhere, never to be brought back to me if I break my heart with longing!"

Tears stood in her eyes. They meant more than she could ever say to another, however close and dear to her. The secret of her mother's life lay in the grave and in her own mind; the one would render it up as soon as the other. For never would Ida tell in words of that moment when there had come to her maturing intelligence clear insight into her mother's history, when the fables of childhood had no longer availed to blind her, and every recalled circumstance pointed but to one miserable truth.

"She's happier than we are," Waymark said solemnly. "Think how long she has been resting."

Ida became silent, and presently spoke with a firmer voice.

"They took her to a hospital in her last illness, and she died there. I don't know where her grave is."

"And what became of you? Had you friends to go to?"

"No one; I was quite alone.--We had been living in lodgings. The landlady told me that of course I couldn't stay on there; she couldn't afford to keep me; I must go and find a home somewhere. Try and think what that meant to me. I was so young and ignorant that such an idea as that I might one day have to earn my own living had never entered my mind. I was fed and clothed like every one else,--a good deal better, indeed, than some of the children at school,--and I didn't know why it shouldn't always be so. Besides, I was a vain child; I thought myself clever; I had even begun to look at myself in the glass and think I was handsome. It seemed quite natural that every one should be kind and indulgent to me. I shall never forget the feeling I had when the landlady spoke to me in that hard, sharp way. My whole idea of the world was overset all at once; I seemed to be in a miserable dream. I sat in my mother's bedroom hour after hour, and, every step I heard on the stairs, I thought it must be my mother coming back home to me;--it was impossible to believe that I was left alone, and could look to no one for help and comfort."

"Next morning the landlady came up to me again, and said, if I liked, she could tell me of a way of earning my living. It was by going as a servant to an eating-house in a street close by, where they wanted some one to wash up dishes and do different kinds of work not too hard for a child like me. I could only do as I was advised; I went at once, and was engaged. They took off the dress I was wearing, which was far too good for me then, and gave me a dirty, ragged one; then I was set to work at once to clean some knives. Nothing was said about wages or anything of that kind; only I understood that I should live in the house, and have all given me that I needed. Of course I was very awkward. I tried my very hardest to do everything that was set me, but only got scolding for my pains; and it soon came to boxes on the ear, and even kicks. The place was kept by a man and wife; they had a daughter older than I, and they treated her just like a hired servant. I used to sleep with the girl in a wretched kitchen underground, and the poor thing kept me awake every night with crying and complaining of her hard life. It was no harder than mine, and I can't think she felt it more; but I had even then a kind of stubborn pride which kept me from showing what I suffered. I couldn't have borne to let them see what a terrible change it was for me, all this drudgery and unkindness; I felt it would have been like taking them into my confidence, opening my heart to them, and I despised them too much for that. I even tried to talk in a rough rude way, as if I had never been used to anything better--"

"That was fine, that was heroic!" broke in Waymark admiringly.

"I only know it was miserable enough. And things got worse instead of better. The master was a coarse drunken brute, and he and his wife used to quarrel fearfully. I have seen them throw knives at each other, and do worse things than that, too. The woman seemed somehow to have a spite against me from the first, and the way her husband behaved to me made her hate me still more. Child as I was, he did and said things which made her jealous. Often when she had gone out of an evening, I had to defend myself against him, and call the daughter to protect me. And so it went on, till, what with fear of him, and fear of her, and misery and weariness, I resolved to go away, become of me what might. One night, instead of undressing for bed as usual, I told Jane--that was the daughter--that I couldn't bear it any longer, and was going away, as soon as I thought the house was quiet. She looked at me in astonishment, and asked me if I had anywhere to go to. Will you believe that I said yes, I had? I suppose I spoke in a way which didn't encourage her to ask questions; she only lay down on the bed and cried as usual. "Jane," I said, in a little, "if I were you, I'd run away as well." "I will," she cried out, starting up, "I will this very night! We'll go out together." It was my turn to ask her if *she* had anywhere to go to. She said she knew a girl who lived in a good home at Tottenham, and who'd do something for her, she thought. At any rate she'd rather go to the workhouse than stay where she was. So, about one o'clock, we both crept out by a back way, and ran into Edgware Road. There we said good-bye, and she went one way, and I another.

"All that night I walked about, for fear of being noticed loitering by a policeman. When it was morning, I had come round to Hyde Park, and, though it was terribly cold--just in March--I went to sleep on a seat. I woke about ten o'clock, and walked off into the town, seeking a poor part, where I thought it more likely I might find something to do. Of course I asked first of all at eating-houses, but no one wanted me. It was nearly dark, and I hadn't tasted anything. Then I begged of one or two people--I forgot everything but my hunger--and they gave me a few coppers. I bought some bread, and still wandered about. There are some streets into which I can never bear to go now; the thought of walking about them eight years ago is too terrible to me. Well, I walked till midnight, and then could stand up no longer. I found myself in a dirty little street where the house doors stood open all night; I went into one, and walked up as far as the first landing, and there fell down in a corner and slept all night."

"Poor child!" said Waymark, looking into her face, which had become very animated as the details of the story succeeded each other in her mind.

"I must have looked a terrible little savage on that next morning," Ida went on, smiling sadly. "Oh, how hungry I was! I was awoke by a woman who came out of one of the rooms, and I asked her if she'd give me something to eat. She said she would, if I'd light her fire for her, and clean up the grate. I did this, gladly enough. Then she pretended I had done it badly, and gave me one miserable little dry crust, and told me to be off. Well, that day I found another woman who said she'd give me one meal and twopence a day for helping her to chop wood and wash vegetables; she had a son who was a costermonger, and the stuff he sold had to be cleaned each day. I took the work gladly. She never asked me where I spent the night; the truth was I chose a different house each night, where I found the door open, and went up and slept on the stairs. I often found several people doing the same thing, and no one disturbed us.

"I lived so for a fortnight, then I was lucky enough to get into another eating-house. I lived there nearly two months, and had to leave for the very same reason as at the first place. I only half understood the meaning of what I had to resist, but my resistance led to other unbearable cruelties, and again I ran away. I went about eight o'clock in the evening. The thought of going back to my old sleeping places on the stairs was horrible. Besides, for some days a strange idea had been in my head. I had not forgotten my friend Jane, and I wondered whether, if I went to Tottenham, it would be possible to find her. Perhaps she might be well off there, and could help me. I had made inquiries about the way to Tottenham, and the distance, and when I left the eating-house I had made up my mind to walk straight there. I started from Hoxton, and went on and on, till I had left the big streets behind. I kept asking my way, but often went long distances in the wrong direction. I knew that Tottenham was quite in the country, and my idea was to find a sleeping-place in some field, then to begin my search on the next day. It was summer, but still I began to feel cold, and this drew me away out of my straight road to a fire which I saw burning a little way off. I thought it would be nice to sit down by it and rest. I found that the road was being mended, and by the fire lay a watchman in a big tub. Just as I came up he was eating his supper. He was a great, rough man, but I looked in his face and thought it seemed good, so I asked him if he'd let me rest a little. Of course he was surprised at seeing me there, for it must have been midnight, and when he asked me about myself I told him the truth, because he spoke in a kind way. Then he stopped eating and gave me what was left; it was a bit of fat bacon and some cold potatoes; but how good it was, and how good *he* was! To this moment I can see that man's face. He got out of his tub and made me take his place, and he wrapped me up in something he had there. Then he sat by the fire, and kept looking at me, I thought, in a sad sort of way; and he said, over and over again, 'Ay, it's bad to be born a little girl; it's bad to be born a little girl; pity you wasn't a boy.' Oh, how well I can hear his voice this moment! And as he kept saying this, I went off to sleep."

She stopped, and played with the pebbles.

"And in the morning?" asked Waymark.

"Well, when I woke up, it was light, and there were a lot of other men about, beginning their work on the road. I crept out of the tub, and when they saw me, they laughed in a kind sort of way, and gave me some breakfast. I suppose I thanked them, I hope I did; the watchman was gone, but no doubt he had told the others my story, for they showed me the way to Tottenham, and wished me luck."

"And you found your friend Jane!"

"No, no; how was it likely I should? I wandered about till I could stand no longer, and then I went up to the door of a house which stood in a garden, and begged for something to eat. The servant who opened was sending me away, when her mistress heard, and came to the door. She stood looking at me for some time, and then told me to come in. I went into the kitchen, and she asked me all about myself. I told her the truth; I was too miserable now to do anything else. Well, the result was--she kept me there."

"For good?"

"Indeed, for good. In that very house I lived for six years. Oh; she was the queerest and kindest little body! At first I helped her servant in the kitchen,--she lived quite by herself, with one servant,--but little by little she made me a sort of lady's maid, and I did no more rough work. You wouldn't believe the ridiculous fancies of that dear old woman! She thought herself a great beauty, and often told me so very plainly, and she used to talk to me about her chances of being married to this and the other person in the neighbourhood. And the result of all this was that she had to spend I don't know how long every day in dressing herself, and then looking at herself in the glass. And I had to learn how to do her hair, and put paint and powder on her face, and all sorts of wonderful things. She was as good to me as she could be, and I never wanted for anything. And so six years passed, and one morning she was found dead in her bed.

"Well, that was the end of the happiest time of my life. In a day or two some relatives came to look after things, and I had to go. They were kind to me, however; they gave me money, and told me I might refer to them if I needed to. I came to

London, and took a room, and wondered what I should do.

"I advertised, and answered advertisements, but nothing came. My money was going, and I should soon be as badly off as ever. I began to do what I had always thought of as the very last thing, look for needlework, either for home or in a work-room. I don't know how it is that I have always hated sewing. For one thing, I really can't sew. I was never taught as a child, and few girls are as clumsy with a needle as I am. I've always looked upon a work-girl's life as the most horrible drudgery; I'd far rather scrub floors. I suppose I've a rebellious disposition, and just because sewing is looked upon as a woman's natural slavery, I rebelled against it.

"By this time I was actually starving. I had one day to tell my landlady I couldn't pay my rent. She was a very decent woman, and she talked to me in a kind way. What was better, she gave me help. She had a sister who kept a laundry, and she thought I might perhaps get something to do there; at all events she would go and see. The result was I got work. I was in the laundry nearly six months, and became quite clever in getting up linen. Now this was a kind of work I liked. You can't think what a pleasure it was to me to see shirts and collars turning out so spotless and sweet--"

Waymark laughed.

"Oh, but you don't understand. I do so like cleanliness! I have a sort of feeling when I'm washing anything, that I'm really doing good in the world, and the dazzling white of linen after I'd ironed it seemed to thank me for my work."

"Yes, yes, I understand well enough," said Waymark earnestly.

"For all that I couldn't stay. I was restless. I had a foolish notion that I should like to be with a better kind of people again--I mean people in a higher position. I still kept answering advertisements for a lady's maid's place, and at last I got what I wanted. Oh yes, I got it."

She broke off laughing bitterly, and remained silent. Waymark would not urge her to continue. For a minute it seemed as if she would tell no more; she looked at her watch, and half arose.

"Oh, I may as well tell you all, now I've begun," she said, falling back again in a careless way. "You know what the end's going to be; never mind, at all events I'll try and make you understand how it came.

"The family I got into was a lady and her two grown-up daughters, and a son of about five-and-twenty. They lived in a small house at Shepherd's Bush. My wages were very small, and I soon found out that they were a kind of people who keep up a great deal of show on very little means. Of course I had to be let into all the secrets of their miserable shifts for dressing well on next to nothing at all, and they expected me--mother and daughters--to do the most wonderful and impossible things. I had to turn old rags into smart new costumes, to trim worn-out hats into all manner of gaudy shapes, even to patch up boots in a way you couldn't imagine. And they used to send me with money to buy things they were ashamed to go and buy themselves; then, if I hadn't laid out their few pence with marvellous result, they all but accused me of having used some of the money for myself. I had fortunately learnt a great deal with the old lady in Tottenham, or I couldn't have satisfied them for a day. I'm sure I did what few people could have done, and for all that they treated me from almost the first very badly. I had to be housemaid as well as lady's maid; the slavery left me every night worn out with exhaustion. And I hadn't even enough to eat. As time went on, they treated me worse and worse. They spoke to me often in a way that made my heart boil, as if they were so many queens, and I was some poor mean wretch who was honoured by being allowed to toil for them. Then they quarrelled among themselves unceasingly, and of course I had to bear all the bad temper. I never saw people hate one another like those three did; the sisters even scratched each other's faces in their fits of jealousy, and sometimes they both stormed at their mother till she went into hysterics, just because she couldn't give them more money. The only one in the house who ever spoke decently to me was the son--Alfred Bolter, his name was. I suppose I felt grateful to him. Once or twice, when he met me on the stairs, he kissed me. I was too miserable even to resent it.

"I went about, day after day, in a dazed state, trying to make up my mind to leave the people, but I couldn't. I don't know how it was, I had never felt so afraid of being thrown out into the world again. I suppose it was bodily weakness, want of proper food, and overwork. I began to feel that the whole world was wronging me. Was there never to be anything for me but slaving? Was I never to have any enjoyment of life, like other people? I felt a need of pleasure, I didn't care how or what. I was always in a fever; everything was exaggerated to me. What was going to be my future?--I kept asking myself. Was it only to be hard work, miserably paid, till I died? And I should die at last without having known what it was to enjoy my life. When I was allowed to go out--it was very seldom--I walked aimlessly about the streets, watching all the girls I passed, and fancying they all looked so happy, all enjoying their life so. I was growing thin and pale. I coughed, and began to think I was consumptive. A little more of it and I believe I should have become so really.

"It came to an end, suddenly and unexpectedly. All three, mother and daughters, had been worrying me through a whole morning, and at last one of them called me a downright fool, and said I wasn't worth the bread I ate. I turned on them. I can't remember a word I said, but speak I did, and in a way that astonished them; they shrank back from me, looking pale and frightened. I felt in that moment that I was a thousand times their superior; I believe I told them so. Then I rushed up to my room, packed my box, and went out into the street.

"I had just turned a corner, when some one came up to me, and it was Mr. Bolter. He had followed me from the house. He laughed, said I had done quite right, and asked me if I had any money. I shook my head. He walked on by me, and talked. The end was, that he found me rooms, and provided for me.

"I had not the least affection for him, but he had pleasant, gentlemanly ways, and it scarcely even occurred to me to refuse his offers. I was reckless; what happened to me mattered little, as long as I had not to face hard work. I needed rest. For one in my position there was, I saw well enough, only one way of getting it. I took that way."

Ida had told this in a straightforward, unhesitating manner, not meeting her companion's gaze, yet not turning away. One would have said that judgments upon her story were indifferent to her; she simply related past events. In a moment, she resumed.

"Do you remember, on the night when you first met me, a man following us in the street?"

Waymark nodded.

"He was a friend of Alfred Bolter's, and sometimes we met him when we went to the theatre, and such places. That is the only person I ever hated from the first sight,--hated and dreaded in a way I could not possibly explain."

"But why do you mention him?" asked Waymark. "What is his name?"

"His name is Edwards," returned Ida, pronouncing it as if the sound excited loathing in her. "I had been living in this way for nearly half-a-year, when one day this man called and came up to my sitting-room. He said he had an appointment with Mr. Bolter, who would come presently. I sat scarcely speaking, but he talked on. Presently, Mr. Bolter came. He seemed surprised to find the other man with me, and almost at once turned round and went out again. Edwards followed him, saying to me that he wondered what it all meant. The meaning was made clear to me a few hours after. There came a short note from Mr. Bolter, saying that he had suspected that something was wrong, and that under the circumstances he could of course only say good-bye.

I can't say that I was sorry; I can't say that I was glad. I despised him for his meanness, not even troubling myself to try and make sure of what had happened. The same night Edwards came to see me again, made excuses, blamed his friend, shuffled here and there, and gave me clearly to understand what he wanted. I scarcely spoke, only told him to go away, and that he need never speak to me any-where or at any time; it would be useless. Well, I changed my lodgings for those I now have, and simply began the life I now--the life I have been leading. Work was more impossible for me than ever, and I had to feed and clothe myself."

"How long ago was that?" asked Waymark, without looking up.

"Four months."

Ida rose from the beach. The tide had gone down some distance; there were stretches of smooth sand, already dry in the sunshine.

"Let us walk back on the sands," she said, pointing.

"You are going home?"

"Yes, I want to rest a little. I will meet you again about eight o'clock, if you like."

Waymark accompanied her as far as the door, then strolled on to his own lodg-ings, which were near at hand. It was only the second day that they had been in Hastings, yet it seemed to him as if he had been walking about on the seashore with Ida for weeks. For all that, he felt that he was not as near to her now as he had been on certain evenings in London, when his arrival was to her a manifest pleasure, and their talk unflagging from hour to hour. She did not show the spirit of holiday, seemed weary from time to time, was too often preoccupied and indisposed to talk. True, she had at length fulfilled her promise of telling him the whole of her story, but even this increase of confidence Waymark's uneasy mind strangely converted into fresh source of discomfort to himself. She had made this revelation--he half believed--on purpose to keep up the distance between them, to warn him how slight occasion had led her from what is called the path of virtue, that he might not delude himself into exaggerated estimates of her character. Such a thought could of course only be due to the fact that Ida's story had indeed produced something of this impression upon her hearer. Waymark had often busied himself with inventing all manner of excuses for her, had exerted his imagination to the utmost to hit upon some most irresistible climax of dolorous circumstances to account for her downfall. He had yet to realise that circumstances are as relative in their importance as everything else in this world, and that ofttimes the greatest tragedies revolve on apparently the most insignificant outward events--personality being all.

He spent the hours of her absence in moving from place to place, fretting in mind. At one moment, he half determined to bring things to some issue, by disregarding all considerations and urging his love upon her. Yet this he felt he could not do. Surely--he asked himself angrily he was not still so much in the thraldom of conventionality as to be affected by his fresh reminder of her position and antecedents? Perhaps not quite so much prejudice as experience which disturbed him. He was well acquainted with the characteristics of girls of this class; he knew how all but impossible it is for them to tell the truth, the whole truth, and nothing but the truth. And there was one thing particularly in Ida's story that he found hard to credit; was it indeed likely that she had not felt more than she would confess for this man whose mistress she became so easily? If she had *not*, if what she said were true, was not this something like a proof of her lack of that refined sentiment which is, the capacity for love, in its real sense? Torturing doubts and reasonings of this kind once set going in a brain already confused with passion, there is no limit to the range of speculation opened; Waymark found himself--in spite of everything-- entertaining all his old scepticism. In any case, had he the slightest ground for the hope that she might ever feel to him as warmly as he did to her? He could not recall one instance of Ida's having betrayed a trace of fondness in her intercourse with him. The mere fact of their intercourse he altogether lost sight of. Whereas an outsider would, under the circumstances, have been justified in laying the utmost stress on this, Waymark had grown to accept it as a matter of course, and only occupied himself with Ida's absolute self-control, her perfect calmness in all situations, the ease with which she met his glance, the looseness of her hand in his, the indifference with which she heard him when he had spoken of his loneliness and frequent misery. Where was the key of her character? She did not care for admiration; it was quite certain that she was not leading him about just to gratify her own vanity. Was it not purely an intellectual matter? She was a girl of superior intellect, and, having found in him some one with whom she could satisfy her desire for rational converse, did she not on this account keep up their relations? For the rest--well, she liked ease and luxury; above all, ease. Of that she would certainly make no sacrifice. How well he could imagine the half-annoyed, half-contemptuous smile which would rise to her beautiful face, if he were so foolish as to become sentimental with her! That, he felt, would be a look not easy to bear. Humiliation he dreaded.

When eight o'clock came, he was leaning over the end of the pier, at the appointed spot, still busy in thought. There came a touch on his arm.

"Well, are you thinking how you can make a book out of my story?"

The touch, the voice, the smile,--how all his sophistry was swept away in a rush of tenderness and delight!

"I must wait for the end of it," he returned, holding out his hand, which she did not take.

"The end?--Oh, you must invent one. Ends in real life are so commonplace and uninteresting."

"Commonplace or not," said Waymark, with some lack of firmness in his voice, "the end of your story should not be an unhappy one, if I had the disposing of it. And I might have--but for one thing."

"What's that?" she asked, with sudden interest.

"My miserable poverty. If I only had money--money"--

"Money!" she exclaimed, turning away almost angrily. Then she added, with the coldness which she did not often use, but which, when she did, chilled and checked him--"I don't understand you."

He pointed with a bitter smile down to the sands.

"Look at that gold of the sunset in the pools the tide has left. It is the most glorious colour in nature, but it makes me miserable by reminding me of the metal it takes its name from."

She looked at him with eyes which had in them a strange wonder, sad at first, then full of scorn, of indignation. And then she laughed, drawing herself away from him. The laugh irritated him. He experienced a terrible revulsion of feeling, from the warmth and passion which had possessed him, to that humiliation, which he could not bear.

And just now a number of people came and took their stands close by, in a gossiping group. Ida had half turned away, and was looking at the golden pools. He tried to say something, but his tongue was dry, and the word would not come. Presently, she faced him again, and said, in very much her ordinary tone--

"I was going to tell you that I have just had news from London, which makes it necessary for me to go back to-morrow. I shall have to take an early train."

"This is because I have offended you," Waymark said, moving nearer to her. "You had no thought of going before that."

"I am not surprised that you refuse to believe me," returned Ida, smiling very faintly. "Still, it is the truth. And now I must go in again;--I am very tired."

"No," he exclaimed as she moved away, "you must not go in till--till you have forgotten me. At least come away to a quiet place, where I can speak freely to you; these people--"

"To-morrow morning," she said, waving her hand wearily. "I can't talk now-- and indeed there is no need to speak of this at all. I have forgotten it."

"No, you have not; how could you?--And you will not go to-morrow; you shall not."

"Yes, I must," she returned firmly.

"Then I shall go with you."

"As you like. I shall leave by the express at five minutes past nine."

"Then I shall be at the station. But at least I may walk home with you?"

"No, please. If you wish me to think you are sincere,--if you wish us still to be friends--stay till I have left the pier.--Good night."

He muttered a return, and stood watching her as she walked quietly away.

When it was nearly midnight, Ida lay on her bed, dressed, as she had lain since her return home. For more than an hour she had cried and sobbed in blank misery, cried as never since the bitter days long ago, just after her mother's death. Then, the fit over, something like a reaction of calm followed, and as she lay perfectly still in the darkness, her regular breathing would have led one to believe her asleep. But she was only thinking, and in deed very far from sleep The long day in the open air had so affected her eyes that, as she looked up at the ceiling, it seemed to her to be a blue space, with light clouds constantly flitting across it. Presently this impression became painful, and a growing restlessness made her rise. The heat of the room was stifling, for just above was the roof, upon which all day the sun had poured its rays. She threw open the window, and drank in the air. The night was magnificent, flooded with warm moonlight, and fragrant with sea breathings. Ida felt an irresistible desire to leave the house and go down to the shore, which she could not see from her window; the tide, she remembered, would just now be full, and to walk by it in the solitude of midnight would bring her that peace and strength of soul she so much needed. She put on her hat and cloak, and went downstairs. The front door was only latched, and, as she had her key, no doubt she would be able to let herself in at any hour.

The streets were all but deserted, and, when she came to the beach, no soul was anywhere visible. She walked towards the place where she had spent the afternoon with Waymark, then onwards still further to the east, till there was but a narrow space between the water and the cliffs. Breakers there were none, not more ripple at the clear tide-edge than on the border of a little lake. So intense was the silence that every now and then could be distinctly heard a call on one of the fishing-boats lying some distance from shore. The town was no longer in sight.

It was close even here; what little breeze there was brushed the face like the warm wing of a passing bird. Ida dipped her hands in the water and sprinkled it upon her forehead. Then she took off her boots and stockings, and walked with her feet in the ripples. A moment after she stopped, and looked all around, as if hesitating at some thought, and wishing to see that her solitude was secure. Just then the sound of a clock came very faintly across the still air, striking the hour of one. She stepped from the water a few paces, and began hastily to put off her clothing; in a moment her feet were again in the ripples, and she was walking out from the beach, till her gleaming body was hidden. Then she bathed, breasting the full flow with delight, making the sundered and broken water flash myriad reflections of the moon and stars.

*   *   *   *   *

Waymark was at the station next morning half an hour before train-time. He waited for Ida's arrival before taking his ticket. She did not come. He walked about in feverish impatience, plaguing himself with all manner of doubt and apprehension. The train came into the station, and yet she had not arrived. It started, and no sign of her.

He waited yet five minutes, then walked hastily into the town, and to Ida's lodgings. Miss Starr, he was told, had left very early that morning; if he was Mr. Waymark, there was a note to be delivered to him.

"I thought it better that I should go to London by an earlier train, for we should not have been quite at our ease with each other. I beg you will not think my leaving you is due to anything but necessity--indeed it is not. I shall not be living at the old place, but any letter you send there I shall get. I cannot promise to reply at once, but hope you will let me do so when I feel able to.

I. S."

Waymark took the next train to town.

CHAPTER XVIII
THE ENDERBYS

Some twenty years before the date we have reached, the Rev. Paul Enderby, a handsome young man, endowed with moral and intellectual qualities considerably above the average, lived and worked in a certain small town of Yorkshire.

He had been here for two years, an unmarried man; now it was made known that this state of things was to come to an end; moreover, to the disappointment of not a few households, it was understood that the future Mrs. Enderby had been chosen from among his own people, in London. The lady came, and there was a field-day of criticism. Mrs. Enderby looked very young, and was undeniably pretty; she had accomplishments, and evidently liked to exhibit them before her homely visitors. She exaggerated the refinement of her utterance that it might all the more strike off against the local accent. It soon became clear that she would be anything but an assistance to her husband in his parochial work; one or two attempts were made, apparently with good will, at intercourse with the poor parishioners, but the enterprise was distinctly a failure; it had to be definitively given up. Presently a child was born in the parsonage, and for a little while the young mother's attention was satisfactorily engaged at home. The child was a girl and received the name of Maud.

Paul Enderby struggled to bate no jot of his former activity, but a change was obvious to all. No less obvious the reason of it. Mrs. Enderby's reckless extravagance had soon involved her husband in great difficulties. He was growing haggard; his health was failing; his activity shrank within the narrowest possible limits; he shunned men's gaze.

Yet all at once there happened something which revived much of his old zeal, and, in spite of everything, brought him once more prominently forward. A calamity had visited the town. By a great explosion in a neighbouring colliery, numbers of homes had been rendered destitute, and aid of every kind was imperatively called for on all sides. In former times, Paul Enderby would have been just the man for this occasion, and even now he was not wanting. Extensive subscriptions were raised, and he, as chief man in the committee which had been formed, had chief control of the funds. People said afterwards that they had often remarked something singular in his manner as he went about in these duties. Whether that was true or not, something more than singular happened when, some two months later, accounts were being investigated and cleared up. Late one evening, Mr. Enderby left home,--and never returned to it. It was very soon known that he must have appropriated to his own use considerable sums which had reached his hands for charitable purposes, and the scandal was terrific. Mrs. Enderby and her child disappeared in a day or two. It was said that ladies from London had come and fetched her away, and she was no more heard of in that little town.

Miss Bygrave, an elder sister of Mrs. Enderby, had received a letter from Paul summoning her to the wife's aid: and this letter, dated from Liverpool, after disclosing in a few words the whole situation, went on to say that the writer, though he would never more be seen by those who knew him, would not fail to send his wife what money he could as often as he could. And, after half a year, sums had begun to be remitted, in envelopes bearing a Californian postmark. They were not much use, however, to Mrs. Enderby. A few days after her arrival at her home in London, she had been discovered hanging, with a rope round her neck, from a nail behind her bedroom door. Cut down in time, her life was saved, but reason had forsaken her.

She was taken away to an asylum, and remained there for five years.

By that time, she seemed to have quite recovered. Her home was now to be with her sister, Theresa Bygrave. Her child, Maud Enderby, was nearly seven years old. Mrs. Enderby returned to the world not quite the same woman as when she left it. She had never lacked character, and this now showed itself in one immutable resolution. Having found that the child had learnt nothing of its parents, she determined that this ignorance should continue; or rather that it should be exchanged for the belief that those parents were both long dead. She dwelt apart, supported by her sister. Finally, after ten years' absence, Paul Enderby returned to England, and lived again with his wife. But Maud, their daughter, still believed herself alone in the world, save for her aunt, Miss Bygrave.

At the time when Waymark and Ida were together at Hastings, Mrs. Enderby called one evening at Miss Bygrave's house--the house of Maud's childhood, still distinguished by the same coldness, bareness and gloom, the same silence echoing to a strange footfall. Theresa Bygrave had not greatly altered; tall, upright, clad in the plainest black garment, she walked into the room with silent dignity, and listened to a suggestion made by her brother-in-law.

"We have talked it over again," said Paul, "and we have decided to take this step."

He paused and watched the listener's face eagerly, glancing quickly away as soon as she looked up.

"And you still wish me to break it to Maud, and in the way you said?"

"If you will.--But I do so wish you would let me know your own thoughts about this. You have so much claim to be considered. Maud is in reality yours far more than she is ours. Will it--do you think now it will really be for our own happiness? Will the explanation you are able to give be satisfactory to her? What will be her attitude towards us? You know her character--you understand her."

"If the future could be all as calm as the past year has been," said Miss Bygrave, "I should have nothing to urge against your wishes."

"And this will contribute to it," exclaimed Enderby. "This would give Emily the very support she needs."

Miss Bygrave looked into his face, which had a pleading earnestness, and a deep pity lay in her eyes.

"Let it be so," she said with decision. "I myself have much hope from Maud's influence. I will write and tell her not to renew her engagement, and she will be with us at the end of September."

"But you will not tell her anything till she comes?"

"No."

Miss Bygrave lived in all but complete severance from the world. When Maud Enderby was at school, she felt strongly and painfully the contrast between her own home life and that of her companions. The girl withdrew into solitary reading and thinking; grew ever more afraid of the world; and by degrees sought more of her aunt's confidence, feeling that here was a soul that had long since attained to the peace which she was vainly seeking.

But it was with effort that Miss Bygrave brought herself to speak to another of her form of faith. After that Christmas night when she addressed Maud for the first time on matters of religion, she had said no second word; she waited the effect of her teaching, and the girl's spontaneous recurrence to the subject. There was something in the very air of the still, chill house favourable to ascetic gravity. A young girl, living under such circumstances, must either pine away, eating her own heart, or become a mystic, and find her daily food in religious meditation.

Only when her niece was seventeen years old did Miss Bygrave speak to her of worldly affairs. Her own income, she explained, was but just sufficient for their needs, and would terminate upon her death; had Maud thought at all of what course she would choose when the time for decision came? Naturally, only one thing could suggest itself to the girl's mind, and that was to become a teacher. To begin with, she took subordinate work in the school where she had been a pupil; later, she obtained the engagement at Dr. Tootle's.

An education of this kind, working upon Maud Enderby's natural temperament, resulted in an abnormal character, the chief trait of which was remarkable as being in contradiction to the spirit of her time. She was oppressed with the consciousness of sin. Every most natural impulse of her own heart she regarded as a temptation to be resisted with all her strength. Her ideal was the same as Miss Bygrave's, but she could not pursue it with the latter's assured calm; at every moment the voice of her youth spoke within her, and became to her the voice of the enemy. Her faith was scarcely capable of formulation in creeds; her sins were not of omission or commission in the literal sense; it was an attitude of soul which she sought to attain, though ever falling away. What little she saw of the world in London, and afterwards at her home by the sea-side, only served to increase the trouble of her conscience, by making her more aware of her own weakness. For instance, the matter of her correspondence with Waymark. In very truth, the chief reason why she had given him the permission he asked of her was, that before so sudden and unexpected a demand she found herself confused and helpless; had she been able to reflect, the temptation would probably have been resisted, for the pleasantness of the thought made her regard it as a grave temptation. Casuistry and sophistical reasoning with her own heart ensued, to the increase of her morbid sensitiveness; she persuaded herself that greater insight into the world's evil would be of aid in her struggle, and so the contents of Waymark's first letter led her to a continuance of the correspondence. A power of strong and gloomy description which she showed in her letters, and which impressed Waymark, afforded the key to her sufferings; her soul in reality was that of an artist, and, whereas the artist should be free from everything like moral prepossession, Maud's aesthetic sensibilities were in perpetual conflict with her moral convictions. She could not understand herself, seeing that her opportunities had never allowed her to obtain an idea of the artistic character. This irrepressible delight and interest in the active life of the world, what could it be but the tendency to evil, most strongly developed? These heart-burnings whenever she witnessed men and women rejoicing in the exercise of their natural affections, what could that be but the proneness to evil in its grossest form?

It was naturally a great surprise to Maud when she received the letter from her aunt, which asked her not to continue her engagement into the new quarter, giving as a reason merely that the writer wished for her at home. It was even with something of dread and shrinking that she looked forward to a renewal of the old life. Still, it was enough that her aunt had need of her. On her return to London, she was met with strange revelations. Miss Bygrave's story had been agreed upon between herself and Paul. It had been deemed best to make Mrs. Enderby's insanity the explanation of Maud's removal from her parents, and the girl, stricken as she was with painful emotions, seemed to accept this undoubtingly.

The five years or so since Paul Enderby's reappearance in England seemed to have been not unprosperous. The house to which Maud was welcomed by her father and mother was not a large one, and not in a very fashionable locality, but it was furnished with elegance. Mrs. Enderby frequently had her hired brougham, and made use of it to move about a good deal where people see and are seen. Mr. Enderby's business was "in the City." How he had surmounted his difficulties was not very clear; his wife learned that he had brought with him from America a scheme for the utilisation of waste product in some obscure branch of manufacture, which had been so far successful as to supply him with a small capital. He seemed to work hard, leaving home at nine each morning, getting back to dinner at half-past six, and, as often as not, spending the evening away from home, and not returning till the small hours. He had the feverish eye of a man whose subsistence depends upon speculative acuteness and restless calculation. No doubt he was still so far the old Paul, that, whatever he undertook, he threw himself into it with surpassing vigour.

Mrs. Enderby was in her thirty-eighth year, and still handsome. Most men, at all events, would have called her so, for most men are attracted by a face which is long, delicate, characterless, and preserves late the self-conscious expression of a rather frivolous girl of seventeen. She had ideals of her own, which she pursued regardless of the course in which they led her; and these ideals were far from ignoble. To beauty of all kinds she was passionately sensitive. As a girl she had played the piano well, and, though the power had gone from long disuse, music was still her chief passion. Graceful ease, delicacy in her surroundings, freedom from domestic cares, the bloom of flowers, sweet scents--such things made up her existence. She loved her husband, and had once worshipped him; she loved her recovered daughter; but both affections were in her, so to speak, of aesthetic rather than of moral quality.

Intercourse between Maud and her parents, now that they lived together, was, as might have been expected, not altogether natural or easy. She came to them with boundless longings, ready to expend in a moment the love of a lifetime; they, on their side, were scarcely less full of warm anticipation; yet something prevented the complete expression of this mutual yearning. The fault was not in the father and mother if they hung back somewhat; in very truth, Maud's pure, noble countenance abashed them. This, their child, was so much the superior of them both; they felt it from the first moment, and could never master the consciousness. Maud mistook this for coldness; it checked and saddened her. Yet time brought about better things, though the ideal would never be attained. In her father, the girl found much to love; her mother she could not love as she had hoped, but she regarded her with a vast tenderness, often with deep compassion. Much of sympathy, moreover, there was between these two. Maud's artistic temperament was inherited from her mother, but she possessed it in a stronger degree, of purer quality, and under greater restraint. This restraint, however, did not long continue to be exercised as hitherto. Life for the first time was open before her, and the music which began to fill her ears, the splendour which shone into her eyes, gradually availed to still that inner voice which had so long spoken to her in dark admonishings. She could not resign herself absolutely to the new delight; it was still a conflict; but from the conflict itself she derived a kind of joy, born of the strength of her imagination.

Yes, there was one portion of the past which dwelt with her, and by degrees busied her thoughts more and more. The correspondence with Waymark had ceased, and by her own negligence. In those days of mental disturbance which preceded her return to London, his last letter had reached her, and this she had not replied to. It had been her turn to write, but she had not felt able to do so; it had seemed to her, indeed, that, with her return home, the correspondence would naturally come to an end; with a strange ignorance of herself, such as now and then darkens us, she had suddenly come to attach little value to the connection. Not improbably, Waymark's last two letters had been forced and lacking in interest. He had never said anything which could be construed into more than an expression of friendly interest, or intellectual sympathy. It may be that Maud's condition, dimly prophetic of the coming change, required more than this, and she conceived a certain dissatisfaction. Then came the great event, and for some weeks she scarcely thought of her correspondent. One day, however, she chanced upon the little packet of his letters, and read them through again. It was with new eyes. Thoughts spoke to her which had not been there on the first reading. Waymark had touched at times on art and kindred subjects, and only now could she understand his meaning. She felt that, in breaking off her connection with him, she had lost the one person who could give her entire sympathy; to whom she might have spoken with certainty of being understood, of all the novel ideas which possessed her; who, indeed, would have been invaluable as a guide in the unknown land she was treading. It was now almost the end of the year; more than three months had gone by since she received that last letter from him. Could she write now, and let him know that she was in London? She could not but give expression to her altered self; and would he be able to understand her? Yet,--she needed him; and there was something of her mother in the fretting to which she was now and then driven by the balked desire. At length she was on the point of writing a letter, with whatever result, when chance spared her the trouble.

One morning in December, she went with her mother to an exhibition of pictures in Bond Street. Such visits had been common of late; Mrs. Enderby could rarely occupy herself at home, and pictures, as everything beautiful, always attracted her. They had been in the gallery a few minutes only, when Maud recognised Waymark close at hand. He was looking closely at a canvas, and seemed quite unaware of her proximity. She laid her hand on her mother's arm, and spoke in a nervous whisper.

"Mother, I know that gentleman."

"This one?" asked Mrs. Enderby, indicating Waymark, with a smile. She showed no surprise, any more than she would have done had Maud been only her friend.

"Yes. If he should notice me, may I introduce him to you? He was at the school where I taught a year ago."

"Why, certainly, my love," replied her mother, with cheerful assent. "It is quite natural that you should have acquaintances I should like to know. Shall I ask him to come and see us?"

There was no opportunity of answering. Waymark, in moving on, had glanced round at the groups of people, and his eye had fallen on Maud. He seemed uncertain; looked quickly away; glanced again, and, meeting her eyes, raised his hat, though still without conviction in his face. Maud came naturally forward a step or two, and they shook hands; then at once she introduced him to her mother. No one ever experienced awkward pauses in Mrs. Enderby's presence; conversation linked itself with perfect ease, and in a minute they were examining the pictures together. Mrs. Enderby had made up her mind with regard to her new acquaintance in one or two gleams of her quick eyes, and then talked on in an eager, intelligent way, full of contagious enthusiasm, which soon brought out Waymark's best powers. Maud said very little. Whenever it was possible unobserved, she gazed at Waymark's face.

She found herself thinking that, in external appearance, he had improved since she last saw him. He had no longer that hungry, discontented look to which she had grown accustomed in the upper schoolroom at Dr. Tootle's; his eye seemed at once quieter and keener; his complexion was brighter; the habitual frown had somewhat smoothed away. Then, he was more careful in the matter of dress. On the whole, it seemed probable that his circumstances had changed for the better.

Waymark, on his side, whilst he talked, was not less full of speculation about Maud. For the change in her appearance was certainly much more noticeable than it could be in his own. Not only that she had put aside her sad-coloured and poor raiment for a costume of tasteful and attractive simplicity--this, of course, her mother's doing--but the look of shrinking, almost of fear, which he had been wont to see on her face, was entirely gone. Her eyes seemed for ever intelligent of new meanings; she was pale, but with the pallor of eager, joy-bringing thought. There was something pathetic in this new-born face; the lips seemed still to speak of past sorrows, or, it might be, to hold unspoken a sad fate half-foreseen.

If this renewal of acquaintanceship came just at the right time for Maud, it was no less welcome to Waymark. When he wrote his last letter to her, it had proceeded more from a sense of obligation than any natural impulse. For he was then only just recovering from a period of something like despair. His pursuit of Ida Starr to London had been fruitless. It was true that she had left her former abode, and the landlady professed to be ignorant of her new one, though she admitted that she had seen Ida scarcely two hours before Waymark's arrival. He wrote, but had no reply. His only comfort was an ever-rising suspicion of the truth (as he would learn it later), but fears were, on the whole, strongest within him. Confidence in her he had not. All the reflections of that last evening on Hastings pier lived and re-lived in his mind; outcome of the cynicism which was a marked feature in his development, and at the same time tending to confirm it. She had been summoned back suddenly by a letter; who but a simpleton could doubt what that meant? He thought of Sally, of course, and the step she had taken; but could he draw conclusions about Ida from Sally, and did ever two such instances come within a man's experience? To Sally herself he had naturally had recourse, but in vain. She said that she knew nothing of the lost girl. So Waymark fought it out, to the result of weariness; then plunged into his work again, and had regained very much his ordinary state of mind when

Maud Enderby unexpectedly came before him.

He called upon the Enderbys, and was soon invited to dine, which necessitated the purchase of a dress suit. On the appointed evening, he found Maud and her mother in a little drawing-room, which had a pleasant air of ease and refinement. It was a new sensation for Waymark as he sank into a soft chair, and, in speaking, lowered his voice, to suit the quietness of the room. The soft lamp-light spreading through the coloured shade, the just perceptible odour of scent when Mrs. Enderby stirred, the crackling of the welcome fire, filled him with a sense of luxury to which he was not accustomed. He looked at Maud. She was beautiful in her evening dress; and, marking the grave, sweet thoughtfulness of her face, the grace of her move- ments, the air of purity which clung about her, his mind turned to Ida Starr, and experienced a shock at the comparison. Where was Ida at this moment? The mere possibilities which such a question brought before his mind made him uneasy, al- most as if he had forgotten himself and uttered aloud some word all unfit for ladies' ears. The feeling was a novel one, and, in afterwards recalling it, he could smile rather contemptuously, If we are enraptured with one particular flower, shall we necessarily despise another, whose beauty and perfume happen to be of quite a dif- ferent kind?

Mr. Enderby appeared, followed by another gentleman. Waymark noticed an unpleasant heat in the hand held out to him; there was a flush in Paul's cheeks, too, and his eyes were very bright. He greeted the visitor with somewhat excessive warmth, then turned and introduced his companion, by the name of Mr. Rudge.

Waymark observed that this gentleman and his hostess were on terms of lively intimacy. They talked much throughout the evening.

During the three months that followed, Waymark's intercourse with the En- derbys was pretty frequent. Mrs. Enderby asked few questions about him, and Maud was silent after she had explained Waymark's position, so far as she was acquainted with it, and how she had come to know him. To both parents, the fact of Maud's friendship was a quite sufficient guarantee, so possessed were they with a conviction of the trustworthiness of her judgment, and the moral value of her impulses. In Waymark's character there was something which women found very attractive; strength and individuality are perhaps the words that best express what it was, though these qualities would not in themselves have sufficed to give him his influence, without a certain gracefulness of inward homage which manifested itself when he talked with women, a suggestion, too, of underlying passion which works subtly on a woman's imagination. There was nothing commonplace in his appearance and manner; one divined in him a past out of the ordinary range of experiences, and felt the promise of a future which would, in one way or another, be remarkable.

The more Waymark saw of Maud Enderby the more completely did he yield to the fascination of her character. In her presence he enjoyed a strange calm of spirit. For the first time he knew a woman who by no word or look or motion could stir in him a cynical thought. Here was something higher than himself, a nature which he had to confess transcended the limits of his judgment, a soul with insight possibly for ever denied to himself. He was often pained by the deference with which she sought his opinion or counsel; the words in which he replied to her sounded so hollow; he became so often and so keenly sensible of his insincerity,--a quality which, with others, he could consciously rely upon as a resource, but which, before Maud, stung him. He was driven to balance judgments, to hesitate in replies, to search his own heart, as perhaps never before.

Artificial good humour, affected interest, mock sympathy, were as far from her as was the least taint of indelicacy; every word she uttered rang true, and her very phrases had that musical fall which only associates itself with beautiful and honest thought. She never exhibited gaiety, or a spirit of fun, but could raise a smile by an exquisite shade of humour--humour which, as the best is, was more than half sadness. Nor was she fond of mixing with people whom she did not know well; when there was company at dinner, she generally begged to be allowed to dine alone. Though always anxious to give pleasure to her parents, she was most happy when nothing drew her from her own room; there she would read and dream through hours There were times when the old dreaded feelings took revenge; night-wakings, when she lay in cold anguish, yearning for the dawn. She was not yet strong enough to face past and future, secured in attained conviction. As yet, she could not stir beyond the present, and in the enjoyment of the present was her strength.

CHAPTER XIX
IN THE MEANTIME

It was one Wednesday evening in early April, that Waymark found a letter awaiting him, addressed in a hand he at once recognised.

"Will you come and see me? I am at home after eight o'clock till the end of the week, and all day on Sunday.

I. S."

No distinct pleasure was aroused in Waymark as he read this. As was always the case for hours after he had left Maud's presence, her face and voice lived with him to the exclusion of every other thought. There was even something of repulsion in the feeling excited by his thus having the memory of Ida brought suddenly before him; her face came as an unwelcome intruder upon the calm, grave mood which always possessed him on these evenings. In returning home each Wednesday night, Waymark always sought the speediest and quietest route, unwilling to be brought in contact with that life of the streets which at other times delighted him. Ida's note seemed a summons from that world which, for the moment, he held at a distance. But the call was not to be silenced at his will. He began to wonder about her life during the past half-year. Why had she written just now, after so long a silence? Where, and under what circumstances, should he meet her? Did she think to find him the same as when they last talked together?

Through the night he woke constantly, and always with thoughts busy about Ida. In the morning his first impulse was to re-read her message; received so carelessly, it had in the meantime become of more account, and Waymark laughed in his wonted way as he saw himself thus swayed between forces he could not control. The ordinary day's task was neglected, and he impatiently waited for the hour when he could be sure of finding Ida at home. The address was at Fulham, and, on reaching it, he found a large new block of the kind known as model lodging-houses. Ida's number was up at the very top. When he knocked, the door opened immediately, and she stood there, holding out her hand to him.

She wore the same dress that she had worn at Hastings, but the gold brooch and watch-chain were missing, and her hair was arranged in a simpler way. She was a trifle pale, perhaps, but that might be due to the excitement of the moment; her voice shook a little as she spoke.

Waymark looked about him as he went in. There appeared to be two rooms, one of them a very small bedroom, the other fitted with a cooking-grate and oven; the kind of tenement suitable to very poor working-people. The floors were bare, and there was nothing in the way of furniture beyond the most indispensable articles: a table, two chairs, and a few cups, saucers, and plates on a shelf; through the half-open door, he saw that the bed-room was equally plain. A fire was burning, and a kettle on it; and in front, on a little square piece of carpet, lay Ida's inseparable friend, Grim. Grim had lifted his head at Waymark's entrance, and, with gathering curiosity in his eyes, slowly stood up; then stretched himself, and, looking first at one, then at the other, waited in doubt.

Ida stooped and took him up in her arms.

"And who's this?" she asked, talking to him as one talks to a child, whilst she pressed his warm black cheek against her own. "Does Grim remember who this is? We still keep together," she added, looking at Waymark. "All day long, whilst I'm away, he keeps house; I'm often afraid he suffers dreadfully from loneliness, but, you see, I'm obliged to lock him in. And he knows exactly the time when I come home. I always find him sitting on that chair by the door, waiting, waiting, oh so patiently! And I often bring him back something nice, don't I, Grimmy? You should see how delighted he is as soon as I enter the door."

Ida was changed, and in many ways. She seemed to have grown younger; in her voice and manner there was a girlishness which was quite new to Waymark. Her motions were lighter and nimbler; there was no longer that slow grace of step and carriage which had expressed absolute leisure, and with it had gone, perhaps, something of dignity, which used to sit so well upon her. She laughed from time to time in a free, careless way; formerly she seldom did more than smile. In the old days, there was nothing about her suggestive of what are called the domestic virtues; now she seemed perfectly at home amid these simple surroundings, and, almost as soon as her visitor had sat down, she busied herself in laying the table in a quick, ready way, which came of the habit of waiting upon herself.

"You'll have a cup of tea with me?" she said, looking at Waymark with the curiosity which seemed to show that she also found something changed in him. "I only get home about eight o'clock, and this is the quietest and pleasantest meal in the day for me."

"What do you do all day, then?" Waymark asked, softening the bluntness of his question with a smile.

She stepped near to him, and held out her hands for him to look at; then, as he met her eyes again, laughed merrily.

"Do you guess?" she asked.

"I believe I can. You have gone back to the laundry again?"

"Yes."

"And how long is it since you did so?"

"How long is it since we last saw each other?"

"Did you begin at once when you returned to London?"

"Yes."

Waymark kept silence, whilst Ida poured out a cup of tea for him, and then took her seat at the table.

"Don't you think I'm comfortable here?" Ida said. "It's like having a house of my own. I see nothing of the other people in the building, and feel independent."

"Did you buy the furniture yourself?"

"Yes; just the things I couldn't do without. I pay only three-and-sixpence a week, and so long as I can earn that, I'm sure at all events of a home, where I can be happy or miserable, as I please."

Waymark wondered. There was no mistaking the genuineness of her tone. What, then, had been the reason for this astonishing change, a change extending, it would seem, almost to temperament? What intermediate phases had led up to this result? He wished to ask her for an explanation, but to do so would be to refer to the condition she had left, and that he did not wish to do. All would no doubt explain itself as they talked; in the meantime she told him how her days were ordered, and the details of her life.

"Have you brought your pipe?" she asked, when they had drank their tea.

"May I smoke?"

"Of course,--just as you used to."

"But it is not the same," Waymark said, half to himself.

"Are you sorry for the change?" Ida asked, as she handed him a box of matches.

"What induced you to make it?"

"Oh, I have strange fancies. The idea came, just like others do. Are you sorry?"

"The opposite. Did the idea come whilst we were at Hastings?"

"Before that. Do you remember my telling you that I had a letter calling me back to London?"

Waymark nodded.

"It was from the laundry, to say I could go to work as soon as I liked."

"And why didn't you tell me that?"

Ida seemed about to reply, but altered her intention, and, after being silent for a moment, asked another question.

"Did you think you would ever hear from me?"

"I had given up hope."

"And did you wonder what had become of me?"

"Often. Why didn't you write before?"

"I wasn't ready."

"What does that mean?" Waymark asked, looking closely at her.

"Perhaps I shall be able to explain some day. If not, well, it won't matter."

"And will you let me see you often?" said Waymark, after thinking a little. "Are we to be friends again, as we used to be?"

"If you would care for it."

Waymark turned away as their eyes met.

"Certainly I should care for it," he said, feeling all at once a difficulty in speaking naturally. Then he looked at Ida again; she was bending down and stroking Grim's ears. There was rather a long silence, which Waymark at length forced himself to break.

"Shall I bring you books again?" he said.

"I have very little time for reading," was Ida's reply. "It's better, perhaps, that it is so."

"But why?"

"Perhaps it would make me discontented with my work, and want all sorts of things I couldn't have."

"You have your Sundays free?" Waymark said, after another rather long silence.

"Yes."

"Then we must have some expeditions again, now that the fine days have come. By the by, do you ever see Sally?"

Ida looked up with a smile and said, "Yes; do you?"

"No; but I hear of her."

"From your friend?"

"Yes, from O'Gree."

"Do your other friends still live near you?" Ida asked, speaking quickly, as if to interrupt what Waymark was about to say.

"The Castis? Oh yes."

"What is Mrs. Casti like?" she said, in a tone which attracted Waymark's attention.

"Well," he replied, "it's difficult to describe her. There's nothing very good about her, and I suppose nothing very bad. I see little of her now; she's almost always ill."

"What's the matter with her?"

"Can't say; general weakness and ill health, I think?"

"But she's so young, isn't she? Has she friends to go and see her?"

"Very few, I think."

"It must be dreadful to be like that," said Ida. "I'm thankful that I have my health, at all events. Loneliness isn't so hard to bear, as it must be in illness."

"Do you feel lonely?"

"A little, sometimes," said Ida. "But it's ungrateful to poor old Grim to say so."

"Have you no acquaintances except the people you work with?"

She shook her head.

"And you don't read? Wouldn't you like to go on reading as you used to? You have a better head than most women, and it's a pity not to make use of it. That's all nonsense about in making you discontented. You won't always be living like this, I suppose."

"Why not?" Ida asked simply.

"Well," said Waymark, without meeting her look, "even if you do, it will be gain to you to cultivate your mind?"

"Do you wish me to cultivate my mind?"

"You know I do."

Waymark seemed uneasy. He rose and leaned against the mantelpiece.

"I will do whatever you bid me," Ida said. "I can get an hour or so each night, and I have all Sunday."

Waymark felt only too well the effect of the tone he was adopting. The situation was by this time clear enough to him, and his own difficulties no less clear. He avoided looking at Ida as much as he could. A change had again come over her manner; the girlishness was modified, the old sadder tone was audible at moments.

"If it's fine on Sunday," he said, "will you go with me to Richmond, and let us have dinner at the old place?"

"No," was Ida's reply, with a smile, "I can't afford it."

"But I invite you. Of course I didn't mean that it should be any expense."

She still shook her head.

"No, I must take my own share, wherever we go."

"Then I shall certainly refuse your cup of tea next time I come," said Waymark jestingly.

"That's quite different," said Ida. "But if you like, we can go in the afternoon, and walk about Roehampton; that I can afford."

"As you please. When shall I call for you?"

"Half-past one."

She opened the door for him, and held out her hand. Their eyes did not meet as they said good-bye. The door closed, and Waymark went so slowly down the stone steps that he seemed at every moment on the point of stopping and turning back.

CHAPTER XX
A SUGGESTION

Waymark and Julian Casti were sitting together in the former's room. It was Saturday evening--two days after Waymark's visit to Ida. Julian had fallen into a sad reverie.

"How is your wife?" asked his friend, after watching the melancholy face for a while.

"She said her headache was worse to-night."

"Curiously," observed Waymark, with a little acidity, "it always is when you have to leave home."

Julian looked up, and seemed to reach a crisis in his thoughts.

"Waymark," he began, reddening as he still always did when greatly moved, "I fear I have been behaving very foolishly. Many a time I have wished to speak out to you plainly, but a sort of delicacy--a wrong kind of delicacy, I think--prevented me. I can't keep this attitude any longer. I must tell you how things are going on, and you must give me what help you can. And perhaps I shall be telling you what you already know?"

"I have suspected."

"Where is the blame?" Julian broke out, with sudden vehemence. "I cannot think that ever husband was more patient and more indulgent than I have been. I have refused her nothing that my means could possibly obtain. I have given up all the old quiet habits of my life that she mightn't think I slighted her; I scarcely ever open a book at home, knowing that it irritates her to see me reading; I do my best to amuse her at all times. How does she reward me? For ever she grumbles that I can't perform impossibilities,--take her to theatres, buy her new dresses, procure for her friends and acquaintances. My wishes, expressed or understood, weigh with her less than the least of her own caprices. She wantonly does things which she knows will cause me endless misery. Her companions are gross and depraved people, who constantly drag her lower and lower, to their own level. The landlady has told me that, in my absence, women have called to see her who certainly ought not to enter any decent house. When I entreat her to give up such associates, her only answer is to accuse me of selfishness, since I have friends myself, and yet won't permit her to have any. And things have gone from bad to worse. Several nights of late, when I have got home, she has been away, and has not returned till much after midnight. Hour after hour I have sat there in the extremest misery, waiting, waiting, feeling as though my brain would burst with its strain! I have no idea where she goes to. If I ask, she only retorts by asking me where I spend the nights when I am with you, and laughs contemptuously when I tell her the truth. Her suspicions and jealousy are incessant, and torture me past endurance. Once or twice, I confess, I have lost patience, and have spoken angrily, too angrily; then she has accused me of brutal disregard of her sufferings. It would hurt me less if she pierced me with a knife. Only this morning there was a terrible scene; she maddened me past endurance by her wretched calumnies--accusing me of I know not what disgraceful secrets--and when words burst from me involuntarily, she fell into hysterics, and shrieked till all the people in the house ran up in alarm. Can you understand what this means to one of my temperament? To have my private affairs forced upon strangers in this way tortures me with the pains of hell. I am naturally reticent and retiring--too much so, I dare say--and no misery could have been devised for me more dreadful than this. Her accusations are atrocious, such as could only come from a grossly impure mind, or at the suggestion of vile creatures. You she hates with a rabid hatred--God only knows why. She would hate any one who was my friend, and whose society relieved me for a moment from my ghastly torments!"

He ceased for very exhaustion, so terribly did the things he described work upon him.

"What am I to do, Waymark? Can you give me advice?"

Waymark had listened with his eyes cast down, and he was silent for some time after Julian ceased.

"You couldn't well ask for advice in a more difficult case," he said at length. "There's nothing for it but to strengthen yourself and endure. Force yourself into work. Try to forget her when she is out of sight."

"But," broke in Julian, "this amounts to a sentence of death! What of the life before me, of the years I shall have to spend with her? Work, forget myself, forget her,--that is just what I *cannot* do! My nerves are getting weaker every day; I am beginning to have fits of trembling and horrible palpitation; my dreams are hideous with vague apprehensions, only to be realised when I wake. Work! Half my misery is caused by the thought that my work is at an end for ever. It is all forsaking me, the delight of imagining great things, what power I had of putting my fancies into words, the music that used to go with me through the day's work. It is long since I wrote a line of verse. Quietness, peace, a calm life of thought, these things are what I *must* have; I thought I should have them in a higher degree than ever, and I find they are irretrievably lost. I feel my own weakness, as I never could before. When you bid me strengthen myself, you tell me to alter my character. The resolution needed to preserve the better part of my nature through such a life as this, will never be within my reach. It is fearful to think of what I shall become as time goes on. I dread myself! There have been revealed to me depths of passion and misery in my own heart which I had not suspected. I shall lose all self-control, and become as selfish and heedless as she is."

"No, you will not," said Waymark encouragingly. "This crisis will pass over, and strength will be developed. We have a wonderful faculty for accommodating ourselves to wretchedness; how else would the world have held together so long? When you begin to find your voice again, maybe you won't sing of the dead world any longer, but of the living and suffering. Your thoughts were fine; they showed you to be a poet; but I have never hidden from you how I wished that you had been on my side. Art, nowadays, must be the mouthpiece of misery, for misery is the key-note of modern life."

They talked on, and Julian, so easily moulded by a strong will, became half courageous.

"One of her reproaches," he said, "is just; I can't meet it. If I object to her present companions it is my duty to find her more suitable ones. She lives too much alone. No doubt it is every husband's duty to provide his wife with society. But how am I to find it? I am so isolated, and always have been. I know not a soul who could be a friend to her."

Waymark grew thoughtful, and kept silent.

"One person I know," he said presently, and in a cautious way, "who might perhaps help you."

"You do?" cried Julian eagerly.

"You know that I make all sorts of queer acquaintances in my wanderings. Well, I happen to know a girl of about your wife's age, who, if she were willing, would be just the person you want. She is quite alone, parentless, and almost without friends. She lives by herself, and supports herself by working in a laundry. For all this, she is by no means the ordinary London work-girl; you can't call her educated, but she speaks purely, and has a remarkably good intelligence. I met her by chance, and kept up her acquaintance. There has been nothing wrong--bah! how conventional one is, in spite of oneself!--I mean to say there has been nothing more than a pleasant friendship between us; absolutely nothing. We see each other from time to time, and have a walk, perhaps a meal, together, and I lend her books. Now, do you think there would be any way of getting your wife to accept her society, say of an evening now and then? Don't do anything rash; it is of course clear that *you* must have no hand in this. I must manage it if it is to be done. Naturally, I can't answer at once for the girl's readiness; but I believe she would do what I asked her to. Do you think it is worth entertaining, this idea?"

"I do, indeed; it would be salvation, I really believe."

"Don't be too sanguine, Casti; that's another of your faults. Still, I know very well that this girl could cure your wife of her ill propensities if any living creature could. She is strong in character, admirably clear-headed, mild, gentle, womanly; in fact, there is perhaps no one I respect so much, on the whole."

"Respect, only?" asked Julian, smiling.

"Ye-es; yes, I believe I am perfectly honest in saying so, though I couldn't have been so sure about it some little time ago. Our relations, no doubt, are peculiar; on her side there is no more warmth than on mine"--Waymark tried so to believe--"and indeed her clear sight has no doubt gauged me fairly well at my true value."

"What is her name?"

"Ida Starr."

"What!" cried Julian startled. "That is a strange thing! You have noticed the scar on Harriet's forehead?"

"Well?"

"Why, it was a wound given her at school by a girl of that very name! I remember the name as well as possible. It was a blow with a slate dealt in passion--some quarrel or other. They were both children then, and Ida Starr left the school in consequence."

"Is it possible that it is the same person?" asked Waymark, wondering and reflecting.

"If so, that puts a new difficulty in our way."

"Removes one, I should have thought"

"Harriet is not of a very forgiving nature," said Julian gravely.

"I shouldn't have supposed she was; but a long time has gone by since then, and, after all, one is generally glad to see an old school-fellow."

At this point the conversation was interrupted by a knock at the door, followed by the announcement that a gentleman named O'Gree wished to see Mr. Waymark. Waymark smiled at Julian.

"Don't run away," he said. "You ought to know O'Gree in the flesh."

The teacher came into the room with a rush, and was much taken aback at the sight of a stranger present. Perspiration was streaming profusely from his face, which was aglow with some great intelligence. After being introduced to Casti, he plunged down on a chair, and mopped himself with his handkerchief, uttering incoherencies about the state of the weather. Waymark made an effort to bring about a general conversation, but failed; O'Gree was so preoccupied that any remark addressed to him had to be repeated before he understood it, and Julian was in no mood for making new acquaintances. So, in a few minutes, the latter took his hat and left, Waymark going with him to the door to speak a few words of encouragement.

"The battle's won!" cried O'Gree, with much gesticulation, as soon as Waymark returned. "The campaign's at an end!--I'm sorry if I've driven your friend away, but I was bound to tell you."

"All right. Let me have a description of the manoeuvres."

"Look here, my boy," said O'Gree, with sudden solemnity, "you've never been very willing to talk to me about her. Now, before I tell you anything, I want to know this. **Why** wouldn't you tell me how you first got to know her, and so on?"

"Before I answer, I want to know this: have you found out why I wouldn't?"

"Yes, I have--that is, I suppose I have--and from her own lips, too! You knew her when she lived near the Strand there, eh?"

"I did."

"Well now, understand, my boy. I don't want to hear anything disagreeable; in fact, I won't listen to anything disagreeable;--all I want to know is, whether I may safely tell you what she has told me. If you don't know it already, there's no need to talk of it."

"I understand, and I don't think you can tell me anything I'm not well aware of."

"Sure, then, I will tell you, and if there's another girl as brave and honest as Sally in all this worruld, I'll be obliged if you'll make me acquainted with her! Well, you know she has a Saturday afternoon off every month. It hasn't been a very cheerful day, but it couldn't be missed; and, as it was too rainy to walk about, I couldn't think of any better place to go to than the British Museum. Of course I wanted to find a quiet corner, but there were people about everywhere, and the best we could manage was in the mummy-room. We looked at all the mummies, and I told her all I knew about them, and I kept thinking to myself: Now, how can I work round to it? I've tried so often, you know, and she's always escaped me, somehow, and I couldn't help thinking it was because I hadn't gone about it in the proper way. Well, we'd been staring at a mummy for about a quarter of an hour, and neither of us said anything, when all at once a rare idea came into my head. 'Sally,' I said, glancing round to see that there was no one by, 'that mummy was very likely a pretty girl like you, once.' 'Do you think so?' she said, with that look of hers which makes me feel like a galvanic battery. 'I do,' I said, 'and what's more, there may once have been another mummy, a man-mummy, standing by her just as I am standing by you, and wanting very much to ask her something, and shaking in his shoes for fear he shouldn't get the right answer.' 'Did the mummies wear shoes when they were alive?' she asked, all at once. 'Wear shoes!' I cried out. 'I can't tell you, Sally; but one thing I feel very sure of, and that is that they had hearts. Now, suppose,' I said, 'we're those two mummies--' 'I'm sure it's bad luck!' interrupted Sally. 'Oh no, it isn't,' said I, seeing something in her face which made me think it was the opposite. 'Let me go on. Now, suppose the one mummy said to the other, "Sally--"' '**Were** the girl-mummies called Sally?' she interrupted again. 'Sure I can't say,' said I, 'but we'll suppose so. Well, suppose he said, "Sally if I can hit on some means of making a comfortable home here by the Nile,--that's to say, the Thames, you know,--will you come and keep it in order for me, and live with me for all the rest of our lives?' Now what do you think the girl-mummy would have answered:'"

Waymark laughed, but O'Gree had become solemn.

"She didn't answer at once, and there was something very queer in her face. All at once she said, 'What has Mr. Waymark told you about me?' 'Why, just nothing at all,' I said, rather puzzled. 'And do you know,' she asked then, without looking at me, 'what sort of a girl I am?' Well, all at once there came something into my head that I'd never thought of before, and I was staggered for a moment; I couldn't say anything. But I got over it. 'I don't want to know anything,' I said. 'All I know is, that I like you better than I ever shall any one else, and I want you to promise to be my wife, some day.' 'Then you must let me tell you all my story first,' she said. 'I won't answer till you know everything.' And so she told me what it seems you know. Well, if I thought much of her before, I thought a thousand times as much after that! And do you know what? I believe it was on my account that she want and took that place in the shop."

"Precisely," said Waymark.

"You think so?" cried the other, delighted.

"I guessed as much when she met me that day and said I might let you know where she was."

"Ha!" exclaimed O'Gree, with a long breath.

"And so the matter is settled?"

"All but the most important part of it. There's no chance of my being able to marry for long enough to come. Now, can you give me any advice? I've quite made up my mind to leave Tootle. The position isn't worthy of a gentleman; I'm losing my self-respect. The she-Tootle gets worse and worse. If I don't electrify her, one of these days, with an outburst of ferocious indignation, she will only have my patience to thank. Let her beware how she drives the lion to bay!"

"Couldn't you get a non-resident mastership?"

"I must try, but the pay is so devilish small."

"We must talk the matter over."

CHAPTER XXI
DIPLOMACY

Waymark had a good deal of frank talk with himself before meeting Ida again on the Sunday. Such conversation was, as we know, habitual. Under the circumstances, however, he felt that it behoved him to become especially clear on one or two points; never mind what course he might ultimately pursue, it was always needful to him to dissect his own motives, that he might at least be acting with full consciousness.

One thing was clear enough. The fiction of a mere friendship between himself and Ida was impossible to support. It had been impossible under the very different circumstances of a year ago, and was not likely to last a week, now that Ida could so little conceal how her own feelings had changed. What, then, was to be their future? Could he accept her love, and join their lives without legal bond, thinking only of present happiness, and content to let things arrange themselves as they would in the years to come?

His heart strongly opposed such a step. Clearly Ida had changed her life for his sake, and was undergoing hardships in the hope of winning his respect as well as his love. Would she have done all this without something of a hope that she might regain her place in the every-day world, and be held by Waymark worthy to become his wife? He could not certainly know, but there was little doubt that this hope had led her on. Could he believe her capable of yet nobler ideas; could he think that only in reverence of the sanctity of love, and without regard to other things, she had acted in this way; then, regarding her as indeed his equal, he would open his heart to her and speak somewhat in this way. "Yes, I do love you; but at the same time I know too well the uncertainty of love to go through the pretence of binding myself to you for ever. Will you accept my love in its present sincerity, neither hoping nor fearing, knowing that whatever happens is beyond our own control, feeling with me that only an ignoble nature can descend to the affectation of union when the real links are broken?" Could Waymark but have felt sure of her answer to such an appeal, it would have gone far to make his love for Ida all-engrossing. She would then be his ideal woman, and his devotion to her would have no bounds.

But he felt too strongly that in thus speaking he would sadden her by the destruction of her great hope. On the other hand, to offer to make her his legal wife would be to do her a yet greater injustice, even had he been willing to so sacrifice himself. The necessity for legal marriage would be a confession of her inferiority, and the sense of being thus bound would, he well knew, be the surest means of weakening his affection. This affection he could not trust. How far was it mere passion of the senses, which gratification would speedily kill?

In the case of his feeling towards Maud Enderby there was no such doubt. Never was his blood so calm as in her presence. She was to him a spirit, and in the spirit he loved her. With Maud he might look forward to union at some distant day, a union outwardly of the conventional kind. It would be so, not on account of any inferiority to his ideal in Maud, for he felt that there was no height of his own thought whither she would not in time follow him; but simply because no point of principle would demand a refusal of the yoke of respectability, with its attendant social advantages. And the thought of thus binding himself to Maud had nothing repulsive, for the links between them were not of the kind which easily yield, and loyalty to a higher and nobler nature may well be deemed a duty.

So far logical arguing. But the fact remained that he had not the least intention of breaking off his intercourse with Ida, despite the certainty that passion would grow upon him with each of their meetings, rendering their mutual relations more and more dangerous. Of only one thing could he be sure: marriage was not to be thought of. It remained, then, that he was in danger of being led into conduct which would be the source of grievous unrest to himself, and for Ida would lay the foundation of much suffering. Waymark was honest enough in his self-communing to admit that he could not trust himself. Gross deception he was incapable of, but he would not answer for it that, the temptation pressing him too hard, he might not be guilty of allowing Ida to think his love of more worth than it really was. She knew his contempt of conventional ties, and her faith in him would keep her from pressing him to any step he disliked; she would trust him without that. And such trust would be unmerited.

It was significant that he did not take into account loyalty to Maud as a help in resisting this temptation. He was too sure of himself as regarded that purer love; let what might happen, his loyalty to Maud would be unshaken. It was independent of passion, and passion could not shake it.

Then came the subject of the proposed acquaintance between Ida and Mrs. Casti. An impulse of friendship had led to his conceiving the idea; together, perhaps, with the recollection of what Ida had said about her loneliness, and the questions she had asked about Mrs. Casti. Waymark had little doubt that those questions indicated a desire to become acquainted with his friends; the desire was natural, under the circumstances. Still, he regretted what he had done. To introduce Ida to his friends would be almost equivalent to avowing some conventional relations between her and himself. And, in the next place, it would be an obstacle in the way of those relations becoming anything but conventional. Well, and was not this exactly the kind of aid he needed in pursuing the course which he felt to be right? Truly; yet--

At this point Waymark broke into that half contemptuous, half indulgent laugh which so frequently interrupted his self-communings, and, it being nearly one o'clock, set out to call for Ida. The day was fine, and, when they left the steamer at Putney, they walked on to the heath in good spirits and with cheerful talk. To be with Ida under these circumstances, in the sunlight and the fresh breeze, was very different from sitting with her yonder in the little room, with the lamp burning on the table, and the quietness of night around. The calm pleasure of passionless intercourse was realised and sufficing. Ida, too, seemed content to enjoy the moment; there was not that wistfulness in her eyes which had been so new to him and so strong in its influence. It was easy to find indifferent subjects of conversation, and to avoid the seriousness which would have been fatal.

When they had found a pleasant spot to rest awhile before turning back, Waymark made up his mind to fulfil his promise to Julian.

"It's rather strange," he said, "that you should have been asking me questions about Mrs. Casti. Since then I've discovered that you probably know her, or once did."

Ida looked surprised.

"Do you remember once having a schoolfellow called Harriet Smales?"

"Is that *her* name?"

"It was, before her marriage."

Ida became grave, and thought for some moments before speaking again.

"Yes, I remember her," she said, "and not pleasantly."

"You wouldn't care to renew her acquaintance then?" said Waymark, half glad, in spite of himself, that she spoke in this way.

Ida asked, with earnestness, how he had made this discovery. Waymark hesitated, but at length told the truth. He explained that Mrs. Casti suffered from the want of companionship, and that he had mentioned Ida's name to Julian; whence the discovery.

"Has *she* been told about me?" asked Ida.

"Nothing was to be said till I had spoken to you."

Waymark paused, but presently continued in a more serious tone. In recurring to that conversation with Julian, his friend's trouble spoke strongly to him once more, and overcame selfish thoughts.

"I said that I had come to know you by chance, and that--strange as it might sound--we were simply friends." He glanced for an instant at Ida; her eyes were turned to the ground. "You will believe me," he went on quickly, "when I tell you that I really said nothing more?"

"I never doubt a word of yours," was Ida's quiet reply.

"Casti was overjoyed at the thought of finding such a friend for his wife. Of course I told him that he must not certainly count either on your consent or on his wife's. Hers I thought to be perhaps more doubtful than yours."

"Could I really be of any use to her," asked Ida, after a silence, "with so little free time as I have?"

"Supposing she would welcome you, I really believe you could be of great use. She is a strange creature, miserably weak in body and mind. If you could get to regard this as a sort of good work you were called upon to undertake, you would very likely be little less than an angel of mercy to both of them. Casti is falling into grievous unhappiness--why, you will understand sufficiently if you come to know them."

"Do you think she bears malice against me?"

"Of that I know nothing. Casti said she had never spoken of you in that way. By-the-by, she still has a scar on her forehead, I often wondered how it came there."

Ida winced.

"What a little termagant you must have been!" exclaimed Waymark, laughing. "How hard it is to fancy you at that age, Ida.--What was the quarrel all about?"

"I can't speak of it," she replied, in a low, sad voice. "It is so long ago; and I want to forget it."

Waymark kept silence.

"Do you wish me to be her friend?" Ida asked, suddenly looking up.

"Certainly not if you dislike the thought."

"No, no. But you think it would be doing good? you would like me to help your friend if I can?"

"Yes, I should," was Waymark's reply.

"Then I hope she will be willing to let me go and see her. I will do my very best.

Let us lose no time in trying. It is such a strange thing that we should meet again in this way; perhaps it is something more than chance."

Waymark smiled.

"You think I am superstitious?" she asked quickly. "I often feel so. I have all sorts of hopes and faiths that you would laugh at."

Ida's thoughts were busy that night with the past and the future. The first mention of Harriet's name had given her a shock; it brought back with vividness the saddest moments of her life; it awoke a bitter resentment which mere memory had no longer kept the power to revive. That was only for a moment, however. The more she accustomed herself to the thought, the easier it seemed to be to bury the past in forgiveness. Harriet must have changed so much since those days. Possibly there would never be a mention between them of the old trouble; practically they would be new acquaintances, and would be very little helped to an understanding of each other by the recollections of childhood. And then Ida felt there was so much to be glad of in the new prospects. She longed for a world more substantial than that of her own imaginations, and here, as she thought, it would be opened to her. Above all, by introducing her to his friends, Waymark had strengthened the relations between her and himself. He was giving her, too, a chance of showing herself to him in a new light. For the first time he would see her under the ordinary conditions of a woman's life in a home circle Ida had passed from one extreme to the other. At present there was nothing she desired so much as the simple, conventional, every-day existence of the woman who has never swerved from the beaten track. She never saw a family group anywhere without envying the happiness which to her seemed involved in the mere fact of a home and relations. Her isolation weighed heavily upon her. If there were but some one who could claim her services, as of right, and in return render her the simple hum-drum affection which goes for so much in easing the burden of life. She was weary of her solitary heroism, though she never regarded it as heroism, but merely as the path in which she was naturally led by her feelings. Waymark could not but still think of her very much in the old light, and she wished to prove to him how completely she was changed. The simple act of making tea for him when he came to see her had been a pleasure; it was domestic and womanly, and she had often glanced at his face to see whether he noticed it at all. Then the fact of Harriet's being an invalid would give her many opportunities for showing that she could be gentle and patient and serviceable. Casti would observe these things, and doubtless would speak of them to Waymark. Thinking in this way, Ida became all eagerness for the new friendship. There was of course the possibility that Harriet would refuse to accept her offered kindness, but it seemed very unlikely, and the disappointment would be so great that she could not bear to dwell on the thought. Waymark had promised to come as soon as he had any news. The time would go very slowly till she saw him.

Waymark had met Harriet very seldom of late. Julian spent regularly one evening a week with him, but it was only occasionally that Waymark paid a visit in turn. He knew that he was anything but welcome to Mrs. Casti, who of course had neither interest nor understanding for the conversation between himself and Julian. Formerly he had now and then tried his best to find some common subject for talk with her, but the effort had been vain; she was hopelessly stupid, and more often than not in a surly mood, which made her mere presence difficult to be endured. Of late, whenever he came, she made her illness an excuse for remaining in her bed-room. And hence arose another trouble. The two rooms were only divided by folding doors, and when Harriet got impatient with what she conceived to be the visitor's undue stay, she would rap on the doors, to summon Julian to her. This rapping would take place sometimes six or seven times in half an hour, till Waymark hastened away in annoyance. And indeed there was little possibility of conversing in Julian's own room. Julian sat for ever in a state of nervous apprehension, dreading the summons which was sure to come before long. When he left the room for a moment, in obedience to it, Waymark could hear Harriet's voice speaking in a peevish or ill-tempered tone, and Julian would return pale with agitation, unable to utter consecutive words. It was a little better when the meeting was at Waymark's, but even then Julian was anything but at his ease. He would often sit for a long time in gloomy silence, and seldom could even affect his old cheerfulness. The change which a year had made in him was painful. His face was growing haggard with ceaseless anxiety. The slightest unexpected noise made him start nervously. His old enthusiasms were dying away. His daily work was a burden which grew more and more oppressive. He always seemed weary, alike in body and mind.

Harriet's ailments were not of that unreal kind which hysterical women often affect, for the mere sake of demanding sympathy, though it was certain she made the most of them. The scrofulous taint in her constitution was declaring itself in many ways. The most serious symptoms took the form of convulsive fits. On Julian's return home one evening, he had found her stretched upon the floor, unconscious, foaming at the mouth, and struggling horribly. Since then, he had come back every night in agonies of miserable anticipation. Her illness, and his own miseries, were of course much intensified by her self-willed habits. When she remained away from home till after midnight, Julian was always in fear lest some accident had happened to her, and once or twice of late she had declared (whether truly or not it was impossible to say) that she had had fits in the open street. Weather made no difference to her; she would leave home on the pretence of making necessary purchases, and would come back drenched with rain. Protest availed nothing, save to irritate her. At times her conduct was so utterly unreasonable that Julian looked at her as if to see whether she had lost her senses. And all this he bore with a patience which few could have rivalled. Moments there were when she softened, and, in a burst of hysterical weeping, begged him to forgive her for some unusual violence, pleading her illness as the cause; and so sensible was he to compassion, that he always vowed in his mind to bear anything rather than deal harshly with her. Love for her, in the true sense, he had never felt, but his pity often led him to effusions of tenderness which love could scarcely have exceeded. He was giving up everything for her. Through whole evenings he would sit by her, as she lay in pain, holding her hands, and talking in a way which he thought would amuse or interest her.

"You're sorry you married me," she would often say at such times. "It's no good saying no; I'm sure you are."

That always made Julian think of her father, and of his own promise always to be a friend to the poor, weak, ailing creature; and he strengthened himself in his resolution to bear everything.

Waymark decided that he would venture on the step of going to see Harriet during the daytime, whilst Julian was away, in order to speak of Ida. This he did on the Monday, and was lucky enough to find her at home. She was evidently surprised at his visit, and perhaps still more so at the kind and friendly way in which he began to speak to her. In a few minutes he had worked round to his subject. He had, he said, a friend, a young lady who was very lonely, and for whom he wanted to find an agreeable companion. It had occurred to him that perhaps he might ask to be allowed to introduce her. Waymark had concluded that this would probably be the best way of putting it; Harriet would perhaps be flattered by being asked to confer the favour of her acquaintance. And indeed she seemed so; there was even something like a momentary touch of colour in her pale cheek.

"Does Julian know her?" she asked, fixing her eyes on his with the closest scrutiny.

"No, he does not."

He would leave her to what conclusion she liked about his relations to Ida; in reality that mattered little.

"She is some one," he went on, "for whom I have a great regard. As I say, she has really no friends, and she earns her own living. I feel sure you would find her company pleasant; she is sensible and cheerful, and would be very grateful for any kindness you showed her. Her name, by-the-by, is Ida Starr."

"Ida Starr?"

"Is the name familiar to you?"

"I used to know some one called that."

"Indeed? How strange it would be if you knew her already. I have spoken to her of you, but she didn't tell me she knew your name."

"Oh no, she wouldn't. It was years and years ago. We used to go to school together--if it's the same."

The way in which this was spoken was not very promising, but Waymark would not be discouraged, having once brought himself to the point of carrying the scheme through. Harriet went on to ask many questions, all of which he answered as satisfactorily as he could, and in the end she expressed herself quite willing to renew Ida's acquaintance. Waymark had watched her face as closely as she did his, and he was able to read pretty accurately what was passing in her mind. Curiosity, it was clear, was her main incentive. Good will there was none; its growth, if at all possible, would depend upon Ida herself. There was even something very like a gleam of hate in her dark eyes when Ida's name was first spoken.

"When may I bring her!" Waymark asked. "Perhaps you would like to talk it over with Julian first? By-the-by, perhaps he remembers her as your schoolfellow?"

"I don't know, I'm sure," she said, with a pretence of indifference. "I don't see what he can have to say against it. Bring her as soon as you like."

"She is not free till seven at night. Perhaps we had better leave it till next Sunday?"

"Why? Why couldn't she come to-morrow night?"

"It is very good of you. I have no doubt she would be glad."

With this understanding Waymark took his departure.

"Do you remember Ida Starr?" was Harriet's first question to her husband when he returned that evening.

"Certainly I do," replied Julian, with complete self-control. "Why?"

"When did you see her last?" followed quickly, whilst she examined him as keenly as she had done Waymark.

"See her?" repeated Julian, laughing. "Do you mean the girl you went to school with?"

"Of course I do."

"I don't know that I ever saw her in my life."

"Well, she's coming here to-morrow night."

An explanation followed.

"Hasn't he ever spoken to you about her?" Harriet asked.

"No," said Julian, smiling. "I suppose he thought it was a private affair, in which no one else had any interest."

"I hope you will like her," he said presently. "It will be very nice to have a friend of that kind, won't it?"

"Yes,--if she doesn't throw one of my own plates at me."

CHAPTER XXII
UNDER-CURRENTS

"Well, how do you like her?" Julian asked, when their visitors had left them.

"Oh, I dare say she's all right," was the reply. "She's got a good deal to say for herself."

Julian turned away, and walked about the room.

"What does she work at?" said Harriet, after glancing at him furtively once or twice.

"I have no idea."

"It's my belief she doesn't work at all."

"Why should Waymark have said so, then?" asked Julian, standing still and looking at her. He spoke very quietly, but his face betrayed some annoyance.

Harriet merely laughed, her most ill-natured and maliciously suggestive laugh, and rose from her seat. Julian came up and faced her.

"Harriet," he said, with perfect gentleness, though his lips trembled, "why do you always prefer to think the worst of people? I always look for the good rather than the evil in people I meet."

"We're different in a good many things, you see," said Harriet, with a sneer. Her countenance had darkened. Julian had learnt the significance of her looks and tones only too well. Under the circumstances it would have been better to keep silence, but something compelled him to speak.

"I am sure of this," he said. "If you will only meet her in her own spirit, you will find her a valuable friend--just such a friend as you need. But of course if you begin with all manner of prejudices and suspicions, it will be very hard for her to make you believe in her sincerity. Certainly her kindness, her sympathy, her whole manner, was perfect to-night."

"You seemed to notice her a good deal."

"Naturally I did, being so anxious that you should find a friend and companion."

"And who is she, I should like to know?" said Harriet, with perfection of subdued acrimony. "How can I tell that she's a proper person to be a friend to me? I know what her mother was, at all events."

"Her mother? What do you know of her mother?"

Julian had never known the whole story of that scar on his wife's forehead.

"Never mind," said Harriet, nodding significantly.

"I have no idea what you mean," Julian returned. "At all events I can trust Waymark, and I know very well he would not have brought her here, if she hadn't been a proper person for you to know. But come," he added quickly, making an effort to dismiss the disagreeable tone between them, "there's surely no need for us to talk like this, Harriet. I am sure you will like her, when you know her better.

Promise me that you will try, dear. You are so lonely, and it would rejoice me so to feel that you had a friend to help you and to be a comfort to you. At all events you will judge her on her own merits, won't you, and put aside all kind of prejudice?"

"I haven't said I shouldn't; but I suppose I must get to know her first?"

Ominous as such a commencement would have been under any other circumstances, Julian was so prepared for more decided hostility, that he was even hopeful. When he met Waymark next, the change in his manner was obvious; he was almost cheerful once more. And the improvement held its ground as the next two or three weeks went by. Ida came to Beaufort Street often, and Julian was able to use the freedom he thus obtained to spend more time in Waymark's society. The latter noticed the change in him with surprise.

"Things go well still?" he would ask, when Julian came in of an evening.

"Very well indeed. Harriet hasn't been out one night this week."

"And you think it will last?"

"I have good hope."

They did not speak much of Ida, however. It was only when three weeks had gone by that Julian asked one night, with some hesitation in putting the question, whether Waymark saw her often.

"Pretty often," was the reply. "I am her tutor, in a sort of way. We read together, and that kind of thing."

"At her lodgings?"

"Yes. Does it seem a queer arrangement?"

"She seems very intelligent," said Julian, letting the question pass by, and speaking with some constraint. "Isn't it a pity that she can't find some employment better suited to her?"

"I don't see what is open. Could you suggest anything?"

Julian was silent.

"In any case, it won't last very long, I suppose?" he said, looking up with a smile which was rather a trembling of the lip.

"Why?"

They gazed at each other for a moment.

"No," said Waymark, shaking his head and smiling. "It isn't as you think. It is perfectly understood between us that we are to be agreeable company to each other, and absolutely nothing beyond that. I have no motive for leading you astray in the matter. However things were, I would tell you frankly."

There was another silence.

"Do you think there is anything like confidence between your wife and her?" Waymark asked.

"That I hardly know. When I am present, of course they only talk about ordinary women's interests, household affairs, and so on."

"Then you have no means of--well, of knowing whether she has spoken about me to your wife in any particular way?"

"Nothing of the kind has ever been hinted to me"

"Waymark," Julian continued, after a pause, "you are a strange fellow."

"In what respect."

"Do you mean to tell me honestly that--that you--"

"Well?--you mean to say, that I am not in love with the girl?"

"No, I wasn't going to say that," said Julian, with his usual bashfulness, heightened in this case by some feeling which made him pale. "I meant, do you really believe that *she* has no kind of regard for you beyond mere friendship?"

"Why? Have you formed any conclusions of your own on the point?"

"How could I help doing so?"

"And you look on me," said Waymark, after thinking for a moment, "as an insensible dog, with a treasure thrown at his feet which he is quite incapable of appreciating or making use of?"

"No. I only feel that your position must be a very difficult one. But perhaps you had rather not speak of these things?"

"On the contrary. You are perfectly right, and the position is as difficult as it well could be."

"You had made your choice, I suppose, before you knew Ida at all?"

"So far from that, I haven't even made it yet. I am not at all sure that my chance of ever marrying Maud Enderby is not so utterly remote, that t ought to put aside all thought of it. In that case--"

"But this is a strange state of mind," said Julian, with a forced laugh. "Is it possible to balance feelings in this way?"

"You, in my position, would have no doubt?"

"I don't know Miss Enderby," said Julian, reddening.

Waymark walked up and down the room, with his hands behind his back, his brows bent. He had never told his friend anything of Ida's earlier history; but now he felt half-tempted to let him know everything. To do so, might possibly give him that additional motive to a clear and speedy decision in the difficulties which grew ever more pressing. Yet was it just to Ida to speak of these things even to one who would certainly not repeat a word? Once or twice he all but began, yet in the end a variety of motives kept him silent.

"Well," he exclaimed shortly, "we'll talk about this another time. Perhaps I shall have more to tell you. Don't be gloomy. Look, here I am just upon the end of my novel. If all goes smoothly I shall finish it in a fortnight, and then I will read it to you."

"I hope you may have better luck with it than I had," said Julian.

"Oh, your time is yet to come. And it's very likely I shall be no better off. There are things in the book which will scarcely recommend it to the British parent. But it shall be published, if it is at my own expense. If it comes to the worst, I shall sell my mining shares to Woodstock."

"After all," said Julian, smiling, "you are a capitalist."

"Yes, and much good it does me."

Since that first evening Julian had refrained from speaking to his wife about Ida, beyond casual remarks and questions which could carry no significance. Harriet likewise had been silent. As far as could be observed, however, she seemed to take a pleasure in Ida's society, and, as Julian said, with apparently good result to herself. She was more at home than formerly, and her health even seemed to profit by the change. Still, there was something not altogether natural in all this, and Julian could scarcely bring himself to believe in the happy turn things seemed to be taking. In Harriet herself there was no corresponding growth of cheerfulness or good-nature. She was quiet, but with a quietness not altogether pleasant; it was as though her thoughts were constantly occupied, as never hitherto; and her own moral condition was hardly likely to be the subject of these meditations. Julian, when he sat reading, sometimes became desperately aware of her eyes being fixed on him for many minutes at a time. Once, on this happening, he looked up with a smile.

"What is it, dear?" he asked, turning round to her. "You are very quiet. Shall I put away the book and talk?"

"No; I'm all right."

"You've been much better lately, haven't you?" he said, taking her hand playfully. "Let me feel your pulse; you know I'm half a doctor."

She drew it away peevishly. But Julian, whom a peaceful hour had made full of kindness, went on in the same gentle way.

"You don't know how happy it makes me to see you and Ida such good friends. I was sure it would be so. Don't you feel there is something soothing in her society? She speaks so gently, and always brings a sort of sunshine with her."

Harriet's lips curled, very slightly, but she said nothing.

"When are you going to see her again? It's hardly fair to let the visiting be always on her side, is it?"

"I shall go when I feel able. Perhaps to-morrow."

Julian presently went back to his book again. If he could have seen the look Harriet turned upon him when his face was averted, he would not have read so calmly.

That same evening Harriet herself was the subject of a short conversation between Ida and Waymark, as they sat together in the usual way.

"I fear there will never be anything like confidence between us," Ida was saying. "Do you know that I am sometimes almost afraid of her; sometimes she looks and speaks as if she hated me."

"She is a poor, ill-conditioned creature," Waymark re plied, rather contemptuously.

"Can you explain," asked Ida, "how it was that Mr. Casti married her?"

"For my life, I can't! I half believe it was out of mere pity; I shouldn't wonder if the proposal came from her side. Casti might once have done something; but I'm afraid he never will now."

"And he is so very good to her. I pity him from my heart whenever I see them together. Often I have been so discouraged by her cold suspicious ways, that I half-thought I should have to give it up, but I felt it would be cruel to desert him so. I met him in the street the other night just as I was going to her, and he thanked me for what I was doing in a way that almost made me cry."

"By-the-by," said Waymark, "you know her too well to venture upon anything like direct criticism of her behaviour, when you talk together!"

"Indeed, I scarcely venture to speak of herself at all. It would be hard to say what we talk about."

"Of course," Waymark said, after a short silence, "there are limits to self-devotion. So long as it seems to you that there is any chance of doing some good, well, persevere. But you mustn't be sacrificed to such a situation. The time you give her is so much absolute loss to yourself."

"Oh, but I work hard to make up for it. You are not dissatisfied with me?"

"And what if I were? Would it matter much?"

This was one of the things that Waymark was ever and again saying, in spite of himself. He could not resist the temptation of proving his power in this way; it is so sweet to be assured of love, even though every voice within cries out against the temptation to enjoy it, and condemns every word or act that could encourage it to hope. Ida generally met such remarks with silence; but in this instance she looked up steadily, and said--

"Yes, it *would* matter much." Waymark drew in his breath, half turned away--and spoke of some quite different matter.

Harriet carried out her intention of visiting Ida on the following day. In these three weeks she had only been to Ida's lodgings once. The present visit was unexpected. She waited about the pavement for Ida's return from work, and shortly saw her approaching.

"This is kind of you," Ida said. "We'll have some tea, and then, if you're not too tired, we might go into the park. It will be cool then."

She dreaded the thought of sitting alone with Harriet. But the latter said she must get home early, and would only have time to sit for half an hour. When Ida had lit her fire, and put the kettle on, she found that the milk which she had kept since the morning for Grim and herself had gone sour; so she had to run out to a dairy to fetch some.

"You won't mind being left alone for a minute?" she said.

"Oh, no; I'll amuse myself with Grim."

As soon as she was alone, Harriet went into the bed-room, and began to examine everything. Grim had followed her, and came up to rub affectionately against her feet, but she kicked him, muttering, "Get off; you black beast!" Having scrutinised the articles which lay about, she quickly searched the pockets of a dress which hung on the door, but found nothing except a handkerchief. All the time she listened for any footfall on the stone steps without. Next she went to the chest of drawers, and was pleased to find that they were unlocked. In the first she drew out there were some books and papers. These she rummaged through very quickly, and at length, underneath them, came upon a little bundle of pawn-tickets. On finding these, she laughed to herself, and carefully inspected every one of them. "Gold chain," she muttered; "bracelet; seal-skin;--what was she doing with all those things, I wonder? Ho, ho, Miss Starr?"

She started; there was a step on the stairs. In a second everything was replaced, and she was back in the sitting-room, stooping over Grim, who took her endearments with passive indignation.

"Have I been long?" panted Ida, as she came in. "The kettle won't be a minute. You'll take your things off?"

Harriet removed her hat only. As Ida went about, preparing the tea, Harriet watched her with eyes in which there was a new light. She spoke, too, in almost a cheerful way, and even showed a better appetite than usual when they sat down together.

"You are better to-day?" Ida said to her.

"Perhaps so; but it doesn't last long."

"Oh, you must be more hopeful. Try not to look so much on the dark side of things. How would you be," she added, with a good-humoured laugh, "if you had to work all day, like me? I'm sure you've a great deal to make you feel happy and thankful."

"I don't know what," returned Harriet coldly.

"But your husband, your home, your long, free days?"

The other laughed peevishly. Ida turned her head away for a moment; she was irritated by this wretched humour, and, as had often been the case of late, found it difficult to restrain some rather trenchant remark.

"It may sound strange," she said, with a smile, "but I think I should be very willing to endure bad health for a position something like yours."

Harriet laughed again, and still more unpleasantly.

Later in the evening Harriet went to call upon her friend Mrs. Sprowl. Something of an amusing kind seemed to be going forward in front of the house. On drawing near and pressing into the crowd of loitering people, she beheld a spectacle familiar to her, and one which brought a smile to her face. A man of wretched appearance, in vile semblance of clothing which barely clung together about him, was standing on his head upon the pavement, and, in that attitude, drawling out what was meant for a song, while those around made merry and indulged in practical jokes at his expense. One such put a sudden end to the exhibition. A young ragamuffin drew near with a handful of rich mud, and carefully cast it right into the singer's inverted mouth. The man was on his feet in an instant, and pursuing the assailant, who, however, succeeded in escaping down an alley hard by. Returning, the man went from one to another in the crowd, holding out his hand. Harriet passed on into the bar.

"Slimy's up to his larks to-night," exclaimed Mrs. Sprowl, with a laugh, as she welcomed her visitor in the bar-parlour. "He'll be losin' his sweet temper just now, see if he don't, an' then one o' them chaps 'll get a bash i' the eye."

"I always like to see him singing on his head," said Harriet, who seemed at once thoroughly at her ease in the atmosphere of beer and pipes.

"It's funny, ain't it? And 'ow's the world been a-usin' you, Harriet? Seen anything more o' that affectionate friend o' yourn?"

This was said with a grin, and a significant wink.

"Have you found out anything about her?" asked Harriet eagerly.

"Why yes, I have; somethin' as 'll amuse you. It's just as I thought."

"How do you mean?"

"Why, Bella, was in 'ere th' other night, so I says to her, 'Bella,' I says, 'didn't you never hear of a girl called Ida Starr?' I says. 'Course I did,' she says. 'One o' the 'igh an' 'aughty lot, an' she lived by herself somewhere in the Strand.' So it's just as I told you."

"But what is she doing now?"

"You say she's turned modest."

"I can't make her out quite," said Harriet, reflecting, with her head on one side. "I've been at her lodgings tonight, and, whilst she was out of the room, I happened to get sight of a lot of pawn-tickets, for gold chains and sealskins, and I don't know what."

"Spouted 'em all when she threw up the job, I s'pose," suggested Mrs. Sprowl. "You're sure she does go to work?"

"Yes, I've had somebody to follow her and watch her. There's Waymark goes to see her often, and I shouldn't wonder if she half keeps him; he's just that kind of fellow."

"You haven't caught no one else going there?" asked Mrs. Sprowl, with another of her intense winks.

"No, I haven't, not yet," replied Harriet, with sudden vehemence, "but I believe he does go there, or else sees her somewhere else."

"Well," said the landlady, with an air of generous wisdom, "I told you from the first as I 'adn't much opinion of men as is so anxious to have their wives friendly with other women. There's always something at the bottom of it, you may bet. It's my belief he's one too many for you, Harriet; you're too simple-minded to catch him."

"I'll have a good try, though," cried the girl, deadly pale with passion. "Perhaps I'm not so simple as you think. I'm pretty quick in tumbling to things--no fear. If they think I don't notice what goes on, they must take me for a damned silly fool, that's all! Why, I've seen them wink at each other, when they thought I wasn't looking."

"You're not such a fool as to leave them alone together?" said the woman, who seemed to have a pleasure in working upon Harriet's jealousy.

"No fear! But they understand each other; I can see that well enough. And he writes to her; I'm dead sure he writes to her. Let me get hold of a letter just once, that's all!"

"And he's orful good-natured to her, ain't he? Looks after her when she has tea with you, and so on?"

"I should think he did. It's all--'Won't Miss Starr have this?' and 'Won't Miss Starr have that?' He scarcely takes his eyes off of her, all the time."

"I know, I know; it's allus the same! You keep your eyes open, Harriet, and you'll 'ave your reward, as the Scriptures says."

When she reached home, Julian was in the uneasy condition always brought about by these late absences. To a remark he made about the time, she vouchsafed no answer.

"Have you been with Ida all the evening?" he asked.

"No, I haven't," was her reply.

She went into the bed-room, and was absent for a few minutes, then reappeared.

"Do you know where my silver spoon is?" she asked, looking closely at him.

"Your silver spoon?" he returned, in surprise. "Have you lost it?"

The article in question, together with a fork, hod been a wedding-present from Mrs. Sprowl, whose character had in it a sort of vulgar generosity, displayed at times in gifts to Harriet.

"I can't find it," Harriet said. "I was showing it to Ida Starr when she was here on Sunday, and now I come to look for it, it's gone."

"Oh, it can't be very far off," said Julian. "You'll find it if you look."

"But I tell you I've looked everywhere. It's gone, that's all I know."

"Well, but--what do you mean? How can it have gone?"

"I don't know. I only know I was showing it her on Sunday."

"And what connection is there between the two things?" asked Julian, almost sternly. "You don't wish me to understand that Ida Starr knows anything about the spoon?"

"How can I tell? It's gone."

"Come," exclaimed Julian, with a laugh, "this is too absurd, Harriet! You must have taken leave of your senses. If it's gone, then some one in the house has taken it."

"And why not Ida Starr?"

Julian stared at her with mingled anger and alarm.

"Why not? Simply because she is incapable of such a thing."

"Perhaps *you* think so, no doubt. You think a good deal of her, it seems to me. Perhaps you don't know quite as much about her as I do."

"I fancy I know much more," exclaimed Julian indignantly.

"Oh, do you?"

"If you think her capable of stealing your spoon, you show complete ignorance of her character. What do you know of her that you should have such suspicions?"

"Never mind," said Harriet, nodding her head obstinately.

There was again a long silence. Julian reflected.

"We will talk about this again to-morrow," he said, "when you have had time to think. You are under some strange delusion. After all, I expect you will find the spoon, and then you'll be sorry for having been so hasty."

Harriet became obstinately silent. She cut a piece of bread and butter, and took it into the other room. Julian paced up and down.

CHAPTER XXIII
THE OPPORTUNITY

One or two days after this, Ida Starr came home from work with a heavy heart. Quite without notice, and without explanation, her employer had paid her a week's wages and dismissed her. Her first astonished questions having been met with silence by the honest but hard-grained woman who kept the laundry, Ida had not condescended to any further appeal. The fact was that the laundress had received a visit from a certain Mrs. Sprowl, who, under pretence of making inquiries for the protection of a young female friend, revealed the damaging points of Ida's story, and gained the end plotted with Harriet Casti.

Several circumstances united to make this event disastrous to Ida. Her wages were very little more than she needed for her week to week existence, yet she had managed to save a shilling or two now and then. The greater part of these small savings she had just laid out in some new clothing, the reason for the expense being not so much necessity, as a desire to be rather better dressed when she accompanied Waymark on those little country excursions which had reestablished themselves of late. By no means the smallest part of Ida's heroism was that involved in this matter of external appearance. A beautiful woman can never be indifferent to the way in which her beauty is arrayed. That Waymark was not indifferent to such things she knew well, and often she suffered from the thought that one strong means of attraction was lost to her. If at one moment Ida was conscious of her claim to inspire a noble enthusiasm, at another she fell into the saddest self-distrust, and, in her hunger for love, would gladly have sought every humblest aid of grace and adornment. So she had yielded to the needs of her heart, and only this morning was gladdened by the charm of some new clothing which became her well, and which Waymark would see in a day or two. It lay there before her now that she returned home, and, in the first onset of trouble, she sat down and cried over it.

She suffered the more, too, that there had been something of a falling off of late in the good health she generally enjoyed. The day's work seemed long and hard; she felt an unwonted need of rest. And these things caused trouble of the mind. With scarcely an hour of depression she had worked on through those months of solitude, supported by the sense that every day brought an accession of the strength of purity, that the dark time was left one more stage behind, and that trust in herself was growing assured.

But it was harder than she had foreseen, to maintain reserve and reticence when her heart was throbbing with passion; the effect upon her of Waymark's comparative coldness was so much harder to bear than she had imagined. Her mind tortured itself incessantly with the fear that some new love had taken possession of him. And now there had befallen her this new misfortune, which, it might be, would once more bring about a crisis in her life.

Of course she must forthwith set about finding new work. It would be difficult, seeing that she had now no reference to give. Reflection had convinced her that it must have been some discovery of her former life which had led to her sudden dismissal, and this increased her despondency. Yet she would not give way to it. On the following morning she began her search for employment, and day after day faced without result the hateful ordeal. Hope failed as she saw her painfully-eked-out coins become fewer and fewer. In a day or two she would have nothing, and what would happen then?

When she returned to London to begin a new life, now nearly a year ago, she had sold some and pawned the rest of such possessions as would in future be useful to her. Part of the money thus obtained had bought the furniture of her rooms; what remained had gone for a few months to supplement her weekly wages, thus making the winter less a time of hardship than it must otherwise have been. One or two articles yet remained capable of being turned into small sums, and these she now disposed of at a neighbouring pawnbroker's--the same she had previously visited on the occasion of pawning one or two of the things, the tickets for which Harriet Casti had so carefully inspected. She spoke to no one of her position. Yet now the time was quickly coming when she must either have help from some quarter or else give up her lodgings. In food she was already stinting herself to the verge of starvation. And through all this she had to meet her friends as hitherto, if possible without allowing any trace of her suffering to become visible. Harriet, strange to say, had been of late a rather frequent visitor, and was more pressing than formerly in her invitations. Ida dreaded her coming, as it involved the unwarrantable expense of obtaining luxuries now unknown in her cupboard, such as tea and butter. And, on the other hand, it was almost impossible to affect cheerfulness in the company of the Castis. At times she caught Julian's eyes fixed upon her, and felt that he noticed some change in her appearance. She had a sense of guilt in their presence, as if she were there on false pretences. For, together with her daily work, much of her confidence had gone; an inexplicable shame constantly troubled her. She longed to hide herself away, and be alone with her wretchedness.

If it came to asking for help, of whom could she ask it but of Waymark? Yet for some time she felt she could not bring herself to that. In the consciousness of her own attitude towards him, it seemed to her that Waymark might well doubt the genuineness of her need, might think it a mere feint to draw him into nearer relations. She could not doubt that he knew her love for him; she did not desire to hide it, even had she been able. But him she could not understand. A struggle often seemed going on within him in her presence; he appeared to repress his impulses; he was afraid of her. At times passion urged her to break through this barrier between them, to bring about a situation which would end in clear mutual understanding, cost her what it might. At other times she was driven to despair by the thought that she had made herself too cheap in his eyes. Could she put off the last vestige of her independence, and, in so many words, ask him to give her money?

This evening she expected Waymark, but the usual time of his coming went by. She sat in the twilight, listening with painful intentness to every step on the stairs; again and again her heart leaped at some footfall far below, only to be deceived. She had not even now made up her mind how to speak to him, or whether to speak to him at all; but she longed passionately to see him. The alternations of hope and disappointment made her feverish. Illusions began to possess her. Once she heard distinctly the familiar knock. It seemed to rouse her from slumber: she sprang to the door and opened it, but no one was there. She ran half way down the stairs, but saw no one. It was now nearly midnight. The movement had dispelled for a little the lethargy which was growing upon her, and she suddenly came to a resolution. Taking a sheet of note-paper, she wrote this:--

"I have been without work for a fortnight. All my money is done, and I am in want. Can you send me some, for present help, till I get more work? ***Do not bring it yourself, and do not speak a word of this when you see me, I beg you earnestly***. If I shall fail to get work, I will speak to you of my own accord.

I. S."

She went out and posted this, though she had no stamp to put on the envelope; then, returning, she threw herself as she was on to the bed, and before long passed into unconsciousness.

Waymark's absence that evening had been voluntary. His work had come to a standstill; his waking hours were passed in a restless misery which threatened to make him ill. And to-night he had not dared to go to Ida; in his present state the visit could have but one result, and even yet he hoped that such a result might not come about. He left home and wandered about the streets till early morning. All manner of projects occupied him. He all but made up his mind to write a long letter to Ida and explain his position without reserve. But he feared lest the result of that might be to make Ida hide away from him once more, and to this loss he could not reconcile himself. Yet he was further than ever from the thought of giving himself wholly to her, for the intenser his feeling grew, the more clearly he recognised its character. This was not love he suffered from, but mere desire. To let it have its way would be to degrade Ida. Love might or might not follow, and how could he place her at the mercy of such a chance as that? Her faith and trust in him were absolute; could he take advantage of it for his own ends? And, for all these fine arguments, Waymark saw with perfect clearness how the matter would end. Self would triumph, and Ida, if the fates so willed it, would be sacrificed. It was detestable, but a fact; as good already as an accomplished fact.

And on the following morning Ida's note reached him. It was final. Her entreaty that he would merely send money had no weight with him for a moment; he felt that there was a contradiction between her words and her wishes. This note explained the strangeness he had noticed in her on their last evening together. He pitied her, and, as is so often the case, pity was but fuel to passion. He swept from his mind all obstinate debatings. Passion should be a law unto itself. Let the future bring things about as it would.

He had risen late, and by the time he had finished a hasty breakfast it was eleven o'clock. Half an hour after he went up the stairs of the lodging-house and knocked at the familiar door.

But his knock met with no answer. Ida herself had left home an hour before. Upon waking, and recalling what she had done, she foresaw that Waymark would himself come, in spite of her request. She could not face him. For all that her exhaustion was so great that walking was slow and weary, she went out and strayed at first with no aim; but presently she took the direction of Chelsea, and so came to Beaufort Street. She would go in and see Harriet, who would give her something to eat. She cared little now for letting it be known that she had left her employment; with the step which she had at last taken, her position was quite changed; she had only kept silence lest Waymark should come to know. Harriet was at first surprised to see her then seemed glad.

"I've only a minute ago sent a note, asking you to be sure to come round to-night. I wanted you to help me with this new hat; you have such good taste in trimming."

Ida would have been astonished at another time; for Harriet to be paying compliments was indeed something novel. There was a flush on the latter's usually sallow face; she did not sit down, and kept moving aimlessly about.

"Give me your hat and jacket," she said, "and let me take them into the other room."

She took them away, and returned. Ida was not looking at her; otherwise she must surely have noticed that weird pallor which had all at once succeeded to the unhealthy flush, and the unwonted gleaming of her eyes. Of what passed during those next two hours Ida had afterwards no recollection. They ate together, and they talked, Ida as if in a dream, Harriet preoccupied in a way quite out of her habit. Ida explained that she was out of employment, news which could scarcely be news to the listener, who would in that case have heard it with far less composure. There were long silences, generally brought to an end by some outburst of forced merriment from Harriet. Ida was without consciousness of time, but her restless imagination at length compelled her to go forth again. Harriet did not urge her to stay, but rose and watched her as she went into the other room to put her things on. In a few moments they had parted.

The instant Harriet, from the head of the stairs, heard the front-door close, she ran back into her bed-room, put on her hat, and darted down. Opening the door, she saw Ida moving away at a short distance. Turning her eyes in the opposite direction, she perceived a policeman coming slowly down the street. She ran towards him.

"I've caught her at last," she exclaimed, as she met him, pointing eagerly after Ida. "She's taken a brooch of mine. I put it in a particular place in my bed-room, and it's gone."

"Was she alone in the room?" inquired the constable, looking keenly at Harriet, then down the street.

"Yes, she went in alone to put her things on. Be quick, or she'll be off!"

"I understand you give her in charge?"

"Of course I do."

A brisk walk of two or three minutes, and they had caught up Ida, who turned at the sound of the quick footsteps, and stood in surprise.

"This lady charges you with stealing some articles of hers," said the constable, looking from face to face. "You must come with me to the station."

Ida blanched. When the policeman had spoken, she turned to Harriet, and gazed at her fixedly. She could neither speak nor move. The constable touched her arm impatiently. Her eyes turned to him, and she began to walk along by his side.

Harriet followed in silence. There were not many people on the way to the police-station in King's Road, and they reached it speedily. They came before the inspector, and the constable made his report.

"Have you got this brooch?" asked the inspector, looking at Ida.

Ida put her hand into one of her jacket-pockets, then into the other, and from the second brought out the object in question. It was of gold, and had been given by Julian to his wife just after their marriage. As she laid it before her on the desk, she seemed about to speak, but her breath failed, and she clutched with her hands at the nearest support.

"Look out," exclaimed the inspector. "Don't let her fall."

Five or six times, throughout the day and evening, Waymark had knocked at Ida's door. About seven o'clock he had called at the Castis', but found neither of them at home. Returning thence to Fulham, he had walked for hours up and down, in vain expectation of Ida's coming. There was no light at her window.

Just before midnight he reached home, having on his way posted a letter with money in it. As he reached his door, Julian stood there, about to knock.

"Anything amiss?" Waymark asked, examining his friend by the light of the street-lamp.

Julian only made a sign to him to open the door. They went upstairs together, and Waymark speedily obtained a light. Julian had seated himself on the couch. His face was ghastly.

"What's the matter?" Waymark asked anxiously. "Do you know anything about Ida?"

"She's locked up in the police cells," was the reply. "My wife has accused her of stealing things from our rooms."

Waymark stared at him.

"Cacti, what's the matter with you?" he exclaimed, overcome with fear, in spite of his strong self-command. "Are you ill? Do you know what you're saying?"

Julian rose and made an effort to control himself.

"I know what I'm saying, Waymark I've only just heard it. She has come back home from somewhere--only just now--she seems to have been drinking. It happened in the middle of the day, whilst I was at the hospital. She gave her in charge to a policeman in the street, and a brooch was found on her."

"A brooch found on her? Your wife's?"

"Yes. When she came in, she railed at me like a fury, and charged me with the most monstrous things. I can't and won't go back there to-night! I shall go mad if I hear her voice. I will walk about the streets till morning."

"And you tell me that Ida Starr is in custody?"

"She is. My wife accuses her of stealing several things."

"And you believe this?" asked Waymark, under his voice, whilst his thoughts pictured Ida's poverty, of which he had known nothing, and led him through a long train of miserable sequences.

"I don't know. I can't say. She says that Ida confessed, and, gave the brooch up at once. But her devilish malice is equal to anything. I see into her character as I never did before. Good God, if you could have seen her face as she told me! And

Ida, Ida! I am afraid of myself, Waymark. If I had stayed to listen another moment, I should have struck her. It seemed as if every vein was bursting. How am I ever to live with her again? I dare not! I should kill her in some moment of madness! What will happen to Ida?"

He flung himself upon the couch, and burst into tears. Sobs convulsed him; he writhed in an anguish of conflicting passions. Waymark seemed scarcely to observe him, standing absorbed in speculation and the devising of a course to be pursued.

"I must go to the police-station," he said at length, when the violence of the paroxysm had passed and left Julian in the still exhaustion of despair. "You, I think, had better stay here. Is there any danger of her coming to seek you?"

Julian made a motion with his hand, otherwise lay still, his pale face turned upwards.

"I shall be back very quickly," Waymark added, taking his hat. Then, turning back for a moment, "You mustn't give way like this, old fellow; this is horrible weakness. Dare I leave you alone?"

Julian stretched out his hand, and Waymark pressed it.

CHAPTER XXIV
JUSTICE

Waymark received from the police a confirmation of all that Julian had said, and returned home. Julian still lay on the couch, calmer, but like one in despair. He begged Waymark to let him remain where he was through the night, declaring that in any case sleep was impossible for him, and that perhaps he might try to pass the hours in reading. They talked together for a time; then Waymark lay down on the bed and shortly slept.

He was to be at the police court in the morning. Julian would go to the hospital as usual.

"Shall you call at home on your way?" Waymark asked him.

"No."

"But what do you mean to do?"

"I must think during the day. I shall come to-night, and you will tell me what has happened."

So they parted, and Waymark somehow or other whiled away the time till it was the hour for going to the court. He found it difficult to realise the situation; so startling and brought about so suddenly. Julian had been the first to put into words the suspicion of them both, that it was all a deliberate plot of Harriet's; but he had not been able to speak of his own position freely enough to let Waymark understand the train of circumstances which could lead Harriet to such resoluteness of infamy. Waymark doubted. But for the unfortunate fact of Ida's secret necessities, he could perhaps scarcely have entertained the thought of her guilt. What was the explanation of her being without employment? Why had she hesitated to tell him, as soon as she lost her work? Was there not some mystery at the bottom of this, arguing a lack of complete frankness on Ida's part from the first?

The actual pain caused by Ida's danger was, strange to say, a far less important item in his state of mind than the interest which the situation inspired. Through the night he had thought more of Julian than of Ida. What he had for some time suspected had now found confirmation; Julian was in love with Ida, in love for the first time, and under circumstances which, as Julian himself had said, might well suffice to change his whole nature. Waymark had never beheld such terrible suffering as that depicted on his friend's face during those hours of talk in the night. Something of jealousy had been aroused in him by the spectacle; not jealousy of the ordinary gross kind, but rather a sense of humiliation in the thought that he himself had never experienced, was perhaps incapable of, such passion as racked Julian in every nerve. This was the passion which Ida was worthy of inspiring, and Waymark contrasted it with his own feelings on the previous day, and now since the calamity had fallen. He had to confess that there was even an element of relief in the sensations the event had caused in him. He had been saved from himself; a position of affairs which had become intolerable was got rid of without his own exertion. Whatever might now happen, the old state of things would never be restored. There was relief and pleasure in the thought of such a change, were it only for the sake of the opening up of new vistas of observation and experience. Such thoughts as these indicated very strongly the course which Waymark's development was taking, and he profited by them to obtain a clearer understanding of himself.

The proceedings in the court that morning were brief. Waymark, from his seat on the public benches, saw Ida brought forward, and heard her remanded for a week. She did not see him; seemed, indeed, to see nothing. The aspect of her standing there in the dock, her head bowed under intolerable shame, made a tumult within him. Blind anger and scorn against all who surrounded her were his first emotions; there was something of martyrdom in her position; she, essentially so good and noble, to be dragged here before these narrow-natured slaves of an ignoble social order, in all probability to be condemned to miserable torment by men who had no shadow of understanding of her character and her circumstances.

Waymark was able, whilst in court, to make up his mind as to how he should act. When he left he took his way northwards, having in view St. John Street Road, and Mr. Woodstock's house.

When he had waited about half an hour, the old man appeared. He gave his hand in silence. Something seemed to be preoccupying him; he went to his chair in a mechanical way.

"I have come on rather serious business," Waymark began. "I want to ask your advice in a very disagreeable matter--a criminal case, in fact."

Abraham did not at once pay attention, but the last words presently had their effect, and he looked up with some surprise.

"What have you been up to?" he asked, with rather a grim smile, leaning back and thrusting his hands in his pockets in the usual way.

"It only concerns myself indirectly. It's all about a girl, who is charged with a theft she is perhaps quite innocent of. If so, she is being made the victim of a conspiracy, or something of the kind. She was remanded to-day at Westminster for a week."

"A girl, eh? And what's your interest in the business?"

"Well, if you don't mind I shall have to go a little into detail. You are at liberty?"

"Go on."

"She is a friend of mine. No, I mean what I say; there is absolutely nothing else between us, and never has been. I should like to know whether you are satisfied to believe that; much depends on it."

"Age and appearance?"

"About twenty--not quite so much--and strikingly handsome."

"H'm. Position in life?"

"A year ago was on the streets, to put it plainly; since then has been getting her living at laundry-work."

"H'm. Name?"

"Ida Starr."

Mr. Woodstock had been gazing at the toes of his boots, still the same smile on his face. When he heard the name he ceased to smile, but did not move at all. Nor did he look up as he asked the next question.

"Is that her real name?"

"I believe so."

The old man drew up his feet, threw one leg over the other, and began to tap upon his knee with the fingers of one hand. He was silent for a minute at least.

"What do you know about her?" he then inquired, looking steadily at Waymark, with a gravity which surprised the latter. "I mean, of her earlier life. Do you know who she is at all?"

"She has told me her whole story--a rather uncommon one, full of good situations."

"What do you mean?"

The words were uttered with such harsh impatience that Waymark started.

"What annoys you?" he asked, with surprise.

"Tell me something of the story," said the other, regaining his composure, and apparently wishing to affect indifference. "I have a twinge of that damned rheumatism every now and then, and it makes me rather crusty. Do you think her story is to be depended upon?"

"Yes, I believe it is."

And Waymark linked briefly the chief points of Ida's history, as he knew it, the old man continually interrupting him with questions.

"Now go on," said Abraham, when he had heard all that Waymark knew, "and explain the scrape she's got into."

Waymark did so.

"And you mean to tell me," Abraham said, before the story was quite finished, "that there's been nothing more between you than that?"

"Absolutely nothing."

"I don't believe you."

It was said angrily, and with a blow of the clenched fist on the table. The old man could no longer conceal the emotion that possessed him. Waymark looked at him in astonishment, unable to comprehend his behaviour.

"Well if you don't believe me, of course I can offer no proof; and I know well enough that every presumption is against me. Still, I tell you the plain fact; and what reason have I for hiding the truth? If I had been living with the girl, I should have said so, as an extra reason for asking your help in the matter."

"What help can I give?" asked Woodstock, again cooling down, though his eyes had in them a most unwonted light. He spoke as if simply asking for information.

"I thought you might suggest something as to modes of defence, and the like. The expenses I would somehow or other meet myself. It appears that she will plead not guilty."

"And what's your belief?"

"I can't make up my mind."

"In that case, it seems to me, you ought to give her the benefit of the doubt; especially as you seem to have made up your mind pretty clearly about this Mrs. What's-her-name."

Waymark was silent, looking at Mr. Woodstock, and reflecting.

"What are your intentions with regard to the girl?" Abraham asked, with a change in his voice, the usual friendliness coming back. He looked at the young man in a curious way; one would almost have said, with apprehensive expectation.

"I have no intentions."

"You would have had, but for this affair?"

"No; you are mistaken. I know the position is difficult to realise."

"Have you intentions, then, in any other quarter?"

"Well, perhaps yes."

"I've never heard anything of this."

"I could scarcely talk of a matter so uncertain."

There was silence. A sort of agitation came upon the old man ever and again, in talking. He now grew absorbed in thought, and remained thus for several minutes, Waymark looking at him the while. When at length Abraham raised his eyes, and they met Waymark's, he turned them away at once, and rose from the chair.

"I'll look into the business," he said, taking out a bunch of keys, and putting one into the lock of a drawer in his desk. "Yes, I'll go and make inquiries." He half pulled out the drawer and rustled among some papers.

"Look here," he said, on the point of taking something out; but, even in speaking, he altered his mind. "No; it don't matter. I'll go and make inquiries. You can go now, if you like;--I mean to say, I suppose you've told me all that's necessary.--Yes, you'd better go, and look in again tomorrow morning."

Waymark went straight to Fulham. Reaching the block of tenements which had been Ida's home, he sought out the porter. When the door opened at his knock, the first face that greeted him was that of Grim, who had pushed between the man's legs and was peering up, as if in search of some familiar aspect.

From the porter he learned that the police had made that afternoon an inspection of Ida's rooms, though with what result was not known. The couple had clearly formed their own opinion as to Waymark's interest in the accused girl, but took the position in a very matter-of-fact way, and were eager to hear more than they succeeded in getting out of the police.

"My main object in coming," Waymark explained, "was to look after her cat. I see you have been good enough to anticipate me."

"The poor thing takes on sadly," said the woman. "Of course I shouldn't have known nothing if the hofficers hadn't come, and it 'ud just have starved to death. It seems to know you, sir?"

"Yes, yes, I dare say. Do you think you could make it convenient to keep the cat for the present, if I paid you for its food?"

"Well, I don't see why not, sir; we ain't got none of our own."

"And you would promise me to be kind to it? I don't mind the expense; keep it well, and let me know what you spend. And of course I should consider your trouble."

So that matter was satisfactorily arranged, and Waymark went home.

Julian spent his day at the hospital as usual, finding relief in fixing his attention upon outward things. It was only when he left his work in the evening that he became aware how exhausted he was in mind and body. And the dread which he had hitherto kept off came back upon him, the dread of seeing his wife's face and hearing her voice. When he parted with Waymark in the morning, he had thought that he would be able to come to some resolution during the day as to his behaviour with regard to her. But no such decision had been formed, and his overtaxed mind could do no more than dwell with dull persistency on a long prospect of wretchedness. Fear and hatred moved him in turns, and the fear was as much of himself as of the object of his hate.

As he approached the door, a man came out whom he did not know, but whose business he suspected. He had little doubt that it was a police officer in plain clothes. He had to stand a moment and rest, before he could use his latchkey to admit himself. When he entered the sitting-room, he found the table spread as usual. Harriet was sitting with sewing upon her lap. She did not look at him.

He sat down, and closed his eyes. There seemed to be a ringing of great bells about him, overpowering every other sound; all his muscles had become relaxed and powerless; he half forgot where and under what circumstances he was, in a kind of deadly drowsiness. Presently this passed, and he grew aware that Harriet was preparing tea. When it was ready, he went to the table, and drank two or three cups, for he was parched with thirst. He could not look at Harriet, but he understood the mood she was in, and knew she would not be the first to speak. He rose, walked about for a few minutes, then stood still before her.

"What proof have you to offer," he said, speaking in a slow but indistinct tone, "that she is guilty of this, and that it isn't a plot you have laid against her?"

"You can believe what you like," she replied sullenly. "Of course I know you'll do your worst against me."

"I wish you to answer my question. If I choose to suspect that you yourself put this brooch in her pocket--and if other people choose to suspect the same, knowing your enmity against her, what proof can you give that she is guilty?"

"It isn't the first thing she's stolen."

"What proof have you that she took those other things?"

"Quite enough, I think. At all events, they've found a pawn-ticket for the spoon at her lodgings, among a whole lot of other tickets for things she can't have come by honestly."

Julian became silent, and, as Harriet looked up at him with eyes full of triumphant spite, he turned pale. He could have crushed the hateful face beneath his feet.

"You're a good husband, you are," Harriet went on, with a sudden change to anger; "taking part against your own wife, and trying to make her out all that's bad. But I think you've had things your own way long enough. You thought I was a fool, did you, and couldn't see what was going on? You and your Ida Starr, indeed! Oh, she would be such a good friend to me, wouldn't she? She would do me so much good; you thought so highly of her; she was just the very girl to be my companion; how lucky we found her! I'm much obliged to you, but I think I might have better friends than thieves and street-walkers."

"What do you mean?" asked Julian, starting at the last word, and turning a ghastly countenance on her.

"I mean what I say. As if you didn't know, indeed!"

"Explain what you mean," Julian repeated, almost with violence. "Who has said anything of that kind against her?"

"Who has? Why I can bring half a dozen people who knew her when she was on the streets, before Waymark kept her. And you knew it, well enough--no fear!"

"It's a lie, a cursed lie! No one can say a word against her purity. Only a foul mind could imagine such things."

"Purity! Oh yes, she's very pure--you know that, don't you? No doubt you'll be a witness, and give evidence for her, and against me;--let everybody know how perfect she is, and what a beast and a liar I am! You and your Ida Starr!"

Julian rushed out of the room.

Waymark could not but observe peculiarities in Mr. Woodstock's behaviour during the conversation about Ida. At first it had occurred to him--knowing a good deal of Abraham's mode of life--that there must be some disagreeable secret at the bottom, and for a moment the ever-recurring distrust of Ida rose again. But he had soon observed that the listener was especially interested in the girl's earliest years, and this pointed to possibilities of a different kind. What was it that was being taken from the drawer to show him, when the old man suddenly altered his mind? Mr. Woodstock had perhaps known Ida's parents. Waymark waited with some curiosity for the interview on the morrow.

Accordingly, he was surprised when, on presenting himself, Mr. Woodstock did not at first appear to remember what he had called about.

"Oh, ay, the girl!" Abraham exclaimed, on being reminded. "What did you say her name was? Ida something--"

Waymark was puzzled and suspicious, and showed both feelings in his looks, but Mr. Woodstock preserved a stolid indifference which it was very difficult to believe feigned.

"I've been busy," said the latter. "Never mind; there's time. She was remanded for a week, you said? I'll go and see Helter about her. May as well come along with me, and put the case in 'artistic' form."

It was a word frequently on Waymark's lips, and he recognised the unwonted touch of satire with a smile, but was yet more puzzled. They set out together to the office of the solicitor who did Abraham's legal business, and held with him a long colloquy. Waymark stated all he knew or could surmise with perfect frankness. He had heard from Julian the night before of the discovery which it was said the police had made at Ida's lodgings, and this had strengthened his fear that Harriet's accusation was genuine.

"How did this girl lose her place at the laundry?" asked Mr. Helter.

Waymark could not say; for all he knew it was through her own fault.

"And that's all you can tell us, Waymark?" observed Mr. Woodstock, who had listened with a show of indifference. "Well, I have no more time at present. Look the thing up, Helter."

On reaching home, Waymark wrote a few lines to Ida, merely to say that Grim was provided for, and assure her that she was not forgotten. In a day or two he received a reply. The official envelope almost startled him at first. Inside was written this:

"You have been kind. I thank you for everything. Try to think kindly of me, whatever happens; I shall be conscious of it, and it will give me strength.

I. S."

The week went by, and Ida again appeared in court. Mr. Woodstock went with Waymark, out of curiosity, he said. The statement of the case against the prisoner sounded very grave. What Harriet had said about the discovery of the pawn-ticket for her silver spoon was true. Ida's face was calm, but paler yet and thinner. When she caught sight of Harriet Casti, she turned her eyes away quickly, and with a look of trouble. She desired to ask no question, simply gave her low and distinct "Not guilty." She was committed for trial.

Waymark watched Mr. Woodstock, who was examining Ida all the time; he felt sure that he heard something like a catching of the breath when the girl's face first became visible.

"And what's your opinion?" asked Waymark.

"I couldn't see the girl very well," said the old man coldly.

"She hasn't quite a fortnight to wait."

"No."

"You're sure Helter will do all that can be done?"

"Yes."

Mr. Woodstock nodded his head, and walked off by himself.

Julian Casti was ill. With difficulty he had dragged himself to the court, and his sufferings as he sat there were horribly evident on his white face. Waymark met him just as Mr. Woodstock walked off; and the two went home together by omnibus, not speaking on the way.

"She will be convicted," was Julian's first utterance, when he had sat for a few minutes in Waymark's room, whilst Waymark himself paced up and down. The latter turned, and saw that tears were on his friend's hollow cheeks.

"Did you sleep better last night?" he asked.

"Good God, no! I never closed my eyes. That's the third night without rest. Waymark, get me an opiate of some kind, or I shall kill myself; and let me sleep here."

"What will your wife say?"

"What do I care what she says!" cried Julian, with sudden excitement, his muscles quivering, and his cheeks flaming all at once. "Don't use that word 'wife,' it is profanation; I can't bear it! If I see her to-night, I can't answer for what I may do. Curse her to all eternity!"

He sank beck in exhaustion.

"Julian," said Waymark, using his friend's first name by exception, "if this goes on, you will be ill. What the deuce shall we do then?"

"No, I shall not be ill. It will be all right if I can get sleep."

He was silent for a little, then spoke, with his eyes on the ground.

"Waymark, is this true they say about her--about the former time?"

"Yes; it is true."

Waymark in turn was silent.

"I suppose," he continued presently, "I owe you an apology."

"None. It was right of you to act as you did."

He was going to say something else, but checked himself. Waymark noticed this, watched his face for a moment, and spoke with some earnestness.

"But it was in that only I misled you. Do you believe me when I repeat that she and I were never anything but friends!"

Julian looked up with a gleam of gratitude in his eyes.

"Yes, I believe you!"

"And be sure of this," Waymark went on, "whether or not this accusation is true, it does not in the least affect the nobility of her character. You and I are sufficiently honest, in the true sense of the word, to understand this."

Waymark only saw Mr. Woodstock once or twice in the next fortnight, and very slight mention was made between them of the coming trial. He himself was not to be involved in the case in any way; as a witness on Ida's side he could do no good, and probably would prejudice her yet more in the eyes of the jury. It troubled him a little to find with what complete calmness he could await the result; often he said to himself that he must be sadly lacking in human sympathy. Julian Casti, on the other hand, had passed into a state of miserable deadness; Waymark in vain tried to excite hope in him. He came to his friend's every evening, and sat there for hours in dark reverie.

"What will become of her!" Julian asked once. "In either case--what will become of her!"

"Woodstock shall help us in that," Waymark replied. "She must get a place of some kind."

"How dreadfully she is suffering, and how dark life will be before her!"

And so the day of the trial came. The pawnbroker's evidence was damaging. The silver spoon had been pledged, he asserted, at the same time with another article for which Ida possessed the duplicate. The inscriptions on the duplicates supported him in this, and he professed to have not the least doubt as to the prisoner's identity. Pressed in cross-examination, he certainly threw some suspicion on the trustworthiness of his assertions. "You positively swear that these two articles were pledged by the prisoner, and at the same time!" asked the cross-examiner. "Well," was the impatient reply, "there's the same date and name, and both in my writing." But even thus much of doubt he speedily retracted, and his evidence could not be practically undermined.

Harriet's examination was long and searching, but she bore it without the slightest damage to her credit. Plain, straightforward, and stubborn were all her replies and assertions; she did not contradict herself once. Waymark marvelled at her appearance and manner. The venom of malice had acted upon her as a tonic, strengthening her intellect, and bracing her nerves. Once she looked directly into Ida's face and smiled.

Mrs. Sprowl had been summoned, and appeared in all the magnificence of accumulated rings, bracelets, necklaces, and watch-chains. Helter hoped to make good use of her.

"Did you on a certain occasion go to the person in whose employ the prisoner was, and, by means of certain representations with regard to the prisoner's antecedents, become the cause of her dismissal?"

"I did. I told all I knew about her, and I consider I'd a right to do so."

Mrs. Sprowl was not to be robbed of her self-assurance by any array of judicial dignity.

"What led you to do this?"

"A good enough one, I think. She'd been imposed on Mr. Casti and his wife as a respectable character, and she was causing trouble between them. She had to be got rid of somehow, and this was one step to it."

"Was Mrs. Casti aware of your intention to take this step?"

"No, she wasn't."

"But you told her when you had done it?"

"Yes, I did."

The frankness of all this had its effect, of course. The case was attracting much interest in court, and the public seats were quite full. Mrs. Sprowl looked round in evident enjoyment of her position. There was a slight pause, and then the examination continued.

"Of what nature was the trouble you speak of, caused by the prisoner between this lady and her husband?"

"Mr. Casti began to pay a good deal too much attention to her."

There was a sound of whispers and a murmuring.

"Did Mrs. Casti impart to you her suspicions of the prisoner as soon as she missed the first of these articles alleged to be stolen?"

"Yes, she did."

"And did you give any advice as to how she should proceed?"

"I told her to be on the look-out."

"No doubt you laid stress on the advantage, from a domestic point of view, of securing this prisoner's detection?"

"Certainly I did, and I hoped and prayed as she might caught!"

Mrs. Sprowl was very shortly allowed to retire. For the defence there was but one witness, and that was the laundress who had employed Ida. Personal fault with Ida she had one at all to find; the sole cause of her dismissal was the information given by Mrs. Sprowl. Perhaps she had acted hastily and unkindly, but she had young girls working in the laundry, and it behoved her to be careful of them.

Julian's part in the trial had been limited to an examination as to his knowledge of Ida's alleged thefts. He declared that he knew nothing save from his wife's statements to him. He had observed nothing in the least suspicious.

A verdict was returned of "Guilty."

Had the prisoner anything to say? Nothing whatever. There was a pause, a longer pause than seemed necessary. Then, without remark, she was sentenced to be imprisoned for six months with hard labour.

Waymark had been drawn to the court in spite of himself. Strangely quiet hitherto, a fear fell upon him the night be fore the trial. From an early hour in the morning he walked about the streets, circling ever nearer to the hateful place. All at once he found himself facing Mr. Woodstock. The old man's face was darkly anxious, and he could not change its expression quickly enough.

"Are you going in?" he said sharply.

"Are you?"

"Yes."

"Then I shall not," said Waymark. "I'll go to your place, and wait there."

But when Abraham, whose eyes had not moved from the prisoner throughout the proceedings, rose at length to leave, a step or two brought him to a man who was leaning against the wall, powerless from conflicting excitement, and deadly pale. It was Waymark. Mr. Woodstock took him by the arm and led him out.

"Why couldn't you keep away?" the old man exclaimed hoarsely, and with more of age in his voice than any one had ever yet heard in it.

Waymark shook himself free, and laughed as one laughs under torment.

CHAPTER XXV
ART AND MISERY

One Monday afternoon at the end of October--three months had gone by since the trial--Waymark carried his rents to St. John Street Road as usual.

"I'm going to Tottenham," said Mr. Woodstock. "You may as well come with me."

"By the by, I finished my novel the other day," Waymark said, as they drove northward.

"That's right. No doubt you're on your way to glory, as the hymn says."

Abraham was in good spirits. One would have said that he had grown younger of late. That heaviness and tendency to absent brooding which not long ago seemed to indicate the tightening grip of age, was disappearing; he was once more active and loud and full of his old interests.

"How's Casti?" Mr. Woodstock went on to ask.

"A good deal better, I think, but shaky. Of course things will be as bad as ever when his wife comes out of the hospital."

"Pity she can't come out heels first," muttered Abraham.

Waymark found that the purpose of their journey was to inspect a large vacant house, with a good garden and some fine trees about it. The old man wished for his opinion, and, by degrees, let it be known that he thought of buying the property.

"I suppose you think me an old fool to want a house like this at my time of life, eh?"

There was a twinkle in his eye, and a moment after he fairly burst into a laugh of pleasure. Waymark asked no questions, and received no more information; but a thought rose in his mind which occupied him for the rest of the day.

In the evening Julian came. He looked like one who had recovered from a long illness, very pale and thin, and his voice had tremblings and uncertainties of key. In fact, a feverish disorder had been upon him for some weeks, never severe enough to prevent his getting about, but weakening him to a serious degree. It would doubtless have developed into some more pronounced illness, but for the period of comparative rest and quietness which had begun shortly after the miseries of the trial. Harriet's ailments had all at once taken such a decided turn for the worse--her fits becoming incessant, and other disorders traceable to the same source suddenly taking hold upon her--that Julian had obtained her admission to the hospital, where she still remained. He went to see her in the ward two or three times a week, though he dreaded the necessity. From little incidents which occurred at such times, he was convinced that all her fellow-patients, as well as the "sister" and nurses of the wards, had been prejudiced against him by her reports and accusations. To meet their looks occasioned him the most acute suffering. Sometimes he sat by the bedside for half an hour without speaking, then rose and hastened away to hide himself and be alone with his misery.

He was earnest and eager to-night in his praise of Waymark's book, which he had just read in manuscript.

"It is horrible," he exclaimed; "often hideous and revolting to me; but I feel its absolute truth. Such a book will do more good than half a dozen religious societies."

"If only people can be got to read it. Yet I care nothing for that aspect of the thing. Is it artistically strong? Is it good as a picture? There was a time when I might have written in this way with a declared social object. That is all gone by. I have no longer a spark of social enthusiasm. Art is all I now care for, and as art I wish my work to be judged."

"One would have thought," said Julian, "that increased knowledge of these fearful things would have had just the opposite effect."

"Yes," exclaimed the other, with the smile which always prefaced some piece of self-dissection, "and so it would in the case of a man born to be a radical. I often amuse myself with taking to pieces my former self. I was not a conscious hypocrite in those days of violent radicalism, working-man's-club lecturing, and the like; the fault was that I understood myself as yet so imperfectly. That zeal on behalf of the suffering masses was nothing more nor less than disguised zeal on behalf of my own starved passions. I was poor and desperate, life had no pleasures, the future seemed hopeless, yet I was overflowing with vehement desires, every nerve in me was a hunger which cried to be appeased. I identified myself with the poor and ignorant; I did not make their cause my own, but my own cause theirs. I raved for freedom because I was myself in the bondage of unsatisfiable longing."

"Well," he went on, after regarding his listener with still the same smile, "I have come out of all that, in proportion as my artistic self-consciousness has developed. For one thing, I am not so miserable as I was then, personally; then again, I have found my vocation. You know pretty well the phases I have passed through. Upon ranting radicalism followed a period of philosophical study. My philosophy, I have come to see, was worth nothing; what philosophy is worth anything? It had its use for myself, however; it made me by degrees self-conscious, and brought me to see that in art alone I could find full satisfaction."

"Yet," urged Julian, "the old direction still shows itself in your choice of subjects. Granting that this is pure art, it is a kind of art only possible to an age in which the social question is predominant."

"True, very likely. Every strong individuality is more or less the expression of its age. This direction may be imposed upon me; for all that, I understand why I pursue it."

After reflecting, Julian spoke in another tone. "Imagine yourself in my position. Could you appreciate the artistic effect of your own circumstances?"

"Probably not. And it is because I recognise that, that I grow more and more careful to hold aloof from situations that would threaten my peace of mind. My artistic egotism bids fair to ally itself with vulgar selfishness. That tendency I must resist. For the artist *ought* to be able to make material of his own sufferings, even while the suffering is at its height. To what other end does he suffer? In very deed, he is the only man whose misery finds justification in apparent result."

"I am not an artist," sighed Julian.

"On the contrary, I firmly believe that you are. And it makes me angry to see the impulse dying in you."

"What am I to do?" Julian cried, almost with a voice of anguish. "I am so helpless, so hopelessly fettered! Release is impossible. No words could express the desperate struggles I go through when I recognise how my life is being wasted and my powers, whatever they may be, numbed and crushed. Something I might do, if I were free; I feel that! But there is no hope of freedom. I shall fall into darker and darker depths of weakness and ruin, always conscious of what I am losing. What will be the end?"

"What the end will be, under the present circumstances, is only too clear to me. But it might easily be averted?"

"How? Give me some practical advice, Waymark! Let us talk of the matter freely. Tell me what you would do!"

Waymark thought for a moment.

"Does there seem any chance of her health being permanently improved?" he asked.

"I can't say. She says she is better. It's no use my asking the doctors; they despise me, and would not think of treating me with any consideration."

"Why don't you do this?" began Waymark, after another pause. "Use all means to find some convalescent home where she can be received when she leaves the hospital. Then, if her fits and the rest of it still continue, find some permanent place for her. You can afford it. Never mind if it reduces you for a time to a garret and a crust."

"She would refuse to go to such places," said Julian despondently.

"Then refuse to take her back! Sell your furniture; take one room for yourself; and tell her she must live where she likes on a sufficient allowance from you."

"I dare not. It is impossible. She would never leave me in peace."

"You will have to do this ultimately, if you are to continue to live. Of that there is no doubt. So why not now?"

"I must think; it is impossible to make up my mind to such a thing at once. I know you advise what is best; I have thought of it myself. But I shall never have the courage! I am so miserably weak. If only I could get my health back! Good God, how I suffer!"

Waymark did his best to familiarise Julian with the thought, and to foster in him something of resoluteness, but he had small hope of succeeding. The poor fellow was so incapable of anything which at all resembled selfishness, and so dreaded the results of any such severity on his part as that proposed. There were moments when indignation almost nerved him to independence, but there returned so soon the souse of pity, and, oftener still, the thought of that promise made to Harriet's father, long ago, in the dark little parlour which smelt of drugs. The poor chemist, whose own life was full of misery, had been everything to him; but for Mr. Smales, he might now have been an ignorant, coarse-handed working man, if not worse. Was Harriet past all rescue? Was there not even yet a chance of saving her from herself and those hateful friends of hers?

This was the natural reaction after listening to Waymark's remorseless counsel. Going home, Julian fought once more the battle with himself, till the usual troubled sleep severed his thoughts into fragments of horrible dreams. The next day he felt differently; Waymark's advice seemed more practical. In the afternoon he should have visited Harriet in the ward, but an insuperable repulsion kept him away, and for the first time. It was a bleak, cheerless day; the air was cold with the breath of the nearing winter; At night he found it impossible to sit in his own room, and dreaded to talk with any one. His thoughts were fixed upon one place; a great longing drew him forth, into the darkness and the rain of the streets, onwards in a fixed direction. It brought him to Westminster, and to the gate of Tothill Fields Prison. The fetters upon the great doors were hideous in the light of the lamps above them; the mean houses around the gaol seemed to be rotting in its accursed shadow. A deadly stillness possessed the air; there was blight in the dropping of the rain.

He leaned against the great, gloomy wall, and thought of Ida. At this hour she was most likely asleep, unless sorrow kept her waking. What unimagined horrors did she suffer day after day in that accursed prison-house? How did she bear her torments? Was she well or ill? What brutality might she not be subjected to? He pictured her face wasted with secret tears, those eyes which were the light of his soul fixed on the walls of the cell, hour after hour, in changeless despair, the fire of passionate resentment feeding at her life's core.

The night became calmer. The rained ceased, and a sudden gleam made him look up, to behold the moon breaking her way through billows of darkness.

CHAPTER XXVI
STRAYING

The Enderbys were at Brighton during the autumn. Mr. Enderby only remained with them two or three days at a time, business requiring his frequent presence in town. Maud would have been glad to spend her holidays at some far quieter place, but her mother enjoyed Brighton, and threw herself into its amusements of the place with spirits which seemed to grow younger. They occupied handsome rooms, and altogether lived in a more expensive way than when at home.

Maud was glad to see her mother happy, but could not be at ease herself in this kind of life. It was soon arranged that she should live in her own way, withholding from the social riot which she dreaded, and seeking rest in out-of-the-way parts of the shore, where more of nature was to be found and less of fashion. Maud feared lest her mother should feel this as an unkind desertion, but Mrs. Enderby was far from any such trouble; it relieved her from the occasional disadvantage of having by her side a grown-up daughter, whose beauty so strongly contrasted with her own. So Maud spent her days very frequently in exploring the Downs, or in seeking out retired nooks beneath the cliffs, where there was no sound in her ears but that of the waves. She would sit for hours with no companion save her thoughts, which were unconsciously led from phase to phase by the moving lights and shadows upon the sea, and the soft beauty of unstable clouds.

Even before leaving London, she had begun to experience a frequent sadness of mood, tending at times to weariness and depression, which foreshadowed new changes in her inner life. The fresh delight in nature and art had worn off in some degree; she read less, and her thoughts took the habit of musing upon the people and circumstances about her, also upon the secrets of the years to come. She grew more conscious of the mystery in her own earlier life, and in the conditions which now surrounded her. A sense which at times besets all imaginative minds came upon her now and then with painful force; a fantastic unreality would suddenly possess all she saw and heard; it seemed as if she had been of a sudden transported out of the old existence into this new and unrealised position; if any person spoke to her, it was difficult to feel that she was really addressed and must reply; was it not all a mere vision she was beholding, out of which she would presently awake! Such moments were followed by dark melancholy. This life she was leading could not last, but would pass away in some fearful shock of soul. Once she half believed herself endowed with the curse of a hideous second-sight. Sitting with her father and mother, silence all at once fell upon the room, and everything was transfigured in a ghostly light. Distinctly she saw her mother throw her head back and raise to her throat what seemed to be a sharp, glistening piece of steel; then came a cry, and all was darkened before her eyes in a rush of crimson mist. The cry she had herself uttered, much to her parents' alarm; what her mother held was in reality only a paper-knife, with which she had been tapping her lips in thought. A slight attack of illness followed on this disturbance, and it was some days before she recovered from the shock; she kept to herself, however, the horrible picture which her imagination had conjured up.

She began to pay more frequent visits to her aunt Theresa, whom at first she had seen very seldom. There was not the old confidence between them. Maud shrank from any direct reference to the change in herself, and Miss Bygrave spoke no word which could suggest a comparison between past and present. Maud tried once more to draw near to the pale, austere woman, whose life ever remained the same. She was not repelled, but neither did any movement respond to her yearning. She always came away with a sad heart.

One evening in the week she looked forward to with eagerness; it was that on which Waymark was generally expected. In Waymark's presence she could forget those dark spirits that hovered about her; she could forget herself, and be at rest in the contemplation of strength and confidence. There was a ring in his voice which inspired faith; whatever might be his own doubts and difficulties--and his face testified to his knowledge of both--it was so certain that he had power to overcome them. This characteristic grew stronger in him to her observation; he was a far other man now than when she first knew him; the darkness had passed from his eyes, which seemed always to look straight forward, and with perception of an end he was nearing. Why could she not make opportunities of speaking freely with him, alone with him? They were less near to each other, it seemed, after a year of constant meeting, than in the times when, personally all but strangers, they had corresponded so frankly and unconventionally. Of course he came to the house for her sake; it could not but be so; yet at times he seemed to pay so little attention to her. Her mother often monopolised him through a whole evening, and not apparently to his annoyance. And all the time he had in his heart the message for which she longed; support and comfort were waiting for her there, she felt sure, could he but speak unrestrainedly. In herself was no salvation; but he had already overcome, and why could she not ask him for the secret of his confidence? Often, as the evening drew to an end, and he was preparing to leave, an impatience scarcely to be repressed took hold upon her; her face grew hot, her hands trembled, she would have followed him from the room and begged for one word to herself had it been possible. And when he was gone, there came the weakest moments her life had yet known; a childish petulance, a tearful fretting, an irritable misery of which she was ashamed. She went to her room to suffer in silence, and often to read through that packet of his letters, till the night was far spent.

It had cost her much to leave London. She feared lest, during her absence, something should occur to break off the wonted course of things, and that Waymark might not resume his visits on their return. After the feverish interval of those first weeks, she tried sometimes to distract her thoughts by reading, and got from a library a book which Waymark had recommended to her at their last meeting--Rossetti's poems. These gave her much help in restoring her mind to quietness. Their perfect beauty entranced her, and the rapturous purity of ideal passion, the mystic delicacies of emotion, which made every verse gleam like a star, held her for the time high above that gloomy cloudland of her being, rife with weird shapes and muffled voices. That Beauty is solace of life, and Love the end of being,--this faith she would cling to in spite of all; she grasped it with the desperate force of one who dreaded lest it should fade and fail from her. Beauty alone would not suffice; too often it was perceived as a mere mask, veiling horrors; but in the passion and the worship of love was surely a never-failing fountain of growth and power; this the draught that would leave no bitter aftertaste, its enjoyment the final and all-sufficient answer to the riddle of life. Rossetti put into utterance for her so much that she had not dared to entrust even to the voice of thought. Her spirit and flesh became one and indivisible; the old antagonism seemed at an end for ever.

Such dreamings as these naturally heightened Maud's dislike for the kind of life her mother led, and she longed unspeakably for the time of her return to London. They had been at Brighton already nearly a month, when a new circumstance was added to her discomfort. As she walked with her mother one day, they met their acquaintance, Mr. Budge. This gentleman dined with them that evening at Mrs. Enderby's invitation, and persuaded the latter to join a party he had made up for an excursion on the following day. Maud excused herself. She did not like Mr. Budge, and his demeanour during the evening only strengthened her prejudice. He was unduly excited and fervent, and allowed himself a certain freedom in his conversation with Mrs. Enderby which Maud resented strongly.

When they were once more in London, Maud did not win back the former quiet of mind. Waymark came again as usual, but if anything the distance between him and herself seemed more hopeless. He appeared preoccupied; his talk, when he spoke with her, was of a more general kind than formerly; she was conscious that her presence did not affect him as it had done. She sank again into despondency; books were insipid, and society irritated her. She began the habit of taking long walks, an aimless wandering about the streets and parks within her reach. One evening, wending wearily homewards, she was attracted by the lights in a church in Marylebone Road, and, partly for a few minutes' rest, partly out of a sudden attraction to a religious service, she entered. It was the church of Our Lady of the Rosary. She had not noticed that it was a Roman Catholic place of worship, but the discovery gave her an unexpected pleasure. She was soothed and filled with a sense of repose. Sinking into the attitude of prayer, she let her thoughts carry her whither they would; they showed her nothing but images of beauty and peace. It was with reluctance that she arose and went back into the dark street, where the world met her with a chill blast, sleet-laden.

Our Lady of the Rosary received her frequently after this. But there were days when the thought of repose was far from her. At one such time, on an evening in November, a sudden desire possessed her mind; she would go out into the streets of the town and see something of that life which she knew only in imagination, the traffic of highway and byway after dark, the masque of pleasure and misery of sin of which a young girl can know nothing, save from hints here and there in her reading, or from the occasional whispers and head-shakings of society's gossip. Her freedom was complete; her absence, if noticed, would entail no questions; her mother doubtless would conclude that she was at her aunt Theresa's. So she clad herself in walking attire of a kind not likely to attract observation, and set forth. The tumult which had been in her blood all day received fresh impulse from the excitement of the adventure. She had veiled her face, but the veil hindered her observation, and she threw it back. First into Edgware Road, then down Oxford Street. Her thoughts pointed to an eastern district, though she feared the distance would be too great; she had frequently talked with Waymark of his work in Litany Lane and Elm Court, and a great curiosity possessed her to see these places. She entered an omnibus, and so reached the remote neighbourhood. Here, by inquiry of likely people, she found her way to Litany Lane, and would have penetrated its darkness, but was arrested by a sudden event characteristic of the locality.

Forth from the alley, just before her, rushed a woman of hideous aspect, pursued by another, younger, but, if possible, yet more foul, who shrieked curses and threats. In the way of the fugitive was a costermonger's stall; unable to check herself, the woman rushed against this, overturning it, and herself falling among the ruin. The one in pursuit, with a yell of triumph, sprang upon her prostrate enemy, and attacked her with fearful violence, leaping on her body, dashing her head against the pavement, seemingly bent on murder. In a moment there was a thick crowd rushing round, amid which Maud was crushed and swayed without possibility of disengaging herself. The screams of the one woman, and the terrific objurgations of the other, echoed through the street. From the words of those about her, Maud understood that the two women were mother and daughter, and that it was no rare occurrence for the younger woman to fall just short of killing her parent. But only for a moment or two could Maud understand anything; horror and physical oppression overcame her senses. Her fainting caused a diversion in the crowd, and she was dragged without much delay to the nearest doorstep.

She was not long unconscious, and presently so far recovered as to know that she was being helped to enter a cab. The cab began to drive off. Then she saw that some one was sitting opposite her. "Who is it?" she asked, trying to command herself, and to see clearly by the light of the street lamps. At the sound of the voice which answered, she started, and, looking again, at length recognised Waymark.

"Do you feel better?" he asked. "Are you able to go on homewards?"

"Quite able," she answered, leaning back again, and speaking with strange calmness.

"What on earth is the meaning of this?" was Waymark's next inquiry. "How came you here at this time?"

"Curiosity brought me," Maud answered, with the same unnatural composure.

"Had you been there long?"

"No; I had asked my way to Litany Lane, and all at once found myself in the crowd."

"Thank goodness I happened to be by! I had just been looking up a defaulting tenant. I couldn't believe my eyes when I saw you lying in that doorway. Why didn't you ask me to come with you, and show you these places?"

"It would have been better," she said, with her eyes closed. Waymark leaned back. Conversation was difficult in the noise of the vehicle, and for a long time neither spoke.

"I told the man to drive to Edgware Road," Waymark said then. "Shall he go on to the house?"

"No; I had rather walk the last part."

They talked brokenly of the Lane and its inhabitants. When at length Maud alighted Waymark offered his arm, and she just laid her hand upon it.

"I have seen dreadful things to-night," she said, in a voice that still trembled; "seen and heard things that will haunt me."

"You give too much weight to the impressions of the moment. That world is farther removed from yours than the farthest star; you must forget this glimpse of it."

"Oh, I fear you do not know me; I do not know myself."

He made no reply, and, on their coming near to the house, Maud paused.

"Mother's sending you a note this evening," she said, as she held out her hand, "to ask you to come on Thursday instead of to-morrow. She will be from home to-morrow night."

"Shall you also be from home?"

"I? No."

"Then may I not come and see you?--Not if it would be troublesome."

"It would not, at all."

"It is good of you. I will come."

CHAPTER XXVII
THE WILL TO LIVE

Waymark made his way to Paddington at the usual time on the following evening, and found Maud alone. There was agitation in her manner as she welcomed him, and she resumed her seat as if the attitude of rest was needful to her. In reply to his inquiries about her health, she assured him she was well, and that she felt no painful results from the previous evening. Waymark also showed an unusual embarrassment. He stood for some moments by the table, turning over the leaves of a book.

"I didn't know you had Rossetti," he said, without looking up. "You never mentioned him."

"I seem to have had no opportunity."

"No. I too have many things that I have wanted to speak to you about, but opportunity was wanting. I have sometimes been on the point of asking you to let me write to you again."

He glanced inquiringly at her. Her eyes fell, and she tried to speak, but failed. Waymark went to a seat at a little distance from her.

"You do not look as well as when I met you in the summer," he said. "I have feared you might be studying too hard. I hope you threw away your books whilst you were at the sea-side."

"I did, but it was because I found little pleasure in them. It was not rest that took the place of reading."

"Are your difficulties of a kind you could speak of to me?" he asked, with some hesitation.

She kept her eyes lowered, and her fingers writhed nervously on the arm of the chair.

"My only fear would be lest you should think my troubles unreal. Indeed it is so hard to make them appear anything more than morbid fancies. They are traceable, no doubt, to my earliest years. To explain them fully, I should have to tell you circumstances of my life which could have little interest for you."

"Tell me--do," Waymark replied earnestly.

"Will you let me?" she said, with a timid pleasure in her voice. "I believe you could understand me. I have a feeling that you must have experienced something of these troubles yourself, and have overcome them. Perhaps you could help me to understand myself."

"If I thought I could, it would give me great happiness."

She was silent a little, then, with diffidence which lessened as she went on, she related the history, as far as she knew it, of her childhood, and described the growth of her mind up to the time when she had left home to begin life as a governess. It was all very simply, but very vividly, told; that natural command of impressive language which had so struck Waymark in her letters displayed itself as soon as she had gained confidence. Glimpses of her experience Waymark had already had, but now for the first time he understood the full significance of her early years. Whilst she spoke, he did not move his eyes from her face. He was putting himself in her position, and imagining himself to be telling his own story in the same way. His relation, he knew, would have been a piece of more or less clever acting, howsoever true; he would have been considering, all the time, the effect of what he said, and, indeed, could not, on this account, have allowed himself to be quite truthful. How far was this the case with Maud Enderby? Could he have surprised the faintest touch of insincerity in look or accent, it would have made a world's difference in his position towards *her*. His instinct was unfailing in the detection of the note of affected feeling; so much the stronger the impression produced upon him by a soul unveiling itself in the *naivete* of genuine emotion. That all was sincere he could have no doubt. Gradually he lost his critical attitude, and at moments surprised himself under the influence of a sympathetic instinct. Then he would lose consciousness of her words for an interval, during which he pondered her face, and was wrought upon by its strange beauty. The pure and touching spirituality of Maud's countenance had never been so present to him as now; she was pale with very earnestness, her eyes seemed larger than their wont, there was more than womanly sweetness in the voice which so unconsciously modulated itself to the perfect expression of all she uttered. Towards the end, he could but yield himself completely to the spell, and, when she ceased, he, like Adam at the end of the angel's speech, did not at once perceive that her voice was silent.

"It was long," she said, after telling the outward circumstances of her life with her aunt, "before I came to understand how differently I had been brought up from other children. Partly I began to see it at the school where we first met; but it only grew quite clear to me when I shared in the home life of my pupils in the country. I found I had an entirely different view of the world from what was usual. That which was my evil, I discovered to be often others' good; and my good, their abhorrence. My aunt's system was held to be utterly unchristian. Little things which I sometimes said, in perfect innocence, excited grave disapproval. All this frightened me, and made me even more reserved than I should have been naturally.

"In my letters to you I began to venture for the first time to speak of things which were making my life restless. I did little more than hint my opinions; I wonder, in looking back, that I had the courage to do even that. But I already knew that your mind was broader and richer than mine, and I suppose I caught with a certain desperation at the chance of being understood. It was the first opportunity I had ever had of discussing intellectual things. With my aunt I had never ventured to discuss anything; I reverenced her too much for that; she spoke, and I received all she said. I thought that from you I should obtain confirmation where I needed it, but your influence was of the opposite kind. Your letters so abounded with suggestion that was quite new to me, referred so familiarly to beliefs and interests of which I was quite ignorant, showed such a boldness in judging all things, that I drifted further and further from certainty. The result of it all was that I fell ill.

"You see now what it is that has burdened me from the day when I first began to ask myself about my beliefs. I was taught to believe that the world was sin, and that the soul only freed itself from sin in proportion as it learned to live apart from and independently of the world. Everything was dark because of sin; only in the still, secret places of the soul was the light of purity and salvation.

"I thought I had passed out of this. When I returned to London, and began this new life, the burden seemed all at once lifted from me. I could look here and there with freedom; the sky was bright above me; human existence was cheerful and noble and justified in itself. I began to learn a thousand things. Above all, my mind fixed on Art; in that I thought I had found a support that would never fail me.

"Oh, why could it not last? The clouds began to darken over me again. I heard voices once which I had hoped were for ever silenced. That sense of sin and horror came upon me last night in the streets. I suffered dreadfully."

She was silent, and, meeting Waymark's eyes so fixed on her own, became conscious of the eagerness and fervour with which she had spoken.

"Have you any experience of such things?" she asked nervously. "Did you ever suffer in the same way?"

"It is all very strange," he said, without answering her question. "This overpowering consciousness of sin is an anachronism in our time. But, from the way in which you express yourself, I should have thought you had been studying Schopenhauer. I suppose you know nothing of him?"

"Nothing."

"Some of your phrases were precisely his. Your doctrine is simply Pessimism, with an element of dogmatic faith added. With Schopenhauer, the will to live is the root of sin; mortify this, deny the first instincts of your being, and you approach righteousness. Buddhism has the same system. And, in deducing all this from the plain teachings of Christianity, I am disposed to think you are right and consistent. Christianity *is* pessimism, so far as this world is concerned; we see that in such things as the thanksgiving for a' person's death in the burial service, and the prayer that the end of the world may soon come."

He paused, and thought for a moment.

"But all this," he resumed, rising from his seat, and going to stand with one arm upon the mantelpiece, "is of course, with me, mere matter of speculation. There are two allegories, which define Pessimism and Optimism. First that of Adam and Christ. Adam falls through eating of the tree of knowledge; in other words, sin only comes with self-consciousness, sin *is* the conscious enjoyment of life. And, according to this creed, it can only be overcome by abnegation, by the denial of the will to live. Accordingly, Christ enters the world, and, representing Humanity, as Adam had done, saves the world by denial, of Himself, even to death. The other allegory is that of Prometheus. He also represents mankind, and his stealing of the fire means man's acquirement of a conscious soul, whereby he makes himself capable of sin. The gods put him in bondage and torment, representing the subjection to the flesh. But Prometheus is saved in a different way from Adam; not by renunciation, but by the prowess of Hercules, that is to say, the triumphant aspiration of Humanity.

Man triumphs by asserting his right to do so. Self-consciousness he claims as a good thing, and embraces the world as his birthright. Here, you see, there is no room for the crushing sense of sin. Sin, if anything, is weakness. Let us rejoice in our strength, whilst we have it. The end of course will come, but it is a wise man's part not to heed the inevitable. Let us live whilst it is called to-day; we shall go to sleep with all the better conscience for having used the hours of daylight."

Maud listened with head bent.

"My own temperament," Waymark went on, "is, I suppose, exceptional, at all events among men who have an inner life. I never knew what goes by the name of religious feeling; impulses of devotion, in the common sense of the phrase, have always been strange to me. I have known fear at the prospect of death; religious consolation, never. Sin, above all, has been a word without significance to me. As a boy, it was so; it is so still, now that I am self-conscious. I have never been a deep student of philosophy, but the doctrine of philosophical necessity, the idea of Fate, is with me an instinct. I know that I could not have acted otherwise than I did in any juncture of my life; I know that the future is beyond my control. I shall do this, and avoid that, simply owing to a preponderance of motives, which I can gauge, but not control. Certain things I hate and shrink from; but I try to avoid, even in thought, such words as vice and crime; the murderer could not help himself, and the saint has no merit in his sanctity. Does all this seem horrible to you?"

Maud raised her eyes, and looked steadily at him, but did not speak. It was the gaze of one who tries humbly to understand, and longs to sympathise. But there was a shadow of something like fear upon her face.

Waymark spoke with more earnestness.

"You will not think me incapable of what we call noble thought and feeling? I have in me the elements of an enthusiast; they might have led me to strange developments, but for that cold, critical spirit which makes me so intensely self-conscious. This restless scepticism has often been to me a torment in something the same way as that burden of which you speak. Often, often, I would so gladly surrender myself to my instincts of passion and delight. I may change; I may perhaps some day attain rest in an absolute ideal. If I do, it will be through the help of one who shall become to me that ideal personified, who shall embody all the purer elements of my nature, and speak to me as with the voice of my own soul."

She hung upon his words, and an involuntary sigh, born of the intensity of the moment, trembled on her lips.

"I have spoken to you," he said, after what seemed a long silence, "with a sincerity which was the due return for your own. I could have shown myself in a more pleasing light. You see how little able I am to help you; the centre-thought of your being is wholly strange to me. And for all that--may I speak my thought?--we are nearer to each other than before."

"Yes, nearer," she repeated, under her breath.

"You think that? You feel that? I have not repelled you?"

"You have not"

"And if I stood before you, now, as you know me--egotistic, sceptical, calm--and told you that you are the only being in whom I have ever felt complete confidence, whose word and thought I felt to be one; that you exercise more power over me than any other ever did or shall; that life in your companionship might gain the unity I long for; that in your presence I feel myself face to face with a higher and nobler nature than my own, one capable of sustaining me in effort and leading me to great results--"

He became silent, for her face had turned deadly pale. But this passed, and in her eyes, as they met his, trouble grew to a calm joy. Without speaking, she held her hand to him.

"You are not afraid," Waymark said, "to link your fate with mine? My life is made up of uncertainties. I have no position; it may be a long time before I can see even the promise of success in my work. I have chosen that work, however, and by it I stand or fall. Have you sufficient faith in me to wait with confidence?"

"I have absolute faith in you. I ask no greater happiness than to have a share in your aims. It will give me the strength I need, and make my life full of hope."

It had come then, and just as he had foreseen it would. It was no result of deliberate decision, he had given up the effort to discover his true path, knowing sufficiently that neither reason nor true preponderance of inclination was likely to turn the balance. The gathering emotion of the hour had united with opportunity to decide his future. The decision was a relief; as he walked homewards, he was lighthearted.

On the way, he thought over everything once more, reviewing former doubts from his present position. On the whole, he felt that fate had worked for his happiness.

And yet there was discontent. He had never known, felt that perhaps he might never know, that sustained energy of imaginative and sensual longing which ideal passion demands. The respectable make-believe which takes the form of domestic sentiment, that everyday love, which, become the servant of habit, suffices to cement the ordinary household, is not the state in which such men as Waymark seek or find repose; the very possibility of falling into it unawares is a dread to them. If he could but feel at all times as he had felt at moments in Maud's presence. It might be that the growth of intimacy, of mutual knowledge, would make his love for her a more real motive in his life. He would endeavour that it should be so. Yet there remained that fatal conviction of the unreality of every self-persuasion save in relation to the influences of the moment. To love was easy, inevitable; to concentrate love finally on one object might well prove, in his case, an impossibility. Clear enough to him already was the likelihood of a strong revulsion of feeling when Ida once more came back, and the old life--if it could be--was resumed. Compassion would speak so loudly for her; her face, pale and illuminated with sorrow, would throw a stronger spell than ever upon his senses. Well, there was no help. Whatever would be, would be. It availed nothing to foresee and scheme and resolve.

And, in the same hour, Maud was upon her knees, in the silence of her own chamber, shedding tears which were at once both sweet and bitter, in her heart a tumult of emotion, joy and thanksgiving at strife with those dark powers which shadowed her existence. *She* had do doubts of the completeness and persistency of her love. But was not this love a sin, and its very strength the testimony of her soul's loss?

CHAPTER XXVIII
SLIMY'S DAY

Waymark had written to Ida just after her imprisonment began, a few words of such comfort as he could send. No answer came; perhaps the prison rules prevented it. When the term was drawing to a close, he wrote again, to let her know that he would meet her on the morning of her release.

It would be on a Tuesday morning. As the time drew near, Waymark did his best to think of the matter quietly. The girl had no one else to help her; it would have been brutality to withdraw and leave her to her fate, merely because he just a little feared the effect upon himself of such a meeting. And the feeling on her side? Well, that he could not pretend to be ignorant of, and, in spite of everything, there was still the same half-acknowledged pleasure in the thought. He tried to persuade himself that he should have the moral courage to let her as soon as possible understand his new position; he also tried to believe that this would not involve any serious shock to Ida. For all that, he knew only too well that man is "*ein erbarmlicher Schuft*," and there was always the possibility that he might say nothing of what had happened, and let things take their course.

On the Monday he was already looking forward to the meeting with restlessness. Could he have foreseen that anything would occur to prevent his keeping his promise, it would have caused him extreme anxiety. But such a possibility never entered his thoughts, and, shortly before mid-day, he went down to collect his rents as usual.

The effect of a hard winter was seen in the decrease of the collector's weekly receipts. The misery of cold and starvation was growing familiar to Waymark's eyes, and scarcely excited the same feelings as formerly; yet there were some cases in which he had not the heart to press for the payment of rent, and his representations to Mr. Woodstock on behalf of the poor creatures were more frequently successful than in former times. Still, in the absence of then but eviction, and Waymark more than once knew what ideal philanthropy, there was nothing for it every now and it was to be cursed to his face by suffering wretches whom despair made incapable of discrimination. "Where are we to go?" was the oft-repeated question, and the only reply was a shrug of the shoulders; impossible to express oneself otherwise. They clung desperately to habitations so vile that brutes would have forsaken them for cleaner and warmer retreats in archway and by roadside. One family of seven, a man and wife (both ill) with five children, could not be got out, even when a man had been sent by Mr. Woodstock to remove the window-frames and take the door away, furniture having already been seized; only by force at length were they thrown into the street, to find their way to perdition as best they might. Waymark did not relish all this; it cost him a dark hour now and then. But it was rich material; every item was stored up for future use.

Among others, the man named Slimy just managed to hold his footing. Times were hard with Slimy, that was clear; still, he somehow contrived to keep no more than a fortnight behind with his rent. Waymark was studying this creature, and found in him the strangest matter for observation; in Slimy there were depths beyond Caliban, and, at the same time, curious points of contact with average humanity, unexpectedly occurring. He was not ungrateful for the collector's frequent forbearance, and, when able to speak coherently, tried at times to show this. Waymark had got into the habit of sitting with him in his room for a little time, whenever he found him at home. Of late, Slimy had seemed not quite in his usual health; this exhibited itself much as it would in some repulsive animal, which suffers in captivity, and tries to find a remote corner when pains come on. At times Waymark experienced a certain fear in the man's presence; if ever he met the dull glare of that one bleared blood-shot eye, a chill ran through him for a moment, and he drew back a little. Personal uncleanliness made Slimy's proximity at all times unpleasant; and occasionally his gaunt, grimed face grew to an expression suggestive of disagreeable possibilities.

On the present day, Waymark was told by a woman who lived on the ground-floor that Slimy had gone out, but had left word with her, in case the collector called, that he should be back in less than half-an-hour. Doubtless this meant that the rent was not forthcoming. The people who lived on the first floor were out as usual, but had left their rent. Of the two rooms at the top, one was just now vacant. Waymark went on to the two or three houses that remained. On turning back, he met Slimy at the door; the man nodded in his wonted way, grinning like a grisly phantom, and beckoned Waymark to follow him upstairs. The woman below had closed her door again, and in all probability no one observed the two entering together.

Waymark sat down amid the collection of nondescript articles which always filled the room, and waited for the tenant to produce his rent. Slimy seemed to have other things in mind. After closing the door, he too had taken a seat, upon a heap of filthy sacking, and was running his fingers through the shock of black hair which made his beard. Waymark examined him. There was no sign of intoxication, but something was evidently working in the man's mind, and his breath came quickly, with a kind of asthmatic pant, from between his thin lips, still parted in the un-canny grin.

"Mr. Waymark," he began at length.

"Well?"

"I ain't got no rent."

"That's bad. You're two weeks behind, you know."

"Mr. Waymark."

The single eye fixed itself on Waymark's face in a way which made the latter feel uncomfortable.

"Well?"

"I ain't a-gem' to pay you no more rent, nor yet no one else, maybe."

"How's that?"

"'Cos I ain't, and 'cos I'm tired o' payin' rent."

"I'm afraid you'll find it difficult to get on without, though," said Waymark, trying to get into the jocular tone he sometimes adopted with Slimy, but scarcely succeeding.

"Mr. Waymark."

There was clearly something wrong. Waymark rose to his feet. Slimy rose also, and at the same time took up a heavy piece of wood, looking like a piece of a cart-shaft, which had lain on the floor beside him. His exclamation elicited no an-swer, and he spoke again, hoarsely as always, but with a calmness which contrasted strangely with the words he uttered.

"Do you believe in the devil and hell?"

"Why?" returned Waymark, trying hard to command himself, and to face down the man as a wild beast has been known to be out-gazed.

"'Cos, by the devil himself, as 'll have me before many weeks is over, and by the fires of hell, as 'll burn me, if you stir a step, or speak a word above your breath, I'll bring you down just like they do the bullocks. Y' understand!"

Waymark saw that the threat was no idle one. He could scarcely have spoken, had he wished. Slimy grinned at the effect he had produced, and continued in the same matter-of-fact way.

"It takes you back a bit, don't it! Never mind; you'll get over it. I don't mean you no 'arm, Mr. Waymark, but I'll have to put you to a little ill-convenience, that's all. See now; here's a bit o' stout rope. With this 'ere, I'm a-goin' jist to tie you up, 'and an' foot, you see. As I said before, if you give me any trouble, well, I'll 'ave to knock the senses out o' you fust, that's all."

Vain to think of grappling with the man, whose strength Waymark knew to be extraordinary. For a moment, the shock of alarm had deprived him of thought and power of movement; but this passed, and he was able to consider his position. He looked keenly into Slimy's face. Had the man gone mad! His manner was scarcely consistent with that supposition. As the alternative before him was of such a kind, Waymark could but choose the lesser evil. He allowed Slimy to remove from his shoulders the satchel which contained the sums of money he had just collected. It was quietly put aside.

"Now," said Slimy, with the same deliberation, "I have to arst you just to lay down on the floor, just 'ere, see. It's better to lay down quiet than to be knocked down, you see."

Waymark mentally agreed that it was. His behaviour might seem cowardly, but--to say nothing of the loathsomeness of a wrestle with Slimy--he knew very well that any struggle, or a shout for help, would mean his death. He hesitated, felt ashamed, but looked at Slimy's red eye, and lay down. In taking the position indicated, he noticed that three very large iron hooks had been driven firmly into the floor, in a triangular shape. Just beside the lower one of these his feet had to rest; his head lay between the other two. Slimy now proceeded to bind his captive's feet together with strong cord, and then attach them firmly to the hook; then bidding him sit up for a moment, he made his hands fast behind his back; lastly, Waymark being again recumbent, a rope was passed once round his neck, and each end of it firmly fastened to one of the remaining hooks. This was not a pleasant moment, but, the operation completed, Waymark found that, though he could not move his head an inch, there was no danger of strangulation as long as he remained quiet. In short, he was bound as effectually as a man could be, yet without much pain. The only question was, how long he would have to remain thus.

Slimy examined his work, and nodded with satisfaction. Then he took up the satchel again, opened it, and for a few moments kept diving his long black fingers into the coins, whilst his face was transformed to an expression of grim joy. Presently, having satisfied himself with the feel of the money, he transferred it all to a pocket inside his ragged coat.

"Now, Mr. Waymark," he recommenced, seating himself on the chair Waymark had previously occupied, "I ain't quite done with ill-conveniencin' you. I'm sorry to say I'll 'ave jist to put a bit of a gag on, to prevent you from 'ollerin' out too soon; but before I do that, I've jist got a word or two to say. Let's spend our last time together in a friendly way."

In spite of his alarm, Waymark observed with astonishment the change which had come over the man's mode of speech. In all their previous intercourse, Slimy had shown himself barely articulate; for the most part it was difficult to collect meaning from his grunts and snarls. His voice was still dreadfully husky, and indeed seemed unused to the task of uttering so many words, but for all that he spoke without hesitation, and with a reserve of force which made his utterances all the more impressive. Having bespoken his hearer's attention in this deliberate way, he became silent, and for a while sat brooding, his fingers still busy among the coins in his pocket.

"I don't rightly know how old I may be," he began at length, "but it's most like about fifty; we'll say fifty. For fifty years I've lived in this world, and in all that time I can't remember not one single 'appy day, not one. I never knowed neither father nor mother; I never knowed not a soul as belonged to me. Friends I *'ave* had; four of 'em; and their names was Brandy, Whisky, Rum, an' Gin. But they've cost me a good deal, an' somehow they ain't quite what they used to be. They used to make me merry for a while, now and then; but they've taken now to burnin' up my inside, an' filling my 'ead with devils; an' I'm gettin' afeard of 'em, an' they'll 'ave to see me through to the end.

"Fifty year," he resumed, after another interval of brooding, "an' not one 'appy day. I was a-thinkin' of it over to myself, and, says I, 'What's the reason on it?' The reason is, 'cos I ain't never 'ad money. Money means 'appiness, an' them as never 'as money, 'll never be 'appy, live as long as they may. Well, I went on a-sayin' to myself, 'Ain't I to 'ave not *one* 'appy day in all my life?' An' it come to me all at once, with a flash like, that money was to be 'ad for the trouble o' takin' it--money an' 'appiness."

The bleared eye rolled with a sort of self-congratulation, and the coins jingled more loudly.

"A pound ain't no use; nor yet two pound; nor yet five pound. An' five pound's what I never 'ad in fifty year. There's a good deal more than five pound 'ere now, Mr. Waymark; I've reckoned it up in my 'cad. What d' you think I'm a-goin' for to do with it?"

He asked this question after a pause, with his head bent forward, his countenance screwed into the most hideous expression of cunning and gratified desire.

"I'm a-goin'," he said, with the emphasis of a hoarse whisper, "I a-goin' to drink myself dead! That's what I'm a-goin' to do, Mr. Waymark. My four friends ain't what they used for to be, an' 'cos I ain't got enough of 'em. It's unsatisfaction, that's what it is, as brings the burnin' i' th' inside, an' the devils in the 'cad. Now I've got money, an' for wunst in my life I'll be satisfied an' 'appy. And then I'll go where there's *real* burnin', an' *real* devils--an' let 'em make the most o' Slimy!"

Waymark felt his blood chill with horror. For years after, the face of Slimy, as it thus glared at him, haunted him in dreamful nights. Dante saw nothing more fearful in any circle of hell.

"Well, I've said my say," Slimy remarked, rising from his seat. "An' now, I'm sorry I'll 'ave to ill-convenience you, Mr. Waymark. You've behaved better to me than most has, and I wouldn't pay you in ill-convenience, if I could help it. But I must have time enough to get off clear. I'll 'ave jist to keep you from 'ollerin'--this way, see--but I won't hurt you; the nose is good enough for breathin'. I'll see as some one comes to let you out before to-morrow mornin'. An' now I'll say good-bye, Mr. Waymark. You won't see Slimy in this world again, an' if I only knowed 'ow to say a prayer, why, I'd pray as you mightn't never see him in the next."

With one more look, a look at once of wild anticipation and friendly regret, Slimy disappeared.

The relief consequent upon the certainty that no worse could happen had brought Waymark into a state of mind in which he could regard his position with equanimity. The loss of the money seemed now to be the most serious result of the affair. Slimy had promised that release should come before the morning, and would doubtless keep his word Waymark had a certain confidence in this, which a less interested person would perhaps have deemed scarcely warrantable. In the meantime, the discomfort was not extreme to lie gagged and bound on a garret-floor for some few hours was, after all, a situation which a philosopher might patiently endure, and to an artist it might well be suggestive of hints. Breathing, to be sure, was not easy, but became more so by degrees.

But with the complete recollection of his faculties came back the thought of what was involved in the question of release before the following day. Early in the morning he had to be at the door of Tothill Fields' Prison. How if his release were delayed, through Slimy's neglect or that of the agent he might employ? As the first hour passed slowly by, this became the chief anxiety in Waymark's mind. It made him forgetful of the aching in his arms, caused by the bind ing together of his hands behind him, and left no room for anticipation of the other sufferings which would result from his being left thus for an indefinite period. What would Ida do, if she came out and found no one to meet her?

His absence would make no one anxious, at all events not till more than a day had gone by. Hitherto he had always taken his rents at once to Mr. Woodstock's office, but the old gentleman was not likely to be disturbed by his non appearance; it would be accounted for in some simple way, and his coming expected on the following morning. Then it was as good as certain that no one would come to Slimy's room. And, by the by, had not there been a sound of the turning of a key when Slimy took his departure? He could not be quite sure of this; just then he had noticed all things so imperfectly. Was it impossible to free a limb, or to ungag his mouth? He tried to turn his head, but it was clear that throttling would be the only result of any such effort; and the bonds on hands and feet were immoveable. No escape, save by Slimy's aid.

He determined not to face the possibility of Slimy's failing in his word; otherwise, anxiety would make him desperate. He recognised now, for the first time fully, how much it meant to him, that meeting with Ida. The shock he had experienced on hearing her sentence and beholding her face as she left the court had not, apparently, produced lasting results; his weakness surprised him when he looked back upon it. In a day or two he had come to regard the event as finally severing him from Ida, and a certain calm ensuing hereupon led to the phase which ultimately brought him to Maud once more. But Waymark's introspection was at fault; he understood himself less in proportion as he felt that the ground was growing firmer under his feet. Even when he wrote the letter to the prison, promising to meet Ida, he had acted as if out of mere humanity. It needed a chance such as the present to open his eyes. That she should quit the prison, and, not finding him, wander away in blank misery and hopelessness, most likely embittered by the thought that he had carelessly neglected to meet her, and so driven to despair--such a possibility was intolerable. The fear of it began to goad him in flesh and spirit. With a sudden violent stringing of all his sinews, he wrenched at the bonds, but only with the effect of exhausting himself and making the walls and ceiling reel before his eyes. The attempt to utter cries resulted in nothing but muffled moaning. Then, mastering himself once more, he resolved to be patient. Slimy would not fail him.

He tried not to think of Ida in any way, but this was beyond his power. Again and again she came before his mind. When he endeavoured to supplant her by the image of Maud Enderby, the latter's face only irritated him. Till now, it had been just the reverse; the thought of Maud had always brought quietness; Ida he had recognised as the disturbing element of his life, and had learned to associate her with his least noble instincts. Thinking of this now, he began to marvel how it could have been so. Was it true that Maud was his good angel, that in her he had found his ideal? He had forced himself to believe this, now that he was in honour bound to her; yet she had never made his pulse quicken, as it had often done when he had approached Ida. True, that warmth of feeling had come to represent merely a temptation to him; but was not that the consequence of his own ambiguous attitude? Suppose he had not known Maud Enderby, how would he then have regarded Ida, and his relations to her? Were these in very deed founded on nothing but selfish feeling? Then he reviewed all his acquaintanceship with her from the first, and every detail of the story grew to a new aspect.

Thinking of Ida, he found himself wondering how it was that Mr. Woodstock appeared to take so much interest in her fate. Several times during the past six months the old man had referred to her, generally inquiring whether Waymark had written to or heard from her. And, only two days ago, he had shown that he remembered the exact date of her release, in asking whether Waymark meant to do anything. Waymark replying that he intended to meet her, and give her what assistance he could, the old gentleman had signified his strong approval, and had even gone on to mention a house in the neighbourhood of the office, where Ida could be lodged at first. A room had accordingly been secured beforehand, and it was arranged that Waymark should take her directly thither on the Tuesday morning. In reviewing all this, Waymark found it more significant than he had imagined. Why, he wondered, had Mr. Woodstock grown so philanthrophic all at once? Why had he been so particular in making sure that Waymark would meet the girl? Indeed, from the very beginning of this affair, he had behaved with regard to it in a manner quite unlike himself. Waymark had leisure now to ponder these things, but could only conjecture explanations.

The hours went by; a church clock kept him aware of their progress. The aching in his arms became severe; he suffered from cold. The floor was swept by a draught which seemed strong and keen as a blast of east wind; it made his eyes smart, and he kept them closed, with some slight hope that this might also have the effect of inducing sleep. Sleep, however, held far aloof from him. When he had wearied his brain with other thoughts, his attention began to turn to sounds in the court below. There, just as it grew dusk, some children were playing, and he tried to get amusement from their games. One of them was this. A little girl would say to the rest:--"I sent my daughter to the oil-shop, and the first thing she saw was C;" and the task was to guess for what article this initial stood. "Carrots!" cried one, but was laughed to scorn. "Candles!" cried another, and triumphed. Then there were games which consisted in the saying of strange incantations. The children would go round and round, as was evident from the sound of their feet, chanting the while:--"Sally, Sally Wallflower, Sprinkle in a pan; Rise, Sally Wallflower, And choose your young man. Choose for the fairest one, Choose for the best, Choose for the rarest one, That you love best!" Upon this followed words and movements only half understood; then at length broke out a sort of hymeneal chorus:--"Here stands a young couple, Just married and settled: Their father and mother they must obey. They love one another like sister and brother. So pray, young couple, come kiss together!" Lastly, laughter and screams and confusion. This went on till it was quite dark.

Pitch dark in Slimy's room; only the faintest reflection on a portion of the ceiling of lamplight from without. Waymark's sufferings became extreme. The rope about his neck seemed to work itself tighter; there were moments when he had to struggle for the scant breath which the gag allowed him. He feared lest he should become insensible, and so perhaps be suffocated. His arms were entirely numbed; he could not feel that he was lying on them. Surely Slimy's emissary would come before midnight.

"One, two, three, four--twelve!" How was it that e had lost all count of the hours since eight o'clock? Whether that had been sleep or insensibility, Waymark could not decide. Intensity of cold must have brought back consciousness; his whole body seemed to be frozen; his eyes ached insufferably. Continuous thought had somehow become an impossibility; he knew that Ida was constantly in his mind, and her image clear at times in the dark before him, but he could not think about her as he wished and tried to do. Who was it that seemed to come between her and him?--some one he knew, yet could not identify. Then the hours sounded uncertainly; some he appeared to have missed. There, at length, was seven. Why, this was morning; and Slimy had promised that he should be set free before this. What was it that tortured his struggling brain so? A thought he strove in vain for a time to grasp. The meaning flashed upon him. By a great effort he regained complete consciousness; mind alone seemed to be left to him, his body was dead. Was he, then, really to be prevented from keeping his promise to Ida? All the suffering of his previous life amassed was nothing to what Waymark endured during the successive quarters of this hour. His brain burned: his eyes had no power to gather the growing daylight. That one name was his single perception; the sound of it, uttered incessantly in thought, alone seemed to keep him conscious. He could feel something slightly warm on his cheeks, but did not know that it was the streaming of tears from his darkened eyes. Then he lost consciousness once more.

The clock struck eight.

CHAPTER XXIX
FREEDOM

Mr. Woodstock was not so indifferent with regard to Waymark's failure to bring the rents as the young man supposed. Under ordinary circumstances he probably would have waited without any anxiety till the following day; already on a previous occasion Waymark had collected on Tuesday instead of Monday, though not without notice of his intention to do so. But Mr. Woodstock had quite special reasons for wishing to see his agent before the following morning; he desired to assure himself once more that Waymark would not fail to be at the prison punctually.

When the afternoon passed without the usual visit, he grew uneasy; he was incapable of attending to matters of business, and walked up and down his office with impatient step. Such a mood was extraordinary in Mr. Woodstock; he had often waxed restive in this or that business difficulty; was, indeed, anything but remarkable for equanimity under trial; but his state of mind was quite different at present, and exhibited itself in entirely different ways. He neither swore nor looked black; his was the anxiety of a man who has some grave interest at stake wherein the better part of his nature is concerned.

At five o'clock he took a cab, and went off to Waymark's lodgings in Chelsea. Here he learned that Waymark had left home at the usual time, and had not yet returned. Just as he was speaking with the landlady at the door, another gentleman came up on the same errand. Mr. Woodstock remembered Julian Casti, and held out his hand to him. Casti looked ill; his handsome features had wasted, and his fair complexion was turned to a dull, unhealthy, yellowish hue. It was a comparatively warm day for the season, but his thin frame was closely muffled up, and still he seemed to be shrinking under the air.

"Have you any idea where he can be?" Mr. Woodstock asked, as they turned away together.

"None whatever. I must see him to-night, though, if possible."

"Ha! And I too."

As he spoke Mr. Woodstock looked at the other keenly, and something seemed to suggest itself to him.

"I'm going to see if he's been for the rents as usual. Would you care to come with me?"

Julian looked surprised, but assented. They got into the cab together, and alighted at the end of Litany Lane, having scarcely spoken on the way. Inquiries here showed that the collector had gone his rounds, and departed, it was said, in the ordinary way.

"Have you an hour to spare, Mr. Casti?" asked the old gentleman, turning suddenly after a moment's reflection.

"Certainly."

"Then I wish you'd just come on with me to St. John's Street Road. It's possible you may have it in your power to do me a great service, if Waymark doesn't turn up. And yet, ten to one, I shall find him waiting for me. Never mind, come along if you can spare the time; you'll find him the sooner."

Mr. Woodstock tried to pooh-pooh his own uneasiness; yet, totally improbable as it seemed that Waymark should disappear at such a juncture, the impatience of the afternoon had worked him into a most unwonted fit of nervousness. Doubts and suspicions which would ordinarily never have occurred to him filled his mind. He was again quite silent till his office was reached.

Waymark had not been. They walked upstairs together, and Mr. Woodstock asked his companion to be seated. He himself stood, and began to poke the fire.

"Do you live in Chelsea still?" he suddenly asked.

"Yes."

"I have left word at Waymark's lodgings that he is to come straight here whenever he returns. If he's not here by midnight, should I find you up if I called--say at half-past twelve or so?"

"I would in any case wait up for you, with pleasure?"

"Really," said Mr. Woodstock, who could behave with much courtesy when he chose, "I must apologise for taking such liberties. Our acquaintance is so slight. And yet I believe you would willingly serve me in the matter in hand. Perhaps you guess what it is. Never mind; I could speak of that when I came to you, if I have to come."

Julian's pale cheek had flushed with a sudden warmth. He looked at the other, and faced steadily the gaze that met his own.

"I am absolutely at your disposal," he said, in a voice which he tried to make firm, though with small success.

"I am obliged to you. And now you will come and have something to eat with me; it is my usual time."

Julian declined, however, and almost immediately took his leave. He walked all the way to Chelsea, regarding nothing that he passed. When he found himself in his lodgings he put a match to the ready-laid fire, and presently made himself some tea. Then he sat idly through the evening, for the most part staring into the glowing coals, occasionally taking up a book for a few minutes, and throwing it aside again with a sigh of weariness. As it got late he shivered so with cold, in spite of the fire, that he had to sit in his overcoat. When it was past midnight he began to pace the room, making impatient gestures, and often resting his head upon his hands as if it ached. It must have been about a quarter to one when there was the sound of a vehicle pulling up in the street below, followed by a knock at the door. Julian went down himself, and admitted Mr. Woodstock.

"What can it mean?" he asked anxiously, when they had walked up to the room together. "What has become of him?"

"Don't know. I stopped at his place on the way here."

"Don't you fear some mischance? With all that money--"

"Pooh! It's some absurd freak of his, I'll warrant. He doesn't care how much anxiety he gives other people."

Mr. Woodstock was excited and angry.

"But he will certainly go--go *there* in the morning, wherever he is," said Julian.

"I'm not so sure of that. I believe it's on that very account that he's keeping out of the way!"

He smote his fist on the palm of the other hand with the emphasis of conviction. Julian looked at him with an expression of wonder. There was a short silence, and then Mr. Woodstock began to speak more calmly. The conversation lasted only about a quarter of an hour. Mr. Woodstock then returned to his cab, which had waited, and Julian bade him good night at the door.

At six o'clock Julian arose. It was still quite dark when he left the house, and the air was piercing. But he did not mind the weather this morning. His step had a vigour very different from the trailing weariness of the night before, and he looked straight before him as he walked. There was a heat on his forehead which the raw breath of the morning could not allay. Before he had gone half a mile, he flung open his overcoat, as if it oppressed him. It was in the direction of Westminster that he walked. Out of Victoria Street he took the same turn as on one miserable night, one which he had taken on many a night since then. But he was far too early at the prison gate. He strayed about the little streets of the neighbourhood, his eyes gazing absently in this or that direction, his hot breath steaming up in the grey light. When it was drawing near the time, he made some inquiries from a policeman whom he passed. Then he went to the spot whither he was directed, and watched. Two or three people, of poor appearance, were also standing about, waiting. Julian kept apart from them. First, a miserable old woman, huddling herself in a dirty shawl; looking on all sides with a greedy eye; hastening off no one knew whither. Then two young girls, laughing aloud at their recovered liberty; they repaired at once to the nearest public-house. Then a figure of quite different appearance, coming quickly forward, hesitating, gazing around; a beautiful face, calm with too great self-control, sad, pale. Towards her Julian advanced.

"Mr. Waymark was unavoidably prevented from coming," he said quickly. "But he has taken rooms for you. You will let me go with you, and show you the house?"

"Thank you," was Ida's only reply.

They walked together into the main street, and Julian stopped the first empty cab that passed. As he sat opposite to her, his eyes, in spite of himself, kept straying to her face. Gazing at her, Casti's eyes grew dim. He forced himself not to look at her again till the cab stopped.

"They are prepared for you here," he said, as they stood on the pavement. "Just give your name. And--you will not go away? You will wait till some one calls?"

Ida nodded.

"No; but your word," Julian urged anxiously. "Promise me."

"I promise."

She went up to the door and knocked. Julian walked quickly away. At the end of the street Mr. Woodstock was waiting.

"What's the matter?" he asked, examining the young man anxiously.

"Nothing--nothing!"

"Does she seem well?"

"I think so; yes," Casti replied, in a stifled voice. Then he asked hurriedly, "Where can Waymark be? What does it all mean?"

Mr. Woodstock shook his head, looking annoyed.

"I am convinced," Julian said, "that something is wrong. Surely it's time to make inquiries."

"Yes, yes; I will do so. But you look downright ill. Do you feel able to get home? If I'd thought it would upset you like this--"

Mr. Woodstock was puzzled, and kept scrutinising the other's face.

"I shall go home and have a little rest," Julian said. "I didn't get much sleep last night, that's all. But I must hear about Waymark."

"You shall. I'll warrant he turns up in the course of the day. Don't be anxious: I'll get to work as soon as possible to find him; but, depend upon it, the fellow's all right."

They shook hands, and Julian took his way homewards. Mr. Woodstock went to the house which Ida had just entered. He knocked lightly, and a woman opened to him and led him into a sitting-room on the ground-floor.

"I'll just have a cup of coffee, Mrs. Sims," he said. "Does she seem to care for her breakfast?"

"I'm afraid not, sir; she looks tired out, and poorly like."

"Yes, yes; the long journey and her troubles. Make her as comfortable as you can. I'll make myself at home with the paper here for an hour or so. Just see if she cares to lie down for a little; If so I won't disturb her."

Abraham did not devote much attention to the news. He sat before the fire, a cup of coffee within reach on the mantel piece, his legs fully stretched out before him, his favourite attitude when thinking. In spite of his fresh complexion and active limbs, you would have seen, had you watched him in his present mood, that Mr. Woodstock was beginning to age. Outwardly he was well-preserved--few men of his years anything like so well. But let the inner man become visible during a fit of brooding, and his features made evident the progress of years. His present phase of countenance was a recent development; the relaxed lines brought to light a human kindliness not easily discoverable in the set expression of wide-awake hours. At present there was even tenderness in his eyes, and something of sad recollection. His strong mouth twitched a little at times, and his brows contracted, as if in self-reproach. When he returned to himself, it was with a sigh. He sat for about an hour; then the woman presented herself again, and told him that Miss Starr had been persuaded to lie down. It seemed likely she might sleep.

"Very well," said Mr. Woodstock, rising. "I'll go to the office. Send some one round when she's stirring, will you?"

Ida, to get rid of her troublesome though well-meaning attendant, had promised to lie down, but she had no need of sleep. Alone, she still kept her chair by the fire, sitting like one worn out with fatigue, her hands upon her lap, her head drooping, her eyes fixed on vacancy. She was trying to think, but thoughts refused to come consecutively, and a dull annoyance at this inability to reason upon her position fretted her consciousness. Not with impunity can the human mind surrender itself for half a year to unvaried brooding upon one vast misery; the neglected faculties revenge themselves by rusting, and will not respond when at length summoned. For months Ida's thoughts had gone round and round about one centre of anguish, like a wailing bird circling over a ravaged nest. The image of her mental state had been presented by an outward experience with which she became familiar. Waking long before daylight, she would lie with her eyes directed to the little barred window, and watch till there came the first glimmer of dawn. Even so was it her sole relief in the deep night of her misery to look forward for that narrow gleam of hope--her ultimate release. As the day approached, she made it the business of her thoughts to construct a picture of the events it would bring. Even before hearing from Waymark, she had been sure that he would meet her; Waymark and freedom grew identical images; to be free meant to see him awaiting her and to put herself absolutely in his hands. Now that everything had turned out differently from what she had grown to anticipate with certainty, she found herself powerless to face the unexpected. Why had Waymark failed her?--she could do no more than repeat the question a thousand times, till the faculty of self-communing forsook her. It was as though the sun should fail one morning to rise upon the world, and men should stand hopeless of day for ever.

She wondered vaguely whither she had been brought. At one moment she seemed to have been waiting an eternity in this unknown room, Julian's face and voice unspeakably remote; then again she would look round and wonder that she no longer saw the hare walls and barred window of her cell, the present seeming only a dream. All the processes of her mind were slow, sinewless. She tried to hope for something, to expect that something would happen, but could not summon the energy. Resentment, revolt, bitterness of spirit, of these things she knew just as little. They had been strong enough within her at first, but how long ago that seemed! She had no thought of time in the present; to sit waiting for an hour meant as little as to wait five minutes; such was the habit that had become impressed upon her by interminable days and nights. When at length she heard a knock at the door it filled her with fear; she started to her feet and looked with unintelligent eyes at the woman who again presented herself.

"Do you feel better, 'm?" the landlady asked. "Have you rested yourself?"

"Yes, thank you."

The woman went away; then came another knock, and Mr. Woodstock entered the room. He closed the door behind him, and drew near. She had again started up, and did not move her eyes from his face.

"Have you any recollection of me?" Abraham asked, much embarrassed in her presence, his voice failing to be as gentle as he wished through his difficulty in commanding it.

Ida had recognised him at once. He had undergone no change since that day when she saw him last in Milton Street, and at this moment it was much easier for her to concentrate her thoughts upon bygone things than to realise the present.

"You are Abraham Woodstock," she said very coldly, the resentment associated with the thought of him being yet stronger than the dead habit which had but now oppressed her.

"Yes, I am. And I am a friend of Osmond Waymark. I should like to talk a little with you, if you'll let me."

The old man found it so hard to give expression to the feelings that possessed him. Ida concluded at once that he came with some hostile purpose, and the name of Waymark was an incentive to her numbed faculties.

"How can you be a friend of Osmond Waymark?" she asked, with cold suspicion.

"Didn't he ever mention my name to you?"

"Never."

Waymark had in truth always kept silence with Ida about his occupations, though he had spoken so freely of them to Maud. He could not easily have explained to himself why he had made this difference, though it had a significance. Mr. Woodstock was almost at a loss how to proceed. He coughed, and moved his foot uneasily.

"I have known him all his life, for all that," he said. "And it was through him I found you."

"Found me?"

"It'll seem very strange, what I have to tell you.--You were a little girl when I saw you last, and you refused to come with me. Had you any idea why I asked you?"

"I hadn't then."

"But you have thought of it since?"

Ida looked at him sternly, and turned her eyes away again. The belief that he was her father had always increased the resentment with which she recalled his face.

"I am your grandfather," Abraham said gravely. "Your mother was my daughter."

A change came over her countenance; she gazed at him with wonder.

"Who did you think I was?" he asked.

She hesitated for a moment, then, instead of replying, said:

"You behaved cruelly to my poor mother."

"I won't deny it," the old man returned, mastering his voice with difficulty. "I ought to have been more patient with her. But she refused to obey me, and I can't help my nature. I repented it when it was too late."

Ida could not know what it cost him to utter these abrupt sentences. He seemed harsh, even in confining his harshness. She was as far from him as ever.

"I can't do anything for *her*," Mr. Woodstock continued, trying to look her in the face. "But you are her child, and I want to do now what I ought to have done long ago. I've come here to ask you if you'll live in my house, and be like a child of my own."

"I don't feel to you as a child ought," Ida said, her voice changing to sadness. "You've left it too late."

"No, it isn't too late!" exclaimed the other, with emotion he could not control. "You mustn't think of yourself, but of me. You have all your life before you, but I'm drawing near to the end of mine. There's no one in the world belonging to me but you. I have a *right* to--"

"No right! no right!" Ida interrupted him almost passionately.

"Then *you* have a duty," said Abraham, with lowered voice. "My mind isn't at ease, and it's in your power to help me. Don't imitate me, and put off doing good till it is too late. I don't ask you to feel kindly to me; all I want is that you'll let me take you to my home and do all I can for you, both now and after I'm gone."

There was pathos in the speech, and Ida felt it.

"Do you know where I came from this morning?" she asked, when both had been silent for some moments.

"I know all about it. I was at the trial, and I did my best for you then."

"Do you believe that I robbed that woman?" Ida asked, leaning forward with eager eyes and quickened breath.

"Believe it! Not I! No one believes it who knows anything about her. Waymark said he wouldn't have believed it if all the courts in England found you guilty."

"*He* said that?" she exclaimed. Then, as if suddenly becoming clearer about her position: "Where is Mr. Waymark? Why didn't he meet me as he promised?"

Abraham hesitated, but speedily made up his mind that it would be best to speak the truth.

"I know as little as you do. He ought to have come to me yesterday, but he didn't, and I can't discover him. I got Mr. Casti to meet you instead."

The keenest trouble manifested itself on Ida's countenance. She asked questions in rapid succession, and thus elicited an explanation of all the circumstances hitherto unknown to her.

"Have you been through the houses?" she inquired, all her native energy restored by apprehension. "Haven't you thought that he may have been robbed and--"

She stopped, overcome by sudden weakness, and sank into the chair.

"Come, come, it isn't so bad as all that," said the old man, observing her closely. "He may turn up at any moment; all sorts of unexpected things may have happened. But I'll go again to his lodgings, and if I can't hear anything there, I'll set the police to work. Will you promise me to wait here quietly?"

"No, that I can't do. I want to move about; I must do something. Let me go with you to look for him."

"No, no; that'll never do, Ida."

The power of speaking tenderly seemed to have been given to him all at once; this and his calling her "Ida," struck so upon the girl's agitated feelings that she began to sob.

"Let me, let me go with you! I will forget everything--I will be your child--I will try to love you.--"

She was as weak as water, and would have sunk to the ground if Abraham had not given her his support just in time. He could not find words to soothe her, but passed his hand very tenderly over her head.

"We are losing time!" she exclaimed, forcing herself into an appearance of calmness. "Come at once."

CHAPTER XXX
ELM COURT

In Beaufort Street they only learnt that Waymark had not yet been home. Thence they drove to the east, and stopped at a police-station, where Abraham saw the inspector. The latter suggested that Mr. Woodstock should go through all the houses which Waymark would have visited; if that search proved fruitless, the police would pursue the matter. Ida insisted on being allowed to accompanying him when the cab stopped at the end of Litany Lane. She gazed about her like one who had been suddenly set down in a new country; this squalor and vileness, so familiar to her of old, affected her strangely under the present conditions. The faces of people at whom she looked remained fresh in her memory for years after; the long confinement and the excitement which now possessed her resulted in preternatural acuteness of observation. Abraham spoke first with several people whom he had already questioned about Waymark, but they had heard nothing since.

"Are you strong enough for this?" he asked Ida. "Hadn't you better go back to the cab and wait for me!"

"Don't ask me to do that!" she entreated earnestly. "I *must* be active. I have strength now for anything."

Just as she spoke, Mr. Woodstock became aware of a disturbance of some kind in a duty little tobacconist's shop close at hand. There was a small crowd at the door, and the sound of wrangling voices came from within. Such an occurrence was too ordinary to suggest any special significance, but Abraham would not pass without making some inquiry. Begging Ida to stand where he left her, he pushed his way into the shop and listened to what was going on. A lad, well known in these parts as "Lushy Dick," was, it appeared, charging the tobacconist with cheating him; he alleged that he had deposited half a sovereign on the counter in payment for a cigar, and the shopman had given him change as if for sixpence, maintaining stoutly that sixpence had been the coin given him, and no half-sovereign at all. When Mr. Woodstock entered, the quarrel had reached a high pitch.

"Arf a quid!" the tobacconist was exclaiming contemptuously. "I'd like to know where such as you's likely to git arf a quid from."

Lushy Dick, stung to recklessness by a succession of such remarks, broke out in vehement self-justification.

" **Would** yer like to know, y' old ----! Then yer shall, ---- soon! I'm ---- if I don't tell jist the ---- truth, an' take the ---- consequences. It was Slimy as give it me, an' if yer want to know where Slimy got it, yer 'll 'ave to ---- well find out, 'cos I don't know myself."

"And how came Slimy to give you half a sovereign?" Mr. Woodstock at once interposed, speaking with authority.

"Is that you, Mr. Woodstock?" exclaimed the boy, turning round suddenly at the sound of the voice. "Now, look 'ere, I'm a-goin' to make a ---- clean breast of it. This 'ere ---- bloke's been a ringin' the changes on me; I'll show him up, an' ---- well chance it. Slimy give me a quid afore he took his ---- hook."

The lad had clearly been drinking, but had not yet reached the incoherent stage. He spoke in great excitement, repeating constantly his determination to be revenged upon the tobacconist at all costs. It was with difficulty that Mr. Woodstock kept him to the point.

"Why Slimy give it me? Well, I'll jist tell yer, Mr. Woodstock. It was to do a job for him, which I never done it after all. Slimy told me as 'ow I was to go to your orffice at ten o'clock last night, 'an tell you from him as he'd no more 'casion for his room, so he'd sent yer the key, an' yer'd better come as soon as possible an' see as he'd left everything square behind him, an' 'cos he was afraid he'd locked in a friend o' yourn by mistake an' in his hurry."

"And why the devil didn't you come?" exclaimed Abraham, looking at him in angry surprise.

"'Cos why, Mr. Woodstock? Well, I'll tell yer just the bloomin' truth, an' charnce it. I loss the key out o' my pocket, through 'avin' a ---- hole in it, so I thought as 'ow I'd best just say nothink about neither Slimy nor his room, an' there y'ave it!"

Abraham was out of the shop again on the instant.

"I've found him," he said to Ida. "A house round there in the court."

She walked quickly by his side, a cluster of people following them. Fortunately, a policeman was just coming from the opposite end of Litany Lane, and Mr. Woodstock secured his services to keep the mob from entering the house where Slimy had lived. As soon as they got inside, the old man begged Ida to remain in a room on the ground floor whilst he went upstairs, and this she consented to do. Reaching the garret, he tried the handle of the door, without effect. Knocking and calling produced no response, and within all was perfectly quiet. Hesitating no longer, he drew back as far as the wall would allow him, and ran with his foot against the door. The rotten woodwork cracked, and a second onset forced the lock away. In the middle of the floor Waymark lay, just as Slimy had left him nearly twenty-four hours ago. Abraham scarcely ventured to draw near; there was no motion in the fettered body, and he dreaded to look closely at the face. Before he could overcome this momentary fear, there was a quick step behind him, and, with a smothered cry, Ida had rushed into the room. She was on her knees beside Waymark, her face close down to his.

"He is alive!" she cried. "His eyes have opened. A knife! Cut these cords!"

That was soon accomplished, but Waymark lay motionless; he showed that he understood what was going on, but he was quite blind, his voice had all but gone, and a dead man could as soon have risen. Ida still knelt by him, chafing one of his hands; when he tried to speak, she gently raised his head and let it rest upon her lap. In a few minutes Abraham had procured a glass of spirits, and, after drinking this, Waymark was able to make himself understood.

"Who is touching me?" he asked in a hoarse whisper. "It is all dark. Whose hand is this?"

"It's Ida," Abraham said, when she herself remained silent. "She and I have had a rare hunt for you."

"Ida?"

He endeavoured to raise himself, but in vain. All he could do was to press her hand to his heart. In the meantime the policeman had come up, and with his help Waymark was carried downstairs, out into the court, and thence to the end of Litany Lane, where the cab still waited.

*   *   *   *   *

Four days after this the following paragraph appeared in the morning papers:--

"The man wanted on a charge of robbery with violence in the East End, and who appears to be known only by the nickname of Slimy, was yesterday afternoon discovered by the police in a cellar in Limehouse. He seems to have been in hiding there since the perpetration of the crime, only going out from time to time to purchase liquor at public-houses in the neighbourhood. Information given by the landlord of one of these houses led to his arrest. He was found lying on the stone floor, with empty bottles about him, also a quantity of gold and silver coins, which appeared to have rolled out of his pocket. He was carried to the police-station in an insensible state, but on being taken to the cell, came to himself, and exhibited symptoms of delirium tremens. Two officers remained with him, but the assistance of a third shortly became necessary, owing to the violence of his struggles. Towards midnight his fury lessened, and, after a very brief interval of unconsciousness, the wretched creature expired."

CHAPTER XXXI
NEW PROSPECTS

Mr. Woodstock's house at Tottenham was a cheerful abode when the months of early summer came round, and there was thick leafage within the shelter of the old brick wall which shut it off from the road.

For the first time in his life he understood the attractions of domesticity. During the early months of the year, slippers and the fireside after dinner; now that the sunset-time was growing warm and fragrant, a musing saunter about the garden walks; these were the things to which his imagination grew fond of turning. Nor to these only; blended with such visions of bodily comfort, perchance lending to them their chief attraction, was the light of a young face, grave always, often sad, speaking with its beautiful eyes to those simpler and tenderer instincts of his nature which had hitherto slept. In the presence of Ida (who was now known, by his wish, as Miss Woodstock) Abraham's hard voice found for itself a more modest and musical key.

He began--novel sensation--to look upon himself as a respectable old gentleman; the grey patches on his head were grateful to him from that point of view. If only he had been able to gather round his granddaughter and himself a circle of equally respectable friends and acquaintances, he would have enjoyed complete satisfaction. Two or three at most there were, whom he could venture to bring over with him from the old life to the new. For Ida he could as yet provide no companionship at all.

But Ida did not feel the want. Since the day of her coming to the new house her life had been very full; so much was passing within, that she desired to escape, rather than discover, new distractions in the world around her. For the week or so during which Waymark had lain ill, her courage had triumphed over the sufferings to which she was herself a prey; the beginning of his recovery brought about a reaction in her state, and for some days she fell into a depressed feebleness almost as extreme as on the first morning of her freedom. It distressed her to be spoken to, and her own lips were all but mute. Mr. Woodstock sometimes sat by her whilst she slept, or seemed to be sleeping; when she stirred and showed consciousness of his presence, he left her, so great was his fear of annoying her, and thus losing the ground he had gained. Once, when he was rising to quit the room, Ida held out her hand as if to stay him. She was lying on a sofa, and had enjoyed a very quiet sleep.

"Grandfather," she murmured, turning to face him. It was the first time she had addressed him thus, and the old man's eyes brightened at the sound.

"Are you better for the sleep, Ida?" he asked, taking the hand she had extended.

"Much; much better. How the sun shines!"

"Yes, it's a fine day. Don't you think you could go out a little?"

"I think I should like to, but I can't walk very far, I'm afraid."

"You needn't walk at all, my dear. Your carriage shall be here whenever you like to order it."

"My carriage?"

The exclamation was like a child's pleased wonder. She coloured a little, and seemed ashamed.

"How is Mr. Waymark?" was her next question.

"Nothing much amiss now, I think. His eyes are painful, he says, and he mustn't leave the room yet, but it won't last much longer. Shall we go together and see him?"

She hesitated, but decided to wait till he could come down.

"But you'll go out, Ida, if I order the carriage?"

"Thank you, I should like to."

That first drive had been to Ida a joy unspeakable. To-day for the first time she was able to sweep her mind clear of the dread shadow of brooding, and give herself up to simple enjoyment of the hour.

Abraham went and told Waymark of all this as soon as they got back. In the exuberance of his spirits he was half angry with the invalid for being gloomy. Waymark had by this time shaken off all effects of his disagreeable adventure, with the exception of a weakness of the eyes; but convalescence did not work upon him as in Ida's case. He was morose, often apparently sunk in hopeless wretchedness. When Abraham spoke to him of Ida, he could scarcely be got to reply. Above all, he showed an extreme impatience to recover his health and go back to the ordinary life.

"I shall be able to go for the rents next Monday," he said to Mr. Woodstock one day.

"I should have thought you'd had enough of that. I've found another man for the job."

"Then what on earth am I to do?" Waymark exclaimed impatiently. "How am I to get my living if you take that work away from me?"

"Never mind; we'll find something," Abraham returned. "Why are you in such a hurry to get away, I should like to know?"

"Simply because I can't always live here, and I hate uncertainty."

There was something in the young man's behaviour which puzzled Mr. Woodstock; but the key to the puzzle was very shortly given him. On the evening of the same day he presented himself once more in Waymark's room. The latter could not see him, but the first sound of his voice was a warning of trouble.

"Do you feel able to talk?" Abraham asked, rather gruffly.

"Yes. Why?"

"Because I want to ask you a few questions. I've just had a call from that friend of yours, Mr. Enderby, and something came out in talk that I wasn't exactly prepared for."

Waymark rose from his chair.

"Why didn't you tell me," pursued Mr. Woodstock, "that you were engaged to his daughter?"

"I scarcely thought it necessary."

"Not when I told you who Ida was?"

This disclosure had been made whilst Waymark was still confined to his bed; partly because Abraham had a difficulty in keeping the matter to himself; partly because he thought it might help the other through his illness. Waymark had said very little at the time, and there had been no conversation on the matter between them since.

"I don't see that it made any difference," Waymark replied gloomily.

The old man was silent. He had been, it seemed, under a complete delusion, and could not immediately make up his mind whether he had indeed ground of complaint against Waymark.

"Why did Mr. Enderby call?" the latter inquired.

"Very naturally, it seems to me, to know what had become of you. He didn't see the report in the paper, and went searching for you."

"Does Ida know of this?" he asked, after a pause, during which Waymark had remained standing with his arms crossed on the back of the chair.

"I have never told her. Why should I have done? Perhaps now you will believe what I insisted upon before the trial, that there had been nothing whatever--"

He spoke irritably, and was interrupted by the other with yet more irritation.

"Never mention that again to me as long as you live, Waymark If you do, we shall quarrel, understand!"

"I have no more pleasure in referring to it than you have," said Waymark, more calmly; "but I must justify myself when you attack me."

"How long has this been going on?" asked the other, after a silence.

"Some three months--perhaps more."

"Well, I think it would have been better if you'd been straightforward about it, that's all. I don't know that I've anything more to say. We know what we're about, and there's an end of it."

So saying, the old man went out of the room. There was a difference in him henceforth, something which Ida noticed, though she could not explain it. On the following day he spoke with her on a matter she was surprised to hear him mention, her education. He had been thinking, he said, that she ought to learn to play the piano, and be taught foreign languages. Wouldn't she like him to find some lady who could live in the house and teach her all these things? Ida's thoughts at once ran to the conclusion that this had been suggested by Waymark, and, when she found that her grandfather really wished it, gave a ready assent. A week or two later the suitable person had been discovered--a lady of some thirty years of age, by name Miss Hurst. She was agreeable and refined, endowed, moreover, with the tact which was desirable in one undertaking an office such as this. Ida found her companionship pleasant, and Mr. Woodstock con gratulated himself on having taken the right step.

At the same time that the governess came to the house, Waymark left it. He returned to his old lodgings, and, with an independence which was partly his own impulse, partly the natural result of the slight coolness towards him which had shown itself in Mr. Woodstock, set to work to find a means of earning his living. This he was fortunate enough to discover without any great delay; he obtained a place as assistant in a circulating library. The payment was small, but he still had his evenings free.

Ida did not conceal her disappointment when Abraham conveyed this news to her; she had been hoping for better things. Her intercourse with Waymark between his recovery and his leaving the house had been difficult, full of evident constraint on both sides. It was the desire of both not to meet alone, and in Mr. Woodstock's presence they talked of indifferent things, with an artificiality which it was difficult to support, yet impossible to abandon. They shunned each other's eyes. Waymark was even less at his ease than Ida, knowing that Mr. Woodstock observed him closely at all times. With her grandfather Ida tried to speak freely of their friend, but she too was troubled by the consciousness that the old man did not seem as friendly to Waymark as formerly.

"This will of course only be for a time?" she said, when told of Waymark's new employment.

"I don't know," Abraham replied indifferently. "I should think it will suit him as well as anything else."

"But he is clever; he writes books. Don't you think he will make himself known some day?"

"That kind of thing isn't much to be depended on, it seems to me. It's a doubtful business to look forward to for a living."

Ida kept silence on the subject after that. She did not seem to brood any longer over sad thoughts, yet it was seldom she behaved or spoke light-heartedly; her face often indicated an absent mind, but it was the calm musing of one whose thoughts look to the future and strengthen themselves with hope. Times there were when she drew away into solitude, and these were the intervals of doubt and self-questioning. With her grandfather she was reconciled; she had become convinced of his kindness to her, and the far-off past was now seldom in her mind. The trouble originated in the deepest workings of her nature. When she found herself comparing her position now with that of former days, it excited in her a restive mood to think that chance alone had thus raised her out of misery, that the conscious strength and purity of her soul would never have availed to help her to the things which were now within her grasp. The old sense of the world's injustice excited anger and revolt in her heart. Chance, chance alone befriended her, and the reflection injured her pride. What of those numberless struggling creatures to whom such happy fortune could never come, who, be their aspirations and capabilities what they might, must struggle vainly, agonise, and in the end despair? She had been lifted out of hell, not risen therefrom by her own strength. Sometimes it half seemed to her that it would have been the nobler lot to remain as she was, to share the misery of that dread realm of darkness with those poor disinherited ones, to cherish that spirit of noble rebellion, the consciousness of which had been as a pure fire on the altar of her being. What was to be her future? Would she insensibly forget her past self, let her strength subside in refinement--it might be, even lose the passion which had made her what she was?

But hope predominated. Forget! Could she ever forget those faces in the slums on the day when she bade farewell to poverty and all its attendant wretchedness? Litany Lane and Elm Court were names which already symbolised a purpose. If ever she still looked at her grandfather with a remnant of distrust, it was because she thought of him as drawing money from such a source, enjoying his life of ease in disregard of the responsibilities laid upon him. The day would come when she could find courage to speak to him. She waited and prepared herself.

Prepared herself, for that, and for so much else. Waymark's behaviour would have cost her the bitterest misery, had she not been able to explain it to her own satisfaction. There could be but one reason why he held aloof from her, and that an all-sufficient one. In her new position, it was impossible for him to be more than just friendly to her. If that had been his attitude in the old days, how could his self-respect allow him to show the slightest change? In his anxiety not to do so, he had even fallen short of the former kindness. No forgiveness was needed, when she felt that she understood him so well. But all the more did it behove her to make herself worthy of him in all things. She had still so much to learn; she was so far his inferior in culture and understanding. Her studies with Miss Hurst were fruitful. Nor were her domestic duties forgotten. Mr. Woodstock had supplied her with a good housekeeper, to help her inexperience, but Ida took an adequate burden on her own shoulders. This again was a new and keen joy.

Waymark dined with them one Sunday in June, and, in the course of the evening, went with Abraham to the smoking-room for some private conversation.

"Do you remember," he began, "once offering to buy those shares of mine?"

"Yes, I do," replied Mr. Woodstock, narrowing his eyes.

"Does the offer still hold good?"

"Yes, yes; if you're anxious to realise."

"I am. I want money--for two purposes."

"What are they?" Abraham asked bluntly.

"One is a private matter, which I don't think I need speak of; but the other I can explain. I have found a courageous publisher who has offered to bring my book out if I take a certain risk. This I have made up my mind to do. I want to get the thing out, if only for the sake of hearing Mrs. Grundy lift up her voice; and if it can't be otherwise, I must publish at my own expense."

"Will it repay you?" Mr. Woodstock asked.

"Ultimately, I have no doubt; but I don't care so much about that."

"H'm. I should think that's the chief matter to be considered. And you won't tell me what the other speculation is?"

"I'm going to lend a friend some money, but I don't wish to go into detail."

The old man looked at him shrewdly.

"Very well," he said presently. "I'll let you have the cash. Could you manage to look in at the office to-morrow at mid-day?"

This was arranged, and Waymark rose, but Mr. Woodstock motioned to him to resume his seat.

"As we're talking," he began, "I may as well have over something that's on my mind. Why haven't you told Ida yet about that engagement of yours?"

"Haven't *you* done so?" Waymark asked, in surprise.

"Did you think I had?"

"Why, yes, I did."

"I've done nothing of the kind," Abraham returned, pretending to be surprised at the supposition, though he knew it was a perfectly natural one.

Waymark was silent.

"Don't you think," the other pursued, "it's about time something was said to her?"

"I can't see that it matters, and--"

"But I *can* see. As long as that isn't known you're here, to speak plainly, on false pretences."

"Then I won't come here at all!"

"Very good," exclaimed the old man irritably, "so long as you explain to her first."

Waymark turned away, and stood gazing gloomily at the floor. Abraham regarded him, and a change came over his hard face.

"Now, look here," he said, "there's something in all this I can't make out. Is this engagement a serious one?"

"Serious?" returned the other, with a look of misery. "How can it be otherwise?"

"Very well; in that case you're bound to let Ida know about it, and at once. Damn it all, don't you know your own mind?"

Waymark collected himself, and spoke gravely.

"I, of course, understand why you press so for this explanation. You take it for granted that Ida regards me as something more than a friend. If so, my manner since she has been here must have clearly shown her that, on my side, I have not the least thought of offering more than friendship. You yourself will grant so much,

I believe. For all that, I don't deny that our relations have always been unusual; and it would cost me very much to tell her of my engagement. I ask you to relieve me of the painful task, on the understanding that I never come here again. I can't make you understand my position. You say my behaviour has not been straightforward. In the ordinary sense of the word it has not;--there let it rest. Tell Ida what you will of me, and let me disappear from her world."

"The plain English of all which," cried Abraham angrily, "is, that, as far as you are concerned, you would be quite willing to let the girl live on false hopes, just to have the pleasure of her society as long as you care for it."

"Not so, not so at all! I value Ida's friendship as I value that of no other woman, and I am persuaded that, if I were free with her, I could reconcile her entirely to our connection remaining one of friendship, and nothing more."

Waymark, in his desperate straits, all but persuaded himself that he told the truth. Mr. Woodstock gazed at him in doubt. He would give him to the end of July to make up his mind; by that time Waymark must either present himself as a free man, or allow Ida to be informed of his position. In the meanwhile he must come to Tottenham not oftener than once a week. To this Waymark agreed, glad of any respite.

He returned to his lodgings in a state of nervous misery. Fortunately, he was not left to his thoughts; in a few minutes a knock at his door announced a visitor in the person of Mr. O'Gree. The Irishman exhibited his wonted liveliness, and at once began to relate an incident to the disadvantage of his archenemy.

"Faith," he cried, "I'd have given a trifle if ye could have heard the conversation between Tootle and me, just after breakfast yesterday. The boys were filing out of the room, when, 'Mr. O'Gree!' cries Pendy.--'Sir!' I reply.--'The boys were called late this morning, I hear.'--'No such thing, sir,' I assure 'um. 'Half-past six to the minute, by my watch.'--'Oh, *your* watch, Mr. O'Gree,' cries the old reprobate. 'I fear your watch doesn't keep very good time.'--'Sure, you're in the right, sir,' said I;' it's been losing a little of late; so only last night I stopped it at half-past six, to make sure it would show me the right calling-time this morning.' And, when I'd said that, I just nod my head, as much as to say, 'There's one for ye, me boy!' and walk off as jaunty as a Limerick bantam."

Then, after a burst of merriment, O'Gree suddenly fixed his face in a very grave expression.

"I'm resolved, Waymark, I'm resolved!" he exclaimed. "At midsummer I break my chains, and stand erect in the dignity of a free man. I've said it often, but now I mean it. Sally urges me to do ut, and Sally never utters a worrud that isn't pure wisdom."

"Well, I think she's right. I myself should prefer a scavenger's existence, on the whole. But have you thought any further of the other scheme?"

"The commercial undertaking? We were talking it over the other night. Sally says: Borrow the money and risk ut. And I think she's in the right. If you enter the world of commerce, you must be prepared for speculation. We looked over the advertisements in a newspaper, just to get an idea, and we calculated the concern could be set afloat for seventy-five pounds. Out of that we could pay a quarter's rent, and stock the shop. Sally's been behind the counter a good bit of late, and she's getting an insight into that kind of thing. Wonderful girl, Sally! Put her in Downing Street for a week, and she'd be competent to supplant the Premier!"

"You have decided for a chandler's?"

"Yes; we neither of us know much about tobacco, and tobacco perhaps isn't quits the thing for a man of education. But to be a chandler is something worthy of any man's ambition. You supply at once the solids and the luxuries of life; you range from boiled ham and pickles to mixed biscuits and preserves. You are the focus of a whole street. The father comes to you for his mid-day bread and cheese, the mother for her half-ounce of tea, the child for its farthing's-worth of sweets. For years I've been leading a useless life; once let me get into my shop, and I become a column of the social system. Faith, it's as good as done!"

"From whom shall you borrow the cash?"

"Sally's going to think about that point. I suppose we shall go to a loan office, and make some kind of arrangement. I'm rather vague on these things, but Sally will find it out."

"I understand," said Waymark, checking his amusement, that you are perfectly serious in this plan?"

"As serious as I was in the moment of my birth! There's no other chance."

"Very well, then, suppose I offer to lend you the money."

"You, Waymark?"

"No less a person."

And he went on to explain how it was that he was able to make the offer, adding that any sum up to a hundred pounds was at his friend's disposal.

"Ye mean it, Waymark!" cried O'Gree, leaping round the room in ecstasy. "Bedad, you are a man and a brother, and no mistake! Ye're the first that ever offered to lend me a penny; ye're the first that ever had faith in me! You shall come with me to see Sally on Saturday, and tell her this yourself, and I shouldn't be surprised if she gives you a kiss!"

O'Gree exhausted himself in capering and vociferation, then sat down and began to exercise his luxuriant imagination in picturing unheard-of prosperity.

"We'll take a shop in a new neighbourhood, where we shall have the monopoly. The people 'll get to know Sally; she'll be like a magnet behind the counter. I shall go to the wholesale houses, and impress them with a sense of my financial stability; I flatter myself I shall look the prosperous shopkeeper, eh? Who knows what we may come to? Why, in a few years we may transfer our business to Oxford Street or Piccadilly, and call ourselves Italian warehousemen; and bedad, we'll turn out in the end another Crosse and Blackwell, see if we don't!"

At the utmost limit of the time allowed him by the rules of The Academy, the future man of business took his leave, in spirits extravagant even for him.

"Faith," he exclaimed, when he was already at the door, "who d'ye think I saw last Sunday? As I was free in the afternoon, I took a walk, and, coming back, I went into a little coffee-shop for a cup of tea. A man in an apron came up to serve me, and, by me soul, if it wasn't poor old Egger! I've heard not a word of him since he left last Christmas. He was ashamed of himself, poor devil; but I did my best to make him easy. After all, he's better off than in the scholastic line."

Waymark laughed at this incident, and stood watching O'Gree's progress down the street for a minute or two. Then he went to his room again, and sitting down with a sigh, fell into deep brooding.

CHAPTER XXXII
A VISION OF SIN

Maud Enderby's life at home became ever more solitary. Such daily intercourse as had been established between her mother and herself grew less and less fruitful of real intimacy, till at length it was felt by both to be mere form. Maud strove against this, but there was no corresponding effort on the other side; Mrs. Enderby showed no dislike for her daughter, yet unmistakably shunned her. If she chanced to enter the sitting-room whilst Maud was there, she would, if possible, retreat unobserved; or else she would feign to have come in quest of something, and at once go away with it. Maud could not fail to observe this, and its recurrence struck a chill to her heart. She had not the courage to speak to her mother; a deadweight of trouble, a restless spirit of apprehension, made her life one of passive endurance; she feared to have the unnatural conditions of their home openly recognised. Very often her thoughts turned to the time when she had found refuge from herself in the daily occupation of teaching, and, had she dared, she would gladly have gone away once more as a governess. But she could not bring herself to propose such a step. To do so would necessitate explanations, and that was what she dreaded most of all. Whole days, with the exception of meal-times, she spent in her own room, and there no one ever disturbed her. Sometimes she read, but most often sat in prolonged brooding, heedless of the hours.

Her father was now constantly away from home. He told her that he travelled on business. It scarcely seemed to be a relief to him to rest awhile in his chair; indeed, Paul had grown incapable of resting. Time was deepening the lines of anxiety on his sallow face. His mind seemed for ever racked with painful calculation. Mrs. Enderby, too, spent much time away from the house, and Maud knew nothing of her engagements. One thing, however, Maud could not help noticing, and that was that her mother was clearly very extravagant in her mode of living. New and costly dresses were constantly being purchased, as well as articles of luxury for the house. Mrs. Enderby had of late provided herself with a *femme de chambre*,

a young woman who arrayed herself with magnificence in her mistresses castoff
dresses, and whose appearance and demeanour had something the reverse of domestic. Maud almost feared her. Then there was a hired brougham constantly in
use. Whenever Mrs. Enderby spent an evening at home, company was sure to be
entertained; noisy and showy people filled the drawing-room, and remained till
late hours. Maud did not even see their faces, but the voices of one or two men and
women became only too familiar to her; even in the retirement of her room she
could not avoid hearing these voices, and they made her shudder. Especially she
was conscious of Mr. Rudge's presence; she knew his very step on the stairs, and
waited in feverish apprehension for the first notes of an accompaniment on the
piano, which warned her that he was going to sing. He had a good voice, and it was
often in request. Sometimes the inexplicable dread of his singing was more than
she could bear; she would hurry on her walking-attire, and, stealing like a shadow
down the stairs, would seek refuge in pacing about the streets of the neighbourhood, heedless of weather or the hour.

Mrs. Enderby never came down to breakfast. One morning, when Paul happened to be at home, he and Maud had finished that meal in silence, and Maud was
rising to leave the room, when her father checked her. He leaned over the table
towards her, and spoke in an anxious undertone.

"Have you noticed anything a little--a little strange in your mother lately,
Maud? Anything in her way of speaking, I mean--her general manner?"

The girl met his look, and shook her head. The approach to such a conversation
affected her as with a shock; she could not speak.

"She has very bad nights, you know," Paul went on, still in a tone just above a
whisper, "and of late she has been taking chloral. It's against my wish, but the relief
makes it an irresistible temptation. I fear--I am afraid it is having some deleteri-
ous effect upon her; she seemed to be a little--just a little delirious in the night, I
thought."

There was something horrible in his voice and face as he uttered these words;
he shuddered slightly, and his tongue seemed to labour for utterance, as though he
dreaded the sound of his own speech.

Maud sat unmoving and silent.

"I thought, also," Paul went on, "that she appeared a little strange last evening, when the people were here.--You weren't in the drawing-room?"

Maud shook her head again.

"Do you--do you think," he asked, "she is having too much excitement? I know she needs a life of constant variety; it is essential to her. I'm sure you understand that, Maud? You--you don't misjudge her?"

"No, no; it is necessary to her," said the girl mechanically.

"But," her father pursued, with still lower voice, "there is always the danger lest she should over-exert herself. Last night I--I thought I noticed--but it was scarcely worth speaking of; I am so easily alarmed, you know."

Maud tried to say something, but in vain.

"You--you won't desert her--quite--Maud?" said her father in a tone of pleading. "I am obliged to be so muck away--God knows I can't help it. And then I--I wonder whether you have noticed? I seem to have little influence with her."

He stopped, but the next moment forced himself to utter what was in his mind.

"Can't you help me a little more, Maud? Couldn't you induce her to live a little more--more restfully at times?"

She rose, pushing the chair back behind her.

"Father, I can't!" she cried; then burst into a passion of tears.

"God help us!" her father breathed, rising and looking at her in blank misery. But in a moment she had recovered herself. They faced each other for an instant, but neither ventured to speak again, and Maud turned and left him.

Waymark came as usual, but now he seldom saw Mrs. Enderby. Maud received him alone. There was little that was lover-like in these hours spent together. They kissed each other at meeting and parting, but, with this exception, the manner of both was very slightly different from what it had been before their engagement. They sat apart, and talked of art, literature, religion, seldom of each other. It had come to this by degrees; at first there had been more warmth, but passion never. Waymark's self-consciousness often weighed upon his tongue, and made his conversation but a string of commonplaces; Maud was often silent for long intervals. Their eyes never met in a steady gaze.

Waymark often asked himself whether Maud's was a passionless nature, or whether it was possible that her reserve had the same origin as his own. The latter he felt to be unlikely; sometimes there was a pressure of her hands as their lips just touched, the indication, he believed, of feeling held in restraint for uncertain reasons. She welcomed him, too, with a look which he in vain endeavoured to respond to--a look of sudden relief from weariness, of gentle illumination; it smote him like a reproach. When the summer had set in, he was glad to change the still room for the open air; they walked frequently about Regent's Park, and lingered till after sunset.

One evening, when it was dull and threatened rain, they returned to the house sooner than usual. Waymark would have taken his leave at the door, as he ordinarily did, but Maud begged him to enter, if only for a few minutes. It was not quite nine o'clock, and Mrs. Enderby was from home.

He seated himself, but Maud remained standing irresolutely. Waymark glanced at her from under his eyebrows. He did not find it easy to speak; they had both been silent since they left the park, with the exception of the few words exchanged at the door.

"Will you let me sit here?" Maud asked suddenly, pushing a footstool near to his chair, and kneeling upon it.

He smiled and nodded.

"When will they begin the printing?" she asked, referring to his book, which was now in the hands of the publisher who had undertaken it.

"Not for some months. It can't come out till the winter season."

"If it should succeed, it will make a great difference in your position, won't it?"

"It might," he replied, looking away.

She sat with her eyes fixed on the ground. She wished to continue, but something stayed her.

"I don't much count upon it," Waymark said, when he could no longer endure the silence. "We mustn't base any hopes on that."

He rose; the need of changing his attitude seemed imperative.

"Must you go?" Maud asked, looking up at him with eyes which spoke all that her voice failed to utter.

He moved his head affirmatively, and held out his hand to raise her. She obeyed his summons, and stood up before him; her eyes had fixed themselves upon his; he could not avoid their strange gaze.

"Good-bye," he said.

Her free hand rose to his shoulder, upon which it scarcely rested. He could not escape her eyes, though to meet them tortured him. Her lips were moving, but he could distinguish no syllable; they moved again, and he could just gather the sense of her whisper.

"Do you love me?"

An immense pity thrilled through him. He put his arm about her, held her closely, and pressed his lips against her cheek. She reddened, and hid her face against him. Waymark touched her hair caressingly, then freed his other hand, and went from the room.

Maud sat in thought till a loud ring at the door-bell made her start and flee upstairs. The room in which she and Waymark sat when they were by themselves was in no danger of invasion, but she feared the possibility of meeting her mother to-night. Her father was away from home, as usual, but the days of his return were always uncertain, and Mrs. Enderby might perchance open the door of the little sitting-room just to see whether he was there, as it was here he ordinarily employed himself when in the house. From her bedroom Maud could hear several people ascend the stairs. It was ten o'clock, but an influx of visitors at such an hour was nothing remarkable. She could hear her mother's laugh, and then the voice of a man, a voice she knew but too well--that of Mr. Budge.

Her nerves were excited. The night was close, and there were mutterings of thunder at times; the cloud whence they came seemed to her to spread its doleful blackness over this one roof. An impulse seized her; she took paper and sat down at her desk to write. It was a letter to Waymark, a letter such as she had never addressed to him, and which, even in writing it, she was conscious she could not send. Her hand trembled as she filled the pages with burning words. She panted for more than he had given her; this calm, half-brotherly love of his was just now like a single drop of water to one dying of thirst; she cried to him for a deeper draught of the joy of life. The words came to her without need of thought; tears fell hot from her eyes and blotted what she wrote.

The tears brought her relief; she was able to throw her writing aside, and by degrees to resume that dull, vacant mood of habitual suffering which at all events could be endured. From this, too, there was at times a retreat possible with the help of a book. She had no mind to sleep, and on looking round, she remembered that the book she had been reading in the early part of the day was downstairs. It was after midnight, and she seemed to have a recollection of hearing the visitors leave the house a little while ago; it would be safe to venture as far as the sitting-room below.

She began to descend the stairs quietly. There was still a light in the hall, but the quietness of the house reassured her. On turning an angle of the stairs, however, she saw that the door of the drawing-room was open, and that just within stood two figures--her mother and Mr. Rudge. They seemed to be whispering together, and in the same moment their lips met. Then the man came out and went downstairs. Mrs. Enderby turned back into the drawing-room.

Maud stood fixed to the spot. Darkness had closed in around her, and she clung to the banisters to save herself from the gulf which seemed to yawn before her feet. The ringing of a bell, the drawing-room bell summoning Mrs. Enderby's maid, brought her back to consciousness, and with trembling limbs she regained her room. It was as though some ghastly vision of the night had shaken her soul. The habit of her mind overwhelmed her with the conviction that she knew at last the meaning of that mystery of horror which had of late been strengthening its hold upon her imagination. The black cloud which lowered above the house had indeed its significance; the voices which wailed to her of sin and woe were the true expression of things amid which she had been moving unconsciously. That instinct which made her shrink from her mother's presence was not without its justification; the dark powers which circled her existence had not vainly forced their influence upon her. Her first impulse was to flee from the house; the air breathed pestilence and death, death of the soul. Looking about her in the anguish of conflicting thoughts, her eyes fell upon the pages she had written. These now came before her as a proof of contagion which had seized upon her own nature; she tore the letter hastily into fragments, and, striking fire with a match, consumed them in the grate. As she watched the sparks go out, there came a rustling of dresses past her door. She flung herself upon her knees and sought refuge in wild, wordless prayer.

A fortnight after this Maud went late in the evening to the room where she knew her father was sitting alone. Paul Enderby looked up from his papers in surprise; it was some time since Maud had sought private conversation with him. As he met her pale, resolute face, he knew that she had a serious purpose in thus visiting him, and his look changed to one of nervous anticipation.

"Do I disturb you, father?" Maud asked. "Could you spare me a few minutes?"

Paul nodded, and she took a seat near him.

"Father, I am going to leave home, going to be a governess again."

He drew a sigh of relief; he had expected something worse than this. Yet the relief was only for a moment, and then he looked at her with eyes which made her soul fail for very compassion.

"You will desert me, Maud?" he asked, trying to convey in his look that which he could not utter in words.

"Father, I can be of no help, and I feel that I must not remain here."

"Have you found a place?"

"This afternoon I engaged myself to go to Paris with a French family. They have been in England some time, and want to take back an English governess for their children."

Paul was silent.

"I leave the day after to-morrow," she added; at first she had feared to say how soon she was to go.

"You are right," her father said, shifting some papers about with a tremulous hand. "You are right to leave us. You at least will be safe."

"Safe?" she asked, under her breath.

He looked at her in the same despairing way, but said nothing.

"Father," she began, her lips quivering in the intensity of her inward struggle, "can you not go away from here? Can you not take mother away?"

They gazed at each other, each trying to divine what it was that made the other so pale. Did her father know?--Maud asked herself. Did Maud know something more than he himself?--was the doubt in Paul's mind. But they were thinking of different things.

"I can't, I can't!" the wretched man exclaimed, spreading out his arms on the desk. "Perhaps in a few months--but I doubt. I can do nothing now; I am helpless; I am not my own master. O God, if I could but go and leave it all behind me!"

Maud could only guess at the meaning of this. He had already hinted to her of business troubles which were crushing him. But this was a matter of no moment in her sight. There was something more terrible, and she could not force her tongue to speak of it.

"You fear for her?" Paul went on. "You have noticed her strangeness?" He lowered his voice. "What can I do, Maud?"

"You are so much away," she said hurriedly, laying her hand on his arm. "Her visitors--she has so many temptations--"

"Temptations?"

"Father, help her against herself!"

"My help is vain. There is a curse on her life, and on mine. I can only stand by and wait for the worst."

She could not speak. It was her duty, clearly her imperative duty, yet she durst not fulfil it. She had come down from her room with the fixed purpose, attained after nights of sleepless struggle, of telling him what she had seen. She found herself alone again, the task unfulfilled. And she knew that she could not face him again.

CHAPTER XXXIII
A GARDEN-PARTY

Waymark received with astonishment Maud's letter from Paris. He had seen her only two days before, and their conversation had been of the ordinary kind; Maud had given him no hint of her purpose, not even when he spoke to her of the coming holiday season, and the necessity of her having a change. She confessed she was not well. Sometimes, when they had both sat for some minutes in silence, she would raise her eyes and meet his gaze steadily, seeming to search for something. Waymark could not face this look; it drove him to break the suspense by any kind of remark on an indifferent subject. He remembered now that she had gazed at him in that way persistently on the last evening that they were together. When he was saying good-bye, and as he bent to kiss her, she held him back for a moment, and seemed to wish to say something. Doubtless she had been on the point of telling him that she was going away; but she let him leave in silence.

It was not a long letter that she wrote; she merely said that change had become indispensable to body and soul, and that it had seemed best to make it suddenly.

"I hope," she wrote in conclusion, "that you will see my father as often as you can; he is very much in need of friendly company, and I should like you to be able to send me news of him. Do not fear for me; I feel already better. I am always with you in spirit, and in the spirit I love you; God help me to keep my love pure!"

Waymark put away the letter carelessly; the first sensation of surprise over, he did not even care to speculate on the reasons which had led Maud to leave home. It was but seldom now that his thoughts busied themselves with Maud; the unreal importance which she had for a time assumed in his life was only a recollection; her very face was ghostlike in his mind's eye, dim, always vanishing. If the news of her departure from England moved him at all, it was with a slight sense of satisfaction; it would be so much easier to write letters to her than to speak face to face. Yet, in the days that followed, the ghostlike countenance hovered more persistently before him than was its wont; there was a far-off pleading in its look, and sometimes that shadow of reproach which our uneasy conscience will cast upon the faces of those we have wronged. This passed, however, and another image, one which had ever grown in clearness and persistency of presentment in proportion as Maud's faded away, glided before him in the hours of summer sunlight, and shone forth with the beauty of a rising star against the clouded heaven of his dreams.

Waymark's mood was bitter, but, in spite of himself, it was no longer cynical. He could not indulge himself in that pessimistic scepticism which had aided him in bearing his poverty, and the restless craving of sense and spirit which had accompanied it. His enthusiasm for art was falling away; as a faith it had failed him in his hour of need. In its stead another faith had come to him, a faith which he felt to be all-powerful, and the sole stay of a man's life amid the shifting shadows of intellectual creeds. And it had been revealed too late. Led by perverse motives, now no longer intelligible, he had reached a goal of mere frustration; between him and the true end of his being there was a great gulf fixed.

To Ida, in the meanwhile, these weeks of early summer were bringing health of body and cheerfulness of mind. She spent very much of her time in the open air. Whenever it was possible she and Miss Hurst took their books out into the garden, and let the shadows of the rose-bushes mark the hours for them. Ida's natural vigour throve on the strength-giving properties of sun and breeze the last traces of unwholesome pallor passed from her face, and exercise sent her home flushed like the dawn.

One afternoon she went to sit with her grandfather on a bench beneath an apple-tree. The old man had his pipe and a newspaper. Ida was quiet, and glancing at her presently, Abraham found her eyes fixed upon him.

"Grandfather," she said, in her gentlest voice, "will you let me give a garden-party some day next week?"

"A party?" Mr. Woodstock raised his brows in astonishment. "Who are you going to invite?"

"You'll think it a strange notion.--I wonder whether I can make it seem as delightful to you as it does to me. Suppose we went to those houses of yours, and got together as many poor little girls as we could, and brought them all here to spend an afternoon in the garden. Think what an unheard-of thing it would be to them! And then we would give them some tea, and take them back again before dark."

The proposal filled Mr. Woodstock with dismay, and the habitual hardness of his face suggested a displeasure he did not in reality feel.

"As you say, it's a strange notion," he remarked, smiling very slightly. "I don't know why you shouldn't have your own way, Ida, but--it'll cost you a good deal of trouble, you know."

"You are mistaking me, grandfather. You think this a curious whim I have got into my head, and your kindness would tempt you to let me do a silly thing just for the sake of having my way. It is no foolish fancy. It's not for my sake, but for the children's."

Her eyes were aglow with earnestness, and her voice trembled.

"Do you think they'd care for it?" asked her grandfather, impressed by something in her which he had never seen before.

"Care for it!--Imagine a poor little thing that has been born in a wretched, poverty-stricken, disorderly home, a home that is no home, and growing up with no knowledge of anything but those four hateful walls and the street outside. No toys, no treats, no change of air; playing in the gutter, never seeing a beautiful thing, never hearing of the pleasures which rich people's children would pine and die without And a child for all that."

Mr. Woodstock cleared his throat and smoothed the newspaper upon his knee.

"How will you get them here, Ida?"

"Oh, leave that to me! Let us choose a day; wouldn't Saturday be best! I will go there myself, and pick out the children, and get their mothers to promise to have them ready. Then I'll arrange to have one of those carts you see at Sunday-school treats. Why, the ride here, that alone! And you'll let me have tea for them,--just bread and butter and a bun,--it will cost not half as much as my new dress this week, not *half* as much--"

"Come, come, I can't stand this!" growled out Abraham, getting up from the seat. "I'd *give* them the garden, for good and all, rather than see you like that. Say Saturday, if it's fine; if not, Monday, or when you like."

On the following morning the details were arranged, and the next day Ida went to Litany Lane. She preferred to go alone, and on this errand Mr. Woodstock would have found a difficulty in accompanying her. Ida knew exactly the nature of the task she had taken in hand, and found it easier than it would have been to the ordinary young lady. She jotted down the names of some twenty little girls, selecting such as were between the ages of eight and twelve, and obtained promises that all should be ready at a fixed hour next Saturday. She met with doubts and objections and difficulties enough, but only failed in one or two instances. Then followed fresh talks with her grandfather, and all the details were arranged.

There was rain on the Thursday and Friday, but when Ida drew up her blind at six o'clock on Saturday morning, the sky gave promise of good things. She was walking in the garden long before breakfast-time, and gladdened to rapture as she watched the sun gain power, till it streamed gloriously athwart cloudless blue. By one o'clock she was at the end of Litany Lane, where the cart with long seats was already waiting; its arrival had become known to the little ones, and very few needed summoning. Of course there were disappointments now and again. In spite of mothers' promises, half the children had their usual dirty faces, and showed no sign of any preparation. Five or six of them had nothing to put on their heads; two had bare feet. It was too late to see to these things now; as they were, the children clambered, or were lifted, on to the cart, and Ida took her seat among them. Then a crack of the driver's whip, and amid the shouts of envious brothers and sisters, and before the wondering stare of the rest of the population, off they drove away.

"Who'd like an apple?" Ida asked, as soon as they were well clear of the narrow streets. There was a general scream of delight, and from a hamper by her side she brought out apples and distributed them. Only for a minute or two had there been anything like shyness in Ida's presence; she knew how to talk and behave to these poor little waifs. Her eyes filled with tears as she listened to their chatter among themselves, and recognised so many a fragment of her own past life. One child, who sat close by her, had been spending the morning in washing vegetables for the Saturday-night market. Did not that call to mind something?--so far off; so far, yet nearer to her than many things which had intervened. How they all laughed, as the big, black houses gave way to brighter streets, and these again began to open upon glimpses of field or garden! Not one of them had the slightest conception of whither they were being taken, or what was to happen to them at length. But they had confidence in "the lady." She was a sorceress in their eyes; what limit could there be to her powers? Something good and joyous awaited them; that was all they knew or cared; leagues of happiness, stretching away to the remote limits of the day's glory; a present rapture beyond knowledge, and a memory for ever.

Mr. Woodstock stood within the gate of the garden, his hands in his pockets, and as the vehicle came in sight he drew just a little back.

They streamed along the carriage-drive, and in a minute or two were all clustered upon the lawn behind the house. What was expected of them? Had an angel taken them by he hand and led them straight from Litany Lane through the portals of paradise, they could not have been more awed and bewildered. Trees and rose-bushes, turf and beds of flowers, seats in the shade, skipping-ropes thrown about on the open--and there, hark, a hand-organ, a better one than ever they danced to on the pavement, striking up to make them merry. That was the happiest thought! It was something not too unfamiliar; the one joyful thing of which they had experience meeting them here to smooth over the first introduction to a new world. Ida knew it well, the effect of that organ; had it not lightened her heart many and many a time in the by-gone darkness? Two of the girls had caught each other by the waist at the first sounds. Might they? Would "the lady" like it?

Miss Hurst had come out as soon as the music began, and Ida ran to talk with her. There was whispering between them, and pointing to one and another of the children, and then the governess, with a pleased face, disappeared again. She was away some time, but on her return two of the children were called into the house. Bare-footed they went in, but came forth again with shoes and stockings on, hardly able to comprehend what had happened to them. Then were summoned those who had nothing on their heads, and to each of these a straw hat was given, a less wonderful possession than the shoes and stockings, but a source of gladness and pride.

In the meantime, however, marvels had accumulated on the lawn. Whilst yet the organ was playing, there appeared two men, one of them carrying a big drum, the other hidden under a Punch and Judy show. Of a sudden there sounded a shrill note, high above the organ, a fluting from the bottom to the top of the gamut, the immemorial summons to children, the overture to the primitive drama. It was drowned in a scream of welcome, which, in its turn, was outdone by thunderous peals upon the drum.

Mr. Woodstock said little during the whole afternoon. Perhaps he thought the more.

Tables had been fixed in one part of the garden, and as the drama of Punch drew to an end, its interest found a serious rival in the spectacle of piled plates of cake. But there was to intervene nearly half-an-hour before the tea-urns were ready to make an appearance. The skipping-ropes came into requisition outside, but in the house was proceeding simultaneously a rather more serious pastime, which fell to Ida's share to carry out. Choosing the little girl whose face was the dirtiest and hair the untidiest of any she could see, she led her gently away to a place where a good bowl of warm water and plenty of soap were at hand, and, with the air of bestowing the greatest kindness of all, fell to work to such purpose that in a few minutes the child went back to the garden a resplendent being, positively clean and kempt for the first time in her life.

"I know you'll feel uncomfortable for a little, dear," Ida said, dismissing the astonished maiden with a kiss, "but the strangeness will wear off; and you'll see how much nicer it is."

One after another, all were dealt with in this way, presently with a good-natured servant-girl's assistance, as time pressed. The result was that a transformed company sat down to tea. The feeling wore off, as Ida said, but at first cleanliness meant positive discomfort, taking the form of loss of identity and difficulty of mutual recognition. They looked at their hands, and were amazed at the whiteness that had come upon them; they kept feeling their faces and their ordered hair. But the appetite of one and all was improved by the process.

"How I wish Mr. Waymark was here!" Ida said to her grandfather, as they stood together, watching the feast. "He would enjoy it. We must give him a full account to-morrow, mustn't we?"

"I forgot," replied the other. "I had a note from him this morning, saying he thought he shouldn't be able to come."

The first shadow of disappointment which this day had brought fell upon the girl's countenance. She made no reply, and presently went to help one or the youngest children, who had spilt her tea and was in evident distress.

After tea the organ struck up again, and again there was dancing on the lawn. Then a gathering of flowers by Ida and Miss Hurst, and one given to each of the children, with injunctions to put it in water on reaching home, and keep it as long as possible in memory of the day. Already the sun was westering, and Litany Lane must be reached before dusk.

"Poor children!" Ida sighed to herself. "If they had but homes to go to!" And added, in her thought, "We shall see, we shall see!"

Every bit as joyous as the ride out was the return to town. With foresight, Ida made the two youngest sit on each side of her; soon the little heads were drooping in her lap, subdued by the very weariness of bliss. Miss Hurst had offered to accompany Ida, that she might not have to come back alone, but Ida wanted her friends all to herself, and was rewarded by the familiarity with which they gossiped to her all the way.

"Hands up, all those who *haven't* enjoyed themselves!" she exclaimed, just as they were entering the noisy streets.

There was a moment's doubt, then a burst of merry laughter.

"Hands up, all those who would like to come again!"

All held up both arms--except the two children who were asleep.

"Well, you've all been good, and I'm very pleased with you, and you *shall* come again!"

It was the culmination of the day's delight. For the first time in their lives the children of Litany Lane and Elm Court had something to look forward to.

CHAPTER XXXIV
A LATE REVENGE

Ida clung to the possibility of Waymark's paying his usual visit on the Sunday, but she was disappointed. This absence had no reason beyond Waymark's choice. It was the last Sunday but one of the month; a week more, and he must keep his word with Mr. Woodstock. The evil day had been put off, and to what purpose? There had been some scarcely confessed hope. Maud's sudden departure from England, and her strange letter, might perhaps mean a change in her which would bring about his freedom; he himself might possibly be driven by his wretchedness to the point of writing to her in a way which would hasten her decision, if indeed she were doubting.

All was over between Ida and himself, so why undergo the torment of still seeing her. In sending his note to Mr. Woodstock, he was on the point of surrendering the week that remained, and begging that Ida might be told at once, but his hand refused to write the words. Through the week that ensued he had no moment's rest. At night he went to places of amusement, to seek distraction; he wished and dreaded the coming of the Sunday. How would Ida receive the revelation? Should he write to her and try to make her understand him? Yet in that he could scarcely succeed, and failure would bring upon him her contempt. The only safety lay in never seeing or communicating with her again.

Even on Saturday night he had not made up his mind how to act. He went to the theatre, but left before the play was half over, and walked slowly homewards. As he drew near to his lodgings, some one hastened towards him with both hands held out. It was Maud Enderby.

"Oh, I have waited so long! I wanted to see you to-night." She was exhausted with fatigue and distress, and still held his hands, as if needing their support. To Waymark, in his then state of mind, she came like an apparition. He could only look at her in astonishment.

"Last night," she said, "I had a telegram from father. He told me to come back at once; he had had to leave, and mother was alone. I was to call for a letter at a place in the city. I was in time to catch the night boat, and when I got his letter it told me dreadful things. Something has happened which compelled him to leave England at once. He could do nothing, make no arrangements. Mother, he said, had a little money; we must sell everything and manage to live somewhere for a little; he would try to send us what he could. Then I went home. There was a police-officer in the house, and mother had gone away, I can't tell where. Father has done something, and--Oh, what shall I do? You can help me, can't you?"

Waymark, whom this news overwhelmed with blank despair, could at first say nothing; but the very greatness of the blow gradually produced in him the strength to bear it. He saw that fate had taken the future out of his hands; there was no longer even the appearance of choice. To Maud he must now devote himself, aiding her with all his strength in the present and through the days to come.

"Shall I go back home with you?" he asked, pressing her hands to comfort her, and speaking with the calmness of one who had made up his mind.

"Yes; perhaps mother will have returned. But what shall we do? What will happen to father? Do you know anything of all this?"

"Nothing whatever. Walk with me to the top of the street, and we will take a cab."

She hung upon his arm, trembling violently; and during the drive to Paddington, she lay back with her eyes closed, holding Waymark's hands in her own, which burned with fever. On alighting, they found that Mrs. Enderby had indeed returned; the servant told them so, and at the same time whispered something to Maud. They went up into the drawing-room, and there found Mrs. Enderby lying upon the couch. She could not understand when she was spoken to, but nodded her head and looked at them with large, woebegone, wandering eyes. Every effort to rouse her was vain.

It was a dreadful night.

The early dawn was in the sky when Waymark reached Beaufort Street. With no thought of sleep, he sat down at once and wrote to Mr. Woodstock, relating what had happened. "So, you see," he concluded, "with the end of July has come the decision of my fate, as we agreed it should. If I had seen you to-morrow, as I proposed, I know not what folly I might have been guilty of. Tell Ida everything at once; I shall never see her again. But do you, if you can, be my friend still. I need your help in this horrible situation. Meet me--will you?--at the office to-morrow night, say at eight o'clock."

This letter would reach Tottenham on Monday morning. Waymark went to the office at the hour he had mentioned, and waited till ten o'clock. But Mr. Woodstock had not been in St. John Street Road that day, and the waiting was in vain.

The garden-party had not been without its effect upon Mr. Woodstock. On the following day, when he was sitting again with Ida in the garden, he recurred to the conversation of a week ago, and seemed desirous of leading the girl to speak freely on the subjects which had such power to stir her. Ida had been waiting for this; she rejoiced at the promise it held out, and unburdened her heart. Would he not do yet more for the poor people in his houses I could not their homes in some way be made more fit for human beings? With careful observation of his mood, she led him on to entertain thoughts he had never dreamt of, and before they parted she had all but obtained a promise that he would go over the whole of his property and really see what could be done. Ida's influence over him had by this time become very great; the old man was ready to do much for the sake of pleasing her.

On the following Tuesday he went down into Litany Lane in company with a builder, and proceeded to investigate each of the houses. In many instances the repairs, to be of any use, would have to be considerable; there would be a difficulty in executing them whilst the tenants remained in possession. One possibility occurred to him in the course of examination, and he determined to make use of it; he would create room by getting rid of the worst tenants, all those, in fact, whose presence was pollution to the neighbourhood, and whom it was hopeless to think of reforming. In this way he would be able to shift about the remaining lodgers without too great a loss to himself, and avoid the necessity of turning helpless people into the street.

Mr. Woodstock had considerably more knowledge of the state of his property, and of the tenants inhabiting it, than is usual with landlords of his kind; for all that, the present examination brought to light not a few things which were startling even to him. Since Waymark had ceased to act as his collector, the office had been filled by an agent of the ordinary kind, and Mr. Woodstock had, till just now, taken less interest in the property than formerly. Things had got worse on the whole. Whereas Waymark had here and there been successful in suppressing the grosser forms of uncleanliness by threats of expulsion, and at times by the actual enforcement of his threat, no such supervision had of late been exercised. There were very few houses in which the air was at all tolerable; in many instances the vilest odours hung about the open door-ways. To pass out of Elm Court into the wider streets around was like a change to the freshness of woods and fields. And the sources of this miasma were only too obvious.

The larger houses which made up Litany Lane had underground cellars; in the court there were fortunately no such retreats. On entering one of these former houses, the two were aware of an especially offensive odour rising from below the stairs. Pursuing, however, their plan of beginning at the garrets, they went up together. In the room at the top they came upon a miserable spectacle. On something which, for want of another name, was probably called a bed, there lay a woman either already dead or in a state of coma, and on the floor sat two very young children, amusing themselves with a dead kitten, their only toy. Mr. Woodstock bent over the woman and examined her. He found that she was breathing, though in a slow and scarcely perceptible way; her eyes were open, but expressed no consciousness. The slightly-parted lips were almost black, and here and there on her face there seemed to be a kind of rash. Mr. Woodstock's companion, after taking one glance, drew hastily back.

"Looks like small-pox," he said, in an alarmed voice. "I wouldn't stand so near, sir, if I was you."

"Isn't there any one to look to her?" said Abraham. Then turning to one of the children, "Where's your father?" he asked.

"Dono," was the little fellow's indifferent reply.

"Are you alone?"

"Dono."

They went down to the floor below, and there found a woman standing at her door.

"What's the matter with her up there?" asked Mr. Woodstock.

"She's very bad, sir. Her Susan's gone to get a order for the parish doctor, I b'lieve. I was just a-goin' to look after the children when you came up. I've only just come 'ome myself, you see."

"What's that horrible stench down below?"

"I didn't notice nothink, sir," said the woman, looking over the banisters as if the odour might be seen.

"Any one living in the kitchen?"

"There **was** some one, I b'lieve, sir, but I don't exac'ly know if they's there yet."

Presently they reached the region below. In absolute darkness they descended steps which were covered with a sort of slime, and then, by striking a light, found themselves in front of a closed door. Opening this, they entered a vile hole where it could scarcely be said to be daylight, so thickly was the little window patched with filth. Groping about in the stifling atmosphere, they discovered in one corner a mass of indescribable matter, from which arose, seemingly, the worst of the effluvia.

"What is it?" asked Mr. Woodstock, holding a lighted match.

"Rotten fish, it seems to me," said the other, holding his nose.

Abraham turned away; then, as if his eye had suddenly caught something, strode to another corner. There lay the body of a dead child, all but naked, upon a piece of sacking.

"We'd better get out of this, sir," said the builder. "We shall be poisoned. Wonder they haven't the plague here."

"Seems to me they have," returned Mr. Woodstock.

They went out into the street, and hailed the first policeman in sight. Then, giving up his investigations for that morning, Mr. Woodstock repaired to the police-station, and after a good deal of trouble, succeeded in getting the attendance of a medical man, with the result that the woman they had seen up in the garret was found to be in truth dying of small-pox. If the contagion spread, as probably it had by this time begun to, there would be a pleasant state of things in Litany Lane.

In the evening, before going home, Abraham had a bath. He was not a nervous man, but the possibilities of the risk he had run were not agreeable to contemplate. Two or three days went by without any alarming symptoms, but as he learnt that another case of small-pox had declared itself in the Lane, he postponed his personal activity there for the present, and remained a good deal at home. On the Sunday morning--when Waymark's letter had already been posted--he awoke with a headache, continued from the night before. It grew worse during the day, and he went to bed early with a dull pain across the forehead, which prevented him from sleeping. On the following morning the headache still remained; he felt a disinclination to rise, and now, for the first time, began to be troubled with vague fears, which blended themselves with his various pre-occupations in a confusing way. The letter which arrived from Waymark was taken up to him. It caused him extreme irritation, which was followed by uneasy dozing, the pain across his forehead growing worse the while. A doctor was summoned.

The same day Ida and Miss Hurst left the house, to occupy lodgings hard by; it was done at Mr. Woodstock's peremptory bidding. Ida at once wrote to Waymark, begging him to come; he arrived early next morning, and learnt the state of things.

"The doctor tells me," said Ida, "there is a case in Litany Lane. It is very cruel. Grandfather went to make arrangements for having the houses repaired."

"There I recognise your hand," Waymark observed, as she made a pause.

"Why have you so deserted us?" Ida asked. "Why do we see you so seldom?"

"It is so late every evening before I leave the library, and I am busy with all sorts of things."

They had little to say to each other, Waymark promised to communicate at once with a friend of Mr. Woodstock's, a man of business, and to come again as soon as possible, to give any help he could. Whether Ida had been told of his position remained uncertain.

For Ida they were sad, long days. Troubles which she had previously managed to keep in the background now again beset her. She had attached herself to her grandfather; gratitude for all that he was doing at her wish strengthened her affection, and she awaited each new day with fear. Waymark seemed colder to her in these days than he had ever been formerly. The occasion ought, she felt, to have brought them nearer together; but on his side there appeared to be no such feeling. The time hung very heavily on her hands. She tried to go on with her studies, but it was a mere pretence.

Soon, she learnt that there was no hope; the sick man had sunk into a state of unconsciousness from which he would probably not awake. She haunted the neighbourhood of the house, or, in her lodging, sat like one who waits, and the waiting was for she knew not what. There was once more to be a great change in her life, but of what kind she could not foresee. She wished her suffering had been more acute; her only relative was dying, yet no tear would come to her eyes; it was heartless, and to weep would have brought relief to her. She could only sit and wait.

When Waymark came, on the evening of the next day, he heard that all was over. Ida saw him, but only for a few minutes. In going away, he paused by the gates of the silent house.

"The slums have avenged themselves," he said to himself sadly, "though late."

CHAPTER XXXV
HOUSE-WARMING

On a Sunday afternoon in October, when Abraham Woodstock had lain in his grave for three months, Waymark met Julian Casti by appointment in Sloane Square, and they set forth together on a journey to Peckham. They were going thither by invitation, and, to judge from the laughter which accompanied their talk, their visit was likely to afford them entertainment. The merriment on Julian's side was not very natural; he looked indeed too ill to enjoy mirth of any kind. As they stood in the Square, waiting for an omnibus, he kept glancing uneasily about him, especially in the direction whence they had come. It had the appearance of a habit, but before they had stood much more than a minute, he started and exclaimed in a low voice to his companion--

"I told you so. She is just behind there. She has come round by the back streets, just to see if I'd told her the truth."

Waymark glanced back and shrugged his shoulders.

"Pooh! Never mind," he said. "You're used to it."

"Used to it! Yes," Julian returned, his face flushing suddenly a deep red, the effect of extraordinary excitement; "and it is driving me mad."

Then, after a fit of coughing--

"She found my poem last night, and burnt it."

"Burnt it?"

"Yes; simply because she could not understand it. She said she thought it was waste paper, but I saw, I saw."

The 'bus they waited for came up, and they went on their way. On reaching the neighbourhood of Peckham, they struck off through a complex of small new streets, apparently familiar to Waymark, and came at length to a little shop, also very new, the windows of which displayed a fresh-looking assortment of miscellaneous goods. There was half a large cheese, marked by the incisions of the tasting-knife; a boiled ham, garlanded; a cone of brawn; a truncated pyramid of spiced beef, released from its American tin; also German sausage and other dainties of the kind. Then there were canisters of tea and coffee, tins of mustard, a basket of eggs, some onions, boxes of baking-powder and of blacking; all arranged so as to make an impression on the passers-by; everything clean and bright. Above the window stood in imposing gilt letters the name of the proprietor: O'Gree.

They entered. The shop was very small and did not contain much stock. The new shelves showed a row of biscuit-tins, but little else, and from the ceiling hung balls of string. On the counter lay an inviting round of boiled beef. Odours of provisions and of fresh paint were strong in the air. Every thing gleamed from resent scrubbing and polishing; the floor only emphasised its purity by a little track where a child's shoes had brought in mud from the street; doubtless it had been washed over since the Sunday morning's custom had subsided. Wherever the walls would have confessed their bareness the enterprising tradesman had hung gorgeous advertising cards. At the sound of the visitors' footsteps, the door leading out of the shop into the parlour behind opened briskly, a head having previously appeared over the red curtain, and Mr. O'Gree, in the glory of Sunday attire, rushed forward with eager hands. His welcome was obstreperous.

"Waymark, you're a brick! Mr. Casti, I'm rejoiced to receive you in my establishment! You're neither a minute too soon nor a minute too late. Mrs. O'Gree only this moment called out from the kitchen that the kettle was boiling and the crumpets at the point of perfection! I knew your punctuality of old, Waymark. Mr. Casti, how does it strike you? Roaring trade, Waymark! Done two shillings and threepence three farthings this Sunday morning. Look here, me boy,--ho, ho!"

He drew out the till behind the counter, and jingled his hand in coppers. Then he rushed about in the wildest fervour from object to object, opening tins which he had forgotten were empty, making passes at the beef and the ham with a formidable carving-knife, demonstrating the use of a sugar-chopper and a coffee-grinder, and, lastly, calling attention with infinite glee to a bad halfpenny which he had detected on the previous afternoon, and had forthwith nailed down to the counter, *in ter-*

rorem. Then he lifted with much solemnity a hinged portion of the counter, and requested his visitors to pass into the back-parlour. Here there was the same perfect cleanliness, though the furniture was scant and very simple. The round table was laid for tea, with a spotless cloth, plates of a very demonstrative pattern, and knives and forks which seemed only just to have left the ironmonger's shop.

"We pass, you observe, Mr. Casti," cried the ex-teacher, "from the region of commerce to that of domestic intimacy. Here Mrs. O'Gree reigns supreme, as indeed she does in the other department, as far as presiding genius goes. She's in all places at once, like a birrud! Mr. Casti," in a whisper, "I shall have the pleasure of introducing you to one of the most remarkable women it was ever your lot to meet; a phenomenon of--"

The inner door opened, and the lady herself interrupted these eulogies. Sally was charming. Her trim little body attired in the trimmest of homely dresses, her sharp little face shining and just a little red with excitement, her quick movements, her laughing eyes, her restless hands graced with the new wedding-ring--all made up a picture of which her husband might well be proud. He stood and gazed at her in frank admiration; only when she sprang forward to shake hands with Waymark did he recover himself sufficiently to go through the ceremony of introducing Julian. It was done with all stateliness.

"An improvement this on the masters' room, eh, Waymark?" cried Mr. O'Gree. Then, suddenly interrupting himself, "And that reminds me! We've got a lodger."

"Already?"

"And who d'ye think? Who d'ye think? You wouldn't guess if you went on till Christmas. Ho, ho, ho! I'm hanged if I tell you. Wait and see!"

"Shall I call him down?" asked Sally, who in the meantime had brought in the tea-pot, and the crumpets, and a dish of slices from the round of beef on the counter, and boiled eggs, and sundry other dainties.

O'Gree, unable to speak for mirth, nodded his head, and presently Sally returned, followed by--Mr. Egger. Waymark scarcely recognised his old friend, so much had the latter changed: instead of the old woe-begone look, Egger's face wore a joyous smile, and his outer man was so vastly improved that he had evidently fallen on a more lucrative profession. Waymark remembered O'Gree's chance meeting with the Swiss, but had heard nothing of him since; nor indeed had O'Gree till a day or two ago.

"How do things go?" Waymark inquired heartily. "Found a better school?"

"No, no, my friend," returned Egger, in his very bad English. "At the school I made my possible; I did till I could no more. I have made like Mr. O'Gree; it is to say, quite a change in my life. I am waiter at a restaurant. And see me; am I not the better quite? No fear!" This cockneyism came in with comical effect. "I have enough to eat and to drink, and money in my pocket. The school may go to ----"

O'Gree coughed violently to cover the last word, and looked reproachfully at his old colleague. Poor Egger, who had been carried away by his joyous fervour, was abashed, and glanced timidly at Sally, who replied by giving him half a dozen thick rounds of German sausage. On his requesting mustard, she fetched some from the shop and mixed it, but, in doing so, had the misfortune to pour too much water.

"There!" she exclaimed; "I've doubted the miller's eye."

O'Gree laughed when he saw Waymark looking for an explanation.

"That's a piece of Weymouth," he remarked. "Mrs. O'Gree comes from the south-west of England," he added, leaning towards Casti. "She's constantly teaching me new and interesting things. Now, if I was to spill the salt here--"

He put his Ii and on the salt-cellar, as if to do so, but Sally rapped his knuckles with a fork.

"None of your nonsense, sir! Give Mr. Casti some more meat, instead."

It was a merry party. The noise of talk grew so loud that it was only the keenness of habitual attention on Sally's part which enabled her to observe that a customer was knocking on the counter. She darted out, but returned with a disappointed look on her face.

"Pickles?" asked her husband, frowning.

Sally nodded.

"Now, look here, Waymark," cried O'Gree, rising in indignation from his seat. "Look here, Mr. Casti. The one drop of bitterness in our cup is--pickles; the one thing that threatens to poison our happiness is--pickles. We're always being asked for pickles; just as if the people knew about it, and came on purpose!"

"Knew About what?" asked Waymark, in astonishment.

"Why, that we mayn't sell 'em! A few doors off there's a scoundrel of a grocer. Now, his landlord's the same as ours, and when we took this shop there was one condition attached. Because the grocer sells pickles, and makes a good thing of them, we had to undertake that, in that branch of commerce, we wouldn't compete with him. Pickles are forbidden."

Waymark burst into a most unsympathetic roar of laughter, but with O'Gree the grievance was evidently a serious one, and it was some few moments before he recovered his equanimity. Indeed it was not quite restored till the entrance of another customer, who purchased two ounces of butter. When, in the dead silence which ensued, Sally was heard weighing out the order, O'Gree's face beamed; and when there followed the chink of coins in the till, he brought his fist down with a triumphant crash upon the table.

When tea was over, O'Gree managed to get Waymark apart from the rest, and showed him a small photograph of Sally which had recently been taken.

"Sally's great ambition," he whispered, "is to be taken cabinet-size, and in a snow-storm. You've seen the kind of thing in the shop-windows? We'll manage that before long, but this will do for the present. You don't see a face like that every day; eh, Waymark?"

Sally, her housewifery duly accomplished in the invisible regions, came back and sat by the fireside. She had exchanged her work-a-day costume for one rather more ornate. Noticeable was a delicate gold chain which hung about her neck, and Waymark smiled when he presently saw her take out her watch and seem to compare its time with that of the clock on the mantelpiece. It was a wedding present from Ida.

Sally caught the smile, and almost immediately came over to a seat by Waymark; and, whilst the others were engaged in loud talk, spoke with him privately.

"Have you seen her lately?" she asked.

"Not for some weeks," the other replied, shaking his head.

"Well, it's the queerest thing I ever knew, s'nough! But, there," she added, with an arch glance, "some men are that stupid--"

Waymark laughed slightly, and again shook his head.

"All a mistake," he said.

"Yes, that's just what it is, you may depend upon it. I more'n half believe you're telling fibs."

Tumblers of whisky were soon smoking on the table, and all except Casti laughed and talked to their heart's content. Casti was no kill-joy; he smiled at all that went on, now and then putting in a friendly word; but the vitality of the others was lacking in him, and the weight which crushed him night and day could not so easily be thrown aside. O'Gree was abundant in reminiscences of academic days, and it would not have been easy to resist altogether the comical vigour of his stories, all without one touch of real bitterness or malice.

"Bedad," he cried, "I sent old Pendy a business prospectus, with my compliments written on the bottom of it. I thought he might perhaps be disposed to give me a contract for victualling the Academy. I wish he had, for the boys' sake."

Then, to bring back completely the old times, Mr. Egger was prevailed upon to sing one of his *Volkslieder*, that which had been Waymark's especial favourite, and which he had sung--on an occasion memorable to Sally and her husband--in the little dining-room at Richmond.

"*Die Schwalb'n flieg'n fort, doch sie zieh'n wieder her; Der Mensch wenn er fortgeht, er kommt nimmermehr!"*

Waymark was silent for a little after that.

When it was nearly eleven o'clock, Casti looked once or twice meaningly at Waymark, and the friends at length rose to take their leave, in spite of much protest. O'Gree accompanied them as far as the spot where they would meet the omnibus, then, with assurances that to-night had been but the beginning of glorious times, sent them on their way. Julian was silent during the journey home; he looked very wearied. For lack of a timely conveyance the last mile or so had to be walked. Julian's cough had been bad during the evening, and now the cold night-air seemed to give him much trouble. Presently, just as they turned a corner, a severe blast of wind met them full in the face. Julian began coughing violently, and all at once became so weak that he had to lean against a palisading. Waymark, looking closer in alarm, saw that the handkerchief which the poor fellow was holding to his mouth was covered with blood.

"We must have a cab," he exclaimed. "It is impossible for you to walk in this state."

Julian resisted, with assurances that the worst was over for the time. If Waymark would give the support of his arm, he would get on quite well. There was no overcoming his resolution to proceed.

"There's no misunderstanding this, old fellow," he said, with a laugh, when they had walked a few paces.

Waymark made no reply.

"You'll laugh at me," Julian went on, "but isn't there a certain resemblance between my case and that of Keats? He too was a drug-pounder; he liked it as little as I do; and he died young of consumption. I suppose a dying man may speak the truth about himself. I too might have been a poet, if life had dealt more kindly with me. I think you would have liked the thing I was writing; I'd finished some three hundred lines; but now you'll never see it. Well, I don't know that it matters."

Waymark tried to speak in a tone of hopefulness, but it was hard to give his words the semblance of sincerity.

"Do you remember," Casti continued, "when all my talk used to be about Rome, and how I planned to see it one day--see it again. I should say? Strange to think that I really was born in Rome. I used to call myself a Roman, you know, and grow hot with pride when I thought of it. Those were dreams. Oh, I was to do wonderful things! Poetry was to make me rich, and then I would go and live in Italy, and fill my lungs with the breath of the Forum, and write my great Epic. How good that we can't foresee our lives!"

"I wish to heaven," Waymark exclaimed, when they were parting, "that you would be a man and shake this monstrous yoke from off your neck! It is that that is killing you. Give yourself a chance. Defy everything and make yourself free."

Julian shook his head sadly.

"Too late! I haven't the courage. My mind weakens with my body."

He went to his lodgings, and, as he anticipated, found that Harriet had not yet come home. She was almost always out very late, and he had learnt too well what t expect on her return. In spite of her illness, of which she made the most when it suited her purpose, she was able t wander about at all hours with the acquaintances her husband did not even know by name, and Julian had no longer the strength even to implore her to have pity on him. He absence racked him with nervous fears; her presence tortured him to agony. Weakness in him had reached a criminal degree. Once or twice he had all but made up his mind to flee secretly, and only let her know his determination when he had gone; but his poverty interposed such obstacles that he ended by accepting them as excuses for his hesitation. The mere thought of fulfilling the duty which he owed to himself, of speaking out with manly firmness, and telling her that here at length all ended between them--that was a terror to his soul. So he stayed on and allowed her to kill him by slow torment. He was at least carrying out to the letter the promise he had made to her father, and this thought supplied him with a flattering unction which, such was his disposition, at times even brought him a moment's solace.

There was no fire in the room; he sank upon a chair and waited. Every sound in the street below sent the blood back upon his heart. At length there came the fumbling of a latch-key--he could hear it plainly--and then the heavy foot ascending the stairs. Her glazed eyes and red cheeks told the familiar tale. She sat down opposite him and was silent for a minute, half dozing; then she seemed suddenly to become conscious of his presence, and the words began to flow from her tongue, every one cutting him to the quick, poisoning his soul with their venom of jealousy and vulgar spite. Contention was the breath of her nostrils; the prime impulse of her heart was suspicion. Little by little she came round to the wonted topic. Had he been to see his friend the thief? Was she in prison again yet? Whom had she been stealing from of late? Oh, she was innocence itself, of course; too good for this evil-speaking world.

Tonight he could not bear it. He rose from his chair like a drunken man, and staggered to the door. She sprang after him, but he was just in time to escape her grasp and spring down the stairs; then, out into the night. Once before, not quite a month ago, he had been driven thus in terror from the sound of her voice, and had slept at a coffeehouse. Now, as soon as he had got out of the street and saw that he was not being pursued, he discovered that he had given away his last copper for the omnibus fare. No matter; the air was pleasant upon his throbbing temples. It was too late to think of knocking at the house where Waymark lodged. Nothing remained but to walk about the streets all night, resting on a stone when he became too weary to go further, sheltering a little here or there when the wind cut him too keenly. Rather this, oh, a thousand times rather, than the hell behind him.

CHAPTER XXXVI
NO WAY BUT THIS

In the early days of October, Waymark's book appeared. It excited no special attention. Here and there a reviewer was found who ventured to hint that there was powerful writing in this new novel, but no one dared to heartily recommend it to public attention. By some it was classed with the "unsavoury productions of the so-called naturalist school;" others passed it by with a few lines of unfavourable comment. Clearly it was destined to bring the author neither fame nor fortune.

Waymark was surprised at his own indifference. Having given a copy to Casti, and one to Maud, he thought very little more of the production. It had ceased to interest him; he felt that if he were to write again it would be in a very different way and of different people. Even when he prided himself most upon his self-knowledge he had been most ignorant of the direction in which his character was developing. Unconsciously, he had struggled to the extremity of weariness, and now he cared only to let things take their course, standing aside from every shadow of new onset. Above all, he kept away as much as possible from the house at Tottenham, where Ida was still living. To go there meant only a renewal of torment. This was in fact the commonplace period of his life. He had no energy above that of the ordinary young man who is making his living in a commonplace way, and his higher faculties lay dormant.

In one respect, and that, after all, perhaps the most important, his position would soon be changed. Mr. Woodstock's will, when affairs were settled, would make him richer by one thousand pounds; he might, if he chose, presently give up his employment, and either trust to literature, or look out for something less precarious. A year ago, this state of things would have filed him with exultation. As it was, he only saw in it an accident compelling him to a certain fateful duty. There was now no reason why his marriage should be long delayed. For Maud's sake the step was clearly desirable. At present she and her mother were living with Miss Bygrave in the weird old house. Of Paul there had come no tidings. Their home was of course broken up, and they had no income of their own to depend upon. Maud herself, though of course aware of Waymark's prospects, seemed to shrink from speaking of the future. She grew more and more uncertain as to her real thoughts and desires.

And what of Ida? It was hard for her to realise her position; for a time she was conscious only of an overwhelming sense of loneliness. The interval of life with her grandfather was dreamlike as she looked back upon it; yet harder to grasp was the situation in which she now found herself, surrounded by luxuries which had come to her as if from the clouds, her own mistress, free to form wishes merely for the sake of satisfying them. She cared little to realise the minor possibilities of wealth. The great purpose, the noble end to which her active life had shaped itself, was sternly present before her; she would not shirk its demands. But there was lacking the inspiration of joy. Could she harden herself to every personal desire, and forget, in devotion to others, the sickness of one great hope deferred? Did her ideal require this of her?

Would he come, now that she was free to give herself where she would, now that she was so alone? The distance between them had increased ever since the beginning of her new life. She knew well the sort of pride he was capable of; but was there not something else, something she dreaded to observe too closely, in the manner of his speech? Did he think so meanly of her as to deem such precautions necessary against her misconstruction? Nay, **could** he have guarded himself in that way if he really loved her? Would it not have been to degrade her too much in his own eyes?

He loved her once. Had she in any way grown less noble in his eyes, by those very things which she regarded as help and strengthening? Did he perchance think she had too readily accepted ease when it was offered her, sacrificing the independence which he most regarded? If so, all the more would he shrink from losing for her his own independence.

She imagined herself wedded to him; at liberty to stand before him and confess all the thoughts which now consumed her in the silence of vain longing. "Why did I break free from the fetters of a shameful life? Because I loved, and loved **you**. What gave me the strength to pass from idle luxury, poisoning the energies of the soul, to that life of lonely toil and misery? My love, and my love for **you**. I kept apart from you then; I would not even let you know what I was enduring; only because you had spoken a hasty, thoughtless word to me, which showed me with terrible distinctness the meaning of all I had escaped, and filled me with a determination to prove to myself that I had not lost all my better nature, that there was still enough of purity in my being to save me finally. What was it that afflicted me with agony beyond all words when I was made the victim of a cruel and base accusation? Not the fear of its consequences; only the dread lest *you* should believe me guilty, and no longer deem me worthy of a thought. It is no arrogance to say that I am become a pure woman; not my own merits, but love of you has made me so. I love you as a woman loves only once; if you asked me to give up my life to prove it, I am capable of doing no less a thing than that. Flesh and spirit I lay before you--all yours; do you still think the offering unworthy?"

And yet she knew that she could never thus speak to him; her humility was too great. At moments she might feel this glow of conscious virtue, but for the most part the weight of all the past was so heavy upon her.

Fortunately, her time did not long remain unoccupied. As her grandfather's heiress she found herself owner of the East-end property, and, as soon as it was assured that she would incur no danger, she went over the houses in the company of the builder whom Abraham had chosen to carry out his proposed restorations. The improvements were proceeded with at once, greatly to the astonishment of the tenants, to whom such changes inevitably suggested increase of rent. These fears Ida did her best to dispel. Dressed in the simplest possible way, and with that kind, quiet manner which was natural to her, she went about from room to room, and did her best to become intimately acquainted with the woman-kind of the Lane and the Court. It was not an easy end to compass. She was received at first with extreme suspicion; her appearance aroused that distrust which with the uneducated attaches to everything novel. In many instances she found it difficult to get it believed' that she was really the "landlord." But when this idea had been gradually mastered, and when, moreover, it was discovered that she brought no tracts, spoke not at all of religious matters, was not impertinently curious, and showed indeed that she knew a good deal of what she talked about, something like respect for her began to spring up here and there, and she was spoken of as "the right sort."

Ida was excellently fitted for the work she had undertaken. She knew so well, from her own early experience, the nature of the people with whom she was brought in contact, and had that instinctive sympathy with their lives without which it is so vain to attempt practical social reform. She started with no theory, and as yet had no very definite end in view; it simply appeared to her that, as owner of these slums, honesty and regard for her own credit required that she should make them decent human habitations, and give what other help she could to people obviously so much in need of it. The best was that she understood how and when such help could be afforded. To native practicality and prudence she added a keen recollection of the wants and difficulties she had struggled through in childhood; there was no danger of her being foolishly lavish in charity, when she could foresee with sympathy all the evil results which would ensue. Her only temptation to imprudence was when, as so often happened, she saw some little girl in a position which reminded her strongly of her own dark days; all such she would have liked to take home with her and somehow provide for, saving them from the wretched alternatives which were all that life had to offer them. So, little by little, she was brought to think in a broader way of problems puzzling enough to wiser heads than hers. Social miseries, which she had previously regarded as mere matters of fact, having never enjoyed the opportunities of comparison which alone can present them in any other light, began to move her to indignation. Often it was with a keen sense of shame that she took the weekly rent, a sum scraped together Heaven knew how, representing so much deduction from the food of the family. She knew that it would be impossible to remit the rent altogether, but at all events there was the power of reducing it, and this she did in many cases.

The children she came to regard as her peculiar care. Her strong common sense taught her that it was with these that most could be done. The parents could not be reformed; at best they might be kept from that darkest depth of poverty which corrupts soul and body alike. But might not the girls be somehow put into the way of earning a decent livelihood? Ida knew so well the effect upon them of the occupations to which they mostly turned, occupations degrading to womanhood, blighting every hope. Even to give them the means of remaining at home would not greatly help them; there they still breathed a vile atmosphere. To remove them altogether was the only efficient way, and how could that be done?

The months of late summer and autumn saw several more garden-parties. These, Ida knew, were very useful, but more enduring things must be devised. Miss

Hurst was the only person with whom she could consult, and that lady's notions were not very practical. If only she could have spoken freely with Waymark; but that she could no longer on any subject, least of all on this. As winter set in, he had almost forsaken her. He showed no interest in her life, beyond asking occasionally what she was reading, and taking the opportunity to talk of books. Throughout November she neither saw him nor heard from him. Then one evening he came.

She was alone when the servant announced him; with her sat her old companion, Grim. As Waymark entered, she looked at him with friendly smile, and said quietly--

"I thought you would never come again"

"I have not kept away through thoughtlessness," he replied. "Believe that; it is the truth. And to-night I have only come to say good-bye. I am going to leave London."

"You used to say nothing would induce you to leave London, and that you couldn't live anywhere else."

"Yes; that was one of my old fancies. I am going right away into the country, at all events for a year or two. I suppose I shall write novels."

He moved uneasily under her gaze, and affected a cheerfulness which could not deceive her.

"Has your book been a success?" Ida asked.

"No; it fell dead."

"Why didn't you give me a copy?"

"I thought too little of it. It's poor stuff. Better you shouldn't read it."

"But I have read it."

"Got it from the library, did you?"

"No; I bought it."

"What a pity to waste so much money!"

"Why do you speak like that? You know how anything of yours would interest me."

"Oh yes, in a certain way, of course."

"For its own sake, too. I can't criticise, but I know it held me as nothing else ever did. It was horrible in many parts, but I was the better for reading it."

He could not help showing pleasure, and grew more natural. Ida had purposely refrained from speaking of the book when she read it, more than a month ago, always hoping that he would be the first to say something about it. But the news he had brought her to-night put an end to reticence on her side. She must speak out her heart, cost her what it might.

"Who should read it, if not I?" she said, as he remained silent. "Who can possibly understand it half so well as I do?"

"Yes," he remarked, with wilful misunderstanding, "you have seen the places and the people. And I hear you are going on with the work your grandfather began?"

"I am trying to do something. If you had been able to give me a little time now and then, I should have asked you to advise and help me. It is hard to work there single-handed."

"You are too good for that; I should have liked to think of you as far apart from those vile scenes."

"Too good for it?" Her voice trembled. "How can any one be too good to help the miserable? If you had said that I was not worthy of such a privilege--Can you, knowing me as no one else does or ever will, think that I could live here in peace, whilst those poor creatures stint and starve themselves every week to provide me with comforts? Do I seem to you such a woman?"

He only smiled, his lips tortured to hold their peace.

"I had hoped you understood me better than that. Is that why you have left me to myself? Do you doubt my sincerity? Why do you speak so cruelly, saying I am too good, when your real thoughts must be so different? You mean that I am incapable of really doing anything; you have no faith in me. I seem to you too weak to pursue any high end. You would not even speak to me of your book, because you felt I should not appreciate it. And yet you do know me--"

"Yes; I know you well," Waymark said.

Ida looked steadily at him. "If you are speaking to me for the last time, won't you be sincere, and tell me of my faults? Do you think I could not bear it? You can say nothing to me--nothing from your heart--that I won't accept in all humility. Are we no longer even friends?"

"You mistake me altogether."

"And you are still my friend?" she uttered warmly. "But why do you think me unfit for good work?"

"I had no such thought. You know how my ideals oppose each other. I spoke on the impulse of the moment; I often find it so hard to reconcile myself to anything in life that is not, still and calm and beautiful. I am just now bent on forgetting all the things about which you are so earnest."

"Earnest? Yes. But I cannot give my whole self to the work. I am so lonely."

"You will not be so for long," he answered with more cheerfulness. "You have every opportunity of making for yourself a good social position. You will soon have friends, if only you seek them. Your goodness will make you respected. Indeed I wonder at your remaining so isolated. It need not be; I am sure it need not. Your wealth--I have no thought of speaking cynically--your wealth must--"

"My wealth! What is it to me? What do I care for all the friends it might bring? They are nothing to me in my misery. But you ... I would give all I possess for one kind word from you."

Flushing over forehead and cheeks, she compelled herself to meet his look. It was her wealth that stood between her and him. Her position was not like that of other women. Conventionalities were meaningless, set against a life.

"I have tried hard to make myself ever so little worthy of you," she murmured, when her voice would again obey her will. "Am I still--still too far beneath you?"

He stood like one detected in a crime, and stammered the words.

"Ida, I am not free."

He had risen. Ida sprang up, and moved towards him.

"*This* was your secret? Tell me, then. Look--*I* am strong! Tell me about it. I might have thought of this. I thought only of myself. I might have known there was good reason for the distance you put between us. Forgive me--oh, forgive the pain I have caused you!

"You asking for forgiveness? How you must despise me."

"Why should I despise you? You have never said a word to me that any friend, any near friend, might not have said, never since I myself, in my folly, forbade you to. You were not bound to tell me--"

"I had told your grandfather," Waymark said in a broken voice. "In a letter I wrote the very day he was taken ill, I begged him to let you know that I had bound myself."

As he spoke he knew that he was excusing himself with a truth which implied a falsehood, and before it was too late his soul revolted against the unworthiness.

"But it was my own fault that it was left so long. I would not let him tell you when he wished to; I put off the day as long as I could."

"Since you first knew me?" she asked, in a low voice.

"No! Since you came to live here. I was free before."

It was the part of his confession which cost him most to utter, and the hearing of it chilled Ida's heart. Whilst she had been living through her bitterest shame and misery, he had given his love to another woman, forgetful of her. For the first time, weakness overcame her.

"I thought you loved me," she sobbed, bowing her head.

"I did--and I do. I can't understand myself, and it would be worse than vain to try to show you how it came about. I have brought a curse upon my life, and worse than my own despair is your misery."

"Is she a good woman you are going to marry?" Ida asked simply and kindly.

"Only less noble than yourself."

"And she loves you--no, she cannot love as I do--but she loves you worthily and with all her soul?"

"Worthily and with all her soul--the greater my despair."

"Then I dare not think of her one unkind thought. We must remember her, and be strong for her sake. You will leave London and forget me soon,--yes, yes, you will *try* to forget me. You owe it to her; it is your duty."

"Duty!" he broke out passionately. "What have I to do with duty? Was it not my duty to be true to you? Was it not my duty to confess my hateful weakness, when I had taken the fatal step? Duty has no meaning for me. I have set it aside at every turn. Even now there would be no obligation on me to keep my word, but that I am too great a coward to revoke it."

She stood near to him.

"Dear,--I will call you so, it is for the last time,--you think these things in the worst moment of our suffering; afterwards you will thank me for having been strong enough, or cold enough, to be your conscience. There *is* such a thing as duty; it speaks in your heart and in mine, and tells us that we must part."

"You speak so lightly of parting. If you felt all that I--"

"My love is no shadow less than yours," she said, with earnestness which was well nigh severity. "I have never wavered from you since I knew you first."

"Ida!"

"I meant no reproach, but it will perhaps help you to think of that. You *did* love her, if it was only for a day, and that love will return."

She moved from him, and he too rose.

"You shame me," he said, under his breath. "I am not worthy to touch your hand."

"Yes," she returned, smiling amid her tears, "very worthy of all the love I have given you, and of the love with which *she* will make you happy. I shall suffer, but the thought of your happiness will help me to bear up and try to live a life you would not call ignoble. You will do great things, and I shall hear of them, and be glad. Yes; I know that is before you. You are one of those who cannot rest till they have won a high place. I, too, have my work, and--"

Her voice failed.

"Shall we never see each other again, Ida?"

"Perhaps. In a few years we might meet, and be friends. But I dare not think of that now."

They clasped hands, for one dread moment resisted the lure of eyes and lips, and so parted.

CHAPTER XXXVII
FORBIDDEN

December was half through, and it was the eve of Maud Enderby's marriage-day. Everything was ready for the morrow. Waymark had been away in the South, and the house to which he would take his wife now awaited their coming.

It was a foggy night. Maud had been for an hour to Our Lady of the Rosary, and found it difficult to make her way back. The street lamps were mere luminous blurs upon the clinging darkness, and the suspension of the wonted traffic made the air strangely still. It was cold, that kind of cold which wraps the limbs like a cloth soaked in icy water. When she knocked at the door of her aunt's house, and it was opened to her, wreaths of mist swept in and hung about the lighted hall. It seemed colder within than without. Footsteps echoed here in the old way, and voices lost themselves in a muffled resonance along the bare white walls. The house was more tomb-like than ever on such a night as thin To Maud's eyes the intruding fog shaped itself into ghostly visages, which looked upon her with weird and woeful compassion. She shuddered, and hastened upstairs to her mother's room.

After her husband's disappearance, Mrs. Enderby had passed her days in a morbid apathy, contrasting strangely with the restless excitement which had so long possessed her. But a change came over her from the day when she was told of Maud's approaching marriage. It was her delight to have Maud sit by her bed, or her couch, and talk over the details of the wedding and the new life that would follow upon it. Her interest in Waymark, which had fallen off during the past half-year, all at once revived; she conversed with him as she had been used to do when she first made his acquaintance, and the publication of his book afforded her endless matter for gossip. She began to speak of herself as an old woman, and of spending her last years happily in the country. To all appearances she had dismissed from her mind the calamity which had befallen her; her husband might have been long dead for any thought she seemed to give him. She was wholly taken up with childish joy in trivial matters. The dress in which Maud should be married gave her thoughts constant occupation, and she fretted at any opposition to her ideas. Still, like a child, she allowed herself to be brought round to others' views, and was ultimately led to consent that the costume should be a very simple one, merely a new dress, in fact, which Maud would be able to wear subsequently with little change. Even thus, every detail of it was as important to her as if it had been the most elaborate piece of bridal attire. In talking with Maud, too, she had lost that kind of awe which had formerly restrained her; it was as though she had been an affectionate mother ever since her daughter's birth. She called her by pet names, often caressed her, and wished for loving words and acts in return. Of Miss Bygrave's presence in the house she appeared scarcely conscious, never referring to her, and suffering a vague trouble if her sister entered the room where she was, which Theresa did very seldom.

The new dress had come home finished this evening whilst Maud was away. On the latter's return, her mother insisted on seeing her at once in it, and Maud obeyed. A strange bride, rather as one who was about to wed herself to Heaven beneath the veil, than preparing to be led to the altar.

Having resumed her ordinary dregs, Maud went downstairs to the parlour where her aunt was sitting. Miss Bygrave laid down a book as she entered.

"We shall not see each other after tonight," Theresa said, breaking the stillness with her grave but not unkind voice. "Is there anything more you would like to say to me, Maud?"

"Only that I shall always think of you, and grieve that we are parted."

"You are going into the world," said the other sadly, "my thoughts cannot follow you there. But your purer spirit will often be with me."

"And your spirit with me. If I had been permitted to share your life, that would have been my greatest joy. I am consciously choosing what my soul would set aside. For a time I thought I had reconciled myself to the world; I found delight in it, and came to look on the promptings of the spirit as morbid fancies. That has passed. I know the highest, but between me and it there is a gulf which it may be I shall never pass."

"It is only to few," said Theresa, looking at Maud with her smile of assured peace, "that it is given to persevere and attain."

As they sat once more in silence, there suddenly came a light knock at the house-door. At this moment Maud's thoughts had wandered back to a Christmas of her childhood, when she had sat just as to-night with her aunt, and had for the first time listened to those teachings which had moulded her life. The intervening years were swept away, and she was once more the thoughtful, wondering child, conscious of the great difference between herself and her companions; in spite of herself learning to regard the world in which they moved as something in which she had no part. Of those school companions a few came back to her mind, and, before all, the poor girl named Ida Starr, whom she had loved and admired. What had become of Ida, after she had been sent away from Miss Rutherford's school? She remembered that last meeting with her in the street, on the evening of Christmas Day, and could see her face.

The house door was opened, and Maud heard a voice outside which held her to the spot where she stood. Then Theresa re-entered the room, and after her came Paul Enderby.

He seemed to be wearing a disguise; at all events his clothing was that of a working man, poor and worn, and his face was changed by the growth of a beard. He shivered with cold, and, as Miss Bygrave closed the door behind him, stood with eyes sunk to the ground, in an attitude of misery and shame. Maud, recovering quickly from the shock his entrance had caused her, approached him and took his hand.

"Father," she said gently. Her voice overcame him; he burst into tears and stood hiding his face with the rough cap he held. Maud turned to her aunt, who remained at a little distance, unmoving, her eyes cast down. Before any other word was said, the door opened quickly, and Mrs. Enderby ran in with a smothered cry. Throwing her arms about her husband, she clung to him in a passion of grief and tenderness. In a moment she had been changed from the listless, childish woman of the last few months to a creature instinct with violent emotion. Her mingled excess of joy and anguish could not have displayed itself more vehemently had she been sorrowing night and day for her husband's loss. Maud was terrified at the scene, and shrunk to Theresa's side. Without heeding either, the distracted woman led Paul from the room, and upstairs to her own chamber. Drawing him to a chair, she fell on her knees beside him and wept agonisingly.

"You will stay with me now?" she cried, when her voice could form words. "You won't leave me again, Paul? We will hide you here.--No, no; I am for getting. You will go away with us, away from London to a safe place. Maud is going to be married to-morrow, and we will live with her in her new home. You have suffered dreadfully; you look so changed, so ill. You shall rest, and I will nurse you. Oh, I will be a good wife to you, Paul. Speak to me, do speak to me: speak kindly, dear! How long is it since I lost you?"

"I daren't stay, Emily," he replied, in a hoarse and broken voice. "I should be discovered. I must get away from England, that is my only chance. I have scarcely left the house where I was hiding all this time. It wouldn't have been safe to try and escape, even if I had had any money. I have hungered for days, and I am weaker than a child."

He sobbed again in the extremity of his wretchedness.

"It was all for my sake!" she cried, clinging around his neck. "I am your curse. I have brought you to ruin a second time. I am a bad, wretched woman; if you drove me from you with blows it would be less than I deserve! You can never forgive me;

but let me be your slave, let me suffer something dreadful for your sake! Why did I ever recover from my madness, only to bring that upon you!"

He could speak little, but leaned back, holding her to him with one arm.

"No, it is not your fault, Emily," he said. "Only my own weakness and folly. Your love repays me for all I have undergone; that was all I ever wanted."

When she had exhausted herself in passionate consolation, she left him for a few moments to get him food, and he ate of it like a famished man.

"If I can only get money enough to leave the country, I am saved," he said. "If I stay here, I shall be found, and they will imprison me for years. I had rather kill myself!"

"Mr. Waymark will give us the money," was the reply, "and we will go away together."

"That would betray me; it would be folly to face such a risk. If I can escape, then you shall come to me."

"Oh, you will leave me!" she cried. "I shall lose you, as I did before, but this time for ever! You don't love me, Paul! And how can I expect you should? But let me go as your servant. Let me dress like a man, and follow you. Who will notice then?"

He shook his head.

"I love you, Emily, and shall love you as long as I breathe. To hear you speak to me like this has almost the power to make me happy. If I had known it, I shouldn't have stayed so long away from you; I hadn't the courage to come, and I thought the sight of me would only be misery to you. I have lived a terrible life, among the poorest people, getting my bread as they did; oftener starving. Not one of my acquaintances was to be trusted. I have not seen one face I knew since I first heard of my danger and escaped. But I had rather live on like that than fall into the hands of the police; I should never know freedom again. The thought maddens me with fear."

"You are safe here, love, quite safe!" she urged soothingly. "Who could know that you are here? Who could know that Maud and I were living here?"

There was a tap at the door. Mrs. Enderby started to it, turned the key, and then asked who was there.

"Emily," said Miss Bygrave's voice, "let me come in--or let Paul come out here and speak to me."

There was something unusual in the speaker's tone; it was quick and nervous. Paul himself went to the door, and, putting his wife's hand aside, opened it.

"What is it?" he asked.

She beckoned him to leave the room, then whispered:

"Some one I don't know is at the front door. I opened it with the chain on, and a man said he must see Mr. Enderby."

"Can't I go out by the back?" Paul asked, all but voiceless with terror. "I daren't hide in the rooms; they will search them all. How did they know that I was here? O God, I am lost!"

They could hear the knocking below repeated. Paul hurried down the stairs, followed by his wife, whom Theresa in vain tried to hold back He knew the way to the door which led into the garden, and opening this, sprang into the darkness. Scarcely had he taken a step, when strong arms seized him.

"Hold on!" said a voice. "You must come back with me into the house."

At the same moment there was a shriek close at hand, and, as they turned to the open door, Paul and his captor saw Emily prostrate on the threshold, and Miss Bygrave stooping over her.

"Better open the front door, ma'am," said the police officer, "and ask my friend there to come through. We've got all we want."

This was done, and when Emily had been carried into the house, Paul was led thither also by his captor. As they stood in the hall, the second officer drew from his pocket a warrant, and read it out with official gravity.

"You'll go quietly with us, I suppose?" he then said.

Paul nodded, and all three departed by the front door.

It was midnight and before Mrs. Enderby showed any signs of returning consciousness. Miss Bygrave and Maud sat by her bed together, and at length one of them noticed that she had opened her eyes and was looking about her, though without moving her head.

"Mother," Maud asked, bending over her, "are you better? Do you know me?"

Emily nodded. There was no touch of natural colour in her face, and its muscles seemed paralysed. And she lay thus for hours, conscious apparently, but paying no attention to those in the room. Early in the morning a medical man was summoned, but his assistance made no change. The fog was still heavy, and only towards noon was it possible to dispense with lamp-light; then there gleamed for an hour or two a weird mockery of day, and again it was nightfall. With the darkness came rain.

Waymark had come to the house about ten o'clock. But this was to be no wedding-day. Maud begged him through her aunt not to see her, and he returned as he came. Miss Bygrave had told him all that had happened.

Mrs. Enderby seemed to sleep for some hours, but just after nightfall the previous condition returned; she lay with her eyes open, and just nodded when spoken to. From eight o'clock to midnight Maud tried to rest in her own room, but sleep was far from her, and when she returned to the sick-chamber to relieve her aunt, she was almost as worn and ghastly in countenance as the one they tended. She took her place by the fire, and sat listening to the sad rain, which fell heavily upon the soaked garden-ground below. It had a lulling effect. Weariness overcame her, and before she could suspect the inclination, she had fallen asleep.

Suddenly she was awake again, wide awake, it seemed to her, without any interval of half-consciousness, and staring horror-struck at the scene before her. The shaded lamp stood on the chest of drawers at one side of the room, and by its light she saw her mother in front of the looking-glass, her raised hand holding something that glistened. She could not move a limb; her tongue was powerless to utter a sound. There was a wild laugh, a quick motion of the raised hand--then it seemed to Maud as if the room were filled with a crimson light, followed by the eternal darkness.

*　　　*　　　*　　　*　　　*

A fortnight later Miss Bygrave was sitting in the early morning by the bed where Maud lay ill. For some days it had been feared that the girl's reason would fail, and though this worst possibility seemed at length averted, her condition was still full of danger. She had recognised her aunt the preceding evening, but a relapse had followed. Now she unexpectedly turned to the watcher, and spoke feebly, but with perfect self-control.

"Aunt, is madness hereditary?"

Miss Bygrave, who had thought her asleep, bent over her and tried to turn her mind to other thoughts. But the sick girl would speak only of this subject.

"I am quite myself," she said, "and I feel better. Yes, I remember reading somewhere that it was hereditary."

She was quiet for a little.

"Aunt," she then said, "I shall never be married. It would be wrong to him. I am afraid of myself."

She did not recur to the subject till she had risen, two or three weeks after, and was strong enough to move about the room. Waymark had called every day during her illness. As soon as he heard that she was up, he desired to see her, but Maud begged him, through her aunt, to wait yet a day or two. In the night which followed she wrote to him, and the letter was this:

"If I had seen you when you called yesterday, I should have had to face a task beyond my strength. Yet it would be wrong to keep from you any longer what I have to say. I must write it, and hope your knowledge of me will help you to understand what I can only imperfectly express.

"I ask you to let me break my promise to you. I have not ceased to love you; to me you are still all that is best and dearest in the world. You would have made my life very happy. But happiness is now what I dare not wish for. I am too weak to make that use of it which, I do not doubt, is permitted us; it would enslave my soul. With a nature such as mine, there is only one path of safety: I must renounce all. You know me to be no hypocrite, and to you, in this moment, I need not fear to speak my whole thought, The sacrifice has cost me much To break my faith to you, and to put aside for ever all the world's joys--the strength for this has only come after hours of bitterest striving. Try to be glad that I have won; it is all behind me, and I stand upon the threshold of peace.

"You know how from a child I have suffered. What to others was pure and lawful joy became to me a temptation. But God was not unjust; if He so framed me, He gave me at the same time the power to understand and to choose. All those warnings which I have, in my blindness, spoken of so lightly to you, I now recall with humbler and truer mind. If the shadow of sin darkened my path, it was that I might look well to my steps, and, alas, I have failed so, have gone so grievously astray! God, in His righteous anger, has terribly visited me. The most fearful form of death has risen before me; I have been cast into abysses of horror, and only saved from frenzy by the mercy which brought all this upon me for my good. A few months ago I had also a warning. I did not disregard it, but I could not overcome the love which bound me to you. But for that love, how much easier it would have been to me to overcome the world and myself.

"You will forgive me, for you will understand me. Do not write in reply; spare me, I entreat you, a renewal of that dark hour I have passed through. With my aunt I am going to leave London. We shall remain together, and she will strengthen me in the new life. May God bless you here and hereafter. MAUD ENDERBY."

After an interval of a day Waymark wrote as follows to Miss Bygrave:--

"Doubtless you know that Maud has written desiring me to release her. I cannot but remember that she is scarcely yet recovered from a severe illness, and her letter must not be final. She entreats me not to write to her or see her. Accordingly I address myself to you, and beg that you will not allow Maud to take any irrevocable step till she is perfectly well, and has had time to reflect. I shall still deem her promise to me binding. If after the lapse of six months from now she still desires to be released, I must know it, either from herself or from you. Write to me at the old address."

CHAPTER XXXVIII
ORDERS OF RELEASE

Waymark and Casti spent their Christmas Eve together. They spoke freely of each other's affairs, saving that there was no mention of Ida. Waymark had of course said nothing of that parting between Ida and himself. Of the hope which supported him he could not speak to his friend.

A month had told upon Julian as months do when the end draws so near. In spite of his suffering he still discharged his duties at the hospital, but it was plain that he would not be able to do so much longer. And what would happen then?

"Casti," Waymark exclaimed suddenly, when a hint of this thought had brought both of them to a pause, "come away with me."

Julian looked up in bewilderment.

"Where to?"

"Anywhere. To some place where the sun shines."

"What an impossible idea! How am I to get my living? And how is she to live?"

"Look here," Waymark said, smiling, "my will is a little stronger than yours, and in the present case I mean to exercise it. I have said, and there's an end of it. You say she'll be away from home to-morrow. Good. We go together, pack up your books and things in half an hour or so, bring them here,--and then off! *Sic volo, sic jubeo, sit pro ratione voluntas!*"

And it was done, though not till Waymark had overcome the other's opposition by the most determined effort. Julian understood perfectly well the full significance of the scheme, for all Waymark's kind endeavour to put a hopeful and common-place aspect on his proposal. He resisted as long as his strength would allow, then put himself in his friend's hands.

It was some time before Julian could set his mind at rest with regard to the desertion of his wife. Though no one capable of judging the situation could have cast upon him a shadow of blame, the first experience of peace mingled itself in his mind with self-reproach. Waymark showed him how utterly baseless any such feeling was. Harriet had proved herself unworthy of a moment's consideration, and it was certain that, as long as she received her weekly remittance--paid through an agent in London,--she would trouble herself very little about the rest; or, at all events, any feeling that might possess her would be wholly undeserving of respect. Gradually Julian accustomed himself to this thought.

They were in the Isle of Wight; comfortably housed, with the sea before their eyes, and the boon of sunshine which Casti had so longed for.

Waymark gave himself wholly to the invalid. He had no impulse to resume literary work; anything was welcome which enabled him to fill up the day and reach the morrow. Whilst Julian lay on the couch, which was drawn up to the fireside, Waymark read aloud anything that could lead them to forget themselves. At other times, Julian either read to himself or wrote verse, which, however, he did not show to his friend. Before springtime came he found it difficult even to maintain a sitting attitude for long. His cough still racked him terribly. Waymark often lay awake in the night, listening to that fearful sound in the next room. At such times he tried to fancy himself in the dying man's position, and then the sweat of horror came upon his brow. Deeply he sympathised with the misery he could do so little to allay. Yet he was doing what he might to make the end a quiet one, and the consciousness of this brought him many a calm moment.

However it might be in those fearful vigils, Julian's days did not seem unhappy. He was resigning himself to the inevitable, in the strength of that quiet which sometimes ensues upon despair. Now and then he could even be, to all appearances, light-hearted.

With the early May he had a revival of inspiration. Strangely losing sight of his desperate condition, he spoke once more of beginning the great poem planned long ago. It was living within his mind and heart, he said. Waymark listened to him whilst he unfolded book after book of glorious vision; listened, and wondered.

There was a splendid sunset one evening at this time, and the two watched it together from the room in which they always sat. Seas of molten gold, strands and promontories of jasper and amethyst, illimitable mountain-ranges, cities of unimagined splendour, all were there in that extent of evening sky. They watched it till the vision wasted before the breath of night.

"What shall I read?" Waymark asked, when the lamp was lit.

"Read that passage in the Georgics which glorifies Italy," Julian replied. "It will suit my mood to-night."

Waymark took down his Virgil.

"Sed neque Medorum silvae, ditissima terra, Nec pulcher Ganges atque auro turbibus Hermus   Laudibus Italiae certent, non Bactra, neque Indi,   Totaque turiferis Panchaia pinguis arenis."

Julian's eyes glistened as the melody rolled on, and when it ceased, both were quiet for a time.

"Waymark," Julian said presently, a gentle tremor in his voice, "why do we never speak of her?"

"*Can* we speak of her?" Waymark returned, knowing well who was meant.

"A short time ago I could not; now I feel the need. It will give me no pain, but great happiness.',

"That is all gone by," he continued, with a solemn smile. "To me she is no longer anything but a remembrance, an ideal I once knew. The noblest and sweetest woman I have known, or shall know, on earth."

They talked of her with subdued voices, reverently and tenderly. Waymark described what he knew or divined of the life she was now leading, her beneficent activity, her perfect adaptation to the new place she filled.

"In a little while," Julian said, when they had fallen into thought again, "you will have your second letter. And then?"

There was no answer. Julian waited a moment, then rose and, clasping his friend's hand, bade him good night.

Waymark awoke once or twice before morning, but there was no coughing in the next room. He felt glad, and wondered whether there was indeed any improvement in the invalid's health. But at the usual breakfast-time Julian did not appear. Waymark knocked at his door, with no result. He turned the handle and entered.

On this same day, Ida was visiting her houses. Litany lane and Elm Court now wore a changed appearance. At present it was possible to breathe even in the inmost recesses of the Court. There the fronts of the houses were fresh white-washed; in the Lane they were new-painted. Even the pavement and the road-way exhibited an improvement. If you penetrated into garrets and cellars you no longer found squalor and dilapidation; poverty in plenty, but at all events an attempt at cleanliness everywhere, as far, that is to say, as a landlord's care could ensure it. The staircases had ceased to be rotten pit-falls; the ceilings showed traces of recent care; the walls no longer dripped with moisture or were foul with patches of filth. Not much change, it is true, in the appearance of the inhabitants; yet close inquiry would have elicited comforting assurances of progressing reform, results of a supervision which was never offensive, never thoughtlessly exaggerated. Especially in the condition of the children improvement was discernible. Lodgers in the Lane and the Court had come to understand that not even punctual payment of weekly rent was sufficient to guarantee them stability of tenure. Under this singular lady-landlord something more than that was expected and required, and, whilst those who were capable of adjusting themselves to the new *regime* found, on the whole, that things went vastly better with them, such as could by no means overcome their love of filth, moral and material, troubled themselves little when the notice to quit came, together with a little sum of ready money to cover the expenses of removal.

Among those whom Ida called upon this afternoon was an old woman who, in addition to her own voluminous troubles, was always in a position to give a ***compte-rendu*** of the general distress of the neighbourhood. People had discovered that her eloquence could be profitably made use of in their own service, and not infrequently, when speaking with Ida, she was in reality holding a brief from this or that neighbour, marked, not indeed in guineas, but in "twos" of strong beverage, obtainable at her favourite house of call. To-day she held such a brief, and was more than usually urgent in the representation of a deserving case.

"Oh, Miss Woodstock, mem, there's a poor young 'oman a-lyin' at the Clock 'Ouse, as it really makes one's 'art bleed to tell of her! For all she's so young, she's a widder, an' pr'aps it's as well she should be, seein' how shockin' her 'usband treated her afore he was took where no doubt he's bein' done as he did by. It's fair cruel, Miss Woodstock, mem, to see her sufferin's. She has fits, an' falls down everywheres; it's a mercy as she 'asn't been run over in the public street long ago. They're hepiplectic fits, I'm told, an' laws o' me! the way she foams at the mouth! No doubt as they was brought on by her 'usband's etrocious treatment. I understand as he was a man as called hisself a gentleman. He was allus that jealous of the pore innocent thing, mem--castin' in her teeth things as I couldn't bring myself not even to 'int at in your presence, Miss Woodstock, mem. Many's the time he's beat her black an' blue, when she jist went out to get a bit o' somethink for his tea at night, 'cos he would 'ave it she'd been a-doin' what she 'adn't ought--"

"Where is she?" Ida asked, thinking she had now gathered enough of the features of the case.

"I said at the Clock 'Ouse, mem. Mrs. Sprowl's took her in' mem, and is be'avin' to her like a mother. She knew her, did Mrs. Sprowl, in the pore thing's 'appy days, before ever she married. But of course it ain't likely as Mrs. Sprowl can keep her as long as her pore life lasts; not to speak of the expense; its a terrible responsibility, owin' to the hepiplectic ailment, mem, as of course you understand."

"Can't she get into any hospital!"

"She only just came out, mem, not two weeks ago. They couldn't do no more for the pore creature, and so she had to go. An' she 'asn't not a friend in the world, 'ceptin' Mrs. Sprowl, as is no less than a mother to her."

"Do you know her name?"

"Mrs. Casty, mem. It's a Irish name, I b'lieve, an' I can't say as I'm partial to the Irish, but--"

"Very well," Ida broke in hastily. "I'll see if I can do anything."

Paying no attention to the blessings showered upon her by the counsel in this case, blessings to which she was accustomed, and of which she well understood the value, Ida went out into the Lane, and walked away quickly. She did not pause at the Clock House, but walked as far as a quiet street some little distance off, and then paced the pavement for a while, in thought. Who this "Mrs. Casty" was she could have little doubt. The calumnies against her husband were just such as Harriet Casti would be likely to circulate.

For a moment it had seemed possible to go to the public-house and make personal inquiries, but reflection showed her that this would be a needless imprudence, even had she been able to overcome herself sufficiently for such an interview. She went home instead, and at once despatched Miss Hurst to the Clock House to discover whether it was indeed Harriet Casti who lay there, and, if so, what her real condition was. That lady returned with evidence establishing the sick woman's identity. Harriet, she reported, was indeed in a sad state, clearly incapable of supporting herself by any kind of work. Her husband--Miss Hurst was told--had deserted her, leaving her entirely without means, and now, but for Mrs. Sprowl's charity, she would have been in the workhouse. This story sounded very strangely to Ida. It might mean that Julian was dead. She wrote a few lines to Waymark, at the old address, and had a speedy reply. Yes, Julian Casti was dead, but the grave had not yet closed over him. Harriet had been in receipt of money, and need have wanted for nothing; but *now* she must expect no more.

The result of it all was that, in the course of a week, Harriet was informed by Miss Hurst that a place was open to her in a hospital near London, where she could remain as long as her ailments rendered it necessary; the expense would be provided for by a lady who had been told of the case, and wished to give what aid she could. The offer was rejected, and with insult. When next she visited Litany Lane, Ida learnt that "pore Mrs. Casty," after a quarrel with her friend Mrs. Sprowl, had fallen downstairs in a fit and broken her neck.

Waymark lived on in the Isle of Wight, until a day when there came to him a letter from Miss Bygrave. It told him that Maud's resolve was immutable, and added that aunt and niece, having become members of "the true Church," were about to join a sisterhood in a midland town, where their lives would be devoted to work of charity.

Not many days after this, Ida, in London, received a letter, addressed in a hand she knew well. There was a flush on her face as she began to read; but presently came the pallor of a sudden joy almost too great to be borne. The letter was a long one, containing the story of several years of the writer's life, related with unflinching sincerity, bad and good impartially set down, and all leading up to words which danced in golden sunlight before her tear-dimmed eyes.

For an hour she sat alone, scarce moving. Yet it seemed to her that only a few minutes were allowed to pass before she took her pen and wrote.

The Codes Of Hammurabi And Moses
W. W. Davies

QTY

The discovery of the Hammurabi Code is one of the greatest achievements of archaeology, and is of paramount interest, not only to the student of the Bible, but also to all those interested in ancient history...

Religion   **ISBN: *1-59462-338-4***   **Pages:132**

MSRP $12.95

The Theory of Moral Sentiments
Adam Smith

QTY

This work from 1749. contains original theories of conscience amd moral judgment and it is the foundation for systemof morals.

Philosophy **ISBN: *1-59462-777-0***   **Pages:536**

MSRP $19.95

Jessica's First Prayer
Hesba Stretton

QTY

In a screened and secluded corner of one of the many railway-bridges which span the streets of London there could be seen a few years ago, from five o'clock every morning until half past eight, a tidily set-out coffee-stall, consisting of a trestle and board, upon which stood two large tin cans, with a small fire of charcoal burning under each so as to keep the coffee boiling during the early hours of the morning when the work-people were thronging into the city on their way to their daily toil...

Pages:84

Childrens   **ISBN: *1-59462-373-2***   *MSRP $9.95*

My Life and Work
Henry Ford

QTY

Henry Ford revolutionized the world with his implementation of mass production for the Model T automobile. Gain valuable business insight into his life and work with his own auto-biography... "We have only started on our development of our country we have not as yet, with all our talk of wonderful progress, done more than scratch the surface. The progress has been wonderful enough but..."

Pages:300

Biographies/   **ISBN: *1-59462-198-5***   *MSRP $21.95*

The Art of Cross-Examination
Francis Wellman

QTY

I presume it is the experience of every author, after his first book is published upon an important subject, to be almost overwhelmed with a wealth of ideas and illustrations which could readily have been included in his book, and which to his own mind, at least, seem to make a second edition inevitable. Such certainly was the case with me; and when the first edition had reached its sixth impression in five months, I rejoiced to learn that it seemed to my publishers that the book had met with a sufficiently favorable reception to justify a second and considerably enlarged edition. ..

Pages:412

Reference   **ISBN:** *1-59462-647-2*   *MSRP $19.95*

On the Duty of Civil Disobedience
Henry David Thoreau

QTY

Thoreau wrote his famous essay, On the Duty of Civil Disobedience, as a protest against an unjust but popular war and the immoral but popular institution of slave-owning. He did more than write—he declined to pay his taxes, and was hauled off to gaol in consequence. Who can say how much this refusal of his hastened the end of the war and of slavery ?

Law   **ISBN:** *1-59462-747-9*   **Pages:48**

MSRP $7.45

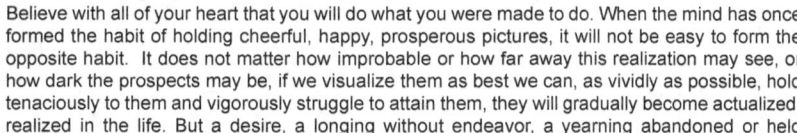

Dream Psychology Psychoanalysis for Beginners
Sigmund Freud

QTY

Sigmund Freud, born Sigismund Schlomo Freud (May 6, 1856 - September 23, 1939), was a Jewish-Austrian neurologist and psychiatrist who co-founded the psychoanalytic school of psychology. Freud is best known for his theories of the unconscious mind, especially involving the mechanism of repression; his redefinition of sexual desire as mobile and directed towards a wide variety of objects; and his therapeutic techniques, especially his understanding of transference in the therapeutic relationship and the presumed value of dreams as sources of insight into unconscious desires.

Pages:196

Psychology   **ISBN:** *1-59462-905-6*   *MSRP $15.45*

The Miracle of Right Thought
Orison Swett Marden

QTY

Believe with all of your heart that you will do what you were made to do. When the mind has once formed the habit of holding cheerful, happy, prosperous pictures, it will not be easy to form the opposite habit. It does not matter how improbable or how far away this realization may see, or how dark the prospects may be, if we visualize them as best we can, as vividly as possible, hold tenaciously to them and vigorously struggle to attain them, they will gradually become actualized, realized in the life. But a desire, a longing without endeavor, a yearning abandoned or held indifferently will vanish without realization.

Pages:360

Self Help   **ISBN:** *1-59462-644-8*   *MSRP $25.45*

The Rosicrucian Cosmo-Conception Mystic Christianity by *Max Heindel*   ISBN: *1-59462-188-8* **$38.95**
The Rosicrucian Cosmo-conception is not dogmatic, neither does it appeal to any other authority than the reason of the student. It is: not controversial, but is: sent forth in the, hope that it may help to clear...   New Age/Religion Pages 646

Abandonment To Divine Providence by *Jean-Pierre de Caussade*   ISBN: *1-59462-228-0* **$25.95**
"The Rev. Jean Pierre de Caussade was one of the most remarkable spiritual writers of the Society of Jesus in France in the 18th Century. His death took place at Toulouse in 1751. His works have gone through many editions and have been republished...   Inspirational/Religion Pages 400

Mental Chemistry by *Charles Haanel*   ISBN: *1-59462-192-6* **$23.95**
Mental Chemistry allows the change of material conditions by combining and appropriately utilizing the power of the mind. Much like applied chemistry creates something new and unique out of careful combinations of chemicals the mastery of mental chemistry...   New Age Pages 354

The Letters of Robert Browning and Elizabeth Barret Barrett 1845-1846 vol II   ISBN: *1-59462-193-4* **$35.95**
by *Robert Browning* and *Elizabeth Barrett*   Biographies Pages 596

Gleanings In Genesis (volume I) by *Arthur W. Pink*   ISBN: *1-59462-130-6* **$27.45**
Appropriately has Genesis been termed "the seed plot of the Bible" for in it we have, in germ form, almost all of the great doctrines which are afterwards fully developed in the books of Scripture which follow...   Religion/Inspirational Pages 420

The Master Key by *L. W. de Laurence*   ISBN: *1-59462-001-6* **$30.95**
In no branch of human knowledge has there been a more lively increase of the spirit of research during the past few years than in the study of Psychology, Concentration and Mental Discipline. The requests for authentic lessons in Thought Control, Mental Discipline and...   New Age/Business Pages 422

The Lesser Key Of Solomon Goetia by *L. W. de Laurence*   ISBN: *1-59462-092-X* **$9.95**
This translation of the first book of the "Lemegton" which is now for the first time made accessible to students of Talismanic Magic was done, after careful collation and edition, from numerous Ancient Manuscripts in Hebrew, Latin, and French...   New Age/Occult Pages 92

Rubaiyat Of Omar Khayyam by *Edward Fitzgerald*   ISBN:*1-59462-332-5* **$13.95**
Edward Fitzgerald, whom the world has already learned, in spite of his own efforts to remain within the shadow of anonymity, to look upon as one of the rarest poets of the century, was born at Bredfield, in Suffolk, on the 31st of March, 1809. He was the third son of John Purcell...   Music Pages 172

Ancient Law by *Henry Maine*   ISBN: *1-59462-128-4* **$29.95**
The chief object of the following pages is to indicate some of the earliest ideas of mankind, as they are reflected in Ancient Law, and to point out the relation of those ideas to modern thought.   Religion/History Pages 452

Far-Away Stories by *William J. Locke*   ISBN: *1-59462-129-2* **$19.45**
"Good wine needs no bush, but a collection of mixed vintages does. And this book is just such a collection. Some of the stories I do not want to remain buried for ever in the museum files of dead magazine-numbers an author's not unpardonable vanity..."   Fiction Pages 272

Life of David Crockett by *David Crockett*   ISBN: *1-59462-250-7* **$27.45**
"Colonel David Crockett was one of the most remarkable men of the times in which he lived. Born in humble life, but gifted with a strong will, an indomitable courage, and unremitting perseverance...   Biographies/New Age Pages 424

Lip-Reading by *Edward Nitchie*   ISBN: *1-59462-206-X* **$25.95**
Edward B. Nitchie, founder of the New York School for the Hard of Hearing, now the Nitchie School of Lip-Reading, Inc, wrote "LIP-READING Principles and Practice". The development and perfecting of this meritorious work on lip-reading was an undertaking...   How-to Pages 400

A Handbook of Suggestive Therapeutics, Applied Hypnotism, Psychic Science   ISBN: *1-59462-214-0* **$24.95**
by *Henry Munro*   Health/New Age/Health/Self-help Pages 376

A Doll's House: and Two Other Plays by *Henrik Ibsen*   ISBN: *1-59462-112-8* **$19.95**
Henrik Ibsen created this classic when in revolutionary 1848 Rome. Introducing some striking concepts in playwriting for the realist genre, this play has been studied the world over.   Fiction/Classics/Plays 308

The Light of Asia by *sir Edwin Arnold*   ISBN: *1-59462-204-3* **$13.95**
In this poetic masterpiece, Edwin Arnold describes the life and teachings of Buddha. The man who was to become known as Buddha to the world was born as Prince Gautama of India but he rejected the worldly riches and abandoned the reigns of power when...   Religion/History/Biographies Pages 170

The Complete Works of Guy de Maupassant by *Guy de Maupassant*   ISBN: *1-59462-157-8* **$16.95**
"For days and days, nights and nights, I had dreamed of that first kiss which was to consecrate our engagement, and I knew not on what spot I should put my lips..."   Fiction/Classics Pages 240

The Art of Cross-Examination by *Francis L. Wellman*   ISBN: *1-59462-309-0* **$26.95**
Written by a renowned trial lawyer, Wellman imparts his experience and uses case studies to explain how to use psychology to extract desired information through questioning.   How-to/Science/Reference Pages 408

Answered or Unanswered? by *Louisa Vaughan*   ISBN: *1-59462-248-5* **$10.95**
Miracles of Faith in China   Religion Pages 112

The Edinburgh Lectures on Mental Science (1909) by *Thomas*   ISBN: *1-59462-008-3* **$11.95**
This book contains the substance of a course of lectures recently given by the writer in the Queen Street Hall, Edinburgh. Its purpose is to indicate the Natural Principles governing the relation between Mental Action and Material Conditions...   New Age/Psychology Pages 148

Ayesha by *H. Rider Haggard*   ISBN: *1-59462-301-5* **$24.95**
Verily and indeed it is the unexpected that happens! Probably if there was one person upon the earth from whom the Editor of this, and of a certain previous history, did not expect to hear again...   Classics Pages 380

Ayala's Angel by *Anthony Trollope*   ISBN: *1-59462-352-X* **$29.95**
The two girls were both pretty, but Lucy who was twenty-one who supposed to be simple and comparatively unattractive, whereas Ayala was credited, as her Bombwhat romantic name might show, with poetic charm and a taste for romance. Ayala when her father died was nineteen...   Fiction Pages 484

The American Commonwealth by *James Bryce*   ISBN: *1-59462-286-8* **$34.45**
An interpretation of American democratic political theory. It examines political mechanics and society from the perspective of Scotsman James Bryce   Politics Pages 572

Stories of the Pilgrims by *Margaret P. Pumphrey*   ISBN: *1-59462-116-0* **$17.95**
This book explores pilgrims religious oppression in England as well as their escape to Holland and eventual crossing to America on the Mayflower, and their early days in New England...   History Pages 268

QTY

The Fasting Cure by *Sinclair Upton*   ISBN: *1-59462-222-1* **$13.95** ☐
In the Cosmopolitan Magazine for May, 1910, and in the Contemporary Review (London) for April, 1910, I published an article dealing with my experi-ences in fasting. I have written a great many magazine articles, but never one which attracted so much attention... New Age/Self Help/Health Pages 164

Hebrew Astrology by *Sepharial*   ISBN: *1-59462-308-2* **$13.45** ☐
In these days of advanced thinking it is a matter of common observation that we have left many of the old landmarks behind and that we are now pressing forward to greater heights and to a wider horizon than that which represented the mind-content of our progenitors... Astrology Pages 144

Thought Vibration or The Law of Attraction in the Thought World   ISBN: *1-59462-127-6* **$12.95** ☐

by *William Walker Atkinson*   Psychology/Religion Pages 144

Optimism by *Helen Keller*   ISBN: *1-59462-108-X* **$15.95** ☐
Helen Keller was blind, deaf, and mute since 19 months old, yet famously learned how to overcome these handicaps, communicate with the world, and spread her lectures promoting optimism. An inspiring read for everyone... Biographies/Inspirational Pages 84

Sara Crewe by *Frances Burnett*   ISBN: *1-59462-360-0* **$9.45** ☐
In the first place, Miss Minchin lived in London. Her home was a large, dull, tall one, in a large, dull square, where all the houses were alike, and all the sparrows were alike, and where all the door-knockers made the same heavy sound... Childrens/Classic Pages 88

The Autobiography of Benjamin Franklin by *Benjamin Franklin*   ISBN: *1-59462-135-7* **$24.95** ☐
The Autobiography of Benjamin Franklin has probably been more extensively read than any other American historical work, and no other book of its kind has had such ups and downs of fortune. Franklin lived for many years in England, where he was agent... Biographies/History Pages 332

Name	
Email	
Telephone	
Address	
City, State ZIP	

☐ **Credit Card**   ☐ **Check / Money Order**

Credit Card Number	
Expiration Date	
Signature	

Please Mail to: Book Jungle
PO Box 2226
Champaign, IL 61825
or Fax to: 630-214-0564

ORDERING INFORMATION

web*: www.bookjungle.com*
email*: sales@bookjungle.com*
fax*: 630-214-0564*
mail*: Book Jungle PO Box 2226 Champaign, IL 61825*
or PayPal *to sales@bookjungle.com*

Please contact us for bulk discounts

DIRECT-ORDER TERMS

**20% Discount if You Order
Two or More Books**
Free Domestic Shipping!
Accepted: Master Card, Visa,
Discover, American Express